Introduction

Finding Audrey by Tracey V. B[illegible]
Raised by the foster system, [illegible] ots
brings her to Brett Canfield's g[illegible] d to
him, his Christianity repels her [illegible] clues
to her search. Through the stories [illegible] finds
pride in her family connections and learns that faith has been the backbone of their success. Will she find the self-worth she has been searching for and be able to look forward to her future?

English Tea and Bagpipes by Pamela Griffin
1822—When Fiona's sister and Alex's brother run off to marry, the families oppose the match between a poor Highlander and an English nobleman. Fiona impulsively goes after her sister, and Alex follows. Joined only in their determination to stop a wedding, both are surprised to find the other quite appealing. Can they find common ground?

Fresh Highland Heir by Jill Stengl
1748—Allan MacMurray is the protégé of the last earl of Carnassis. When Celeste's father takes over Kennerith Castle, he retains Allan for Celeste's bodyguard. She is determined to think the worst of Allan, until someone is out to get rid of him and the true heir of the castle comes into question. Will Celeste find the truth before it is too late to help Allan?

Fayre Rose by Tamela Hancock Murray
1358—Fayre has been brought to Kennerith Castle to tend the rose garden in payment for her father's taxes. When the Laird Kenneth falls ill with the Black Death plague, only Fayre is brave enough to play nursemaid. How can a laird and serf openly profess their love?

(Note—*Finding Audrey* is segmented in four parts between the other three stories.)

Highland Legacy

Four Generations of Love Are Rooted in Scotland

Tracey V. Bateman
Pamela Griffin
Tamela Hancock Murray
Jill Stengl

ISBN 1-59310-082-5

Illustrations by Mari Goering

All Scripture used in *Fayre Rose* taken from the Douay-Rheims translation of the Latin Vulgate, 1899 edition, published by Tan Books and Publishers, Rockford, IL.

All other Scripture taken from the King James Version.

Published by Barbour Publishing, Inc., P.O. Box 719, Uhrichsville, Ohio 44683, www.barbourbooks.com

Our mission is to publish and distribute inspirational products offering exceptional value and biblical encouragement to the masses.

Printed in the United States of America.
5 4 3 2 1

Highland Legacy

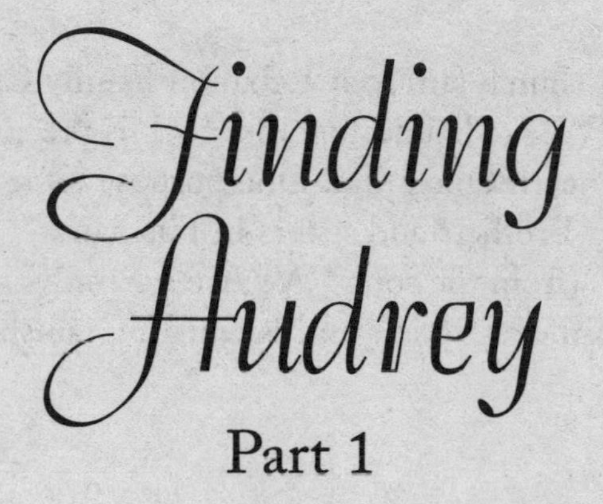

Part 1

by Tracey V. Bateman

Dedication

To my church family at Lebanon Family Church.
"We are bound together by His precious blood.
One heart. One mind. One purpose. One love.
Brothers and sisters in His name"
(from the song "We Are a Family"
by Aimee Flanders and Kevin E. Crainshaw).

Chapter 1

Audrey MacMurray paid the taxi driver, then pivoted just in time to catch a blast of freezing lakefront wind across her neck. She shivered and turned up the collar on her long trench coat. Her breath formed a cloud as she glanced up at the brick building before her and sighed in relief. A few short steps to warmth.

She would have preferred staying inside her cozy home to braving an unseasonably cold and wintry November evening, but after six months of trying to find specific information about some of her ancestors, this genealogy class seemed like her last recourse before she gave up altogether.

"Going in?"

Audrey's heart sped up at the deep, throaty voice behind her, and she whirled around. Sudden heat crept to her cheeks despite the frigid air. Gorgeous eyes, which were either blue-green or green-blue, stared back at her from beneath dark lashes. His thick, dark hair was uncovered and blew attractively across his forehead. Despite the arctic air, he didn't seem a bit cold. No red nose or quivering lips. Looking like something out of a fashion magazine, he wore a black wool coat, and a scarf hung loosely down either side of his neck. Black leather gloves covered his hands.

Audrey arranged her half-frozen face into what she hoped was an alluring yet vulnerable expression and consciously curved her numbed lips ever so slightly.

After ten months without a date, she knew this was too much to be coincidence. The fates had dealt her a winning hand, and she wasn't about to disappoint them. Who knew when they'd smile upon her again?

"Yes, I'm going in. Of course I am. Why else would I be standing out in the cold in front of the library?" A dreadful, high-pitched giggle, which could only have come from her throat, cut through the air like the annoying sound of nails scraping a chalkboard. Audrey cringed inwardly. *Oh, gravy.* She needed a class on social skills worse than this genealogy class.

Idiot, idiot, idiot, she chided herself. *Why can't you ever deliver a great comeback?*

"Then, let's get you inside where it's warm," he said without even a hint that he thought her reply to be anything other than brilliant. "May I?" He motioned toward her arm.

Dumbstruck and utterly charmed, Audrey nodded. Cute and sweet! She was in love. Visions of candles and flowers and, yes, a white silk gown danced through her mind.

"God surely has a sense of humor, doesn't He?" her future husband asked, his eyes sparkling in the glow of the streetlights.

"Huh?" Audrey's brow furrowed. Why did he have to go and wreck the moment by bringing God into it?

He grasped her elbow and led her up the steps to the door. "Two days ago, I wore a pair of shorts to walk my dog; now it's full-blown winter again." He gave a great-sounding chuckle.

"Sometimes I think God must have a lot of fun with His creation."

Audrey felt the disappointment to her toes. Religious people had no business being that great-looking. It wasn't fair to the normal people of the world. At the very least he should have worn a cross as a warning. Irritation flashed through her, and she jerked away from his light grip.

His eyebrows lifted as he opened the door.

"Thanks," Audrey mumbled, ducking under his arm.

Inside the double glass doors, Audrey shook off the light dusting of snow covering her shoulders and hair and rubbed vigorously at her arms in an attempt to warm herself.

Her formerly future husband cleared his throat. "I guess I'll be going. It was nice talking to you."

"Yeah," Audrey said, unable to conceal a sniff of disgust at her own foolish fantasy. "Wonderful talking to you, too."

She watched his broad-shouldered form saunter away with all the appeal and confidence of a male model on a runway. What a shame.

She smiled at the librarian sitting behind a round desk.

"May I help you?"

"Yes, I'm taking the genealogy class meeting here tonight. Can you point me in the right direction?"

An amused grin tipped the thin woman's too-red lips. "Just follow him."

Turning, Audrey felt a groan rising in her throat. "You mean him?" she asked, pointing to Mr. Fashion Mag's retreating form.

"Yes. That's Brett Canfield. He teaches your class."

"Figures," she muttered.

"Excuse me?"

"Never mind. Thanks." Audrey glanced back toward the entrance and contemplated bowing out of the class, but she dismissed the thought almost as quickly as it had come. She had gone as far into her family history as she could go alone, and she needed the help this class offered. After her years of growing up in one foster home after another, Audrey had been thrilled to meet a real, blood-related great-aunt—her only living relative—a few months ago. To Audrey's delight, her aunt had been a historian and had traced the family back generations. Audrey was hooked. She made a copy of the documents and went to work trying to discover anything personal about the names on the lists. It hadn't been too hard to get a firm idea of just who these people were throughout the last part of the nineteenth century and through the twentieth century.

From the great-great-grandmother who was rumored to have been a Yankee spy during the Civil War, to the moonshining great-uncle who was arrested and served prison time during prohibition, Audrey loved her family and the unraveling of each new ancestor. But she had hit a dead end with her great-great-great-grandfather, Rory MacMurray. He appeared to have been something of a rogue—a sea captain and possibly a pirate. Yet she couldn't find any record of his father or mother.

A bitter grin twisted Audrey's lips. With all the salty characters in her genealogical line, she wondered how her parents had ever become missionaries. The only religious people in her whole family tree, they were the ones who had died young, leaving a little girl to be raised in foster homes. So much for good living keeping you alive longer.

Shaking off the familiar ache in her heart, Audrey watched Mr. Religious open a door to a small room. A huge glass window revealed a round table with seven or eight men and women seated in metal chairs. She waited just a moment, then gathered a fortifying breath and stepped forward. "Rory MacMurray," she muttered, "this had better be worth it."

Brett snatched up his briefcase and hurried outside the classroom. "Miss MacMurray," he called in a subdued, library voice. "Could you wait for a minute?"

She stopped short and turned to face him, reluctance clouding her freckled features. She didn't speak, but her brow lifted as though waiting for him to get to the point. After four weeks of class two nights each week, he still couldn't get more than three words out of this woman. Clearly, she wasn't interested in him, but something about her made him keep going back for more punishment.

Brett felt heat rise up his neck. "I thought you might like to borrow this." He offered her a large, hardback book.

She glanced at the cover and tentatively accepted the book. *"How to Pick the Fruits Off Your Family Tree?"* Her laugh filled the air with a pleasant ring.

Brett caught his breath at the sight of her beautifully curved lips and forced his gaze to meet the unusual silvery gray eyes, which were filled with question.

"Don't let the title fool you. The author shares some really great research tips. Especially for someone like you, who wants to delve deeper into your ancestry than just learning names."

"Well, thanks. I'll get it back to you as soon as I finish with it." She turned to go.

His heart lurched. If he didn't take advantage of this opportunity, he deserved to be blown off like an autumn leaf.

Stepping forward quickly, he touched her arm. "Could I interest you in stopping for a cup of coffee? There's a little coffeehouse just down the street." He saw instant refusal leap to her eyes and quickly went on before it had the chance to drop to her lips. "I'd guess you're a mocha latte sort of woman. I'm hardly ever wrong when it comes to matching people with their companion java. Come on. One cup? I'll even spring for some white chocolate syrup thrown in for extra flavor."

A quick smile lifted the corners of her lips, then she frowned, instantly wiping out the smile and Brett's hopes. A deep breath lifted her chest, then she let out a sigh. "Look, Brett. You're a great guy. Everything a girl could want. A *religious* girl. I just couldn't, in good conscience, date someone like you. It wouldn't be fair to either of us."

Taken aback, Brett frowned. "How did you know I'm a youth pastor?"

She gave him a blank stare. "A youth pastor? I figured you went to church. But a minister. . .that's even worse."

"But how do you know I'm a Christian?" Perplexed, Brett couldn't help his frown. He knew he should be glad people could pick him out of a crowd of unbelievers. Still it was a little confusing.

"You said something about God laughing that first night of class. That sort of tipped me off that you're religious."

"Ah." Brett nodded. Now it all made sense. The reason she had seemed so interested at first only to completely disregard him before they got inside the building. "Thank you for being honest. And now I'll be honest with you. I couldn't entertain thoughts of a romantic relationship with a woman who doesn't share my faith, anyway."

Her eyes clouded for an instant, then took on a look of disinterest. She shrugged. "Well, then," she said and, once again, turned to go.

"You know," Brett said, surprising himself by speaking up. "There's nothing wrong with a couple of people sharing coffee and conversation, is there? And really, it takes the tension out of the whole situation because we both know we aren't going to date each other. What do you say? Will you come along with me if I promise not to pay for yours or hold out your chair for you like I would for a woman I'm trying to impress?"

Her lips twisted in a wry grin. "Well, when you put it that way, it's almost too much to resist. But there have to be some ground rules," she said, as he fell into step beside her.

"Besides making you pay for your own coffee?"

She nodded, without cracking a smile at his last attempt at humor. "Do not try to convert me, because it will never happen. Understand?"

Brett hesitated, pondering the Great Commission to preach the gospel to every creature.

Noting his reluctance, Audrey stopped short. "Look, let's just forget it, okay? You're not going to be able to resist trying to preach. No hard feelings."

"Let's make a deal," Brett replied. "I promise not to bring up God unless you bring Him up first. But if you mention Him, then you have to listen to what I have to say. Deal?"

A twinkle lit her eyes, and she reached out and accepted his proffered hand. "You will never, ever hear me bring up the subject of God or religion," she said. "So I think this is one deal I can safely accept."

Relieved, Brett sent a silent plea to heaven. *Father, now You'll have to have her bring it up so I can keep my promise and still tell Audrey about You.*

"You were right, you know." Audrey's husky voice broke through Brett's prayer.

"I was?"

She flashed him an impish grin. "I am a mocha latte kind of girl."

"With a white chocolate twist?"

"Mmmm."

Brett chuckled. "My favorite, too. I think this is the beginning of a beautiful friendship."

Chapter 2

True to his word, the good reverend refrained from acting like a date. Still, as cute as he was, Audrey didn't mind pretending, especially when she observed the look of envy she received from their perky blond waitress. Brett didn't seem to notice the college-aged flirt trying to make eye contact, and he actually apologized when the girl's French-manicured claws brushed his hand.

Audrey grinned, then covered it by taking a sip of the chocolate coffee.

"That's a pretty smile. What's it for?"

"What do you think?" she asked in mock incredulity. "Chocolate is a girl's best friend."

He blew on his latte. Audrey's gaze fixed on his puckered lips, and her mind flew into unguarded territory.

He swallowed and nodded. "Mmm. That *is* good. But what about diamonds?"

She forced her mind back to the reality that those lips were never going to pucker over hers and sighed. "What about diamonds?"

His half grin nearly threw her for a loop. "Girl's best friend?"

Oh, duh. Diamonds. Snap out of it. You are not kissing a preacher—not even a junior preacher. So knock it off!

Shaking her head emphatically, Audrey fingered the rim of her enormous coffeehouse mug and focused on keeping things light. "Oh, no. That's a common fallacy. What's really true—and don't ever forget this—is that chocolate heals all manner of heartache and symptoms. Diamonds only make you remember the giver of the jewels. If something goes horribly wrong with the relationship, a girl is compelled to flush said diamonds down the—well, you know."

He chuckled, and Audrey's heart lifted. She rewarded him with a wide smile and continued her instruction. "Chocolate, on the other hand, can be eaten and enjoyed whether a girl's in love or mending from a broken heart."

He gave an understanding nod, his face a mask of mock consideration. "So, just to recap: Never give a girl a diamond and expect it back?"

"That's right. Because if you marry her, she'll cherish it forever. But if you break her heart, the sparkly rock goes into the sewer, Babe, and there's not a thing you can do to get it back."

Brett's pleasant laugh filled the air between them. "Note to self. Hold off on buying of engagement ring until day before wedding."

Audrey sent him a smug grin. "Or you could make sure you find the right person in the first place. Then you won't have to worry about it."

He leaned in, his torso skimming the edge of the Formica table. "And how does one go about doing that?"

Wishing her heart wasn't pounding in her ears, Audrey returned his gaze, taking in the fashion-model square jawline, the way his mouth tilted slightly at the edges, and most of all, the way he looked at her as though he really cared what she thought.

Watch yourself, Audrey. Friendship only, remember? Even if you were interested in dating a religious guy, he's already made it clear he's looking for Mother Teresa.

With a shrug, she sipped more of the mocha. She cleared her throat as she set the cup back onto the table. "I'm thirty-two and single, remember? How do I know how to find the one?"

He leaned back and stretched his arm over the chair beside him. Tilting his head, he studied her.

Heat crept to her cheeks under his appraisal. "What?"

"Nothing. I'm just going to enjoy getting to know you, that's all."

"Thanks. Same here." A nice witty comment would have come in handy, but an unfamiliar blank filled her mind instead. She silently stared at him, feeling utterly foolish.

Undoubtedly mistaking her silence for disbelief, he forged ahead. "No, really. It's nice to know there's no pressure to try to find out if you're the one or not, because we both know the rules. You don't want to date me."

"And let's not forget the other important fact. I'm not good little preacher's wife material."

A frown darkened his expression, and Audrey inwardly kicked herself. Now she was going to get the inevitable sermon. He'd break his word for her own good, and then they wouldn't be friends after all. She braced herself, a knot forming in her stomach.

"I'm not forgetting the other fact," he said quietly. "But I promised you I wouldn't bring up your spiritual condition or the remedy to that tragic state." A rakish grin spread across his too-cute-not-to-be-surgically-enhanced face. "Although, one could argue that your comment was a cry for help. Taken literally, *you* brought it up. So, I'd be within my right to—"

With a pointed glance at her watch, Audrey *tsk-tsked.* "Would you *look* at the time." She gave a fake yawn. "Boy, oh, boy. Way past this girl's bedtime."

Reaching out, Brett covered her hand. "Okay. You win. Stay. Tell me about yourself."

Hesitating only a moment, Audrey resisted the urge to turn her hand over and lace her fingers with his. Instead, she nodded, and he pulled back.

She slunk down in her chair, feeling suddenly like a rebellious teen sitting in the principal's office. All she needed was some gum to smack and she'd have the image nailed. Ten minutes of conversation, and she was out of there. She'd just have to find another genealogy class. "All right, Rev. What would you like to know?" Nine minutes, fifty-five seconds.

"For starters, where were you born?"

She scowled. "You don't ask the easy ones, do you?"

"That's a toughie?"

"It is for an orphan."

For the first time in their scant, four-week association, Brett's composure fled. His face—from chin to hairline—reddened. "I'm sorry. No wonder you're working so hard to trace your roots. How did you know where to start?"

The concern in his voice warmed her to her toes, and she decided to have an adult conversation after all. She straightened in the chair. "Actually, my aunt found me a few years ago. She was something of a historian and amateur genealogist. But to answer your question, I was born in Georgia. Atlanta to be precise. My parents were missionaries who, I'm told, never planned to have kids. Mom was in her late thirties when she found out she was pregnant with me." She gave a bitter snort. "I can just imagine her disappointment. Anyway, they left me with my maternal grandparents three days before my second birthday. A month later they were killed in a plane crash on the way back from a mission trip to Spain."

"You were raised by your grandparents then?"

Audrey swallowed another sip of the now-cool latte. "Nope. My grandfather passed away soon after my parents, and my grandmother was in poor health. She didn't feel she could raise a little girl all by herself."

"Your dad's parents?"

Audrey shook her head. "My dad was twenty years older than my mom, so my paternal grandparents were really old." She took a deep breath, knowing that by allowing it, she was revealing her feelings of betrayal by her entire family. Might as well spell it out for the good preacher. "The grandparents got together—like one happy little family—and decided it was best to put me up for adoption. So they found me a wonderful mom and dad who couldn't have children of their own, and I went to live with them. Only guess what? Before the adoption was final, Mom got a miracle."

"She found out she was going to have a baby?"

"Bingo! And they couldn't afford two children on his salary at the jeans factory, so can you figure out which kid got the boot?"

"That's terrible. I'm sorry."

The kindness in his voice brought a lump to Audrey's throat, and out came the tough girl again. "Well, hey. How many kids get to play musical families?"

He took her hand again and regarded her, tenderness radiating from his eyes. "Too many."

She pulled her hand free, determined not to give him the chance to see her cry. "Yeah, well. That's life."

"You were never adopted?"

"Surprisingly, no. It's a real mystery, too. I was such a cute kid, you'd have thought someone would have snatched me right up." She gave what she hoped was a saucy grin.

He humored her with a return smile. A sympathetic one.

She sighed. So much for keeping things light. "I stayed in the same foster family until I was six. Then they moved out of state, so I changed homes. And from then until I was grown, I was passed around. Lucky for me, I had a brain and knew how to use it, so I got a scholarship."

"Good for you." His eyes twinkled. "I knew you were smart."

He was just so sweet! "Thanks. Anyway, that's it." Keeping things platonic wasn't going to be easy. But she knew she had no choice in the matter. Even if she wanted to date a religious man, she'd never date anyone who had pledged his life to being a preacher. . .or missionary. . .or whatever. No ministers of any kind. The price they were required to pay was just too high. And the price their families paid was even higher.

Brett's snapping fingers startled her. "What?" she asked, frowning.

"Does your mind wander a lot?" He let out a chuckle.

"Sorry," she muttered. "As a matter of fact, I'm usually pretty focused."

"It's okay. I was just kidding. I asked what you majored in during college."

"Education."

"You're a teacher?" His eyes sparked with interest.

She looked away. "In theory."

"What's that mean?"

"What it means, Mr. Nosy, is that I have a degree and a teaching certificate, but I own and run a flower shop."

"Makes sense." He grinned.

"Actually, it does. I wasn't cut out to shape the minds of fourth graders."

"How did the flower shop come about?"

"My great-aunt. The one I told you about?"

"Yes. . ."

"I got to know her in the last three years of her life. She left me her house and flower shop. The sad thing is that she said if she'd known about me all those years ago, she'd have taken me in a heartbeat. She never married." Regret passed over Audrey's heart as it often did when she allowed herself to think about what might have been.

"Why didn't she know about you?"

"She'd had a falling-out with my grandparents and didn't reconcile until near their deaths. She started looking me up and found me during my sophomore year in college. We had a nice three years together."

"And you moved to Chicago after she died?"

"No. I transferred to Northwestern and finished up here. I lived with her. I–I was there when she died."

"It was good of God to allow those three years."

Resentment welled up in Audrey. She wanted to rail at him. To remind him that *God* had given her to parents who never wanted her, who ran off to work for *Him* and then died in the process. So this God placated her after she was already grown up and didn't need family?

She glared at Brett, about to set him straight, but stopped when the waitress showed up and leaned over him to retrieve his empty cup. Jealousy shot through her. With determination, she gave it a violent mental shove. No way would she be jealous. Brett would be a friend. She liked him, and he was easy to talk to. But she couldn't allow herself to be dragged onto an emotional roller coaster with a man clearly unsuited to her.

"Do you want another latte?" Brett's voice captured her attention.

Shaking her head, she picked up her mug. "I still have half of mine left." She glanced up at the waitress. "Can I get it nuked to warm it up?"

The girl gave her a friendly smile. Audrey noticed a gold collar pin in the shape of a cross.

"No prob." The waitress took the mug and sashayed toward the kitchen.

"There's a nice Christian girl who's drooling over you."

Brett shot her a startled glance, then frowned and swept the coffeehouse with his gaze. "Where?"

"The waitress. Didn't you notice her not-so-subtle hints?"

His face reddened, a surefire indication that he'd noticed. "What makes you think she's a Christian?"

"She's wearing a cross on her collar. Are you interested?" Again the jealousy surged.

"Oh." He cleared his throat, and his face grew even redder when the perky female returned with Audrey's mug and a fresh cup of regular coffee for Brett. He said a hurried thank-you.

The waitress's expression clouded, and she walked away like a whipped pup.

"I think you broke her heart," Audrey teased.

He cleared his throat again and this time didn't return her smile. "Okay. If you can have ground rules about this friendship, it's only fair I get some, too. Right?"

Her stomach jumped at the intensity in his blue-green eyes. She gave a nonchalant shrug. "Sure, sounds reasonable."

He squared his shoulders and leaned slightly forward. He definitely meant business. "Okay. My only ground rule is that you don't try to set me up with another girl." He scowled. "It's like throwing a dog a bone."

Unable to resist, Audrey laughed and said the first thing that sprang to mind. "Which one of you is the dog?"

His lips twitched in response. "Seriously. It's the lowest insult possible for a pretty girl to try to set a guy up with someone she doesn't even know just to get rid of him."

"Hey, that's not what I—"

"You don't have to explain." He smiled. "I agreed that we'll only be friends, and I happen to like you a lot, so that's not going to be difficult. What will be difficult is trying not to fall in love with a beauty with the most unusual silverish eyes, with a witty sense of humor, and with more intelligence than ninety percent of the population. So, do we have a deal?"

Audrey drew a sharp breath. He wasn't the only one who would be fighting the attraction between them. But he was right. She wasn't the one to fix him up. She extended her hand and nearly sighed when his warmth enveloped her icy fingers. "We have a deal. You don't try to hook me up with the man upstairs, and I won't try to hook you up with any women."

He hedged, and Audrey held her breath. Was he about to renege on his end of the deal? "All right. But remember, if you bring it up, all bargains are off. Right?"

Relieved, Audrey nodded.

"Great. Now let's talk about what you've been able to learn about your family tree."

The remainder of the evening passed in pleasant excitement as Audrey shared her research results and Brett offered his suggestions. Before she knew it, they were saying good-bye and promising to meet again the following week.

Later, lying in her four-poster bed inside her newly remodeled, 1940s, two-story home, Audrey stared at the ceiling, replaying her evening with Brett. Resentment rose inside, a comfortable and familiar companion.

"God, why do You keep putting people into my life who I can't keep?" Tears slipped from the corners of her eyes and slid down the sides of her head, soaking into the hair at her temples. "When will You realize that I won't make the same mistakes my parents made? The price of serving You is just too high." She flopped onto her stomach as if doing so would shut Him out. "And throwing a great guy like Brett at me isn't playing fair. I won't fall for him."

But the memory of Brett's smile wreaked havoc with her determination. And when she finally drifted off to sleep in the wee hours of the morning, she could already feel her resolve weakening.

Chapter 3

The measles?" Audrey's voice filtered through the phone line with a definite ring of suspicion. "I didn't think adults could get the measles."

Heat crept up Brett's neck at her insinuation that he'd made the whole thing up. "Apparently they can because my brother's wife is covered with spots. So what do you say? Can you take her place helping me chaperone the young people tonight?"

She hesitated. "Don't you have any other friends?"

He chuckled at the cornered-animal panic in her voice. "I have other friends but no one I can ask. There will be girls in the group. I can't get another guy to chaperone. And it wouldn't be appropriate to ask a married woman."

"You don't know any single women besides me?"

Brett smiled at the guarded question. He had a feeling she was just as attracted to him as he was to her. Unfortunately, it wasn't a situation that could go anywhere unless she allowed the Lord to soften her heart. He wasn't exactly happy Marlene, his sister-in-law, had gotten the childhood disease, but it did give him the opportunity to share Jesus with Audrey without breaking the rules of their friendship—if she would agree to help him chaperone the youth Bible study and game night. He just needed to convince her that he couldn't do it alone—which was basically true at this eleventh hour. "Okay, I know a lot of single ladies from church. But what do you think would happen if I invited one of them to co-chaperone a youth event at my house?"

"I don't know. What?"

"Rumors would fly, and before I knew it, the girl's mother would be inviting me to Sunday dinner so her dad could ask me my intentions. Do you really want to put me through that?"

She laughed.

The spontaneous response swelled Brett's chest with a sense of well-being. He took advantage of her obvious weakening and pushed his cause. "So, you'll help out a friend in need? Otherwise, I'll have to cancel and disappoint all those kids."

"Hey, no fair bringing out the heavy artillery." Her breathy voice revealed that she was most likely talking on a cordless phone and moving around.

He imagined her surrounded by flowers of all shapes, sizes, and colors. The image picked up his pulse. He cleared his throat. "I also came across something you might find interesting. Something to do with a certain ancestor of yours."

"First guilt, now bribery? And you call yourself a preacher?" She sighed deeply into the receiver. "Okay, first tell me what you found out, and I'll decide if it's worth the trouble."

"Nope. You want the info, you'll have to help me out."

"Oh, all right. But this isn't exactly my thing, so I'll probably ruin the whole evening for the kids. What time and what's your address?"

Brett closed his eyes and mouthed a silent, "Yes!"

So far they had only seen each other on class nights. For the past month, they'd made a point to walk together to the coffee shop afterward. It wasn't nearly enough for Brett. His heart was on dangerous ground, but he had the feeling Audrey needed a friend. And he knew for certain she needed to learn to trust Jesus. He could keep his feelings in check and let the Lord use him, even if there was never anything in the relationship for him.

Walking up the steps to Brett's duplex apartment, Audrey tried to still her pounding heart. Why had she agreed to this lunacy? How could she chaperone a bunch of church kids? She didn't even go to Sunday school herself, for crying out loud. Furthermore, she had no intention of darkening the doorstep of a church, cathedral, or synagogue for as long as she lived.

Forget it. This was a huge mistake. She was getting back into the cab and heading for the hills. *Nice knowing you, Rev.*

She spun around to stop the taxi and lifted her hand just in time to see her getaway car's tail lights whiz down the quiet street. "Wait!" she called with a moan. A sigh of defeat hissed from her lips. Her shoulders slumped, and she turned around to face the inevitable disaster awaiting her behind the forest green door.

"Hi. Wrong address?"

Audrey glanced in startled surprise at a pretty teenaged girl coming down the sidewalk toward the duplex. "No. Just cold feet."

The girl laughed, charming Audrey immediately. If there was such a thing as a sweet laugh, this girl had one. "You must be Pastor Brett's partner tonight."

"You guessed it." Audrey bit back a groan. *Pastor* Brett? She was in way over her head and sinking fast. She didn't want to see him in that role. To remind herself that he was always going to be just out of reach. Like a carrot dangling in front of a horse just to keep the animal running. Only God was holding the Brett-carrot, and she was just tagging along, hoping to eventually catch up, even if she knew there was no way she ever would.

"Hey, don't look so worried. We'll go easy on you."

Audrey grinned at the girl. "Thanks. I'm Audrey."

"Cassie." She shook Audrey's hand. "I'll knock."

Audrey braced herself as they waited for the door to open. When it did, she sucked in a breath. Brett, the genealogy teacher, always looked nice and professional in his jackets and slacks. But *this* Brett had on a pair of Tommy jeans and a red, long-sleeved pullover. He looked *good.* Too good for a preacher.

He greeted Cassie first. "Glad you could make it."

"Thanks, Pastor." She jerked her thumb toward Audrey, who pulled herself together in time to keep from making an idiot of herself. The girl gave them each an impish grin, then addressed Brett. "Met your friend outside. Your taste is improving."

Cheeks burning, Audrey stepped over the threshold.

Brett gave Cassie's unruly blond curls a slight tug. "Very funny. Get out of here." The teen's laughter followed her down the hall. His brow rose in apology. "Sorry about that."

"No problem." A shrug lifted Audrey's shoulders. "At least she didn't say I was a step down from the last one."

"Hardly." He leaned closer, and before Audrey knew what was happening, he brushed her cheek with his lips. "Thanks for coming."

Her senses reeled from the scent of his aftershave, and she had trouble forming words. So she simply nodded, trying to remember her name, age, and where she was born.

"Let me have your jacket," Brett said.

Thankfully or regrettably, depending on how she decided to look at it, Audrey didn't seem to have the same effect on Brett. His suggestion eased the tension surrounding Audrey. She smiled and shrugged out of her windbreaker. Glad she'd opted for jeans, she pushed up the sleeves of her Northwestern sweatshirt and hid her hands in her back pockets. "So, what do I do tonight?"

After hanging her jacket on the coat rack, he turned and motioned her to head down the hall in front of him. "Nothing much, really," he said. "We'll start out with a game. Then I'll say a prayer, and I thought you could lead us in a couple of songs."

Audrey gasped and swung around.

Brett frowned. "What? Surely you know 'Kumbaya' or something."

Panic beat a rapid cadence within her chest, and the room temperature rose to about 104 degrees. "Brett. . ." Her voice squeaked around the Ping-Pong-ball-sized lump in her throat.

"Relax." He tweaked her nose. "I'm kidding. You're mainly here for decoration."

Relief mingled with irritation as her heart slowed to a non-lethal beat. She scowled. "Mainly?"

He took her shoulders and turned her around in the narrow hallway. "You can help the girls get the refreshments ready after the lesson."

"The girls serve the boys? What kind of message does that send?"

"Believe me," he said next to her ear. "The girls would rather take care of it. Otherwise there's nothing left for them.

Besides, what's wrong with girls waiting on boys?"

Audrey sniffed. "Neanderthal."

He laughed as they entered the living room, where at least twenty kids, all shapes, sizes, and a pretty even mix of genders, hung out in various huddles.

Audrey scanned the room for a familiar face and frowned as she located Cassie. The girl sat alone at the edge of the couch, pretending interest in a magazine. Frequent upward glances, however, betrayed her anxiety, but apparently no one but Audrey noticed. Indignation rose inside of Audrey. She made a beeline for the couch. Cassie glanced up and gave her an infectious all-American-girl smile.

"Mind if I sit?" Audrey asked. "I could use an ally."

"Me, too," the girl replied, patting the cushion next to her.

"Thanks." Audrey plopped down, folded her hands in her lap, and rested her ankle on the opposite knee. "So, what kinds of games are we playing?"

"Tonight we're playing 'Who Wants a Free Ticket to the Newsboys Concert?' "

"That's a game?"

"It's our version of the TV game show." Cassie smiled—the same sweet smile that had charmed Audrey a few minutes before—and Audrey couldn't help but wonder what a great kid like this one was doing sitting all by herself in a room full of peers.

She glanced around for Brett. Why didn't he know Cassie didn't fit in? She located him in the center of a group of boys, each trying to outdo the others to gain Brett's attention. As if drawn by her perusal, he turned his head slightly and caught her eye. Audrey's heart nearly stopped as he smiled and nodded to her.

Caught off guard, she looked away and focused her attention on Cassie, trying to remember what they'd been talking about. Oh, yeah, some game.

"Pastor Brett's pretty cute," Cassie mused.

With great effort, Audrey refrained from swallowing her tongue. She shrugged. "I really hadn't noticed. Besides, we're just friends. So, how do you play this game?"

The teen lifted her eyebrows, but she apparently decided not to push the Pastor Brett issue. "Okay, here's how we play. Two people compete at a time. Pastor Brett asks questions, and we go back and forth until one gets the wrong answer. Then someone takes the loser's place until there's only one person left. The winner. And to make it easier, we each get one lifeline—not three like the TV game."

"What kind of lifeline?"

"We get to ask someone in the group to give us the answer."

Audrey smiled. "Sounds like fun."

"It is." Her face clouded. "Only almost everyone asks friends to be their lifeline. And a person can only be a lifeline to one person."

"So what's the problem?"

A shrug lifted her shoulders as pain flickered in her eyes. "Not everyone has friends here."

Brett saw Cassie's face go white as she sat in the hot seat, groping for the right answer to his question. His heart went out to her. After all, the other kids had parents who would gladly spring for tickets to a concert—and could afford to do so. For Cassie, winning the game was a must if she was going to go to the concert without feeling like a charity case.

But she was up against tough competition. Ephraim Todd was the pastor's son. He'd cut his teeth on the Ten Commandments and had memorized a verse a day from the time he could talk. The kid was a rock. A living testimony to his parents' dedication to raising him with a full knowledge and understanding of the Word of God. Unfortunately, that did nothing to help Cassie's situation. Ephraim's face held a smug expression. Sure, he might not have known the question, but he'd beaten six opponents already. If Cassie missed the last question, Ephraim automatically won the game—and the ticket.

"Remember, Cassie," Brett said. "You still have that lifeline."

"Yes, Sir," she said dully. She glanced about and received a roomful of blank stares. Brett inwardly sighed. He loved these kids, but some of them just didn't have any sympathy whatsoever. Besides, he seriously doubted they would be able to help Cassie. After all, how many of them were likely to know the name of Caleb's daughter?

A loud cough erupted from the couch. Brett frowned in concern as Audrey hacked as though she were about to pass out. Cassie looked at her, too. Audrey grinned at the girl and nodded. "Pastor," Cassie whispered and motioned to him.

He leaned in. "Yeah?"

"Can Audrey be my lifeline?"

Alarm shot through him. Asking Audrey anything about the Bible was a surefire way to lose, but there was no rule stating an adult couldn't be a lifeline. Only he was excluded. "You sure?"

"Yes." Her eyes twinkled.

Dread hung over Brett as he shrugged, certain she was sealing her fate. "Go for it." He looked at Audrey. "Is that okay with you?"

Audrey nodded. "Yep."

"Okay. What was the name of Caleb's daughter? Was it Othniel, Esther, Michal, or Acsah?"

He cringed, about to hand the ticket over to Ephraim.

"Acsah." Audrey's voice rang through the silent room.

"Cassie. . ." His mouth dropped open at the same time her words penetrated his mind. "What did you say?"

"Acsah. And that's the right answer." Audrey frowned as though ready to take him on. "It's in the book of Judges, and I can prove it."

"No, no. You don't have to prove it. Cassie, Audrey thinks it's Acsah. Do you want to take her advice? Or do you think it's one of the other answers?"

"I'm going to take Audrey's advice and say Acsah."

Wings of joy fluttered inside of Brett's chest. "Final answer?"

Cassie's face said it all. "Final answer."

He could barely contain himself as he handed her the ticket. "Congratulations! You're the winner of a very fine ticket to the Newsboys concert next Friday night."

Always a great sport whether winning or losing, Ephraim shot the girl a sheepish grin and extended his hand. "Congratulations, Cassie."

Her face turned red. "Thanks," she whispered. "You played a good game." Without awaiting his answer, she spun around and headed for the couch—her haven during get-togethers. Brett smiled as she flung her arms around Audrey.

Brett caught Audrey's wide-eyed gaze over Cassie's shoulder. He was unable to offer his own thanks as the kids surrounded him. That she knew anything of the Bible was a surprise. That she knew such an obscure fact was downright shocking. He grinned to himself. There was an awful lot to learn about Audrey.

Audrey smiled to herself as she stuffed the last paper plate inside the tall kitchen garbage bag she'd shuffled around the apartment. The look on Brett's face when she'd gotten the right answer was priceless.

"You're smiling all by yourself?"

His voice startled her, and she jumped and squeaked.

"For crying out loud, Brett. Warn a girl first."

"So, how'd you know the answer was Acsah?"

"Just because I don't go to church, you think I don't know anything about the Bible?"

"This wasn't just anything," he shot back, completely undaunted by her challenge. "I would have expected you to get a question like, 'Who killed Goliath?' But the name of Caleb's daughter? No one knows that. Even I wouldn't have known it if the answer hadn't been right in front of me."

She couldn't resist a laugh. "All right. One of my foster families was made up of a preacher and his wife and three kids. Anytime we got in trouble, we had to write an essay taken from the Bible. These people believed that women were little more than household slaves, so once, when I got in trouble, I wrote a five-page masterpiece entitled 'God Likes Girls Too.' "

Brett laughed, and Audrey joined in.

"I'm intrigued. Go on." He took the bag from her and tied it up.

"I combed through the Bible and studied all the major women players. Esther, Ruth, Deborah—who was a judge of Israel. Then I saw Acsah. I figured my foster dad wouldn't have heard of her." She grinned. "I was a little full of myself. Anyway,

Caleb, Acsah's father, gave her to the man who defeated his enemy. At first I was mad, but then I noticed that she asked her dad for more land than he'd originally given to her husband, and Caleb granted his daughter's request. Caleb's daughter secured a great piece of land for her family just by asking her father for it." She shrugged. "I don't know. . .just seemed important to me."

"It is important. And I think the significance is that God loves His daughters and wants to bless them with more than He offers, if they will ask."

"Yeah, well." She took in a quick breath of air, rested her hands on her hips, and looked at him expectantly. "Okay, so where is this bit of information you have for me?"

Brett smiled, obviously willing to look past her abrupt change of subject. "Right here." He pointed toward the bottom shelf of an end table next to his recliner. Snatching a pile of photocopied papers, he handed them to her. "I found these pages in a book while I was researching an old English family for a client. I thought this might be the Rory MacMurray you were telling me about."

Audrey's eyes widened, and she took the papers. "It has to be!" She scanned the pages. "Brett, listen to this. 'For twenty years, Rory eluded capture by fleeing England to the United States. There he dropped his English family name and took on MacMurray, the name of his maternal great-grandparents. He was eventually caught and taken back to England, where he bargained his way out of imprisonment but was forced to leave the country as part of the arrangement. Rather than returning to the United States, which by now was embroiled in Civil War, he traveled to Scotland, his mother's homeland, and lived out his days at Kennerith Castle. Two of his American-born children joined him in Scotland, along with his wife, Anna. One married daughter remained behind and became a spy for the Union Army. Rory was buried in the MacMurray graveyard on the castle grounds.' "

Audrey's heart raced. She glanced up at Brett. "No wonder I haven't been able to go back any farther in my family line. He wasn't using his given name. Thank you so much for copying these for me, Brett. I don't know what to say."

An insistent honk sounded from the curb outside.

"Your cab's here." He reached for her hand and held it as he led her down the hall toward the door. "And you don't have to say anything. I'm just glad that you're on the right track again."

"I'd like to repay you. Will you come to my house for dinner tomorrow night?"

She noted the hesitation and felt heat rising in her face. "I'm sorry. Dumb idea."

"Probably not the smartest," he agreed, his smile taking the sting out of the words. "We have to remember the bargain and stick with it."

"Yeah. Okay. You're right."

"I wish things were different."

Regret slashed at Audrey's heart, and she swallowed past the tears threatening to make an untimely appearance. She was about to turn to the door when he stepped forward and took her face in his hands. Before either could speak, he bent and pressed a tender kiss to her forehead. "I'll see you Monday night at class."

She met his gaze and found much more than friendship lurking in the depths of his eyes. Her emotions went wild, muddling her brain. Everything she wanted to say fled her mind. She opened the door and stepped onto the porch. "See ya, Brett."

She sat quietly as the cab sped toward her home. If circumstances had been different, would Brett have accepted her invitation? Would they be halfway to the altar by now? She pondered the possibilities until she reached her home. When she walked in the door, she made a beeline for her computer. While it booted, she filled the kettle with water, set it on the stove, and went to change into her comfy sweats.

Twenty minutes later, armed with a cup of tea and the pages Brett had copied for her, she began to search. Her gritty eyes were beginning to droop after three hours, but then she found the name Kennerith Castle associated with the name Spencer. A surge of energy gave her a second wind and she read on and on, finding another piece of her heritage in the story of an Englishman and a Scottish lass. . . .

English Tea and Bagpipes

by Pamela Griffin

Dedication

Thanks to all those who helped and encouraged me,
especially to Mom and my local crit group.
And to Tracey, Tamela, and Jill—my online critique partners
and fellow writers in this collection—
it's so wonderful to be in a novella anthology with you lassies!
grin
In the beauty of the gloamin',
in the dismal gray of storms, my God is ever faithful.
It is to Him I devote this story.
For without the Lord in my life,
accepting me when few others would,
you wouldn't be reading this now.

Only by pride cometh contention:
but with the well advised is wisdom.
PROVERBS 13:10

Chapter 1

Scotland, 1822

Fiona moved up the slippery path with care, clutching a plaid underneath her chin to block her head from the light shower. The long rectangular cloth did little to keep her completely dry, but then, she was accustomed to rain. It was her previous talk with the Finlays that gave her distress. Frowning, she paused to look up and study the familiar landmarks.

Endless steep-sided hills speckled with gray granite rose on either side and before her in the deep glen, adding their distinct signature to the untamed beauty of the region. Peaks of distant snow-covered mountains could be seen in the gap between hills at her right. To her left, a loch glimmered as drops ruffled the surface of the lake's waters. The cool, soft rain touched the rugged land, watering the earth of her Highland home.

Directly ahead, Fiona spotted a man sitting bolt upright on Ian MacGregor's shaggy nag, Dunderhead. From the navy coat, top hat, and black shiny boots he wore, the man must be a stranger, though she could only see him from the back. Why he was on Ian's horse was the real puzzle. Still, Fiona kept herself far removed from her neighbors' affairs, and likewise they left her to her own. The gentleman didn't seem the type to be a horse thief. What's more, who would want to steal old Dunderhead?

Fiona pulled her plaid farther over her hair as she walked past, her shoes squelching in the puddles.

"I say—wait a moment!" he called.

Fiona grimaced in her distaste for anything English.

"Can you help me?" he yelled more loudly over the tapping rain.

"There's nae need t' screech like a banshee." Fiona pivoted to face him. "I'm no' deaf."

She forced herself to calm. Often, when she was excited or upset, the thick Highland brogue rolled off her tongue rather than the proper speech she'd been taught as a child. She took her first real look at the dark-haired rider. Even wet, his countenance and form appeared pleasing to the eye, she had to admit. For an Englishman, that is.

"Thank you." He tipped his hat, civilly inclining his head. "I have twice been given erroneous directions to the place I seek and feel as though I've traversed this entire countryside. To make matters worse, I made the dreadful mistake of purchasing this nag that seems to know only one speed. Slow. So if you could assist me, I would be most obliged."

Fiona hid a smile. "Any halfwit knows just t' look at the beast that Ian's horse isna worth a shilling."

"Yes," he said, his voice bearing a slight edge. "I, too, have arrived at that conclusion. However, as much as I would like to stay and hold a discussion concerning the idiosyncrasies of the locals, I don't relish doing so in a downpour."

"What? This wee bit of rain?" she asked with an innocent smirk, lifting her palm to shoulder level to catch the drops.

He shook his head slowly, as though dealing with a backward child. "In that assessment we most assuredly differ, Miss. Yet perhaps my view is colored by the fact that I've been traveling in this 'wee bit of rain' for a matter of hours. That said, I would be most grateful if you could tell me, is this the way to Kennerith Castle?"

"Kennerith Castle?" Fiona repeated in bewilderment.

"Yes," he said wearily. "Kennerith Castle."

Suddenly suspicious, Fiona took several seconds to examine his upright bearing and expensive attire. She gave a curt nod. "Aye. 'Tis that."

"Thank you *ever* so much," he replied, sarcasm coating his words.

Narrowing her eyes, Fiona left him and took a shortcut near a stand of birches that forked off the road. Englishmen! He could go and get lost in a bog, for all she cared.

When she reached home a short time later, she hurried through the entryway of the crumbling gatehouse to the living quarters beyond and slipped off her plaid. Squeezing the water from the tartan wool, she hung the cloth over the back of a chair near the peat fire to dry, all the while assessing her meager surroundings. Her grandmother huddled in a chair close to the hearth.

"Gwynneth has not yet come down from her chambers, and it's nearing noonday. Go and see what keeps her."

"Aye, *Seanmhair,*" Fiona said, using the Gaelic endearment for *grandmother.* Though the language had trickled away and all but disappeared, her family had passed down the dialect over the generations. Fiona was proud of that, intending never to let it fully die.

Exasperated with her irresponsible sister, mostly because searching her out was an interruption she didn't need, Fiona headed for the east tower. If Gwynneth were immersed in one of those idealistic novels with which she wasted her time, she would receive an earful from Fiona—that was certain!

The repeated bangs of the doorknocker resounded through the area, halting Fiona's steps. Deciding that Gwynneth could wait, Fiona whirled around and hurried to the entryway before old Agatha could get there. Checking to see that her tunic was properly tucked in, Fiona noticed that mud covered the bottom of her ankle-length skirt. She grimaced, but there wasn't time to change into another. Smoothing her damp, riotous curls away from her face, she straightened her shoulders and, as she opened the huge, heavy door, assumed the dignified air befitting the granddaughter of the earl of Carnassis.

The Englishman stood in the rain and stared, shock written in eyes that Fiona could now see were blue-gray. An impish hint of satisfaction swept through her, but she struggled to keep her face expressionless and inclined her head graciously. "Welcome to Kennerith Castle."

The rain continued to beat down on Alex as he took in the smug expression of the bright-eyed wisp of a woman standing inside the door. Her eyes, a shade lighter than the overcast sky, glistened silver. Briefly he wondered how the slim column of her neck could hold up her head, as weighed down as it was by the mass of ginger-colored ringlets trailing to her waist. The plaid she'd worn earlier had hidden them. Yet what she lacked in size, she made up for in spirit.

"You could have told me," he said, giving her a mildly reproving look.

She shrugged. "You didna give me the chance. You were not exactly of a cordial mind."

"Nor were you."

She gave a grudging nod. " 'Tis true enough, I suppose."

Despite his irritation, Alex couldn't help but appreciate the lilting way she spoke and rolled her *R*s. Of course everyone in Scotland spoke in such a manner, but with her smooth, pleasantly pitched voice, it sounded especially nice. If only her disposition were as sweet.

"I am Dr. Alexander Spencer, recently arrived from England, and I have need to speak with your mistress, Miss Gwynneth Galbraith, on a most urgent matter."

She straightened to her full height—the top of her head still only coming to his shoulders—and glared at him with disdain. "Now see here, Dr. Alexander Spencer of England Gwynneth Galbraith isna me mistress, nor will she ever be. I am Fiona Galbraith, Gwynneth's elder sister and the granddaughter of Hugh Galbraith—the sixth earl of Carnassis, eighth viscount of Dalway, and eleventh baron—and laird—of Kennerith. If ye have need to speak with Gwynneth—though for what reason I canna ken—ye will need t' speak through me."

Her sister! Alex sobered. "Forgive my error. Actually, the matter concerns Gwynneth. It is your audience I desire." He motioned with one hand. "Might I come inside, out of the rain?"

The mystified expression on her face proved that she'd not yet heard the news. A measure of relief swept through Alex. Perhaps he wasn't too late.

Her manner still suspicious, Fiona stepped back, allowing him entrance. With a quick, calculating glance, he pulled off his hat, shook water from its brim, and surveyed the interior of the drafty citadel. The imposing exterior of the stone fortress, with its four square towers, moat, and keep, didn't reveal the true condition of the ivy-covered castle. Furnishings appeared worn and in need of replacement. The flagstone floor was in dire need of repair. Everywhere he cast a glance, evidence of neglect and poverty was visible, and Alex imagined the other chambers fared just as badly.

As though she discerned his thoughts, Fiona stepped into his line of vision, blocking his quiet perusal. "Ye wish to speak with me?" she asked, narrowing her eyes.

"Fiona?" a woman called from somewhere nearby. "Who is that you're talking to?"

"Only a strange Englishman who wandered here in the rain," Fiona retorted, her rigid gaze never leaving his face. "He soon will be leaving."

"Bring him to me!"

Fiona blew out a breath. "Aye, *Seanmhair.*" Her eyes narrowed at Alex. "Come on with ye, then. But I warn you, if it's mischief you're aboot, you've come t' the wrong place!"

The woman was impossible. Alex just managed to hold his tongue and followed her to a nearby chamber. The obvious scarcity of furnishings made the room seem larger. Near the fire, an elderly woman sat in one of four chairs in the room and looked at him, narrowing her eyes over her half-moon glasses. Two portraits hung side by side over the mantel. The one on the left was of a kind-faced gentleman in a plain, gray tie-wig, the other of a fierce-looking warrior with curly ginger-colored hair much like Fiona's. Both men and the girl shared the same feature of silver-gray eyes. The warrior in the painting wore a kilt with a long plaid of matching red, black, yellow, blue, and green clasped to his shoulder, and he bore a broadsword in his hand.

"That is my grandfather, Angus MacMurray, once a clan chieftain," the old woman said, following Alex's gaze. "And the first portrait is of my husband's father, Allan, who was also Angus's nephew." Her sober gaze turned his way. "Angus MacMurray fought—and died—at Culloden."

The stern words carried with them a warning Alex recognized. He was English; they were Scots. And though close to a hundred years had passed since the battle at Culloden Moor, these people had not forgotten it. That being the case, they would never approve of what Gwynneth Galbraith had done. Alex's lips turned upward in a dry smile. Without the women realizing it, they were on his side.

He quickly introduced himself to the old woman and withdrew the letter from his coat pocket, grateful to find the message only slightly damp. "While on an unannounced visit to my brother, Lord Beaufort Spencer, a scholar at the University of Edinburgh, I did not find him but came across this instead," Alex explained. "My brother had delivered it into the hands of a friend along with directions to mail it to our father next week. In short, the letter states that Beaufort met a woman visiting there, fell in love, and they have eloped. He doesn't say where they've gone."

"I dinna see what that has to do with us," Fiona argued.

"The woman is your sister—Miss Gwynneth Galbraith of Kennerith Castle." At Fiona's gasp of disbelief, Alex added, "It's all here in the letter, if you care to see it."

Glaring, she covered the short distance between them and snatched the paper from his outstretched hand. She scanned the missive, her face paling.

"Fiona?" the old woman rasped. "Tell me it's not true, Lass."

"Aye, *Seanmhair,*" she murmured. " 'Tis that."

"Perhaps it's not too late," Alex said, understanding their shock, for he'd been rocked by the same emotion. "Beaufort left only the day before I arrived, and surely, if this is as much a surprise to you as it was to me, then there's a strong chance Gwynneth might still be on the premises?"

Fiona's countenance lightened. "Aye! She must be. I was on my way t' talk with her when your knock came."

Without waiting for a response, Fiona whirled around and headed for the opposite end of the castle. She took the winding and narrow tower stairs, passing a portrait of the ghoulish-looking Olivia Galbraith, who'd once occupied this same tower chamber. Many female ancestors had stayed in the well-fortified east tower, including Fiona's great-grandmother, Lady Celeste, whose love for a servant brought peace between the once-feuding Clan MacMurray and Clan Galbraith, and her other great-grandmother, Beryl, who'd been a simple ladies' maid. Now Fiona's sister occupied the tower that legend said had a reputation for bearing doomed women.

Fiona threw open the door to Gwynneth's sitting room. Seeing it unoccupied, she moved to the adjoining bedchamber, disheartened to find it empty, as well. She mustn't jump to conclusions. Perhaps the lass had gone to the crag that jutted out near the loch. She often enjoyed sitting there and looking out over the lake's waters.

On a nearby table, atop a copy of Sir Walter Scott's *Ivanhoe,* lay a novel Fiona had never seen—*Pride and Prejudice.* Beneath its title, the cover only said: "by the author of *Sense and Sensibility.*" Fiona grimaced at the book, whose script lettering seemed to accuse her, and wondered how her sister had come by it. She spotted a paper rectangle peeking from within the pages. With heavy heart, she slid it out and read her name on the parchment in Gwynneth's flowery hand. Fingers trembling, she opened the note.

Dearest Fiona,

When you read this, I will long be gone. I have fallen in love with a most wonderful man, Lord Beaufort Spencer of Durrencourt. Aye, he is an Englishman. I met him when I visited our cousin in Edinburgh last spring. I knew you and our grandmother would not approve, so I thought it best to keep our acquaintance secret. Beaufort also thought it wise not to inform his family of our wedding plans. Yet the love we share is strong, and we'll not be denied a life together due to prejudices that are centuries old. As you read this, we are on our way to Gretna Green, and when next you see me—if you will see me—I will be Lady Spencer. I pray that you can look beyond your intolerance for anything English and can share in my happiness. . . .

Fiona's hand holding the letter dropped to her side as she sank against the four-poster bed. After awhile, the stunned feeling dissipated, and she marched to her chamber, resolute.

There was nothing to be done but go after the foolish girl. And Fiona was up to the task.

Wondering what was keeping the young woman, Alex stood, clasping his wrist behind his back, his hat in his hand, and gazed at the paintings, though he was very aware of the elderly matriarch's stern eye on him. The musty scent from the smoky fire coupled with the faint odor of mildew fit in well with these primitive surroundings. From the little Alex had seen, it was a wonder the castle still stood.

A quick, light tread on the flagstones made him turn, and Fiona rushed into the room. She stopped short at seeing Alex, as if just remembering he was there, narrowed her eyes at him, and moved toward her grandmother. Alex noticed Fiona had taken time to change from her muddy clothes into a serviceable dark blue wool dress. He wondered why. Certainly she hadn't done so for him.

"Well, Child—speak." The old woman leaned forward. "Dinna keep me in suspense."

Fiona's woebegone expression told all. "She's gone, as he said. I found this letter in her room. She must have taken the secret stairway."

The woman put a hand to her heart, skimming the parchment. "Gretna Green! Such news may give your grandfather another stroke. . .though likely he's beyond understanding."

"She willna get far," Fiona assured her grandmother, retrieving the letter from the woman's limp hand now lying in her lap. "I'll see to that."

"Excuse me." Alex stepped forward, earning him a cold stare from both women, as though he'd been the one to steal their relation away and not his brother. From the little he'd seen of the castle, he doubted Gwynneth Galbraith had needed much enticing. "Might I see the letter? If I'm to find them, I'll need to know what it says."

"That willna be necessary." Fiona folded the letter and stuck it within the high neckline of her dress. "I'm capable of findin' my own sister."

Alex could barely restrain a laugh. "You? Surely you jest. Traveling to Gretna Green in this weather could take many days, even weeks."

"Perhaps for an Englishman," Fiona retorted, a gleam in her eye. "But no' for a Scot."

"I'm sorry, Miss Galbraith, but I simply don't have the time or the inclination to act as companion—which is preposterous in any case. Surely you realize the impropriety of a man escorting an unmarried woman without a chaperone present?" He didn't add that should she produce such a chaperone, the two would only slow him down.

Challenge sparked her eyes. "Who said anything about me goin' with the likes o' you? I'm perfectly capable of findin' the place on my own."

"What?" Alex couldn't believe what he was hearing. "You can't travel alone!"

"And why not?" She faced him, hands balled on her hips. "Because I'm only a wee slip of a lass and not a laddie?" she challenged.

"Yes—no." Alex twisted his hat around in his hands. The girl was confusing him. "It's a hazardous journey. You might not be safe."

"To be sure, I'm well able to take care o' myself."

"Fiona, you are certain?" her grandmother interrupted.

Incredulous, Alex glanced at the old woman. Surely, she

couldn't be in favor of such a preposterous plan!

The expression in the girl's eyes softened. "Aye, *Seanmhair.* I'll find her."

"And how do you propose to get there?" Alex inserted triumphantly. "Obviously you've no horse, or you wouldn't have been walking in this downpour. And I certainly won't give you the nag I was saddled with, poor beast that she is."

After a long silence, Fiona lowered her head in evident defeat and turned her back to him, shoulders slumping. "Aye. Perhaps ye speak wisely. Perhaps 'tis best I stay. For surely, I canna walk across all o' Scotland and make it there in time to stop the wedding."

A little off balance by her unexpected change of heart, Alex paused before replying. "I'm relieved that you see things my way at last. It's best for all concerned. Do not fear; I shall see to it that your sister returns safely."

"How good of ye."

Alex stared hard at the mass of ginger-red curls flowing down her back. Had he detected a note of mockery in the words?

"Grandmother, ye've not yet had your broth," Fiona said, as though the thought had just occurred. "I'll see what keeps Agatha." She directed a cool gaze toward Alex. "I suppose you'll be wantin' food as well before continuin' your search?"

Alex considered the prospect. "That would be splendid. Also a cup of tea, if you have it."

"Ye'll not be findin' English tea at Kennerith Castle," she said proudly. "As to the other, I'll see to it."

Alex watched Fiona whisk from the room. Though the offer for refreshment had been less than charming, Alex looked forward to a quick, hot meal to warm him before heading into the chill rain again. Moreover, somewhere he must find a better piece of horseflesh if he were to catch up to his brother in time. Alex's father wouldn't tolerate failure in accomplishing this task.

Minutes passed, the low crackle of fire in the hearth the only sound heard. The old woman sat upright, staring out a nearby window as though looking for someone. Evidently she desired no idle drawing room chitchat, if this indeed could be considered a drawing room. Alex eyed every object in the sparse chamber twice, fiddling with his hat, turning it round and round, wishing the girl would hurry so he could be gone from this place.

From outside, the clatter of galloping hooves followed by muffled pounding—the sound of a horse exiting the drawbridge and tearing up sod—caught his attention. He rushed to glance out the same window the woman stared at. Through the paned glass, he made out a cloaked figure astride a fine gray mount flying like the wind. The hood fell away, and an abundant banner of long red hair unfurled behind the rider.

The old woman chuckled and turned her proud gaze toward Alex. "My granddaughter isna easily crossed, Dr. Spencer. She has the spirit of her forebears. You would do well to remember that."

Alex stared in disbelief and watched Fiona ride away along the high moor.

Chapter 2

Hours had elapsed since Fiona's escape. She still grinned when she thought of how she'd outwitted the annoying Englishman. Imagine, telling her what she could and could not do! The need for a hasty departure had been crucial; otherwise they would have wasted precious time arguing the matter, and Fiona didn't take kindly to anyone ordering her about.

Nigh unto two years had passed since her grandfather's stroke that left him an invalid and void of his mental faculties. Since that time, Fiona had needed to unofficially assume any pressing duties that her frail grandmother or the earl's secretary couldn't handle. Fiona and Gwynneth had been orphaned at an early age and had come to live at Kennerith with her mother's parents. Her fondest memories were the nights of the *ceilidh*, when young and old in their household, along with any visiting family or friends, would gather cozily 'round the fire while outside the fierce winds howled.

Grandfather had played the part of the bard and regaled them with stories of their long-dispersed clan and of battles fought, once against the Vikings and more recently against the

English, passing the family history on to the next generation, often in Gaelic song. Fiona's head barely reached the kitchen table so she could help Agatha whip the cream and add the raspberries and oats for the delicious *cranachan* she favored before she knew all about the noble Bonnie Prince Charlie and his final victory at Falkirk, followed so swiftly by his defeat at Culloden Moor. Fiona's courageous ancestors had played a vital role in those battles.

After Grandfather wove his tales, Grandmother played the ancient *clarsach,* a triangular harp whose use disappeared many years ago along with the clans—thanks to British interference. Her uncle sawed on his fiddle, her cousin played the pipes, and there would be dancing and singing.

Fiona missed those days.

Seeing a white ribbon of waterfall in the craggy hills ahead, Fiona prodded her mare to climb that direction. The gentle spraying sound of water was pleasing to her soul, and she slid off the gray's back. She stroked Skye's soft muzzle before trudging to the edge of the rippled water, white with froth from the pounding fall. Kneeling on the damp loam, Fiona dipped her hands into the ice-cold pool and drank her fill. The rains had stopped long ago, the weather a fickle companion to this ruggedly beautiful land. One minute the sun kissed the earth, causing the mountain burns and lochs' waters to shimmer as though jewels hid beneath their crystalline depths. The next, rain slapped the ground, streaming from beneath low-lying clouds that often skimmed the heather hills and glens and broad, rolling straths—all of which looked as if they'd been covered with an abundance of rich green velvet, whose nap waved in the constant breezes.

A soft whinny—not Skye's—ruffled the air behind Fiona.

She stiffened and looked over her shoulder.

His bearing rigid, the Englishman sat atop a cream-colored steed Fiona recognized as Barrag, a horse belonging to the castle stables. The interloper tipped his hat, inclining his head her way. A most peculiar heat bathed her face, and she hurriedly returned her gaze to the pool. While she shook her hands free of drops, she heard him dismount. The rustle of his booted steps came close. She sensed him crouch by the water's edge and tensed.

"I wish to make a suggestion," he finally said, making her jump from the suddenness of his voice—closer than she'd thought. She darted a glance his way. He stared over the pool, his eyes seemingly on the tall waterfall in the rocks ahead.

"Aye?" The word came warily.

"It would be folly to escort you back to the castle. I would lose a half day's ride at least, and I have as fervent a desire to prevent this wedding from taking place as you do."

Fiona bristled at his inference that, had there been time, he would have forced her to return home. As if he could! She narrowed her eyes. "Go on."

"I propose we band forces and journey together. For reasons earlier stated, I was formerly opposed to such a plan. However, now that matters have changed and you've taken it on yourself to set out alone, I see it as the best recourse for all involved. Together, we might reach Dumfriesshire that much faster. You know the lay of the land better than I, and in return, I could offer you any protection you might need."

"You?" She stood and laughed. "An Englishman offering a Highlander protection? If I should need protection—and I dinna need any such thing—perhaps 'twould be wiser t' seek someone t' protect me from you!"

He let out a weary breath and stood, facing her. "You have my word, I'll not touch you. You've no reason to fear me."

"Hmph." Fiona crossed her arms. "And how am I t' ken that you're not cut from the same cloth as your brother? I'm certain 'twas his talk of trinkets that led poor Gwynneth astray."

"Is your sister the type of woman to marry a man solely for his money?"

She balled her hands at her sides to prevent herself from slapping his aristocratic, planed cheek. Raising her chin high, she said, "Ye dare speak ill of me sister after your brother has committed so heinous a crime as t' snatch her from her home?"

"By her letter, your sister was willing. It was no abduction, this."

"Oh!" Fiona spun around and made for her horse.

"Besides protection, I can think of another reason why we should accompany one another in our search," he called after her.

Curiosity at what he would say next compelled her to stop. Yet she didn't turn or address him.

"Though Beaufort and I are not cut from the same cloth, as you suggested, I know how he thinks. You do not. Should he and your sister encounter problems during their journey, I can better surmise the steps he may have taken to meet them. Also. . ." The sound of his footsteps came closer until he was standing before her. She met the disturbing blue-gray of his eyes and looked away.

"You may be disinclined to hear this," he continued, "but the truth of the matter is that I, being an English gentleman, likely will receive more aid from the villagers than will you, being a Highland lass. We shall be traversing country different from your own. Especially in the Lowlands, from the little I've witnessed, the Scots do not abhor the English. Neither do they hold any ancient grudges against them. Indeed, they've come to recognize the benefits of living under British rule. Yet I've also heard it said there are those Scottish Lowlanders who think poorly of Highlanders. For that reason, you may find it difficult to retrieve any information you seek."

Fiona stiffened, thinking of the land clearances, still in progress. Tenants were being driven from their homes in droves to make wider sheep runs so that the lairds could grow wealthier. Kennerith Castle needed to do the same but for different reasons. They could no longer support their tenants and thrive. Bad crops and the tenants' inability to pay rent had forced the decision neither Fiona nor her grandmother wanted to make. Both realized that to keep the castle and remain in the Highlands, there was no other way for them but to raise the money-producing sheep, which thrived well on rocky soil ill fit for farming. This morning, when Fiona broke the news to the Finlays at her grandmother's request, she'd given them several weeks to move, even offering to help relocate them to crofts by the sea or to the Lowland's cities to work in the factories there—unlike other lairds whom she'd heard gave their tenants only an hour's notice, even burning their homes so they couldn't return to them.

" 'Twas you English who encouraged the land clearances," Fiona stated in an effort to assuage the guilt. "So why should any Lowlander be opposed t' me or my kinsmen—and no' to you as well?"

"It's not merely the land clearances which make them prejudiced." He hesitated, as if he would say more, then shook his head and moved toward Barrag.

She followed him. "Speak, then! What is it that would turn my countrymen against me?" Another thought struck. "Or perhaps ye lie t' seek your ain way, Englishman?"

He stopped walking and abruptly faced her. She barely refrained from barreling into him.

"I speak no falsehoods," he said. "I merely do not wish to repeat ill words spoken about another."

"If ye dinna tell me, I'll be sure 'twas a lie, and I'll go nowhere with you." Fiona was surprised by her words and quickly added, "Not that I plan to go with you in any case."

He released a breath, clearly exasperated. "Very well. If speaking will persuade you to join me, I'll make an exception this once, though to do so goes against my nature. Those Lowlanders of whom I spoke are of the opinion that all Highlanders are a wild, brutal, and uncouth lot."

"That's a lie, if ever I heard one! A Scotsman wouldna have said such about another Scot."

Or would he? Fiona had no idea. She only had knowledge of those things that her grandparents told her, mainly the history of her clansmen, but very little about the land or people outside her Highland home, except to say that the Lowlanders were weak for so readily giving in to the English and making their homes in cities there. Nor had her childhood nurse or tutor taught her anything but the rudiments of a girl's learning.

Alex looked at her with pity, and Fiona marched back to her horse.

"Will you accept my offer of protection and aid?" he called.

"No!" she fumed, mounting Skye. She guided the mare closer to the Englishman. Lifting her chin, she stared him down. "I need protection from no man. Especially, if that man be you!"

Bouncing her heels into Skye's flanks, Fiona urged the horse into a full gallop. She needed no one's protection except the Almighty's. Her grandmother had raised Fiona to fear the Lord, and Him only did she serve. Her own people feared her, in the truest sense of the word, and some had accused her of being a witch or possessing an evil spirit until she saved a tenant's son from the loch's deep waters. Then the hurtful words finally ceased from all except the older children. Yet the people kept their distance. And their superstitions.

Sadness enveloped a heart Fiona thought fully hardened against the taunts she'd endured since childhood. No, she needed no man's protection. Likely, all would flee in the opposite direction should the curse visit itself upon her while she was in their midst.

Alex guided his horse south, far behind Fiona's gray. Whether she was aware of his presence or not, he didn't know. She gave no outward indication. To allow a woman to travel unaccompanied went against his nature, and he'd appointed himself her guardian. If she wouldn't travel with him, then he planned to follow her—all the way to Dumfries and Gretna Green if necessary. She made good time and didn't dally, so perhaps she wasn't the burr under his saddle that Alex had thought she would be.

He frowned when he remembered her firm declaration of needing no man's protection. Stubbornness had made her eyes glint like a sword's honed edge. Yet her proud bearing was in direct opposition to the betraying tremble of her lower lip, which hinted at her vulnerability. Her ancestor may have been a fierce clan chieftain; however, Fiona wasn't as tough as she pretended. What had put such pain in her heart—enough to make her almost crumble when she spoke of needing no man's protection? Had someone hurt her? A lover, perhaps?

Irritated with his mind's wanderings, Alex shifted in the saddle and assessed the scope of treeless moors they crossed. Different from his home in Darrencourt, these primitive surroundings possessed a wild, eerie beauty—dangerous yet beguiling. Mauve-colored heather, wild bracken, and tufts of yellow broom carpeted the ground while barren crags etched a murky sky. High above, a golden eagle sailed. A breath of silver mist uncurled like smoke in the air for miles around, yet Alex could see well enough to travel safely, and his charge showed no inclination toward stopping. Soon, they would need to find somewhere to rest for the night. Hopefully a village would emerge before twilight fell.

A thick batting of angry gray clouds loomed closer, shadowing the land and bringing with it rain. When the drops grew more furious, Alex was relieved to note Fiona guide her gray toward an outcropping of rock. She sought shelter under an overhang, and Alex did the same, glad for the respite though his cloak helped to keep some of the moisture off. Like these Highlands, his English home was known for its frequent rain showers.

In the cramped twelve feet of dry space with a recess no more than six feet deep, Fiona went as far to the other side as possible, and Alex stayed on his end. The cream-colored steed nudged his shoulder, as though looking for a treat, and Fiona gave a disgusted snort.

Alex looked her way. She leaned back against the rock wall, chewing on a hunk of bread. Remembering his own meal, Alex withdrew a wrapped napkin from inside his coat. Unknotting the cloth, he saw a crust of bread like Fiona's, a single smoked piece of fish, and a hunk of hard cheese.

Wondering if the woman only had bread, he held out the napkin. "Would you like to share?"

"I want nothing from you, Englishman," she said in a voice rivaling the cold rain.

He lifted his brows in a shrug and began to eat the cheese.

"So tell me, did ye steal that food from Kennerith, as you stole our horse from the courtyard stables?" Fiona's words held rancor, as did her expression. "Your kind makes a habit of ripping away what belongs t' others, is that no' so?"

"My kind?"

"You English. You stole our way of living, our traditions, even our dress. Why no' steal our food and horses, as well?" She tore away a large hunk of bread with her teeth, no doubt wishing it were the back of his hand instead.

"I seem to recall that much of what you named has been reinstated to your kinsmen. The dress, the traditions—"

"But no' the clans," Fiona interrupted.

"No, not the clans." Alex knew his history. The clan system of which she spoke had been considered too dangerous and was abolished decades ago after the Scots' defeat at Culloden. Likewise, all Highland customs and dress were done away with and stiff penalties invoked on those who opposed the ordinance, except on those soldiers who'd given over their loyalties to serving Britain. Approximately forty years ago, Highland dress and customs were restored to the people. Yet evidently that wasn't enough for this fiery slip of a girl, who stared at him with daggers in her eyes. Alex thought it wise to change the subject.

"Your accusation is false. Your grandmother gave me the horse in exchange for a few pounds."

"My grandmother wouldna have sold Barrag! Nor anything else belonging t' Kennerith—no' to an Englishman!"

"The horse is only borrowed. I shall return it to the castle upon completion of my task. Your grandmother was naturally anxious about your sister's welfare. Her primary concern was that I find her in time to stop the wedding."

"I dinna believe you. She knows I went after Gwynneth."

Alex decided it best not to repeat that a well-traveled Englishman would likely entertain more success than a girl who'd never left the Highlands—and her grandmother had realized that. He trod carefully. "She arrived at the conclusion that two seeking out the couple would garner more success than one. At any rate, she did grant me use of this horse and, while I saddled the beast, also had your cook prepare food for me—food, I will remind you, which you so graciously offered before your hasty departure from the castle."

Fiona smiled sweetly. "Let's hope she poisoned it."

Alex withheld an answering grin and brought the smoked fish to his mouth. He stopped short of biting into it, her words fully registering, and stared at the silver morsel. He thought he heard her softly laugh, but when he looked, her focus was entirely on the rain.

Alex discreetly sniffed the fish, then, feeling ten times the fool, bit into it. Fiona might be as wild as the buffeting wind and as obstinate as the endless rain, but Alex was certain neither she nor her frail grandmother would be an accomplice to murder.

At least he hoped such was the case.

Chapter 3

With the vast ocean on their right, Fiona and her unwelcome escort approached a scattering of white crofts shortly before nightfall. The Englishman inquired about a place to sleep from an old man mending a net, and he and Fiona were directed to a humble stone croft nearby. A thatched roof topped the single-story dwelling, and a large bundle of cut and dried brown peat lay stacked high against a wall. Plots of farmland ran right up to the front of each cottage, unhindered by boundaries of hedges. Even flower gardens were absent, and Fiona thought of Kennerith's beautiful rose garden started centuries ago by a serf maiden who married a laird. Girls like Gwynneth swooned over such a legend, but a romantic, Fiona was not. Still, she loved to stroll through the well-kept garden and breathe deeply of the roses' sweet scent.

At Alex's knock, a rotund woman came to the door. She nodded to Alex, who explained their need for a place to stay. Casting a cursory glance over both of them, she offered shelter and food for ten shillings, including lodging and feed for the horses.

"Have another couple like us, an Englishman and a Scottish woman, been through here?" Alex asked, handing over a gold half sovereign, which the woman eyed greedily. "The gentleman is approximately my age and has fair hair. The woman looks much like my companion, except her hair is dark." At Fiona's gasp of surprise that he should be so knowledgeable about Gwynneth's appearance, he glanced her way. "Your grandmother told me."

"Sich a couple rode through here late this mornin'," the crofter's wife responded.

Alex smiled. "Thank you. If you have separate quarters for us to sleep, I would be most obliged."

"Give him a bed," Fiona inserted. "As for myself, I'm in need of a fresh horse and lantern, if you have them."

Alex faced her, incredulous. "Surely, you jest. You cannot mean to travel by night."

"If ye feel the need for rest, Englishman, dinna let me keep you from it." Fiona drew herself up. "We Galbraiths are a strong lot. My ancestors endured many a night without sleep while in battle, and I will do the same."

"A foolish lot, I daresay," Fiona thought she heard him mumble. She peered closely at him, but his attention was focused on their hostess. He addressed her with a polite smile. "If you'll excuse us a moment?"

She looked back and forth between them and nodded. "I've bu' one empty bed, since my Sean jist married. The lady can sleep wit' my daughter." She moved away.

"Thank you, but I dinna need a bed," Fiona called after her. "I need a horse."

The woman gave no sign of hearing.

Frustrated, Fiona snapped her gaze to Alex's. "Now see what you've done?"

Alex's eyes were serious. "Miss Galbraith, it would be most foolhardy of you to continue in the black of night with no moon to guide you. Rest the evening here, and we'll leave before dawn. Beaufort isn't an early riser. Wherever the two have chosen to stay the night, I doubt he'll break that lifelong habit. Especially since it's doubtful he knows he's being pursued."

His words, "Wherever the two have chosen to stay the night," struck an icy shaft of awareness deep within Fiona's heart. Her expression must have betrayed her, for Alex quickly spoke. "I assure you, my brother may be many things, but he is a gentleman and will treat your sister as a lady." A flush of red crawled up his neck. "They'll have separate quarters, as will we."

"I told you, I'll not stay."

Alex exhaled a weary breath. "At least come inside and allow me to buy you a meal."

The hunk of bread she'd thought to grab before fleeing the castle had done little to sustain Fiona. Good food did sound appealing. Deciding that to tarry one hour wouldn't hurt, she brushed past him and through the door. "I have my own money, Englishman. I want nothing from you."

Inside, a warm peat fire welcomed her deeper into the room. A wooden table filled the area, with a bench on either side. On the other end of the big room, two beds had been built into the wall, each with a curtain for privacy. At one end of the table sat a red-faced man, seeming to enjoy the barley juice he tippled more than the steaming bowl of soup before him. He directed a cursory glance their way, nodded, then looked back to his cup.

Alex took a seat across the table from Fiona. Immediately her attention went to the peat glowing red in the stone pit. A rosy-cheeked young girl stoked and blew on the smoldering fire underneath the kettle that hung on a hook, urging it, until it burst into yellow flame.

The woman set a platter of oatmeal bannocks between them followed by two steaming containers of *partan bree.* With Fiona's stomach close to rumbling from the pleasant smell of the peppery crab and fish, she picked up her wooden spoon and dipped it into the rich, creamy soup.

She trained her attention on her food and noticed Alex also made quick work of his meal, even asking for a refill. Halfway through the meal, he leaned closer, as though about to confide a secret. "Miss Galbraith?"

Fiona looked at him over the spoon she targeted toward her mouth.

"I propose we call a truce."

"A truce?" The uneaten spoonful plopped into what was left of the soup, and she scoffed at him in disbelief. "Tell me. How is it that a Galbraith can make peace with a Spencer?"

His brows lifted slightly, as if surprised she remembered his name. "The century-old battles on which you dwell are recorded in the annals of history. They shouldn't affect the present in which we live. Even Almighty God has commanded that we not strive with our fellow man but learn to live peaceably with one another."

His words made Fiona uncomfortable, almost guilty. She shook the undesirable feeling away. "Did your ancestors fight at Culloden?"

"Truthfully, Miss Galbraith, I do not know."

"Ye dinna know?" The admission surprised her. "Did ye have no bard to tell you stories 'round the fire about your family history?"

His loch-blue eyes gentled, and an awkward lump rose to her throat—probably due to the thick soup. She tore away a hunk of bread and ate it, hoping to dislodge the discomfort.

"That is solely a Scottish custom, I do believe," he said. "However, my father did speak to us of recent ancestors, as well as briefly outlining the Spencer history and our lineage, time and again. Since I'm not in line for the title, he chose not to prepare me as thoroughly as he did Beaufort."

"Title?"

He studied her before speaking. "My father is the earl of Darrencourt. My brother is viscount and shall inherit the title and all that goes with it one day."

"Hmph. No doubt he enticed Gwynneth to her destruction with his talk o' wealth. Poor simple lass that she is, t' fall for such a trick."

Fiona hadn't realized she'd spoken her thoughts aloud until Alex narrowed his eyes. "And is your sister so easily enticed, Miss Galbraith? Perhaps, to her, wealth is a matter to be pursued, even grasped?"

Fiona stiffened. "Are ye implying that my sister would marry a man for his title and money?"

"Such a prospect is not unheard of. It has been done before this," Alex said soberly. "After living in such, shall we say, meager conditions, it's understandable that she should want to seek a better life."

Fiona swiftly rose to her feet. "So ye think us t' be wallowin' in poverty, is that it? That we're so destitute as t' snatch whatever morsels we can from whoever'll give them—even if it be from our foes?"

She drew herself up, reached into the small drawstring bag

she carried on a belt around her waist, and slapped down onto the planked table two silver shillings for her meal. "Ne'er let it be said that a Galbraith took anything from a Spencer, in this lifetime or in the lifetime t' come. If Gwynneth be guilty of any folly, 'tis in believin' the lies of a cloven-tongued Englishman, who likely dallies with every poor lass he meets!"

Realizing what she'd just spewed in her anger and seeing Alex's mouth drop, as well as the other man's, Fiona felt humiliation's fire scorch her face. Her eye began to twitch and grow heavy. Swiftly she turned and headed for the door.

She would find another horse or die trying! She would not tarry another moment in *his* presence.

Before dawn the next morning, after a filling bowl of porridge and cream accompanied by oatcakes, the grain of which Alex thought better suited to a horse's food intake than a person's diet, he hurried to the stables. He hadn't ceased thinking of the Scottish spitfire since her hasty departure last night. When a heavy thunderstorm began only minutes after she left, Alex felt obliged to go on foot in search of her. Yet the wind had proven too beastly, blowing the slicing rain at a slant into his eyes and causing the ocean's waters to crash high upon the rocks. Soon Alex returned to the cottage, assuring himself that Fiona would know how to take care of herself, having lived in the Highlands all her life. Surely she would have found shelter elsewhere and not attempted to ride in such weather.

In the predawn light, Alex made out the building that housed the stables. He moved across the muddy ground and, not seeing anyone about, pulled open the ancient wooden door. It gave a low, protesting squeak. A horse's whinny greeted him, but it was a woman's sleepy groan that stopped him cold.

In the dim shaft of blue light forcing its way into the darkened building, Alex noticed a blanketed form on the ground at the end of a stall. The blanket undulated, the form rose, and a pair of half-open eyes underneath a matted tousle of ginger-colored ringlets blinked his way. The apparition sneezed.

"Miss Galbraith," he said in surprise.

She clapped her hand over her nose and mouth. "Be it mornin' already?" The voice came groggily through her fingers.

"Yes. Just." Alex hesitated, awkward. "I came to ready the horse for departure. I shall do so now." Hurriedly he moved toward the cream-colored steed.

Fiona put her hand to the wall, using it for balance, and rose to her feet, clutching the blanket to her throat. Alex wondered if he should excuse himself and give her privacy, but before he could speak, she turned her back on him and loosely folded the blanket. Alex was relieved to note that she wore not only her dress but her cloak as well. By her nervous actions, he feared she'd been clothed only in her undergarments.

"The crofter's wife has porridge bubbling on the hearth," Alex offered.

Fiona shook her head. "There isna time. And I'm no' that hungry. There's. . .there's something I must say. I–I wish. . ."

"Yes?" Alex prompted, curious about what incited such self-conscious behavior.

She faced him. "I wish t' go now." With awkward steps, Fiona moved to her gray, threw the blanket over the horse's back, and reached for the saddle. "What do I owe for lodging Skye?"

"The debt is paid in full."

"I canna take money from you," she all but whispered.

"And neither can I receive payment from you." He injected lightness into his next words. "So you see, it seems we've reached a stalemate. Now we can both stand here and argue all day about who will concede, or we can leave things as they are and continue on our journey—which is the reason we're here in the first place, I'll remind you. To reach my brother and your sister in time to stop the wedding."

"Aye." She nodded but still didn't look at him.

He returned his attention to the horse. The steed tossed its head when Alex tried to slip the bridle over its muzzle. Alex tried again but got the same response.

"Barrag can be irritable of a mornin'." Fiona came up beside Alex. "Sometimes, when Grandmother used to ride him, she would first stroke his nose and sing to him. Like this."

Bedazzled, Alex watched Fiona rub the horse between the eyes and down its muzzle, softly crooning to it in a language unfamiliar to him. Dawn's pale light streamed from the stable's open door, making her face glow. Indeed, her countenance had softened as she dealt with the horse and slipped the bridle over its head. A peculiar twinge clutched Alex's stomach when he noticed the red splotch on her pale cheek where her arm had evidently pressed against it while she slept. Her hair was frizzled with wild ringlets, an indentation at the back coupled with the way it bunched up on one side making it appear as though she'd lain down while it was wet.

"You should have taken shelter in the cottage," he said quietly. "You could have caught your death of cold sleeping on the ground after having been out in the rain and with no fire to warm you."

Her gaze flitted to his, surprise making her light gray eyes shimmer like precious metals. "I've slept in a stable before, when Skye birthed her foal. You needna worry, Englishman. I'll not slow you down."

Alex stood, rooted in shock, and watched her lead the gray outside. So she had changed her mind and decided to ride with him. What spurred such a decision? He wondered if this was another of her tricks, but what purpose would it serve? Even if she did slip away, she must know by now that he would follow.

Fiona rode silently beside the Englishman, aware of his frequent glances her way but unable to explain her behavior. Earlier, when they stood inside the stables, the apology concerning her ill conduct last night had shuddered to a stop.

An admission of guilt was often difficult for her. She'd been raised to believe that a Galbraith or a MacMurray apologized to no man—and she still felt rattled over the dream. The dream captured her attention, left her confused. Her grandmother had taught Fiona that the Lord sometimes spoke to people through dreams. Yet surely such a dream could not have come from the Almighty Himself!

Last night, when the affliction came over her and she'd been caught in the rain, Fiona slipped into the byre with the cows and horses to hide. Unfortunately, an older lad, a simpleton who cared for the animals, was inside mucking out the stables. She pleaded with him to let her stay until the storm stopped, when she would be on her way again. But he only gaped at her, as if she were the frightening, rarely sighted creature from Loch Ness, and backed out of the building.

Shivering and wet, Fiona had grabbed the blanket off her

dry horse, thrown it around her shoulders, and huddled in a corner. A pervading cloud of despair loomed over her, making her feel as weak and hopeless as a starving kitten. Why had God made her this way? Why? Did He not accept her either?

Over and over she asked herself those questions before falling into exhausted slumber. The dream revisited her, as it had many times over the years. She was fleeing across a barren heath—at first on Skye, then on foot—while clouds boiled overhead and some unknown pursuer chased her. She raced toward a shimmering loch, knowing that if she could cross it, she would be safe. Always, before she could swim across, a monstrous shadow fell over her from behind and rocklike appendages encircled her, squeezing the breath from her lungs. This time, however, the dream ended differently.

Before she could reach the loch's cool blue waters, feeling the pursuer's breath hot on her neck, sensing his shadow creep over her, Fiona unexpectedly ran into a pair of open arms that closed around her back. Only these arms weren't cruel or harsh; they were gentle and comforting. The shadow lifted, the sun broke through the clouds, and Fiona raised her head from the man's strong chest to thank him.

Again, as had happened when she'd abruptly awakened from the dream to see the Englishman standing in the stable entryway, Fiona experienced a breathless, almost dizzying sensation.

Her rescuer's face had been his.

Chapter 4

The road took them beyond one of numerous hills, and Fiona heard the lonely wail of bagpipes. Up ahead, she saw a line of people. By the look of their clothes and the belongings they carried over their shoulders, they were tenant farmers. Several men guided beasts of burden that carried woven baskets and other goods. Midway up a nearby hill, a Highlander stood wearing a kilt and tartan plaid. The wheezing yet shrill notes of his bagpipes from the slow, haunting *pibroch* he played swept through the deep glen, as though bidding farewell to the people and the way of life they'd known.

Tears stung Fiona's eyes, and she blinked them away. "Likely they've been driven from their homes and seek new ones. Such has been the way of it for many years." She threw an unsmiling glance Alex's way. "Behold the 'improvement' of which ye speak so highly."

Without waiting for Alex to remark and feeling a twinge of guilt that she and her grandmother were forced to do the same with their tenants, Fiona tapped her heels into Skye's flanks and guided the horse along the road. Once she drew closer to the refugees, she saw what appeared to be five families, nearly twenty people, all with a lost look in their eyes.

"Where do you travel?" Alex's voice came from behind, and Fiona looked over her shoulder to see him address an old, bent woman.

"Tae the first burgh in the Lowlands we come tae wi' a factory," she said tiredly. "Tae seek work. Five days o' walk we've had."

"You must be weary," Alex said. To Fiona's surprise, he slid off Barrag. "Ride my horse. My companion and I are traveling in the same direction, if you don't mind the company?"

Relief swept across the woman's features, and she nodded. Alex helped the woman mount, then took the reins, leading the horse. A blond-haired giant of a man moved Alex's way.

"Thank ye fer helpin' my *mathair*. You're welcome t' travel with us as long as ye have a care to. I'm Hugh MacBain, formerly of Inverness near Moray Firth."

"And I'm Dr. Alexander Spencer of Darrencourt."

"A doctor!" the old woman exclaimed from atop Barrag. "The Lord love ya, Laddie, fer surely He sent ye tae us this day." She motioned behind her, and Fiona saw two children pulling a small cart where a little girl lay. Her head was nestled on a collie's sleek fur. "My gran'daughter isna well. She fell while runnin' doon a hill."

"I shall see to her." Alex offered Barrag's reins to a fair-haired youth and moved toward the cart. Hugh announced to the others that they would stop for a rest, and Fiona reined in Skye as well, turning her horse so that she could watch Alex inspect the wee girl's foot. He asked for a strip of cloth and bound the dirty, bare foot tightly. " 'Tis only a slight sprain," he announced to her family, who stood nearby. "I recommend she stay off of it for a few days."

"She can ride my horse," Fiona found herself saying. Everyone turned to look at her as though just remembering she was there. Heat crept up her face. "There's room enough for the other two children as well. They look in need of a rest."

Alex's eyes were gentle as they studied Fiona. "Her foot should be elevated, but since that's not possible under such circumstances, perhaps riding atop your mare would be more comfortable for her than having her leg jiggled in the back of a cart."

Hugh nodded as though Alex's word were law. "The wee ones would ride best bareback. Ne'er have they used a saddle the likes o' yours."

Fiona dismounted and readied the horse. The injured child's eyes widened as another man, obviously her father, set down the straw container he carried and lifted her from the cart. An older boy picked up Fiona's saddle and threw it where the girl had lain, then took hold of the cart handles, preparing to pull it. Gently the man set the child atop Fiona's horse, placed the small boy behind her, and the other girl in front. None of them looked over the age of eight. Their little legs stuck out to the sides on Skye's wide back as each wrapped their arms tightly around the waist of the person in front of them and the older girl gripped Skye's dark mane. The boy turned Fiona's way.

"Thank ye, Miss. I'm Kiernan, and these are my sisters, Rose and Mary. Mary is the one who was hurt. She's but three and is forever runnin' o'er the place. Like a wee fairy, she is."

Rose giggled, and Mary stared at Fiona with huge eyes, the same misty green as the other two children's.

Fiona wasn't certain how to reply. She was unaccustomed

to speaking with people, except those at Kennerith, of course, and she rarely spoke to children. The tenants' offspring habitually taunted her, and Fiona found it best to steer clear of them.

She offered a hesitant smile to the MacBain children, then directed her attention to the long road ahead.

Hours later, the gloaming painted the sky with rose, blue, and amber once the sun dipped below the horizon. Twilight followed the lengthy afterglow of the sunset and purpled the glen, and they stopped for the night. Fiona had no idea of the expanse they'd covered nor of the distance yet to go, but she strongly was beginning to feel the discomforts of traveling and wished for a vat of steaming hot water with which to bathe. She felt so dirty, and her hair was a matted, frizzled mess. One kind woman had given her a piece of soft leather so she could tie her hair back, and Fiona gratefully did so. Now, as the chill night cloaked them, the white stars winking from a thankfully cloudless sky, Fiona drew close to the fire one of the MacBains had built.

"Dinna worry, Lass," the elderly woman said. From a basket she plucked up a smoked herring and an oatcake and handed both to Fiona. "Ye maun eat. Yer sister will be all right. If it be God's purpose that ye find her, ye will."

The words hardly comforted Fiona, but she nodded. Shortly after Fiona and Alex had joined the MacBains, Alex had inquired if they'd seen other travelers on the road, and Hugh admitted to seeing a man and woman, each on horseback, ride past a few hours prior to Fiona and Alex's arrival.

"Which means," Alex told Fiona in an aside later, "if the riders were our siblings, we should be catching up to them soon. Hugh mentioned they weren't traveling with speed, so

Beaufort must be unaware that we're following them. He had no idea I was coming to Scotland, and I'm sure he doubts you would pursue them either. Before meeting you, I never would have believed such a thing possible."

Fiona wondered if Gwynneth suspected. Surely she must know Fiona wouldn't have simply stood by and done nothing.

They had lost some time since joining the MacBains. Still, Fiona was glad they'd done what they could to help these people and were now all traveling together as one large group. Such a situation was preferable to sharing Alex's sole company, though Fiona grudgingly had to admit the prospect of being with him hadn't been entirely distasteful. There'd even been times, such as when Alex offered his horse to the old woman or when he'd so tenderly bound the child's foot, that she'd actually found herself drawn to him.

"The doctor is a grand man," Hugh's mother abruptly said, as though discerning Fiona's thoughts. "Ye could do nae better."

"Oh, but—" The words shocked Fiona into raising her head. "We arenna together—that is, we only ride together in search of his brother and my sister."

The woman chuckled. "With the way I see him starin' at ye an' ye at him when neither of ye think the other is looking?" She chuckled again. "Ye could ha'e fooled me, t' be sure!"

Fiona quickly rose, brushing off the back of her dress. "Such an idea is—is bizarre. Why, 'twould be like having English tea and bagpipes together. And anyone kens, the two dinna mix."

"An' why not? Others ha'e done so. 'Twould appear ye are well suited."

Fiona made a sound of disbelief, somewhere between a snort

and a laugh. She couldn't help herself.

The woman eyed her. "What aught have ye against him, Lass?"

"He's English."

The woman let out a scoffing sound that matched the one Fiona had just given. "Is that all that ails ye? A more foolish excuse I've ne'er heard."

Fiona drew her shoulders back. "My *Seanair* raised me on stories of what the English did to our clan."

"Aye. I, too, have heard sich stories in my day, an' from my ain gran'father as well," the woman replied softly. "Perhaps ye think I've nae right tae be speakin' t' ye so. Bu' I'm the oldest in what's left o' my clan, and I speak t' everyone the same." She eyed Fiona, her blue eyes wise amid the wrinkles. "Ye can take what I be tellin' ye t' heart, or ye can forget the words ever were spoken—'tis a choice you alone maun make. But I've found it wise no' t' blame the sons for the sins o' their fathers—especially for sins nigh unto a century old."

Fiona kept her gaze on the crackling fire.

"The doctor is a braw man, undeservin' of yer scorn. I kenna the two of ye, but I've two eyes with which t' see. Instead of judgin' through auld stories spoken in days gone by or lookin' at himself with only yer eyes, see him as he is, Lass. From yer heart. 'Tis said, the heart is the best judge o' matters, showin' things as they truly are."

Some time elapsed before Fiona spoke. "I must be away to my bed of heather if I'm t' rise before dawn," she said quietly, more disturbed by the woman's words than she let on.

"Aye." The woman nodded and bit into her fish. "Sleep well."

Fiona moved toward Skye, intending to bed down near

her mare. On her way, she met Alex, who'd just left the four MacBain men.

"Are you all right?" he asked, concern evident in his tone. "You look upset."

"I'm fine!" Fiona clipped out, walking past him. She was grateful he didn't follow.

Wrapping her cloak more tightly about her to ward off the chill, Fiona sank to the damp grass, spotted with heather, and looped an arm around her upraised knees. She ate the fish and bread while staring above the steep hills at the numerous stars in the blue-black sky and tried to sort through her thoughts. That many of these musings contained the Englishman didn't sit well with her, and Fiona scowled. Despite her weariness, a long span of time elapsed before she lay down and fell asleep.

Three days had passed since Alex and Fiona had joined the MacBains. The steep hills and rolling straths were beginning to level out, the expanses of valley becoming flatter and easier to travel, with thicker stands of trees spotting the hedged land. At a wide river, they crossed a long stone bridge single-file, and Alex watched Fiona guide her gray ahead of his horse. Each day, she gave all ten of the MacBain children turns riding Skye, usually three at a time, then took a turn as well.

Alex watched her now, sitting as regal as a Highland princess atop the gray mount, the setting sun transforming her hair into blazing ringlets of fire, and thought to himself that even dirty with her face lightly sunburned she was more attractive than many fine ladies of his acquaintance. Fiona possessed passion. Spirit. Strength. If the sister was anything like Fiona, Alex could begin to understand why Beaufort had done such a thing as to elope with a Highlander. Yet the earl, their father, would be less forthcoming, of that Alex was certain.

He could almost hear his father rant and rave, see him throw his arms about and declare, "If Beaufort marries this miserable Scottish wench, I shall disinherit him! Go to Edinburgh. Watch him. If he defies me and again meets with this wild creature, bring him to me!"

Alex had gone gladly. If Beaufort were disinherited, Alex would receive the title—a title he didn't want. He'd spent ten years watching and aiding his uncle in medicine, fascinated by the prospect of healing, until, at the age of twenty, he took up the profession as well. Now, at twenty-six, Alex was satisfied with his life and didn't need the burden of being next in line. From what Alex had observed of his father's duties, an earl must oversee his land and tenants and would have scant time to pursue doctoring. His father certainly had little enough time for his family, though any anger Alex once harbored for his father's neglect had long since passed.

Once they crossed the bridge, Alex glanced toward Fiona. She stared at him, a mystified expression on her face.

"Miss Galbraith, is anything the matter?"

It took her awhile to answer. When she did, it was as though she'd just heard his words, and a deeper pink enhanced her already rosy face. She gave a slight shake of her head. "No. 'Tis nothing." Hurriedly she turned Skye southward and resumed following the others.

Alex was curious but didn't pursue the matter. She'd been acting peculiar all day.

A band of pale gold stretched across the hilly horizon, the thick clouds above it deep indigo blue when the group crossed a narrow, high, stone bridge that stretched over the River Forth and left the Highlands behind. Lush, flat land bordered with trees cloaked the area. Pillars of smoke erupted from factories and marred the pale sky. Nearby, a huge stone fortress loomed on a crag ringed by a thick patch of trees, the town spread out below it.

"We'll be takin' oor leave of ye," Hugh MacBain said. "A place t' live I must be findin', before I seek work at a factory."

They said their farewells, and Alex inspected little Mary's foot one last time. To his surprise, she clasped him around the neck. "Thank ye, Dr. Spencer, fer makin' me foot all better," she whispered, then hurried away. He watched as she skipped beside her sister, no sign of injury evident. The young always did mend quickly, at least in the physical sense.

Alex's gaze drifted to Fiona, who couldn't be more than twenty, if that. Sometimes he caught a wounded look in her eyes, one she quickly masked, and again wondered who'd hurt her so deeply. Fiona prodded Skye to a walk, and Alex guided Barrag beside her.

"We also should seek shelter before nightfall," Alex said. "I shall see to securing each of us a room at a hostel, then will make inquiries about town concerning Beaufort and your sister. There's a chance he might have decided to stop here for the night. Beaufort never was one for long-distance traveling, and I presume that he chose the destination of Gretna Green for the marriage due to the fact that it's on the way to our home in Darrencourt. I suppose you and I should count ourselves blessed that they decided to wait and marry there. With Scotland's lax marriage laws, they could have married anywhere in the country, so I've been told."

"I would think my sister had her say in it," Fiona admitted rather grudgingly. "Gwynneth is idealistic. Gretna Green has quite a reputation, I've heard, and is just the type o' setting she would fancy for a wedding."

Alex held his tongue. He didn't see how an irregular marriage outside the church could be considered romantic but knew English literature had made it seem such, and there were those who sought the small village as sanctuary. Many mismatched English couples whose parents weren't in favor of a union eloped to Gretna Green on Scotland's border, near neighboring England, to exchange marriage vows. Oftentimes, they were pursued by irate fathers or vengeful brothers or even wronged suitors in a mad chase of horse and coach. Yet all too often, the rescuers were late in arriving.

Alex hoped he would reap better success. To push the mares harder would be folly, because a horse could go lame from such ill treatment. Now that they'd reached the Lowlands and better roads, perhaps he should seek out a coach and fresh horses, like he had used earlier in his journey. At that time and with no explanation, the driver had taken him no farther than the rugged Highland border, and Alex had to continue on foot until he'd bought the old horse that took him the rest of the way to Kennerith Castle, where he'd met Fiona. That was an encounter he likely would never forget.

Soon they entered the bustling city. Crowded rows of multilevel stone buildings faced one another across the long street. Narrow alleyways branched off the cobbled lane. Alex found an adequate hostel with two rooms, but no available stable for the horses. Nor had the innkeeper seen Beaufort.

"It might be wise for you to rest here while I try to locate accommodations for the horses," Alex said to Fiona. "Upon my return, we'll search the city for another mode of lodging where your sister and my brother may have taken rooms." If he found the errant couple, Alex realized that Gwynneth might not agree to come with him, since he was a stranger. With Fiona there, he hoped the sister wouldn't make a scene. He hadn't yet decided what he would say when he confronted Beaufort.

At the sound of men's boisterous laughter nearby, Fiona's eyes darted to the street. She drew her cloak more tightly under her throat and clutched its black folds together. She seemed anxious, and Alex realized she'd probably never seen a crowded city.

"I shall return as soon as I'm able," he said, regaining her attention. "You'll be safe here."

Her gaze snapped to his, then lowered, but she remained mute. Apparently she didn't want to admit her fright.

Alex took his leave, wishing he didn't have to go. It took him longer than he thought it would to find lodging for the horses, and at a steep price, though he handed over the silver crown without arguing. He quickly left the stables and hurried toward the inn, anxious to rejoin Fiona.

Once he arrived at the hostel, alarm grabbed hold of him. She wasn't where he'd left her. He made inquiries to the pleasant-faced woman inside and searched the first floor's public rooms, but to no avail.

Fiona was gone.

Chapter 5

A light shower watered the cobbles as Fiona hurried along the narrow wynd. She stayed close to the buildings that towered on either side of the road and away from the livestock and carts that clattered through the area. Nervousness propelled her feet faster, and she gripped the damp woolen cloak around her at the waist, keeping her arms crossed.

Not long after Alex left, when she'd first seen the woman enter the building up the road, Fiona had been sure it was Gwynneth by the cloud of dark hair and familiar-looking green hat she wore. However, having hurried in that direction to reach the place where she'd seen the girl, Fiona was uncertain which of the close buildings the young woman had entered. She knocked on a few doors, earning her one or two grumpy replies but no sister.

One kindly woman suggested she try the inn three streets over. Fiona gave her thanks and hurried in the direction the woman told her to go. She didn't need Alex's help and still felt a little miffed that he thought her so weak as to require protection, leaving her behind and telling her she'd "be safe" at the hostel.

Two streets down, the shower grew heavier. Fiona drew the

cloak over her head, muttering at the unpredictable weather. With the rain impairing her vision, she darted into an open doorway shrouded in welcome lantern light. Maybe whoever owned the building would allow her to stay close to the entrance until the rain let up.

Boisterous talking trickled to murmurs, and Fiona saw that she'd entered a tavern. Three youths walked from the long bar toward her, interest putting a gleam in their eyes. Anxious, Fiona flattened her back against the wall. She searched for a sly remark, to show them that she wasn't afraid of them, when her right eye began to twitch. . . .

Alex hurried along the wet pavement in the direction the hostel worker told him Fiona had run. Whatever possessed her to leave the shelter of the inn and dash out into the rain, into an unfamiliar city? Did her desire to leave his presence compel her to engage in hazardous forays in the dark of night, the moment his back was turned? Frowning, Alex pulled his hat farther over his brow, though it did little to keep his face dry, and stalked onward.

He should leave the foolhardy girl to her own devices. She was so determined to prove herself capable of going it alone. He should give her the benefit of doing so and resume his task, giving no further thought to her whereabouts. He should allow her to do as she pleased and forget her existence. He should. . . But he couldn't. Her safety had become imperative to him, and he would tear this town apart, if need be, and knock on every door, until he found the strong-willed vixen and assured himself that she was all right.

"Witch! Begone frae here!" a man yelled into the storm.

Alex halted, shocked, as a cloaked figure with downcast head quickly stumbled from a nearby tavern, as if thrown from it, and lurched into the rain. A man appeared on the stoop, cursed, and bent to scoop up some mud. He lumbered after the cloaked person and threw the clod at the slender back. The figure staggered and almost fell but continued running in Alex's direction. The hood fell away.

Alex gasped and rushed toward Fiona. She barreled into his arms before she saw him. He closed his arms around her trembling form, raw anger pumping his blood and making him wish he could slam his fist into the cruel drunkard's face, though he'd never hit a person in his life.

"Fiona, look at me," Alex insisted, pulling an arm away from her back and trying to lift her chin. He thought he'd seen a trickle of blood near her brow. "Did he hurt you?"

She kept her head down. "Nae—please. . ." Her shaky wisp of a voice could scarcely be heard over the rain. "Leave me be."

"I'm afraid that's impossible," Alex retorted staunchly. She seemed determined to shield her face. Nevertheless, he realized, standing in the middle of the street in a downpour was not an acceptable place to hold this conversation. Seeing no coach or wagon nearby, he draped his cloaked arm over her shoulder, drawing her chilled, wet body close to his side, and steered her in the direction of the inn. "We must see to getting you dry. Then I shall want to examine you."

He felt her slim shoulders jerk then tense. "Nae—you canna—please! I'm—I'm all right."

"Miss Galbraith, as a physician, I shan't get a good night's rest until I'm assured that you are indeed well."

She said nothing more, and Alex chose not to press the

matter. This time, he would have his way.

Once they reached the hostel and he turned her over to the innkeeper's wife, ordering her to see that Fiona change into dry clothing, Alex waited until he was sure she would be presentable, then tapped on her closed door. The innkeeper's wife opened it.

"If you'll stay," Alex said, "I think it will ease the lady's qualms."

"As ye wish." The woman moved aside to let Alex pass.

Fiona sat among the pillows on a high, four-poster bed, engulfed in a voluminous white nightgown with a neck-high collar, obviously belonging to the stout innkeeper's wife. Her head was lowered, her fiery, damp ringlets cascading to the ivory sheet.

An invisible hand gripped Alex's heart. She looked adorable. . .and vulnerable. . .and altogether too frightened. Switching off his emotions before he said something he shouldn't and aroused her ire, he adopted his clinical doctor-patient attitude and proceeded with the examination. He wished he'd at least thought to bring his bag with his stethoscope, but when he'd left Darrencourt, he hadn't known he would need it.

Tapping her back and chest through the gown and placing his ear close to her heart, Alex heard no matter that could point to pneumonia or other illness. As many times as she'd been caught in the rain since they'd met, that was a relief. Seeing purple bruises the shape of meaty finger marks above her tiny wrist where the wide sleeve of the nightgown had fallen back, Alex tensed, trying to keep his anger in check. How dare that drunken sot touch her!

Frowning, he brushed his finger along the marks and felt her startled jump. "Did he hit you?" Alex asked softly.

Fiona shook her head. "One of them pushed me, and I fell against the wall, but no one hit me."

Alex closed a gentle hand over her wrist to take her pulse. Again, he felt her give a little jump. "Relax, Miss Galbraith, I'm almost finished with the examination. Please lift your head so I can look into your eyes."

"My eyes?" she asked, her words soulful.

Alex was confused by her behavior. "Often matters can be determined about a patient's health by looking into their eyes."

Underneath his fingertips, her pulse quickened, and he felt her arm begin to tremble. My word! Was she crying?

"Miss Galbraith?"

"Tell her t' leave," she whispered at last.

"The innkeeper's wife?"

Fiona nodded.

Puzzled, Alex motioned for the woman to step outside. She did so, leaving the door partly open.

"She's gone," Alex assured.

Slowly, Fiona lifted her head. Her right eyelid hung halfway down, as though stuck, and twitched madly, causing the thin ivory skin around it to pulse.

"Did something get into your eye?" Alex asked, at once concerned. He brushed his thumb near her throbbing temple and was startled when she jerked backward, as though he'd struck her.

"It oft happens when I grow upset and weary. Ever since I was a child. It starts and stops withoot warning."

"Have you been to see a physician?"

"There isna one near Kennerith."

Alex considered her words and hoped she wouldn't get angry by the suggestion he was about to offer. "Miss Galbraith, I know little about afflictions of the eye, though I suspect this has to do with the nerves and not the actual eye itself. However, my uncle has studied the subject in depth and is a good friend of Dr. Thomas Young, who is quite knowledgeable in matters concerning the eye. Perhaps they could be of service to you. There is still much in the field of medicine that we as physicians do not understand and are only just discovering, but if anyone would know how to help you, these two men should."

She sat very still, her one good eye looking at him. He was relieved to see that it was clear and alert, the pupil normal. She appeared in fine health despite her earlier encounter. If there had been any blood on her brow, it was gone now. Looking closer, Alex discerned a shallow scrape near her temple.

"You dinna think me cursed?" she asked quietly. "Or a witch?"

"Of course not!" Alex wondered how she could arrive at such a conclusion. He smiled. "At times I might think you overly determined and a little reckless, but I've never thought evil of you." He cupped her face, his thumb again brushing the skin near her eye above her cheekbone, and was relieved to note that the twitching had slowed.

Her good eye lowered. "Thank ye, Dr. Spencer."

Suddenly he became aware of how soft her skin felt, how silky her damp curls were as they brushed his fingers. He withdrew his hand from her cheek and stood. "I prescribe a good night's sleep." He hoped his tone sounded professional. "I shall see you in the morning."

She looked up. "Will ye search for them this night?"

"No. To seek them in such weather would prove fruitless. I've given some consideration to the matter. Chances are Beaufort continued on to Glasgow, in the hopes of finding better accommodations since that city is quite large—much larger than this. Perhaps with God's help we shall waylay our siblings on the road tomorrow. And now, I shall bid you a good night, Miss Galbraith. Pleasant dreams."

He moved to the doorway, barely hearing her wispy "good night" in return.

Fiona watched Alex's back as he rode ahead of her. They were in unfamiliar territory and had been since they'd left Glasgow two days ago where he'd taken the lead. Just like her brief interlude in the small burgh of Stirling, Glasgow was a frightening experience for Fiona. Thousands upon thousands of people hurried amid huge buildings that loomed in all directions, making her want to flee the teeming city and run back to her empty, wild Highland hills, where only deer and sheep and what amounted to fewer than fifty people dotted the burgh near the castle.

Alex had seemed to understand how overwhelmed Fiona felt, for he paid solicitous attention to her without belittling her. It came as a shock that she hadn't minded his courtesies one bit. Since the night Alex had rescued her from those drunken men, showing nothing but kindness after learning of her affliction—and not calling her evil, as others had done—Fiona had moved past the point of merely tolerating Alex's company. She actually was starting to like it.

If her great-great-grandfather Angus knew, he would roll over in his grave.

Uneasy, Fiona fidgeted in the saddle, focusing her attention beyond Alex to the scenic area they'd entered only that morning. The gently rolling hills were mostly uniform in size with trees at their base and granite at their tops—but nothing like the untamed beauty of her Highland mountains. Black-faced sheep spotted the fertile grasses, the white wooly animals as plentiful as they were at Kennerith.

She looked ahead to a river they were approaching. At this point, it wasn't wider than any others they'd crossed, but the bridge was in sad repair, the stones soft and crumbling away at a few places, and it didn't look capable of bearing their weight.

Fiona guided Skye beside Alex, who halted his horse and stared at the flowing peat-brown water. Here it must be deep, for Fiona couldn't see bottom. Alex's expression reflected the doubt she felt. He looked up and down for another way across, then guided Barrag along the rocky bank. Soon, they saw a lad of about eleven years. He was crouched near the water's edge and appeared to be looking for something. At their approach, he lifted his head.

"Do you know of another way across?" Alex asked. "The bridge doesn't appear safe. We are headed to Gretna Green."

The lad eyed them a moment before he straightened and pushed a tangle of wild, barley-colored hair from his eyes. "Aye, that I may, bu' it'll be costin' you." He spoke in the familiar Highland brogue, making Fiona feel less homesick. For the past few days she'd heard nothing but the broad Lowland way of talk from a Scotsman.

Alex raised his eyebrows. "What is your price?"

"I dropped me reed in the river." He pointed to a slim stick with holes, floating out of his reach. It was stuck against some tall grasses growing in the water. "Fetch it, and I'll show ye the way across. I even ken a shortcut, if ye've the stomach for it."

"My, but that does sound intriguing," Alex said with an amused smirk. He swung down from Barrag. "Very well. Show me this reed, and I'll do my best to retrieve it."

The boy again pointed it out, and Alex hunched down, putting one hand to a rock on the bank and reaching toward the reed with the other. His fingertips barely brushed the stick. He stretched farther, lost his balance, and fell into the river with a loud splash.

"Oh, my!" Fiona chuckled and nudged Skye closer. She watched Alex surface, then grab the bank and hoist himself out. He snatched up his hat floating nearby and stood, river water streaming from his clothes.

The boy let out a delighted whoop. "Me reed!" He plucked it from the water. Alex's thrashing about had caused the stick to move within the lad's reach. "It's thanks I'm owin' t' ye."

Alex's expression was stiff. "So happy to oblige," he muttered, removing his coat and waistcoat and wringing out the dripping material. "And now if you'll show us your shortcut?"

"Aye." Smiling, the boy raised the reed to his mouth and fingered the holes, producing pathetic gurgling notes. He shrugged. "It needs only t' dry. Come along then."

Alex moved to Barrag, his polished black boots making squishing sounds. "How well I can relate," he said under his breath, and Fiona chuckled. Once he mounted, he looked her way.

She couldn't prevent the grin that flickered on her lips at the sight he made. His dark hair was plastered to his head in little waves. His pantaloons and shirt clung to him, outlining upper arms and a chest that looked surprisingly toned and accustomed to a hard day's work. Fiona would have thought that doctors engaged in little exercise except to visit their patients.

Alex returned her smile as he donned his dry cloak. "Indeed, judging by your expression, I must look a sight. Happily, the sun is shining, and the day is quite pleasant."

Fiona was certain his explanation of the sun's warmth must be what made her insides glow. She couldn't remember feeling this light and carefree in a long time. Forcing her focus on the wee piper leading the way and not on the tall Englishman riding beside her, Fiona sobered, reminding herself that she was on a mission. There was no place for foolish thought.

They followed the lad through a cool forest. Here, a shallow burn bubbled over gray rocks, and birdsong filled the trees. A woodpecker's taps clattered from somewhere upstream. The boy continued to lead them, playing his gurgling reed.

"Christopher!" A fair-haired girl with freckles burst through a stand of firs and came running toward them. "The bairn comes, and Mam says I maun fetch Daddy. There be trouble. She canna stop screaming." Terror etched the delicate features of the child smaller than Christopher.

"Am I to understand your mother is in childbirth?" Alex asked.

The girl looked his way, surprise in her eyes—whether from his drenched condition or the sudden realization that her brother wasn't alone, Fiona wasn't sure. The child nodded.

"Is there a midwife present?"

The girl shook her head, her lower lip beginning to tremble as her eyes filled with tears. "An' we havena doctor, either."

Alex hesitated, pensive. His gaze went to Fiona, and in his eyes, she sensed an apology. He looked at the frightened girl. "You have a doctor now. Take me to her."

Chapter 6

With little recourse, Fiona also decided to delay the journey and followed the trio. Her own mother had died in childbirth, and Fiona's heart ached in empathy at the fear she'd seen on the children's faces. If she could do something to help, she would. She could still remember Gwynneth and herself as wee children, huddled in each other's arms as they listened to their mother's screams from a far-off chamber. Later, their father came to tell them that the baby and their mother were dead. Months later, he was killed in an accident—his neck broken from a fall off his horse, an accident no doubt aided by the endless drams of ale he'd drunk in a futile effort to numb his grief.

Fiona hoped these children weren't to experience a similar childhood. She had lived a pleasant life at Kennerith, once she and Gwynneth moved in with their grandparents, but rarely a day went by that she didn't miss her mother or wonder about her.

They approached a small cottage. Instantly Alex dismounted and hurried inside after the boy and girl. Fiona followed.

A glance in the next room revealed a woman who lay deathly still on a crudely made bed. At first Fiona feared it was too late, but when Alex took her hand, the woman stirred. "I'm Dr. Spencer," he said reassuringly, "and I'm going to try to help you."

The woman said nothing, only closed her eyes. As Alex bent over her, Fiona turned to the children behind her. Beside Christopher and his sister, a child of approximately three years stood, her curled index finger hanging from her mouth, and stared at her mother's inert form. Fiona closed the door and gently drew the small lass away. She studied the humble dwelling, noticing the distinct smell of cooked *haggis*. Obviously the woman had been preparing a meal before her pains struck.

"Are you hungry?" Fiona asked the children.

All three shook their heads no.

A low, eerie moan from the next room quickly grew into a pitiful wail, then a scream. The small child ran to her sister, throwing her arms around the girl and burying her face in her frock. After the scream died away, Alex stepped outside, closing the door behind him.

"Miss Galbraith, if I might have a word with you?"

Fiona moved his way, the grave look on his face sharpening her apprehension.

"The baby is turned around," he said, his voice low, "and I must confess, I've never been faced with a breech presentation. Your prayers would be most appreciated."

"Of course."

Alex eyed the three sober faces of the children. "Perhaps it would be best if you took them outside. If I need you, I'll call."

He reentered the small room, and Fiona herded the children outdoors. The sunlight warmed her shoulders, chasing away the chill of death that seemed to pervade the hut. The children stood as though uncertain. She must give them something to do to get their minds off what was happening inside the cottage.

Fiona looked at Christopher. "Have you any idea where your father might be?"

The boy nodded. "He went to a nearby burgh."

"Perhaps you should fetch him?"

"I am no' allowed, bu' Garth may do so."

"Garth?"

"My brother. He tends the sheep in the high pasture."

Fiona felt a measure of relief. "Fetch Garth, then, and be quick aboot it."

"Aye." The boy raced toward one of the nearby hills.

Fiona felt a tug at her skirt and looked down at the smallest girl.

"Please t' tell me," she whispered, her blue eyes huge. "Is my mither t' die?"

A rush of emotion swept through Fiona, threatening to close her throat. She crouched low and took gentle hold of the girl's shoulders. "We'll pray for her—aye? And for the bairn. My grandmother oft spoke that the Almighty protects what is His own and listens t' the prayers of His children. Will ye pray with me?"

The girl nodded.

"What's your name?"

"Marget."

"And I'm Sadie," her sister said.

"I'm Fiona. Sit ye doon, the both of you, and let us pray."

"Are we no' t' kneel?" Sadie asked.

Fiona's limbs were tired from the long ride, and the cool grass felt good. "I dinna think the Lord should mind this once."

The two girls sat cross-legged on the ground with Fiona,

the three of them forming a circle. Closing her eyes, Fiona murmured a heartfelt prayer. She felt first Marget's cool hand slip into hers, where it lay on her lap, then Sadie's slid into her other one. At the unexpected contact, Fiona's words abruptly stopped, and she almost lost all train of thought. Then with eyes still closed, she continued the prayer and gently squeezed each of the girls' hands.

Alex released a weary breath. He wiped off his hands and arms with a spare cloth he'd found, directing a smile toward the exhausted but happy mother and the sleeping babe beside her. There for awhile, he had thought he might lose them both. He'd heard of physicians' attempts to manually turn the child while in the womb, but most all such cases ended in death for both mother and child. Alex had stood, uncertain, as he debated on the right course to take, trying to reassure the tortured woman, do his work, and pray at the same time. Miraculously, the babe turned of its own accord—or perhaps the Lord's hand had nudged it? In his profession, Alex occasionally witnessed wonders that couldn't be attributed to medicine, and with the many prayers being lifted up on this woman's behalf, Alex wouldn't be surprised if divine intervention had been the cause this time as well.

Now, many hours after their arrival to the cottage, Alex pulled down his rolled-up sleeves, fastened them, donned his wrinkled and damp waistcoat and overcoat, grabbed his hat, and stepped into the next room.

A stocky man with a red face immediately rose from a chair, fear written upon his features. Earlier, when the husband arrived, he had rushed into the room, paled, and stumbled back out.

"She's dead," he now whispered.

"She's alive and well," Alex contradicted. "As is your son."

"Son?" A radiant smile crossed the man's craggy features. "Might I see them?"

"Of course. She's weak, as is to be expected, but she's awake."

The man walked into the next room, closing the door behind him, and Alex took a chair at the table. Fiona set a bowl of stew in front of the oldest girl and then eyed him.

"You look wearied," she said. "Are ye hungry? There's a good barley stew t' fill your belly. . .unless you would prefer the *haggis*."

At the spark of mischief in her eyes, Alex couldn't resist. "Which is. . . ?"

"The liver, heart, and lungs of a sheep cooked in its stomach, along with suet, oats, and onions. Make no mistake about it, 'tis a food for warriors. All my ancestors ate *haggis* before doin' battle."

He didn't point out that the sheepherder and his wife hardly looked like warrior material, though after what that woman had been through the past several hours, perhaps they were. The ingredients didn't sound appealing, but Alex had a fondness for steak and kidney pie, which was somewhat similar, he supposed—though baked in a crust and not a sheep's stomach.

He watched her walk to the fire pit in the middle of the room and dish stew into a bowl. "I shall take a serving of the *haggis*," he said.

She spun around in surprise, then gave a slight nod. "Very well."

When she began to tip the stew back into the hanging

pot, Alex added, "No—I'll take that, too. I'm quite famished, actually."

Fiona set the food before him and sank to a chair. Alex looked at the shiny brown and unappealing mass, a mix of mashed potato and rutabagas on the side, tentatively took a bite of the *haggis* and chewed. She watched him as though waiting for him to retch or explode, Alex wasn't sure which. The dish wasn't as tasty as the favored kidney pie, rather gamey with a strong distinctive flavor, but it was edible. He took another bite.

"You like it?" she asked in surprise.

"I wouldn't ask our cook to put it on Darrencourt's menu, but it will suffice." He smiled at her, and she looked at the fire, seeming uneasy.

"About this delay, you have my apologies, Miss Galbraith, but I simply couldn't ignore a woman in need."

"You didna hold me here. I stayed of my own accord."

Wishing to reassure her, Alex said, "I'm reasonably certain we still have a chance to reach our siblings in time."

"Aye," she said quietly.

But the next day brought with it a pelting rain that seemed bent on attacking the small dwelling. Lightning flashed through the one window of the cottage and thunder rumbled. Water trickled in through the roof in a far corner, and together Fiona and Sadie cleared the large kettle of the last trace of porridge left and set the black pot underneath the small stream, emptying it outside as needed. They ate smoked fish and bread that day.

"Do not fret, Miss Galbraith," Alex said, hoping to console her. "This same storm will keep Beaufort and your sister from traveling if they are in the area."

From where he stood near the window, Kyle, the man of the house, looked at Fiona and Alex where they sat at the table. He pulled his pipe from his mouth and stared. "Do ye seek an Englishman and a Scottish lass?" he asked.

"Yes," Alex said in some surprise. "You know of such a couple?"

"Aye. Yesterday, when I was in the burgh seein' aboot my wagon, I saw two such as they in the smithy's shop. From what I ken, and it isna much for I came as they were leavin' the place, one o' their horses threw a shoe, and they were seekin' a coach. The smithy told them there was no' one available, and they maun wait 'til he finish with Laird MacClooney's horse."

"How far is this burgh?" Alex asked, encouraged by the news.

Kyle appeared to consider. "Two hours' journey by foot."

"The shortcut I be showin' ye is faster," the boy said with a pout.

"Christopher," Kyle admonished. "I'll no' have ye speakin' in sich a disrespectful tongue, or it's boxin' yer ears I'll be doin'."

"Bu' it is faster, Daddy. They ride t' Gretna Green."

"Gretna Green?" Kyle asked in surprise.

Alex shared a look with Fiona. "Yes."

"Then it's congratulations I'm offerin' t' ye," Kyle said, a huge smile cracking his weathered face. "Though you needna wait to reach the Green. We have a priest who'll marry ye in the kirk. 'Tis the least I can do t' fetch him, if ye have a mind t' wed."

Fiona blushed. "No—I—"

"We do not wish to marry," Alex inserted, as flustered as she. "We travel to Gretna Green to stop a wedding."

Kyle's smile dissipated. "Och, I see." He stared at both Fiona and Alex. "Are ye for a certain ye dinna wish t' marry? I've been watchin' the both of ye this day past, and ne'er have I seen two people who seem so well fitted t' another."

Fiona choked on the cider she was drinking. Alex listened to her cough while Sadie slapped her back. Bewildered by a new revelation, Alex couldn't pose an answer to Kyle's comment. He realized as he sat watching Fiona fan her face and try to catch her breath that the prospect of having her for a wife wasn't at all unappealing.

She'd been a tremendous help to him during the birth. Strong and steadfast, she stood at his side near the end, often seeming to read his mind and bring him those things he needed before he asked. Any of the English young ladies of his acquaintance would have probably fainted dead away at the first signs of labor. A doctor needed a strong, loyal wife who would aid him in his profession, if necessary, as well as be a good mother to his children, if the Lord should bless them with any. He observed the kindness Fiona bestowed on these young ones, the tender care, and he had witnessed her unswerving loyalty to family. Moreover, he and Fiona had been talking civilly with one another for a few days now, and he found himself enjoying her company.

Alex was thankful when the baby's sudden crying from the next room put an end to all thoughts trailing through his mind and Kyle left the table, letting the matter drop. Yet Fiona wouldn't meet Alex's gaze, and he couldn't draw her into conversation.

Christopher merrily played his reed, masking the uneasy silence that fell in the room.

Chapter 7

"Cross that bridge," Christopher said, pointing to a stone arch on the far side of the forest, "and when ye reach the other side, go on 'til ye come t' the gap between hills. Turn t' the left, and ye'll come back t' the road. If ye be followin' my lead, ye should reach Gretna Green by nightfall."

"Many thanks," Alex said with a tip of his hat.

"Mind ye, take care of your mother and your sisters and the new wee bairn," Fiona said, feeling strangely choked. "And help your father and Garth with the sheep."

"I will," the lad promised.

As they rode over a vista of rolling farmland, Fiona felt strangely sad to leave the sheepherder's family. In caring for the children these past two days, she had discovered a part of herself she hadn't known existed. Always, she had tried to shield herself from people, hiding within Kennerith and its surrounding mountains to protect herself from the scorn others might show. During this journey with Alex, she had been forced not only to converse with strangers but also to live among them, with no thick castle walls to protect her. In taking a chance by reaching out to others, she, in turn, had been blessed.

Last night, when her eye unexpectedly began to twitch while she tucked the children into the one bed they shared, little Marget hadn't run away in horror but instead placed her wee hand against Fiona's face, her blue eyes wide with concern, and asked, "Does it hurt?"

Tears had choked Fiona as she grabbed the little hand and kissed the palm, her heart full with the knowledge that the child didn't fear her. Nor did Marget think her affliction a curse, but instead had shown love and concern, as had Sadie and Christopher. Perhaps there were people outside Kennerith like these children, like Alex, who wouldn't reject her and might even come to accept her. Through his patient ministrations and kind words, Alex had shown her an acceptance she'd never known. And through them, Fiona came to realize that God accepted her also. Just as she was—flawed and all.

She watched cool, blue shadows slant across the flowing hills while confectionary-white clouds crept past a low sun. Alex was different than she'd first thought. Indeed, if Beaufort were as kind as his brother, perhaps it wasn't so horrible that Gwynneth had eloped with an Englishman.

The random thought shocked her, and she quickly spoke to cover the confusion she felt. "Tell me about your home at Darrencourt. What's it like?"

If Alex thought it strange that she should so suddenly ask such a question, he didn't show it. "The manor is a brown-and-white, sixteenth-century Tudor with elaborate gardens and a deep forest beyond, where I often go to hunt." He directed a look her way. "Darrencourt is in the country, with an abundance of green meadows in which to ride."

"No moors or mountains?"

"There's a stretch of moorland within a short distance of Darrencourt, but no mountains. Only wooded hills, much like these, only not so barren at the top." He motioned to the slopes on either side of them.

"And what do you hunt?"

"Venison, pheasant, quail—whatever meat my mother expresses a culinary desire for at the moment." He grinned.

Fiona was surprised. "Do you not have servants to take care o' such matters?"

"We do. Yet I enjoy the hunt. Fencing, too."

"Fencing?"

"Swordplay."

"Aye." That would explain why he was in such fine shape. "Are you accomplished?"

"I can hold my own."

Fiona studied his aristocratic profile and proud bearing, then looked to his strong hands holding the reins. She didn't doubt his words for a minute. "And have ye found the need to also treat your opponents?"

He looked at her curiously. "Treat them?"

"From the cuts o' your sword."

He let out a loud, delighted laugh. The sound cheered Fiona. His eyes sparkled with mirth, and she noticed attractive creases bracketing his mouth. Had they always been there?

"I assure you, Miss Galbraith, the points are tipped for safety's sake. Fencing is considered a sport, and we use stilettos, not swords."

Fiona thought about that. From tales told at the *ceilidh*, her ancestors fought with weapons to kill, not for game play. "The only time I've heard of a sword being used for purposes other than the battles for which it was made is in a dance o' my kinsmen—but even that dance is connected with war."

"Oh?" He sounded interested.

She nodded. "Centuries ago, King Malcolm slew a chief of MacBeth. Afterward, he laid his sword o'er the chief's sword and did a victory dance—what my kinsmen call a sword dance. My cousin David is adept at that, though he canna toss a caber for the life of him." She chuckled when she remembered David's attempts at carrying and throwing the upright tree trunk during the games of skill and strength her kinsmen played.

A comfortable stretch of silence settled between them before he spoke again. "Tell me about Kennerith. What do you do there?"

"Often I climb the hills. On a clear day, you can see the ocean and some of the islands while standing atop Mount MacMurray."

"Mount MacMurray?" he repeated with upraised brow.

"What our family named it generations ago. 'Tis the steepest mountain on our land. Pines and alders cover its base and trail upward, but at the top lies nothing but granite."

He nodded, his expression meditative.

"We also named the roses in our garden MacMurray Roses," she added. "Gwynneth and I take turns tending them. 'Tis a family tradition we dinna leave t' the servants. The garden is ancient, as ye can see by the Celtic cross in its midst." She thought back to something her grandmother had said. "I was told the roses began through an ancestor named Fayre. And legend has it that throughout past centuries, no matter what hardships Kennerith underwent, every new owner of the castle found at least one bush still living. The roses are lovely, of the most unusual color ye will find. Like the sunset before the gloamin', they are."

"The gloaming. Twilight?" Alex questioned.

"Aye." Fiona smiled. " 'Tis the afterglow once the sun disappears beyond the horizon. The gloamin' lasts a long while."

The day passed in pleasant conversation as they continued southward. They reached a pass where the road narrowed, and they had to travel single file. Fiona felt almost saddened to end their discussion. When Alex pulled Barrag to a sudden stop, Fiona walked Skye closer to the trees crowding the lane so she could bring her horse next to Alex's. A small village could be seen in the distance.

"Is something wrong?" she asked.

He didn't answer for a moment, then looked at her, his eyes no longer laughing. "We have reached our destination. Beyond lies Gretna Green."

Fiona said nothing, but Alex sensed by the faint frown on her lips that she hovered in a state of indecision, even remorse. In an instant, the sober look was gone, and she bounced her heels into Skye's flanks, prodding the horse into a wild gallop.

Alex followed, wondering if he'd imagined her earlier hesitation. She seemed anxious to reach the small village, whereas Alex now had reservations. What right did he have to tell his older brother not to marry? Certainly the fact that Gwynneth was not merely a simple peasant girl but the granddaughter of an earl must hold some sway with his father. Indeed, if the sister was as amazing and lovely as Fiona, Beaufort should count himself blessed.

It was then that Alex realized he was smitten with his

redheaded collaborator, though he couldn't pinpoint the exact moment she'd found her way into his heart. Little did it matter; she considered him as repulsive as the filth scraped from the bottom of his boots. Alex withheld a sigh. Duty to family prevailed. He might have experienced a change of heart, but it was of no account. He would remain loyal in carrying out his father's wishes.

Gretna Green appeared to be no more than a cluster of white cottages at a crossroads. Alex spotted an inn, a tavern, and other places of business. People walked through the streets, going about their daily duties. Alex slowed his horse to a walk, and Fiona did the same. He guided Barrag up to the first person they met, a short man with a bulbous nose and large ears.

"Excuse me," Alex said. "Could you tell me where marriages are performed?"

The man cracked a wide smile, showing several gaps where his teeth had been. "Where'er ye like. Most are wedded at Gretna Hall, others at the Sark Tollbar—the first cottage ye come to when ye cross the border and pay the toll. Especially if the pursuit be hot, ye may want t' go there. Others share vows in private cottages or e'en here, outside among the gorse bushes." He spread his arms wide to encompass the village. "There's nary a place a weddin' canna be performed in all o' Gretna Green."

A slight man wearing an apron strode from a cobbler's shop. "If it's a marriage ye be wantin', come this way," he called out to Alex.

"Nae," a stout man on the other side of the road cried out. "He has just come from the asylum this week. I can show ye t' a respected man t' give ye yer vows, a Robert Elliot."

"Nae," the other man cried out good-naturedly, "my friend is drunk on ale. Bishop Lang is the man ye seek."

The two continued their easy, competitive bantering, and Alex questioned the man they'd first met. "You have a bishop presiding over weddings?"

"In name only," the man said. "David Lang was but a peddler in his youth before he served in the British navy. He's been in the marriage trade thirty years and has performed many a ceremony." He scratched his head. "Come t' think of it, he was called on only minutes ago to wed a couple."

Alex grew alert. "Where?"

"Gretna Hall. Many a fine lord and lady ha'e married there. Ye will be in good company." Chuckling, the man gave them directions, and Alex prodded Barrag into a fast gallop.

Fiona stared after Alex, then urged Skye to follow. Heat bathed her face at the villagers' assumptions that she and Alex had eloped and were looking for a place to wed. Even more shocking was her discovery that the idea was not detestable. Quite the opposite, really. And Fiona realized that somehow, at some point, she, Fiona Galbraith, a Highland Scot, had fallen in love with Alexander Spencer, a noble Englishman.

The abrupt awakening nearly unseated her from her horse.

Her grandmother might one day forgive her, but her grandfather, God bless him, never would stand for such a match, if he were cognizant of his surroundings. Fiona creased her brow, thinking of all she'd learned from those she'd met on their journey. Indeed, a whole new world had been opened to her, one not entirely without merit. The elderly MacBain woman's sage words were accurate. This was a new era, a time for change.

Surely, then, it was time to let go of prejudices almost a century old as well as of the pride that had fostered them.

Perhaps Gwynneth wasn't as foolish as Fiona had reckoned her. Indeed, she might be the only intelligent Galbraith alive.

With each pounding of Skye's hooves on the road, Fiona felt more uncertain. What right did she have to try to stop her sister from marrying the man she loved? Gwynneth was seventeen, of marriageable age, and if Beaufort were as wonderful as his brother, as kind and considerate of others' feelings, then surely Gwynneth would enjoy a happy life. Wasn't that all that mattered?

Yet Alex's family considered Gwynneth unfit, and Fiona didn't think he'd understand her sudden change of heart if she were to speak. She didn't wholly understand it herself. After the rudeness she'd shown him those first days, Alex probably was anxious to be rid of her, though he was too much a gentleman to say so. Fiona only had herself to blame. Never mind that she was unaccustomed to strangers or the art of being sociable. She knew what the Good Book said about being charitable toward one's fellow man, and no excuse would erase the fact that Fiona had acted shamefully. The revelation was sobering, and she issued a silent plea for God to intervene and steam out the wrinkles in her rutted character.

Soon, they approached a long carriage drive. A wide, lush lawn covered in hardwood trees and evergreens fronted a white stone manor with gray trim along its many windows. Numerous chimneys rose above its gray roof. In front stood a shiny black coach, empty of its passengers, and a team of fine horses, prancing and snorting, their red coats glistening as if they'd just come to a quick stop. The driver worked to steady them.

Alex hurriedly dismounted, and Fiona followed him inside Gretna Hall. He threw open the door, looked around the empty foyer, and hurried through the open door of a parlor. A man, approximately in his late sixties with black clerical robes and broad-brimmed hat, faced a couple who had their backs to Fiona. The woman wore a bonnet, but the dark hair was familiar.

"Stop this wedding at once!" Alex cried.

The couple turned in terrified shock, and Fiona felt strangely relieved.

Alex's face darkened a shade. "You have my apologies," he told the unknown couple. "I thought you were someone else."

"May we continue?" the young woman said, her fearful gaze on the door. "I'm afraid Papa might come charging in here at any moment." She slipped her hand into the fair-haired man's, they exchanged a few words, saying they agreed to take one another for man and wife, and the older man officiating proclaimed them married.

It was over so quickly, Fiona wasn't certain it had happened, but she couldn't miss the joyous kiss the man bestowed on his blushing bride before escorting her from the parlor.

Alex moved toward the old man. "Have you wed an Englishman and a Scottish woman today?"

The man's full face beamed and his dark eyes sparkled. "Aye. I married them an hour ago. Sich a fine couple. They took a room here as well."

Alex quieted. "May I see the register? If we speak of the same couple, the man is my brother."

The old man nodded and pointed to the open page of a thick ledger where names and dates had been penned. Fiona stepped beside Alex and read the last entry:

> *On Wednesday 22nd inst at Gretna, Lord Beaufort Spencer of Darrencourt to Gwynneth Galbraith of Kennerith in Scotland. A polite young lady and a dignified nobleman. Paid one hundred guineas.*

"Then we're too late," Fiona murmured.

"You sound almost relieved," Alex said in surprise.

Fiona turned her gaze fully upon him. "If the truth be told, I am."

He showed no astonishment, but his eyes intently focused on her, as though looking deep into her soul. "Might I ask why?"

"Aye," she responded just as softly. "When first we met at Kennerith, you were just a name, a class o' people I'd been taught to dislike, and I was bitter about other things as well. But during our journey, you've become a person t' me. One I greatly admire." Fiona tried to keep her words blithe, yet her heart pounded madly at the light that entered his eyes. "To be sure, if Beaufort be anything like you are, Dr. Spencer, then Gwynneth couldna have made too horrid a match."

"Miss Galbraith, if you'll permit me to speak?" Alex seemed suddenly flustered, searching for words. When he took hold of her hands, Fiona forgot to breathe. "Before setting out for Scotland, I never dreamed I would find a woman I might grow to love, if that is indeed what this emotion is. All I know is that I desire to spend each moment in your presence, to walk by your side and learn of all that interests you, to never refrain from looking into your lovely silver eyes. . . ."

"I can marry ye this moment, if ye so desire," the elderly

man suddenly said, reminding the two of his presence. "If ye have no ring, I can provide one as well."

Heat bathed Fiona's face, and her heart sped up with nervous expectancy. Her hands grew slick in his, but Alex didn't release his hold. This was so sudden, but it was what she wanted. To marry this man. It was as though the reason for her existence, for God putting her on this earth, instantly became clear to her. She was to become Alex's wife and bear his children.

"No," Alex said, never breaking eye contact with her.

"No?" Fiona repeated, her dreams spiraling to dust.

The elderly man tsk-tsked and left the parlor, leaving the two alone.

"My dearest Fiona—if you'll allow me to take the liberty of addressing you as such?"

Fiona nodded, confused.

"The love I have for you seems quite real to me at this moment. However, this swift change regarding our feelings toward one another should be tested with time. Before engaging in the holy institution of marriage—and it is a wondrous and holy institution—I feel we should spend time getting to know one another. I shall make it a priority to visit Scotland whenever possible. In time, if we should decide to marry, I would rather the wedding take place in a church, before God, with a true minister presiding, and with our families' blessings. Rather than on the sly, in the front parlor of an inn, with an ex-peddler speaking the vows—and against our families' wishes." He tightened his grasp. "Do you understand, my dearest Fiona?"

"Aye." Her earlier disappointment evaporated, and she smiled. "I've always wanted to marry in the castle chapel at Kennerith and have the reception in the rose garden there."

Alex grinned. "I'm anxious to see these famous MacMurray roses. Perhaps when I escort you home, you'll show them to me?"

The awareness that he would be returning with her to Kennerith made her smile all the wider. "Aye, that I will. It willna take you long to win o'er my grandmother. She never would have allowed someone she didna trust t' take her beloved horse. And my grandfather is no longer mindful of his surroundings, so ye'll have no problem with him. But what about your father? Will he come to accept me? Or Gwynneth, for that matter?"

Alex sobered. "I'll talk to him. It may take some time, but I'm convinced that my father eventually will realize what wonderful additions the Galbraith sisters will make to our family. He's an intelligent man."

Fiona laughed. "I once thought myself the same, but this past week I've come t' ken that I've much to learn."

"You're one of the most remarkable women I've ever met." Alex's expression softened, and he raised her hands to his lips and kissed them. "Shall we see about acquiring two rooms and then go in search of a meal? Before they leave, I have a sudden desire to wish my brother a hearty congratulations and your sister the best of wishes!"

Epilogue

In the midst of the castle chapel, decorated with an abundance of sunset-colored roses, Alex kissed his new bride. At the warmth of his lips on hers, the strength of his embrace, Fiona's heart beat with wonder that her beloved Alex was now her husband. She felt brighter than the streams of sunbeams that shone down at them from one of five stained-glass windows, encasing them and the Scottish minister in an aura of jewel-toned light.

Pulling away, she smiled and looked into Alex's blue-gray eyes with their familiar sparkle. She could never doubt his love; it shone from his eyes. He took hold of her hand, and together they moved to accept their families' blessings.

As Fiona predicted, her grandmother hadn't greatly argued the point that Fiona loved an Englishman. The fact that King George IV had visited Scotland during the same year Fiona first met Alex and they had embarked on their journey together had helped matters. It was said the English king had appeared in a kilt, and Fiona knew, thanks to the author Sir Walter Scott, that Highland dress and customs had been embraced by many of the British, even romanticized.

Alex and Fiona's courtship was more wonderful than Fiona dared dream. On the occasions Alex had visited the castle, he and Fiona climbed mountains, rode horses, and fell more deeply in love. The most amazing thing was that the twitching in Fiona's eye disappeared. She hadn't had an episode in months. Yet even if the affliction were to return, and Alex's uncle wasn't able to treat her successfully, Fiona was confident that her new husband would never cease to love her.

Gwynneth moved forward to hug Fiona. "I'm so happy for you," she said. "And so glad that you'll come to live at Darrencourt."

"I'll miss this castle and our grandparents," Fiona admitted, "but Alex assured me that we'll visit every summer. I canna explain it. I never thought anything would entice me to leave these mountains, but I look forward to living at Darrencourt. I canna imagine a life without Alex."

"Aye. 'Tis the same way I feel about Beaufort."

"I scarcely can believe it! Both of us married—and to Englishmen as well!"

They laughed, and Gwynneth glowed from the promise of the child she carried within her. Fiona was pleased that she would soon be an aunt and relieved for Gwynneth, whose first months at Darrencourt had been difficult. Beaufort's father hadn't disowned him, as he'd threatened, but he'd had nothing to do with Gwynneth at first and avoided her presence. Beaufort's mother, dismayed but resigned to Beaufort's choice of a bride, had insisted they properly marry in the Church of England, and they had honored her wish. As the months passed, both Spencers came to see what a delightful and polite girl Gwynneth was and apologized for wrongly judging her.

Their acceptance of Gwynneth made Alex's announcement of his own impending marriage to Fiona easier to accept.

Gwynneth pulled away, brushing the wrinkles from the shoulders of Fiona's best gown of shimmering emerald green. Beaufort stepped forward to hug his new sister-in-law. "You're perfect for my brother. I'm confident after meeting you that Alex has found a woman who'll stand up to him and not always let him have his way." He directed an amused grin toward Alex.

"Shall we move to the garden?" Alex asked, his color heightened at his brother's ribbing.

Fiona slipped her arm through his. "Aye. I have yet to give you your gift."

They walked into the spacious garden, fragrant with MacMurray roses. So many of the orange-red roses still grew on the vines that the absence of the ones Fiona used to decorate the chapel didn't show.

"Sit ye doon," Fiona instructed, her hands impatiently going to Alex's shoulders to seat him in one of two chairs that stood by a table off to the side. Agatha had helped her move the furniture into the garden that morning.

Alex chuckled. "My, I am intrigued by what has my new wife so flustered."

"Hush now," Fiona said with a smile. She nodded toward her cousin, and he lifted his bagpipes to his mouth. Soon the wheezing wail of pipes erupted into a carefree jig. Two of her cousins began to dance in the center clearing, and others quickly joined in. Fiona was surprised to see Alex's father, Lord Spencer, attempt a turn beside her grandmother, though Lady Spencer only looked on with a smile. Caught up in the music and dancing, no one paid attention to Fiona or Alex, which suited Fiona just fine.

Agatha walked toward them, bearing a platter with a very English-looking tea set and a platter of small cakes, then left. At the curious lift of Alex's brow, Fiona smiled, poured liquid from the pot into a cup, and set it before him.

"I once told you that ye'll not be findin' English tea at Kennerith Castle," Fiona explained. "At the time, false pride led me t' believe that English tea and bagpipes didna mix—I even told others so. Well, I was wrong. Please accept this gesture as a token of my love."

"Fiona," he breathed and grabbed her hand, pulling her down to his lap.

"Alex!" she protested with a laugh. "What's gotten into ye?"

"Perhaps it's this wild Highland air or the realization that the woman I adore is truly my wife. I don't know. But I doubt there's a man alive who's as happy as I am at this moment." He kissed her until Fiona forgot about all else but him.

When he pulled away, his gaze sheepishly went to the dancing guests as though just remembering their existence. "Perhaps we should save this for later. If Mother were to see us, she would be scandalized—even if this is my wedding and the woman I hold is my wife."

Fiona laughed and cupped his face with her palms, brushing her lips over his once more. "Aye, Alex. I do love ye so." Smiling, she stood and took hold of his hands. "Come, and I'll teach you a Highland jig. Later, we'll drink our tea, when we're alone together."

He allowed her to pull him up. "Mrs. Spencer," he whispered near her ear before taking her arm to escort her to the dancing. "I must confess I eagerly await that moment."

Fiona shared a secret smile with her Englishman. To be sure, so did she.

PAMELA GRIFFIN

Pamela Griffin lives in North Central Texas and divides her time among family, church activities, and writing. Her main goal in writing Christian romance is to encourage others and plant seeds of faith through entertaining stories that minister to the wounded spirit. She has contracted twenty novels and novellas and would love for you to visit her Web site at: http://members.cowtown.net/PamelaGriffin/.

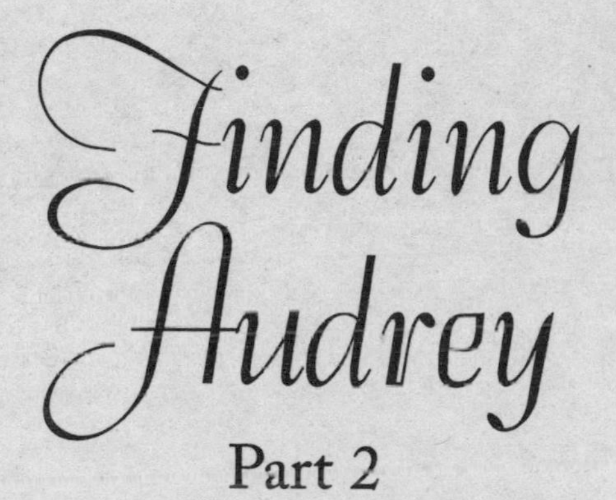

Part 2

by Tracey V. Bateman

Chapter 4

You seem so happy lately."

Audrey blinked at Cassie, her new employee. "I do?"

"You sure do." The girl grinned. "Does it have anything to do with Pastor Brett?"

An indulgent smile played on Audrey's lips. "Not in the way you think. He gave me some research material that opened up a section of my family tree that I couldn't seem to find."

Disappointment clouded the girl's expression for a second. "Oh, well. Not exactly what I'd hoped for. But I'm happy for you."

Cassie wasn't the only one who wished the relationship could move forward. Still, Audrey loved the steady friendship, even if it couldn't grow into anything romantic.

"How's this?" Cassie held up an arrangement she'd been creating off and on all day.

The girl had real talent and a knack for working with flowers. Audrey smiled, delighted as she observed Cassie's arrangement. Three pink carnations placed between baby's breath. A single red rose in the center. "That's wonderful, Cassie! Your foster mother will love that."

Cassie flushed under the praise. She gave Audrey a tight hug and pulled away with a grin. "I've never been able to get her anything for Mother's Day before. I hope she likes this."

"Who wouldn't?"

Uncertainty clouded the teen's eyes for just a second. Then she nodded. "You're right. She'll love it." Her tone was a little too bright. Audrey frowned.

"Cass, is everything all right at your house?"

"What? Oh, sure."

She wouldn't admit in a million years if something were wrong. Audrey knew that. To complain was to take a risk of switching foster homes. Who wanted to be moved around and forced to change schools over and over? Cassie had been in the same foster house now for two years, she had told Audrey. Worry flooded Audrey, but she understood the girl's hesitance. She didn't press.

Audrey fished in the register. "Here's your check. You're doing a great job, Cass. You should seriously consider working with flowers and plants as a career."

"You really think so?"

"Yep. Just don't open a shop on the next corner and put me out of business."

Tucking her check inside her back pocket, Cassie laughed and picked up her vase of flowers. She headed toward the door. "I promise I'll keep my distance. Thanks again for giving me the knockoffs for my arrangement."

Audrey smiled and, grabbing her keys, followed the girl to the door. "My pleasure." She typically threw out flowers that she didn't consider to be perfect. Cassie had sorted through and found the best of those and had asked if she could take them.

Through the glass door, Audrey watched Cassie walk to the corner a half block away. A foster child. How on earth did Cassie keep herself together and happy when she had no family?

Being a foster child had grated on Audrey all through her growing-up years. She'd learned to cope, but she hadn't been a happy girl. Cassie was different. She wasn't faking it. She'd been working at the Rosie Posie Flower Shop after school and on Saturdays for the past few months. Brett had asked Audrey to hire the girl because Cassie's waitressing job had required she work on Sundays.

The stretch to pay the girl's salary was worth every pinched penny of Audrey's own budget. Cassie's sunny personality and natural ability to work with flowers brought a source of joy into Audrey's life that she hadn't realized she'd been missing. And having someone else to cover the front counter gave Audrey more time to research on her computer and plow through the piles of books she'd checked out from the library.

After all the frustrating months when the genealogical trail had been cold, Audrey welcomed the sense of belonging that made an appearance in her heart from discovering the story of Fiona and Alex. She now knew with certainty that she wasn't some pod woman grown from a seed. There were really and truly people from whom she'd descended. The most amazing discovery by far was uncovering the information that Fiona Galbraith Spencer's eyes were silvery gray like Audrey's. Audrey no longer felt like a freak of nature. She'd come by the unusual trait honestly.

She stood at the door and waited until Cassie stepped onto the bus, then she locked the door and grabbed the broom. The phone chirped just as she swept up the last of the dirt and dried leaves from the floor.

A smile tipped her lips. Right on time. Her heart skipped a beat at the sound of Brett's voice. "We still on for tonight?" he asked.

A short laugh escaped her throat.

"Did I say something funny?" His voice was guarded.

"No. I just enjoy your predictability." His class had been over for several weeks, but they'd kept their Monday night coffee date—or non-date. Brett never failed to call and confirm. As if she'd stand him up. All week she looked forward to their three hours together. And it wasn't because of the mocha.

"Some people might consider my weekly confirmation call to be reliability rather than predictability."

Grinning to herself, she absently cleaned dirt from her nails with a file she kept under the register for just that reason. "Reliability then. Feel better?"

"Much."

She could hear the humor in his voice, and it warmed her. Brett was going to make some woman awfully happy. Just the sound of his voice brightened her day. What would it be like to belong to such a man?

"So you never answered me," he said.

"I'll be there." *Like always. Isn't that what pals do? Have coffee together and discuss their week?*

"Look, I was thinking. . . ."

"You were?" she quipped, trying to remove the sting in her own heart and get her own thoughts focused on lightness and friendship. "Good move."

"Very funny," he answered dryly. "I'm trying to be serious."

"I'm sorry. Continue, please. What were you thinking? Inquiring minds want to know."

He chuckled. "It's such a nice day, I thought maybe I'd walk along the beach. Want to join me?"

She hesitated. A walk along the beach sounded an awful lot like a date.

"I'll buy you a hotdog."

The thought of the two of them walking on the moist sand, watching the sun go down filled Audrey with such a pleasant sensation that she decided immediately.

"Sounds great. What time?"

"Now, actually. I'm right outside."

Audrey glanced toward the door and saw his forest green Ford Explorer parked along the curb. He grinned and waved. Instinctively her hand went to her hair. She had to be a mess.

Brett laughed. "You look great."

"Yeah, if you're looking through both a car window and a store window," she said dryly. "Give me ten minutes, will you?"

"All right. I'll be here."

Brett slid the gearshift to park and killed the motor but decided to keep his sunglasses on for now. The sun shone brilliantly over the waters of Lake Michigan, promising a glorious sunset in another few minutes. He scanned the beach. On a Monday evening in early June, the main traffic would be teenagers out of school for the summer and joggers and walkers following the paths along the Rocks—the trails between the beaches, aptly named for the massive rocks flanking either side.

He glanced at Audrey, who was staring out the window, no doubt taking in the view of the shimmering water. "Do you want to walk along the trails or the beach?"

"The beach," she replied without missing a beat.

That was one thing Brett admired about Audrey. She knew her mind. No games. "You sure? It's going to be romantic."

She turned to him, her beautiful, silver eyes soft and revealing. "I'm in the mood for romantic."

Alarm shot through him, a check in his spirit. A warning that he knew was most certainly from God. Romantic wasn't possible. His stomach clenched. The circumstances were the same now as they had been seven months ago. Despite their friendship, things would never go any further until Audrey made a true and lasting commitment to Jesus Christ.

Her face paled, then she turned away and slipped off her sandals. "Get the panic off your face, Rev. I didn't say I was in the mood to be romantic with you. A nice barefoot walk along the beach will hit the spot."

Heat crept up Brett's neck. She was bluffing. He knew her feelings for him were as strong as his. He regretted that her resolve seemed to be weakening when he had no choice but to keep his as strong as ever. Even stronger if she'd decided she was willing to pursue a relationship that went deeper than friendship. *Oh, Lord. Give me strength.*

"Come on," he said, opening his door.

"Don't forget you promised me a hotdog," she said as she closed the door and joined him.

They stopped at a stand. "Give me lots of onions," Cassie told the vendor.

Brett laughed. She was obviously making sure that he knew she didn't want him to kiss her. As though a few onions would keep him from wanting to draw her into his arms and press his lips to hers. His heart responded to the direction of his thoughts and sped up. Quickly, he pushed away the image and laughed again.

She sent him a sheepish grin, then her laughter joined his, and suddenly everything was all right again. Breathing a sigh of relief, he paid for their hotdogs and Cokes.

They walked along the water's edge, occasionally catching a surge of water over their feet and ankles. It felt wonderful. Would have been perfect if he had been free to snatch her hand and hold it while they walked.

He fought his desire to make this evening personal and finally settled on a safe topic of mutual interest. "How's Cassie doing?"

Audrey wiped the catsup off her lip with her napkin, sipped her Coke, and looked at him. "She's doing great. Such a natural, Brett. She has an eye for what colors and varieties go together. Better than I do, really. I'll probably end up giving her some free rein soon and see what she can really do."

Pleased, Brett nodded his approval. "It's good to see Cassie find something she can excel at."

"She's such a great kid, Brett. It just kills me that she doesn't have a family. Why does God do this to the best kids?"

"What do you mean?" Taken aback by the bitterness in Audrey's voice, Brett stared at the sand and waited for her to explain.

"I mean, if Cassie had the advantages that those other kids in your group have, there's no telling how far she could go. Instead, she's stuck living in a low-income home with a foster mother who can't even buy her a ticket to a concert and probably wouldn't do it if she could."

"I know; it's hard to understand sometimes. But God has a bright future in mind for that girl. She's special, and I know she has a tough time at home."

"No, Brett. You *don't* know. You couldn't possibly understand how it is for Cassie. She has no parental guidance. No love. She's stuck for two more years, and then what?"

"Then we'll help her with college applications, financial-aid packets, whatever we have to do to give her every chance."

"That's a pretty pat answer. It doesn't let God off the hook though. What good is the bright future He has planned for her, as you say, if she's emotionally scarred from years of being unwanted or only being given a place to stay because of the money the state pays her foster parents?"

"Not all foster parents are like that, Audrey. God never promised a life without struggle. We all have our share of heartache and disappointment. It's called the human condition."

"How come some humans don't have the same level of disappointment and heartache, Brett?"

Her question came, not in the defensive tone of a moment before, but with real vulnerability. Brett stopped. "Let's sit for awhile and watch the sun go down."

She nodded. "Hang on a sec." She tossed what remained of her Coke and hotdog into a nearby trashcan. Brett followed her example, his appetite suddenly gone.

Audrey dropped to the sand and cradled her knees to her chest. "So, Rev. What's the verdict? If God is so impartial, why does the human condition seem to swing in certain people's favor while others are left parentless?"

"Who are we discussing now, Audrey? You or Cassie?"

She shrugged and tossed a broken shell into the water. "I

don't know. Both, I guess. All I ever wanted was to know I belonged somewhere."

The wind whipped off the lake, blowing Audrey's strawberry blond hair around her face. Brett swallowed hard. She was so beautiful. And out of his reach. His heart ached.

You do belong somewhere, Audrey. With me.

With you, Son?

The nudge of correction pricked his heart. "You've been given a family, Audrey."

She gave a short laugh and pulled her hair away from her face. "Yeah, an old aunt who died before I could really know her and hundreds of years of dead ancestors. Our holiday get-togethers are downright ghoulish."

Brett snatched her hand and held it in his. "Audrey, I'm not speaking of your physical family. God has called you into His eternal family. You know that."

She jerked her hand free. "We have a deal, Buster. No preaching."

"You brought it up."

A moan escaped her, and she hugged her knees again and rocked. "You're right. Okay. Can we let it go now and resume our previous arrangement?"

He grinned. "Chicken."

She grinned back. "Nag."

"Touché."

Chapter 5

How's the research coming along back here?"

"Not great." Audrey rubbed her aching temple and forced a smile as Cassie walked into her office. "You remember me telling you I'm trying to find a link between Allan Galbraith and Allan MacMurray?"

Cassie set a cup of tea on the desk in front of her. "You mean where one was a servant and the other an earl?"

Audrey took the tea gratefully. "Thanks, Cass."

"You're welcome."

"I think they're the same man."

"The same man? You mean he went by two different names? Do you think he was a criminal?"

"I just don't know." Frustrated, Audrey snatched off her glasses and tossed them on the desk. "He could have been a criminal. It seems to run in the family." She thought of Rory MacMurray and his high-seas angst, and Dane MacMurray, who went to prison for running moonshine during prohibition. "My family tree isn't without its salty dogs. That's for sure. And. . ." She grinned at the girl. "I share my birthday with a great-great-great-aunt who single-handedly defended her homestead from marauding Indians after an arrow pierced her husband's heart. Their sod walls kept fiery arrows from doing much damage. Just as she ran out of bullets, the four or five remaining Indians had enough and took off."

"Wow."

Audrey glanced back at her notes. "Not only that, she was also buried on her birthday. I've never heard of anyone who was born and died on the same date. Have you?"

"No, I haven't." Cassie raised her brow, her eyes beautiful pools of innocence. "What date would that happen to be?"

Audrey grinned. "Are you fishing around to find out my birthday?"

"Of course."

"Two weeks from today, July 27."

"And the year?"

"Ha! Nice try."

The bell chimed from the front of the store. Cassie headed that way. "Duty calls."

Audrey watched her bouncy steps and shook her head. *What a great kid.* Even her incessant invitations to join her for church didn't turn Audrey off. Cassie spoke with a sincerity that Audrey had never encountered before. The girl truly believed Audrey would be happier if she attended services on a regular basis. Audrey couldn't hold it against her. She simply politely thanked her and declined each time Cassie brought it up—which happened to be every Saturday, without fail.

Clicking off the computer, Audrey decided to put off the research for now. Maybe some time away would help. She rested her elbows on her desk and covered her face with her hands. Cassie would be leaving soon, and Brett would make his "reliable" Monday evening call. But Audrey had made a decision. The risk associated with their friendship had become too great. For a couple of reasons. One, she loved him. And that was impossible. Two, he watched her constantly. As though waiting for her to "come to the Lord."

Why did things have to be so complicated? She knew the answer all too well. God. He complicated things.

My way or the highway. That's the way You are, right, God? No room for compromise. I wouldn't mind negotiating if You'd let me have Brett in my life as more than a friend. What do You say? I'll give a little if You will.

I already gave everything I could give. There's only one thing I want from you.

Audrey gasped as the silent words hit her full force. She continued her railing. *You've done what You wanted with my life from the moment You decided I should be given to two parents who wanted You more than they wanted a child. I can't give You what You've already taken.*

Only silence answered.

"Earth to Audrey."

Startled, Audrey opened her eyes. "What?"

"I said I'm leaving now. Do you want me to lock up when I go?"

"Huh? Oh yeah. Go ahead. Just use your key."

"Okey-dokey." Cassie hesitated and frowned. "You okay?"

"Yeah."

"You don't look okay. Want me to call Pastor Brett to come and get you?"

"It's just a headache from looking at the computer screen all day." Audrey attempted a smile but knew she hadn't managed more than a grimace. "I can drive. I promise."

Looking unconvinced, Cassie took a step toward the door. "Are you sure, Audrey? I hate to leave you here like this."

"Go before you miss your bus, Cass. I need to finish cleaning up, then I'm making an early night of it."

"Will you call me later, just so I know you're okay?"

Tenderness rose up inside of Audrey. Cassie would make a great mom someday. "You got it, Kid. Now get out of here."

She turned to go.

"Hey, Cass," Audrey called after her.

"Yeah?"

"Thanks for caring so much about me." This time she managed a real smile.

Cassie winked and grinned. "You got it, Kid."

Audrey chuckled at Cassie's imitation of her.

True to tradition, Brett called ten minutes after Cassie locked the door and left the flower shop.

"We on for tonight?"

Audrey's heart drummed like tom-toms in her ears. "I don't think so, Brett."

"You feeling all right? I could bring you some chicken soup."

Oh, man! Why was he so perfect?

"Actually, I've been thinking," she said in halting rhythm.

"Careful with that."

"I'm serious, Brett."

"Want to talk about it? Say, over lattes?"

"Nice try." Audrey doodled on a note pad. She gathered a quick breath. "I don't think we should see each other anymore."

"I disagree. That's one vote yea, one vote nay. Now what?"

Audrey frowned. This wasn't the reaction she'd expected.

She thought he'd bow out gracefully and most likely be relieved. "It's not up for a vote. I've decided."

"You can't just decide not to see me anymore. We're friends. I should have a say in the matter."

"I don't believe this! You carry your male domination a bit too far, Brett. You might believe in female submission and all that garbage, but don't try to force me to play into your little world. If I say we're not seeing each other anymore, we're not!"

Her hands shook as she put down the receiver, disconnecting the call.

The phone rang again immediately. After a ten-ring inward debate, Audrey snatched it up.

"I'm sorry, Audrey. You have a right to end our friendship if you choose to do so. But please tell me what I've done and give me a chance to make it up to you."

Tears stung her eyes at the regret in his tone. "Nothing, Brett. The thing is, we started this relationship knowing that we aren't right for each other. But that doesn't stop my heart from having ideas of its own. If things were different. . .well, then things would be different."

Silence buzzed over the line between them until Audrey thought Brett might have disconnected the line. She was just about to say his name when she heard his breathing, long and shaky as he fought for control.

Tears trickled down her cheeks. This was the way it had to be. She felt she was making a noble sacrifice. Brett needed to get on with his life. Find the right girl to be a minister's wife.

"I understand perfectly, Audrey." His voice was hoarse. "I'm falling in love with you, too." He gave a short laugh. "Actually, I'm way past the 'falling' part. I love you."

"But you love God more, right?"

"Yes. Always. I couldn't love you if I didn't first love God."

"Then I don't see how we have anything to say to each other. Our friendship is ruined now that we've said the *L* word."

"Audrey. . ."

She steeled her heart against the pleading in Brett's voice. "Don't ask, Brett."

"I know you believe in Jesus Christ. You have more knowledge of the Bible than most of the people in our congregation. Why can't you live for Him?"

"Because God expects too much from the people who live for Him. I could never leave my child and run off to some land and take care of someone else's child."

"Oh, Sweetheart. God doesn't expect that. I'm sorry your parents did that to you. But you can't blame God forever."

"Watch me."

A sigh of defeat threaded through the line and caused a lump in Audrey's throat when it reached her ears.

"All right. I won't argue with you anymore. But I want you to know one thing."

"What's that?"

"I'll be praying for you every day of my life until Jesus convinces you."

"Good-bye, Brett."

"Good-bye. I love you."

Audrey hung up, laid her head on the desk, and sobbed.

Brett felt his jaw go slack at Pastor Turner's words. The elderly preacher chuckled. "You have no need to feel unqualified. The board is seriously considering you to be my replacement. I thought you should be prepared."

"But why are you retiring, Sir? You have plenty of days ahead of you."

"Oh, don't get me wrong. I'm not retiring from my ministry. No one in God's service really ever retires until they see Jesus face to face in heaven. I've been offered a teaching position at Bethany Bible College. My alma mater. I have prayed extensively and feel God is calling me to help raise up a new generation to be ministers of the gospel. It's a great honor."

"But I don't feel ready to take over for you. I'm only the youth pastor." *And I'm in love with an unbeliever.*

Pastor Turner stood and extended his hand, still sure and steady. "You pray about it. I won't tell you what the Lord is calling you to do. This is something you'll have to hear His voice tell you about yourself."

Brett sighed and accepted the proffered hand. "Yes, Sir."

He returned to his office, shaken and feeling a bit like a freshman on the first day of high school. Completely out of his element and yet excited at new possibilities. He'd believed for years that he was called to be a pastor. But he'd grown content over the last few years, teaching youth, attending all the sports activities and high school endeavors. He'd settled into a comfort zone. Maybe God was moving him on. . . .

He was still pondering the possibility a few moments later when he spied a note on his desk. His secretary must have placed it there before she left for lunch.

Cassie Reynolds called to remind you that today is Audrey's birthday. She knows for a fact that Audrey plans to spend the evening alone at home. Cassie is ill and can't spend the evening with her.

Brett's heart sped up at the mere sight of Audrey's name on

the page. It had been two weeks since she'd severed ties with him. Would she be angry if he showed up with a gift? The gift he'd found while searching through a used bookstore. A one-of-a-kind or definitely a rare find, even if she was the only person alive who might value the gift. He grinned and picked up the phone.

"Rosie Posie Flower Shop. How may I help you?" Her lovely throaty voice nearly took away his own voice. "Hello?"

"Sorry. This is Brett."

She hesitated. "I thought we had an understanding," she finally said with a firmness that almost made Brett change his mind.

Instead he bucked up. "I can take my business elsewhere, I guess."

"What?"

"I called to place an order."

"Oh. Okay, fine. What can I get for you?"

"A dozen red roses. Long stems."

"A dozen. . .do you know how much those cost?"

"No."

"Too much for a girl you haven't been seeing very long."

"I'm in love with this girl."

A whoosh of air traveled the line. "Oh."

Brett thought about setting her straight but decided not to ruin her surprise for later.

"Do you want them delivered or are you picking them up?" she asked, her voice cool, collected, and altogether miffed.

"Hmm. I'll pick them up. Can you have them ready by the time I get off work?"

"No problem. Your total is seventy-five dollars. Can you afford it?"

"Do you grill all your customers about their financial status before filling their orders?"

"Just letting you know roses aren't cheap."

He chuckled. "I'll manage."

"Fine. There is tax on those, too."

"I'll be sure to allow for the extra percentage. Do you include tips? Or should I plan for that?"

She sniffed. "We don't expect a tip on pick-ups."

"That's a relief." He couldn't help baiting her. It was so good to hear her voice, he would have stayed and bantered all day, except he had to run a few errands before picking up the flowers.

"Is that all, Brett? I'm busy. Cassie is sick today and couldn't come to work, so I'm trying to fill orders and run the register all by myself."

"That's it. I'll see you later."

"Fine." She disconnected the call without saying good-bye.

Brett fought the urge to call her back and set her mind at ease that there was no other woman in his life. But he didn't want to take the chance she'd cancel the roses and tell him to get lost.

He placed the receiver in its cradle and sat back in his chair, clasping his hands behind his head. He grinned, imagining her face when he showed up at her door, roses in hand. Only later, when he left the church and was on his way to the flower shop, did he consider the fact that he was making a romantic gesture.

He rejected the thought as he maneuvered through congested rush-hour traffic. He was only doing what anyone would do—not letting a friend spend her birthday all alone. Audrey had no family and no friends in town but Cassie, who wasn't feeling well.

He wouldn't stay long. Only long enough to share Chinese takeout and present her with her flowers and the gift he'd purchased.

Unease nipped at the heels of reason. Was God dangling the pastorate and Audrey before him as a test? A choice? If so, was Audrey to be sacrificed once more for the sake of the gospel?

Audrey stepped over the threshold of her home, closed her door, and turned the lock. Slipping off her shoes, she finally gave into the tears she'd fought off since Brett's phone call. She'd had other customers when he picked up the beautiful flowers, so she'd accepted his payment and watched while he left without so much as a backward glance. Her head kept telling her this was for the best, but the cavern in her heart felt hollow and told her otherwise.

She missed Brett. His companionship, laughter, details of his episodes with some of the kids in his group. She loved him, and she missed him. And besides, if a girl couldn't share her birthday with the man she loved just because they didn't have the same beliefs, then there was something very, very wrong with the world. And she had every right to cry a little. A lot actually. And eat rocky road ice cream for supper without worrying about the calories and fat.

She had just changed into a pair of sweats and an "I Love Goofy" T-shirt when the doorbell rang. In no mood for company, she gave a half-growl and decided to ignore whoever it was. She padded to the kitchen instead. Taking a carton of rocky road from the freezer, she grabbed a bowl, then put it back and grabbed a spoon instead. The doorbell continued to ring. She returned to the living room in time for the ringing to change to knocking.

This bozo was *not* going to leave.

She walked to the door. "Who is it? I'm not decent."

"It's Brett."

Brett?

"What about the *love of your life?* Did she stand you up?"

"I hope not. Can you open the door? The lady across the street is staring. I think she's about to sic her Doberman on me."

Audrey giggled, then forced herself to stop. "What do you want?" she growled to make up for the giggle.

"Open the door, and I'll tell you."

With a sigh, she turned the deadbolt and opened the door.

"These are for you." Brett presented her with the roses she'd prepared earlier.

She gasped. "These are for me?"

"I told you they were for the woman I love. Happy birthday."

If she had known they were for her, she wouldn't have picked the worst flowers she could get away with. But that would be her little secret for the rest of her life.

"Thank you," she whispered.

"Can I come in? My arms are about to fall off."

Her eyes widened at the load he was carrying. "What do you have there?"

"A birthday present and Chinese food. You haven't eaten, have you?"

She felt her cheeks grow hot. "Not yet."

He set the bags down on the coffee table and motioned toward the carton of ice cream. A smirk tipped his lips, but his eyes held her fast with a look of tenderness that took her breath away. "That was your supper?" he asked.

"Yeah. I didn't think anyone but Cassie knew it was my birthday." For some reason, all of her emotions rose to the surface, and tears filled her eyes.

"Come here." He stepped forward and opened his arms for her. She went into them willingly and rested her head against his broad chest.

"Oh, Brett. I'm so tired of being all alone." She lifted her head to gaze into his eyes. They were filled with emotion, love, desire, reservation. She'd take the love and desire and do her best to melt away the reservation. God took everything from her. He couldn't have Brett. She was going to do whatever it took to win him away.

Smiling, she pressed closer. She slipped her arms upward and clasped them behind his neck.

"Audrey," he said, his voice choked. "Please don't. . ."

"I love you," she whispered, rising onto her tiptoes. "Let me thank you for coming through for me on my birthday." Without awaiting his answer, she pressed his head down. Satisfaction surged within her as she felt his resistance melt. He crushed her to him and took her lips with his.

He's mine, God. You can have everyone else. But I want him.

Reveling in his embrace, Audrey matched him kiss for kiss, until finally, he pulled away, shaken and fighting for control. Knowing it was now or never, Audrey stroked the back of his neck with her manicured nails. "Let's go upstairs," she whispered.

He gripped her upper arms and pushed her away from him, his eyes wide with horror. "Audrey. I–I can't. You know that. What are you trying to do?"

"I want you," she said simply.

"Not like this. I. . .you know this is sin. I shouldn't have given in to my weakness and held you to begin with. I never meant the kiss to happen. Audrey. Forgive me. I can't choose you over the Lord."

All her fight was gone. She'd tried and she'd lost. As usual.

"All right, Brett. Go. Please don't come back again. I can't bear it."

He cradled her cheek in his palm and forced her to meet his gaze. His eyes filled with tears. "I'm sorry. I wish there was another way. But you've made your choice. And I have to make another."

Closing her eyes, she nodded. She remained where she stood until the door clicked behind him, then she sat weakly on the couch and realized that once again, she was alone.

Chapter 6

Audrey knocked for the third time on the one-hinged screen door. If she banged any harder, she'd tear the dilapidated thing completely off. A frustrated growl escaped her throat. The screen was hooked from the inside, so she knew someone was home and ignoring the knocks.

She was about to go to a window and bang on the glass, when she heard heavy footsteps coming from the other side of the thin door. "All right, all right. Keep your pants on!" a hoarse, female voice groused as the locks turned.

A blast of cold air hit the sweltering front porch as Audrey tried not to stare at the unkempt woman through the screen door. She swallowed hard to hide her revulsion.

"Well?" The woman stood in a pair of torn sweatpants and a too-tight, coffee-stained T-shirt.

"Mrs. Groves?"

"Yeah, who's asking?" She spoke around the red glow of a cigarette hanging from her mouth.

Audrey held onto the screen door and waited for the woman to move out of the way and invite her in. "Audrey MacMurray." She attempted a smile. "I'm Cassie's boss at the flower shop."

"So what's her boss doing coming to her house? Checking up on her?"

"Actually, no. I'm a little worried. She called yesterday to tell me she was sick, but she didn't call in today. I just wanted to make sure everything's okay."

"I ain't seen her all day. She might still be in bed."

Hadn't seen her all day? This woman made any of Audrey's former foster mothers look like June Cleaver. Good grief. Audrey had every intention of making a call to social services as soon as she left.

Fighting to keep her anger in check, Audrey stepped forward with determination. Her efforts paid off as the woman stepped back and let her in. "I just want to check on Cassie, then I'll be out of your hair."

The woman gave a shrug. "Suit yourself. Her room's down there." Waving toward a dingy hallway, she turned and shuffled back through the cluttered room. She plopped down on the stained, sagging couch. Audrey stared in disbelief as the woman clicked the remote and the TV volume rose significantly. No wonder she hadn't seen Cassie all day. She was too engrossed in daytime TV.

Clenching her teeth, Audrey headed down the hallway, past a foul-smelling bathroom, past a closed door, and finally to the room on the right at the end of the hall. She tapped on the doorframe. "Cass?"

A groan came from the bed. Audrey hurried inside. "Cassie, Honey. Are you all right?"

She sat on the edge of the bed. Cassie rolled over to face her, the poor girl's face bleached white, her sweat-covered hair plastered to her head.

"Honey, it's Audrey. I'm going to call an ambulance." She fished inside her purse for her cell phone.

Cassie weakly pressed her hand. "No, please. They'll take me away."

"Of course they will. You need to go to the hospital."

Shaking her head, Cassie turned and groaned, holding her stomach. "They'll send me to a group home."

"Well, Cass. You need to go to another home. This one isn't good."

Her pleading gaze met Audrey's. Audrey understood Cassie's reasoning, but she couldn't give in. "Listen, Honey. You're very ill. You have to go to a doctor."

"First, promise me something."

"What?"

"If I go to the hospital, will you come to church with me?"

"Oh, Cassie."

"Please?" Her face crunched in pain.

"Okay. Fine. You go to the hospital without causing anyone trouble, and I'll go to church with you."

"Promise?"

Breathing a heavy sigh, Audrey nodded. "I promise." She dialed 9-1-1. "Okay, Cassie. Hang on a little longer, Hon, the ambulance will be here in a few minutes."

"Call Pastor Brett."

"Brett?"

Cassie whimpered and doubled over again. "I need him to pray with me."

"Are you sure?" The thought of yesterday's humiliation seared Audrey's heart like a branding iron. But how could she refuse Cassie's request just because she dreaded facing Brett again after she'd ineffectively tried her hand at seduction?

The sounds of sirens in the distance spurred her to action. "Okay, Cass. I'll have him meet us at the hospital."

Brett's heart turned over at the sight of Audrey sitting alone in the waiting room. He'd been angry with her last night. Angry at himself for his own weakness. He'd obeyed the Word to "flee youthful lusts." But in his heart, he hadn't wanted to let her go. He had wanted to give in to the pleading in her beautiful, silver-gray eyes. They both would have regretted it later. Whether she wanted to admit it or not, God was tugging at Audrey's heart. Brett had seen the signs over the last few months. Some days she resisted and acted as worldly as someone who had never heard about Jesus. Other times, she was sensitive, caring, warm, and showed the fruits of the Spirit better than he did. She was in a tug-of-war with the Convictor, the Holy Spirit. The problem for Brett was that he was in the middle.

She looked up as he stepped into the room. A pretty blush colored her cheeks, and Brett knew she was reliving last night, too. He smiled in an effort to put her at ease. She stood and met him across the room.

"How's Cassie?"

"She's in surgery. Appendicitis." Her eyes flashed. "That foster mother of hers could have killed her with neglect, Brett. I called social services and talked to Cassie's caseworker. She said the only other option for her right now is to go into a group home. There are no available foster parents for girls Cassie's age."

"I've been talking to a couple in our church who have taken

a special interest in Cassie over the last year. I think they plan to call and see what they can do about getting Cass."

Audrey's face washed with relief. "Oh, Brett. Thank you. That's wonderful." She stepped forward as though she might hug him, then checked herself and diverted her attention to the mauve, indoor/outdoor carpet covering the waiting room floor.

She was a ball of nervous energy about to burst into a million flames if she didn't calm down.

"Let's sit, Audrey." Without waiting for an answer, he took her arm and led her back to her seat.

"Listen, Brett." She cleared her throat. "About last night. . ."

Feeling heat creep up his neck, Brett shook his head. "It's all right. Let's forget it."

"I–I agree, but first I wanted to tell you that I've never. . .I mean I haven't. . ."

Catching her meaning, Brett again felt a rush of tenderness for her. He took her hand and pressed it back against his chest. "I'm glad to hear that, Audrey."

She looked down at her feet.

Brett cleared his throat. "I want to talk about your relationship with God."

Her head turned sharply. "We had a deal."

"Not anymore. You broke off our friendship, so all bets are off."

"That's not. . .okay, fine. But it won't do you any good."

"I want to talk about God's love for you. I know last night was a power struggle. You wanted to get me away from Him."

"Don't be ridiculous!"

"Come on. Be honest."

"He takes everything away from me, Brett," she whispered.

"Mom and Dad, family, even you. If He loves me so much, why did He do that?"

A heavy sigh escaped Brett. Audrey didn't start with the easy questions.

"When a person makes a choice to serve Jesus, they take the bad with the good. It's like a marriage. For better or worse."

She gave a snort. "Exactly the reason I'm not making either of those choices."

"Playing it safe isn't all it's cracked up to be either. If you don't risk your heart, you can't find true happiness. Think of all you miss out on by not marrying and having children. You miss out on even more by choosing not to serve Jesus."

"Like what? Potluck dinners and church bake sales?"

"There's something to be said for fellowshipping with other believers. But I'm not just talking about the things you miss out on here on earth. Mainly, I'm speaking of eternity."

"Eternity's a long way off."

"Maybe, maybe not."

She released a long breath. "I understand everything you're saying, Brett. Really I do. But how can I give myself to God when I don't even know who I am? I'd be the worst kind of hypocrite to accept His salvation and then not really give Him my life. The most important thing to me is finding myself in my family."

"You rationalize it too much, Honey. The decision for Jesus Christ is made with the heart. Not the head. What follows is the process of learning to serve Him. He won't take you beyond your ability to serve. At least not until you're ready to stretch your faith."

She leaned toward him as though she would argue further,

but a beep from the pager in the chair beside her stopped her. "It's the doctor. They gave me this so he could page me when Cassie was finished."

She walked across the room and called the number. Brett could see the relief in her posture. Turning to him, she grinned and gave him a thumbs-up while she listened to what the doctor was saying. Brett sent up a silent prayer of thanks.

Lord, I should never have agreed to friendship with Audrey under her terms. But please let today's conversation take root and grow into her making a commitment to You.

Audrey stepped inside and slipped off her shoes. With a weary sigh, she shuffled into the kitchen and grabbed a pre-made protein shake from the fridge and picked up a banana from the counter. She checked for messages on her cordless phone, then plopped onto the couch. Stretching her legs onto the coffee table, she frowned when they landed on the all-but-forgotten present Brett had brought by the night before. She couldn't bear to look at it last night and had been running late this morning. She'd gone straight to Cassie's after she closed the shop. So putting her feet on the gift wasn't a subconscious anger-management technique. She leaned forward and grabbed it. Thought maybe she'd toss it aside, then gave in to her insatiable curiosity and tore into the lovely—and most certainly professional—wrapping.

A squeal of glee flew from her lips as soon as she saw the title of the book beneath the wrapping. *Kennerith Castle Past and Present.* She drank in the sight of the tan stone castle, her ancestral home, set against a backdrop of beautiful high green hills rolling endlessly behind the castle.

She forgot about her banana and protein drink and devoured page after page of the wonderful book. The familiar names of Galbraith, Spencer, and MacMurray shot wonder to her heart. Toward the end of the book, the name Allan Galbraith shot from the pages, causing her to draw a sharp breath. Her jaw went slack as the mystery of Allan Galbraith came to light, and she finally understood. . . .

Fresh Highland Heir

by Jill Stengl

Prologue

Crash! Thunk.

Icy air ruffled the bed curtains like groping hands.

"Papa!" Celeste shrieked. Visions of tattooed, spear-brandishing savages slithered through her imagination. Clutching her blankets to her chest, she pulled aside the bed curtain and felt about on a table until she found her eyeglasses.

Her father rapped at the door connecting their chambers before he entered, bedshoes flopping, nightcap hanging in his face. "Are ye safe, Lass?" He held up a candle and studied the shattered glass on the inn floor.

"No harm has come to me, but look." Celeste pointed, still hooking a wire behind her ear with the other hand. "Another message. Someone follows us."

A rock lay amid the shards beneath the window, wrapped in paper and tied with string. Her father picked it up, slid the note free, and read. The candle highlighted frown lines on his brow.

"Papa, what does it say?"

He threw the rock out the window and crumpled the note. "Come, let us trade chambers until morn. Have a care for your feet."

"Papa, is it another threat? Why didna ye let me marry Roderick and remain in Edinburgh? He would have protected me."

"We'll discuss this another time. Be off with ye now."

Chapter 1

Scotland, 1748

Through the thick lenses of her lorgnette, Lady Celeste Galbraith studied the passing landscape with avid interest. White clouds cast fleeting shadows across high green hills. Pine-scented air brushed her face. The heavy carriage swayed and bumped over ruts in the primitive road, its wheels passing alarmingly close to a steep drop-off. She looked behind, searching for pursuit, but the winding road lay empty in the wake of the earl's procession of coaches and riders.

"Sit back, please, my lady," moaned Mr. Ballantyne.

Celeste turned her lorgnette to survey her traveling companions in the opposite seat. Mr. Ballantyne covered his mouth with a lacy handkerchief. His wig sat askew upon his bald head, and heavy bags hung beneath his faded eyes. His daintily shod feet dangled above the floorboards.

"I am sorry ye're ill, Mr. Ballantyne, but I've an interest in our surroundings." She focused her gaze upon the earl. "This is a desolate land, Papa. These mountains roll on forever like the sea."

Mr. Ballantyne moaned.

A twinkle appeared in the earl's dark eyes. "I forget that ye dinna remember our last visit to Kennerith Castle, my dearie. Ye were but a lass."

"I remember Uncle Robert from his visits to us in Edinburgh." Celeste recalled a stern gentleman.

"Aye, 'tis not a year since last we saw him." Her father looked pensive.

"Struck down in his prime, he was. A judgment from God." Mr. Ballantyne shifted his handkerchief to speak.

Celeste saw a cloud cross her father's face, but he said nothing.

"D'ye recognize these hills, Papa?" Celeste found it difficult to imagine him as a lad. Over one shoulder she regarded his narrow face and scholarly brow.

"Aye, that I do. This fresh Highland air nurtures many a hearty lad and forms him into a doughty warrior." She saw his gaze slide to Mr. Ballantyne. "Else it breaks a man's health, and he retires to the fireside, books, and ledgers."

"Doughty warriors," muttered Mr. Ballantyne. "Heathen barbarians, more like. These hills teem with painted, kilted savages. Nary a step up from the beasts, most of them." His watery eyes focused upon Celeste. "Tales abound of their treachery. How they'll skin a man alive and drag his woman into the hills and—"

"Fireside tales and legends. Enough, Ballantyne." When Malcolm Galbraith spoke in that tone, few men dared oppose him. He coughed into his fist, frowned, and subsided into the corner. Ballantyne retreated behind his handkerchief.

Celeste returned her attention to the scenery framed by the

carriage window. Did danger truly lurk amid these rocky peaks and sylvan glens?

The warble of a horn caught her attention. Craning her neck to peer forward, she saw the attendant riders ahead disappear over a rise. The coach horses strained, their sweaty haunches driving upward. A whip cracked, and the postilions shouted encouragement to the six-horse team. A lurch, and the carriage leveled out.

The earl joined his daughter at the window. "Kennerith Castle." His voice held a breathless hush.

Beside the windswept surface of a loch, ancient stone turrets glowed against their emerald backdrop of hills. Then scudding clouds hid the sun, and the fortress plunged into gloom. With a great clacking of hooves upon paving stones, the entourage swept over a bridge and through a stone archway. Ahead, servants lined the castle's stone steps and curving drive, shoes polished, wigs brushed, buttons gleaming. The brisk spring breeze turned coattails into banners and skirts into sails.

Celeste blinked and lowered her lorgnette, wondering at her sense of dread. "So many servants."

"Ye're the daughter of a laird now, my lady," Mr. Ballantyne reminded her. "Remain seated until a footman places the step. Let me disembark first so that I may make proper introductions."

As soon as Mr. Ballantyne looked away, Celeste rolled her eyes. Irritating little man. He seemed to have made a miraculous recovery when the castle came into sight. Papa should put Mr. Ballantyne in his proper place. Papa was the new earl; Mr. Ballantyne was a mere secretary, related distantly to the family.

The carriage stopped. Celeste heard a confusion of barking dogs, clopping hooves, laughter and shouts of greeting, and the rumble of the baggage coach arriving behind. Servants in the earl's scarlet-and-silver livery passed the windows.

The coach door opened, and a footman placed the step. Mr. Ballantyne climbed down, his spindly legs tottering with fatigue, and began to speak to a waiting lackey.

"You next, Papa," Celeste requested, dreading the scrutiny of so many servants. How did they feel about a new earl taking over Kennerith Castle? Would they welcome the earl's daughter? The hand gripping her lorgnette handle trembled, making it difficult for her to see clearly. Vanity forbade Celeste to wear her eyeglasses in public, but the stylish lorgnette had its disadvantages.

Her father descended from the coach and surveyed his new domain. Mr. Ballantyne's reedy voice announced into a sudden hush: "Malcolm Galbraith, fifth earl of Carnassis, seventh viscount of Dalway, and tenth baron of Kennerith."

Cheering broke out, and Papa bowed. Still smiling, he turned back to the coach and reached a hand to Celeste. "Keep your head high and win them with your smile."

Celeste followed her billowing skirts out into the sunlight and wind, holding her straw hat to her head. Everything was a blur until she let go of her skirts and lifted her lorgnette.

A middle-aged servant stepped forward and bowed. "Welcome back to Kennerith Castle, your lairdship. I am Crippen, the house steward."

"Good afternoon, Crippen. May I present Miss. . .uh, Lady Celeste Galbraith." Papa had not yet adjusted to his own august role, let alone to his daughter's honorary title.

With Mr. Ballantyne leading the way, the earl and Celeste passed along the line of servants, nodding with polite reserve after each introduction. Celeste felt as if she were an actress playing a part. She did not catch even one name, and not one servant looked her in the eye. As they passed the lead coach horses, amid the animals' heavy breathing, Celeste heard a whisper. Curious, she turned with a swirl of skirts and lifted her lorgnette.

Mr. Ballantyne gripped the sleeve of the manservant holding the bridle of one lead coach horse. Scrawny neck extended, standing on tiptoe, the earl's secretary attempted to whisper into the servant's ear, "His lairdship has need of ye."

Celeste took one backward step and twisted her foot on a cobblestone. Stumbling sideways, she gave a little squeal. Someone caught her by the elbows, and she scrambled to regain her footing. The world was a blur of scarlet-and-silver uniforms except for the wrinkled face inches from hers. "Air ye hurt, me lady?"

The old servant released her elbows and backed away until he, too, became a smudge. Celeste tried to laugh. "This terrible stony road! Just call me 'Your Grace.' " She quelled rising panic. "I seem to have dropped my lorgnette."

"My lady." One scarlet figure detached itself from the general haze. Celeste took a step forward and discerned an outstretched arm. "My lady, your spectacles."

She reached to accept them, but her hand closed upon empty space. A gloved hand gripped her arm, and she felt the handle of her lorgnette press against her palm. Her face felt hot. Now everyone knew her infirmity. "Th–thank you." She lifted the lorgnette. Silvery gray eyes met her gaze and widened. She caught a flash of amusement before he bowed.

"A pleasure it is to serve ye, my lady." It was the man to

whom Ballantyne had been whispering.

"Be thankful the lenses didna break," her father remarked, then shifted his address to the helpful servant. "Ye've a familiar aspect. Have ye been at the castle long?"

The man bowed again. "I served the late earl many years, your lairdship. Perhaps ye've seen me attend him during visits in Edinburgh."

"Ah." The earl moved on. Celeste followed, her chin held high, bestowing a regal nod upon each person in the remaining lineup of servants. Her forearm still felt the firm grip of a leather glove. Was he watching? Her posture was perfect, her smile bright as she turned on the top step for one last overview of the serving staff.

Her eyes sought the coach horses. Her hopes drooped. The carriage was just disappearing into the stable yard below.

"Come in, Lad. Come in." Mr. Ballantyne and the earl lounged beside the hearth, smoking clay pipes.

Celeste did not look up from her needlework when the manservant stepped inside and stood at attention, but her heart picked up its pace.

"I've been telling his lairdship about ye," Mr. Ballantyne said. Celeste distrusted the old man's hearty manner. She pulled through a stitch of gold thread and arranged the strands with her thumbnail until they lay flat.

"Strong enough, aye, but he looks o'er-young. Are ye sure he's the man we want?" Celeste recognized her father's evaluation voice, usually reserved for oral examination of university students. For what task did he require this servant's strength?

"Certain-sure. Take a seat here, Allan." Ballantyne waved a

withered hand. "Despite the lad's Highland lineage, the late earl favored him. Sent him to school in Aberdeen, where Allan distinguished himself. After the lad's graduation, the earl hired him as bodyguard."

"Where was this Allan the night my brother Robert died?"

"No bodyguard could have saved his lairdship. The coroner said 'twas a stroke. If it means aught to ye, I saw this lad weep for your brother that night. I wept meself, if the truth be known."

Celeste glanced up to see Mr. Ballantyne wipe his nose with a handkerchief. He would be wearing his sanctimonious expression, she was certain.

The servant named Allan perched on the edge of a chair. Celeste picked up her lorgnette and sneaked a look. He was as comely as she remembered. Those black brows and fine gray eyes! He must have dark hair beneath his wig, she decided. His hand picked at the buttons at the knee of his breeches.

He glanced right and caught her staring. He smiled. The lorgnette fell to her lap, and she picked up her needlework, holding the fabric mere inches from her nose.

"Are ye a supporter of the Jacobite cause?" the earl inquired gruffly.

"Nay—" His voice cracked. He coughed. "Nay, your lairdship. Some of my relations sympathized with the Stuarts, but I couldna support the cause. My loyalty and service are yours."

"Which clan?" the earl asked.

"I have taken the name Croft."

"I asked which clan."

A pause before Allan said, "MacMurray."

At her father's exclamation, Celeste hastily retrieved her

lorgnette. She could not interpret the earl's expression, a combination of disgust and amusement.

"Och, Robert!" The earl shook his head, then pinned Allan with a glare. "Lad, ye must ken that we Galbraiths are sworn enemies to your clan these two hundred years and more. Blackmailers, thieves, pillagers, and worse are the MacMurrays."

"I've heard equally dire account of the Galbraiths. I disapprove the violent acts of both sides. Before her death just ere my ninth birthday, my mother advised me to come to the earl of Carnassis."

"And your clan didna object?"

"My mother's wish overrode any objection. I believe some connection existed in the family, though I am unaware of its nature. Your brother, his lairdship, once told me I had no need to ken."

The earl wiped a hand across his mouth and studied his slipper-clad feet. His gaze lifted to the portrait of his late brother that hung above one door. Celeste's blood ran cold as she read her father's thoughts, and she gazed upon the servant with empathy.

Mr. Ballantyne cleared his throat. "One reason I called ye here, Allan, was to deliver this. I found it among the late earl's effects." He produced a note with a broken seal and handed it to Allan MacMurray.

Celeste watched Allan turn the note over and over, then unfold and scan the message. His gaze lifted to the large Bible upon a reading stand in one corner of the room, and his face went red.

"Can ye tell us its meaning?" Ballantyne asked.

"Nay. It seems. . .out of character." Allan read the message aloud. " 'My son, all ye need to know is found in the Holy Scriptures. C. IV' " After clearing his raspy voice, he interpreted the signature. "Carnassis the fourth."

"So my brother turned to religion before the end," the earl said.

"Yet ne'er did he confess his sins," Ballantyne added with a lifted brow. "Now what do ye think, your lairdship?" He seemed to stress the term of address.

"I think ye've a brilliant mind," the earl replied.

Celeste laid aside her sewing and arose. The three men started to rise, but she shook her head. "Prithee, pay me no mind." They settled back into their chairs.

She began to stroll about the room, running her fingers across the spines of priceless volumes. Because of her voluminous skirts, she had to turn sideways to fit between the bookcase and an armchair.

"Are ye married?" the earl asked Allan abruptly.

"Nay."

"Pledged?"

"I have ties to no woman or man."

"Ballantyne tells me ye're trustworthy with women. Is this true?"

"In God's strength, I strive to treat all people as my kin in Christ Jesus."

The earl sat back. "Ah, a sincere man of religion. I am satisfied. This is a delicate situation, Allan MacMurray."

"Croft, if ye please, your lairdship."

"Croft it will be. Ye see, Lad, I neither expected nor desired to become a peer. I am a man of books, not of politics nor business, and the responsibilities that come with a title are odious to me. My brother, James, was Robert's heir, and he had two sons. All three perished last year of influenza."

Celeste pulled out a book and fluttered its musty pages. A silence and conferring whispers brought her attention back to the men. Unfortunately, her lorgnette lay on the table, so she was unable to read their expressions. At times she wondered if appearing more beautiful was worth being unable to see.

"Celeste, 'twould be best if ye retired," the earl said, sounding ill at ease.

She closed the book. "If this concerns me, Papa, I wish to hear your arrangements." Too many secrets had been kept from her already.

"Very well." He turned back to the servant. "Allan, I wish to hire ye as personal bodyguard to my daughter."

"I?" Allan's voice cracked again. "What could anyone hope to gain by harming the lady?"

"I dinna ken. But twice I have received threatening letters. One arrived in Edinburgh ere our departure, the other last night at an inn along the way. Both poorly written, as ye'll note." He handed something to the servant—presumably the letters.

"Papa, why do I need a bodyguard?" Celeste asked. "I thought the threats were against you."

"The first threat demanded that I remain in Edinburgh and abdicate the Galbraith family claim to title and lands. Last night's note threatened your safety if I dinna return immediately to Edinburgh. The rogue knows the vulnerability of a father's heart."

The sincerity in her father's voice startled Celeste. Did he truly care so much? A month ago she would have taken his love for granted, but now. . .

The earl addressed Allan. "I want my daughter attended at all times, night and day."

Celeste turned back to the bookshelf lest the servant behold her crimson cheeks. Whatever was Papa thinking?

"At *all* times? Would not a woman be a more appropriate custodian?"

"I'm hiring ye to guard my daughter, not to question my judgment. I'm sure ye'll come to a balance 'twixt protection and propriety. Her safety, not her convenience, will be your primary concern. I'll so task ye only until the day Lady Celeste is wedded."

Wedded? Celeste's heart took wing. Papa must be considering Cousin Roderick's matrimonial offer after all! Soon she would be married and living back in Edinburgh, far away from this castle. Closing her eyes, she pressed one hand to her throbbing bosom. *Roderick knows me better than anyone, and he loves me.*

"That day may yet be years away, your lairdship," Allan protested.

"Ooh!" Celeste whirled about, and her skirts knocked a candlestick to the floor. Wax spattered in an arc across the rug. The flame extinguished.

"As ye see, I have other reasons for requiring her close supervision," the earl replied calmly.

"Papa!" Mortified, she hurried to her worktable. Her groping hands knocked her embroidery to the floor. Her lorgnette—where was it?

Allan knelt at her feet. "My lady." Once again he caught her arm and placed the lorgnette handle against her palm.

She lifted it to give him a baleful stare, but he was busy

picking bits of embroidery thread from the Oriental rug. Folding her needlework, he replaced it on the table. Sweat beaded his brow and upper lip. His irritatingly angelic grin had vanished.

As Allan returned to his seat, Celeste confronted her father, ready for a fight. The earl wore a bemused smile. To her surprise, he lowered one lid in an affectionate wink.

"Ballantyne tells me scattered bands of Highlanders hide out in my hills," the earl said, "and these heathen folk dare to raid local villages and farms despite the military stationed nearby."

"They raid because they would otherwise starve." Allan shifted in his seat. "Are ye certain, your lairdship, that a guard need be put upon her ladyship while she is *inside* the castle? And what of your own safety?"

"I am armed. With numerous servants in my employ, many of them no doubt Highlanders, the danger to my daughter could arise from within these walls. I can take no chances. While Celeste is well educated for a woman, she lacks practical understanding. Her fortune has made her the desire of more than one impecunious scoundrel, and her artlessness leads her to believe them sincere. She canna see beyond the end of her nose either figuratively or in fact."

"Papa! I am no fool," Celeste protested in a choked voice. "And I need no armed eunuch at my gate as if my room housed a harem." She approached Allan's chair and glared down at him. "Be warned that should ye choose to become my guardian, I shall make your life miserable!"

Chapter 2

Heels clicked on flagstone floors. "Sirra?"

A dark figure appeared above the back of a bench. "It is arranged?"

"Aye, and his lairdship suspects naught. 'Twill keep the rascal under our eyes and the peerage safe. Ye're keeping your part?" The smaller figure glanced around fearfully. Moonlight shining through stained glass turned his wig orange and blue.

"Trust me. Meet here again in a fortnight."

"Ye'll be comfortable in this chamber, m'lady. 'Twas furnished by your grandmother, Lady Elizabeth Galbraith. Your aunt Olivia died in that bed at the tender age of eighteen. Her portrait hangs beside the door." The house steward, Crippen, spoke in a monotone brogue.

"Indeed." Celeste knew the steward's inspection was mere protocol. A complaint from her would produce no change—the earl had insisted she occupy the chambers in the east tower, which were accessible only by use of a spiral staircase. Celeste's legs already ached from ascending and descending those narrow stone steps.

"Beryl Mason will be your personal maid," Crippen continued.

Celeste nodded at the white-capped woman beside him. "Aye, we met earlier today."

The steward said, "If ye have any need, m'lady, dinna hesitate to ring. Our desire is to serve ye well."

"Many thanks, Mr. Crippen," Celeste said in her best lofty manner. "This bedchamber is chilled. I require a larger fire."

" 'Twill be attended, m'lady." Crippen bowed and retired. The wooden door closed behind him with a hollow boom, and a small chunk of plaster fell from the wall.

Shivering, Celeste glanced around her bedchamber. It looked, if possible, worse by candlelight than by daylight. Faded tapestries lined the outer walls. A high, four-poster bed hung with brocaded curtains nearly touched the mildewed ceiling. One of the lathe-and-plaster interior walls seemed to bulge inward, and the floor had a definite slant. Nevertheless, aside from its architectural flaws, it was a chamber befitting a princess. . .a consumptive princess doomed to pine her life away in seclusion, or maybe a doddering maiden princess whose one lover died sixty years earlier on the eve of their wedding.

Pushing her glasses higher on her nose, Celeste met her maid's gaze and forced herself to smile. "I am certain we shall suit each other, Beryl."

The maid appeared to be in her early twenties, a few years older than Celeste. Her square face was handsome with its full lips and black-lashed blue eyes. A large knot of red hair and a generous figure completed her somewhat earthy attractions.

Someone rapped at the chamber door.

"Enter."

The latch lifted, and the heavy door creaked open. "My lady? I bring fuel for your fire." Celeste's unwanted bodyguard carried a sack over his shoulder. His beatific smile was back.

"I am grateful." Too late Celeste remembered to remove her eyeglasses. With an inward grimace, she realized that he would often see her wearing the ugly device during his stint as her guardian. She might as well swallow her pride and pretend unconcern. The admiration of a servant was inconsequential, after all.

Celeste watched him kneel beside her hearth and poke at the smoldering peat. He added two additional bricks of fuel and blew until they began to burn.

Beryl joined Allan at the fire and slowly ran a finger across his shoulders until her body pressed against his. "Meet me in the rose garden tonight?" she murmured in a seductive tone. Feeling her face burn, Celeste turned to arrange her hairbrushes on the dressing table.

"I have duties, as have you." Allan's voice sounded friendly yet detached. "Why not ask Dougal?"

"Wherefore would I be wanting to meet me own brother?" Beryl snapped.

He ignored her. "My lady?"

Celeste met his direct gaze and felt as if she should curtsy. "Aye?" *He is a servant,* she reminded herself, lifting her chin.

"By the earl's command, I shall sleep in your drawing room to keep watch o'er your chamber door. Should ye have need of protection, my sword and my life are yours." He bowed and made a hasty exit.

"As if I need a bodyguard," Celeste said. "Where do ye sleep, Beryl?"

"In the servants' quarters o'er the kitchen."

Celeste studied the maid's flaming hair, met her fiery gaze, and decided not to inquire further. "Assist me with my gown, if ye please."

Beryl lifted the gown over Celeste's head, then unlaced the corset and helped her mistress step out of the hooped bustle and underskirts. Celeste tried not to stare at Beryl's arms, which were hairier and more muscular than many a man's.

While Celeste sat in a padded chair, Beryl unpinned her mistress's hair and brushed until it crackled. Celeste closed her eyes and groaned with pleasure. "Ye've a gentle touch, Beryl. After the tales Mr. Ballantyne told, I expected a wilderness inhabited by half-naked, tattooed savages clad in kilts. I was almost disappointed to find ye civilized."

Beryl remained silent, so Celeste chattered on. "I ne'er had a personal maid until last autumn when Papa hired Marie. She refused to leave Edinburgh, professing fear of the Highlanders, which is purely nonsense. Certain I am that ye'll be an excellent replacement maid, Beryl."

Celeste tipped her head back to smile at the Highland woman.

"Why d'ye wear that?" Beryl pointed the brush at Celeste's glasses.

"I canna see without them," Celeste admitted.

"Not at all?"

"Only a blur. Have ye lived at the castle long?" she asked. Establishing rapport with this maid would require concentrated effort.

"Nigh a year. Allan got me the work. We are soon to wed."

"Ah," Celeste said, concealing her skepticism. "I, too, intend to wed soon. Roderick is my father's heir. I first met him only last month, yet I feel as though I have loved him always."

"In his mate, Allan requires strength and courage to match his own. He despises weakness and timidity—such women he uses and tosses aside." Beryl's tone implied that Celeste was the useless type.

"Ye wish to marry a man who uses and discards women?" Celeste turned in her chair. "Allan claimed high principles. I must inform my father of his deceit. Perhaps he'll be relieved of this ridiculous duty. I should prefer to have ye near, if attended I must be."

Beryl's gaze traveled over her mistress in a way that made Celeste uncomfortable. On further consideration, she would prefer not to have this fierce maiden too near. Wishing she had donned her bed gown, she drew her chemise up over her shoulders and tightened its drawstring. "Roderick will come soon and marry me. He promised to love me forever."

Taking Celeste's hair in her hands, Beryl divided it into three sections and began to braid. "He is rich?"

"Nay, but he is fine and good." Smiling, Celeste recalled her cousin's burning dark eyes. "In his presence, I feel womanly. But Papa insists he courts me only for. . ." Her voice and her smile faded.

Roderick was not her only beau. Lord Werecock had also promised eternal fidelity; and, but a fortnight past, the viscount of Downeybeck had knelt at her feet in the university gardens and composed a sonnet "To the Ringlet Upon Her Shoulder."

Papa insisted these admirers cared solely for her fortune. It was true that no suitors had approached Celeste until news spread of the comfortable inheritance in English funds left to her upon her eighteenth birthday by her mother's mother. Celeste preferred to believe that her youth and reclusive lifestyle accounted for the gentlemen's previous lack of attentiveness. Surely such tender admiration could not be feigned. They must truly love her. . .mustn't they?

Beryl tied off the brown braid with a ribbon and dropped it over her mistress's shoulder. "I'd advise ye to make haste and marry ere ye join the ranks of maidens who've perished in this tower. Your aunt wasna the first."

Startled, Celeste looked up. An enigmatic smirk curled Beryl's lips. "I changed the water in your basin, and I'll bank the fire. D'ye need aught besides?"

"I–I think not."

When Beryl had retired, Celeste paced the chamber's warped floorboards. Pausing before Lady Olivia's portrait, she wrinkled her nose. "Ye're no true relation to me, my lady. Which fact disturbs me not at all, for either the artist had no talent or ye were a bloodless weakling. I'll be fearing not your haunt or any other."

She rubbed her upper arms. "Bodyguard, indeed. Personal maid, indeed." Disappointment at her failed efforts to befriend Beryl pushed out her lower lip. "I need no friends; I need no one. When Roderick comes for me, I'll run away with him if Papa refuses his consent."

Not even to herself could she speak aloud the doubts that gnawed like mice at the fringes of her self-respect. Only recently had Roderick brought to her attention certain disturbing truths. Celeste had often heard her father relate the tale of her parents' whirlwind romance—they had married within three weeks of meeting. He also frequently told of his joy at

Celeste's birth. The one fact he omitted was the two-month interval between these important dates.

She opened one of the casement windows and leaned upon the sill. The castle rooftops below lay in shadow. Only a squirrel could escape by that route. Flashes of lightning glared upon hilltops far beyond the fortress walls and revealed lowering black clouds. The drapes billowed behind her, and several candles snuffed out.

Celeste's chin lifted. She spread her arms wide and felt her chemise whip about her legs. Heart pounding in strange ecstasy and defiance, she laughed aloud. "I am strong!"

A knock at the door whipped her around. "Who is there?" She grabbed her bed gown off a hook and slipped it on, buttoning with shaking fingers.

"Are ye alone, my lady?"

The bodyguard. Celeste pressed a hand to her racing heart and hurried to lean against the door. There was neither lock nor bar.

"To whom were ye speaking just now?" he persisted.

"Am I not allowed a soliloquy?"

A pause. "Ye needna fear me, my lady. Sleep well."

She hardened her heart against his beguiling voice. "Beryl says ye plan to wed her."

Silence.

"Allan MacMurray? D'ye hear me?"

His reply sounded distant. "Allan Croft is my name. If ye must ken, I hear your every word. The walls and door are none too sturdy."

"So ye o'erheard my conversation with Beryl? How impolite!"

"I coughed and made noise, hoping ye'd take the hint. In

future, please say naught ye'd desire no man to hear."

Celeste recalled what he had already overheard, and her face flamed. "Are ye pledged to marry Beryl? Ye told my father otherwise."

"Beryl may say what she will, but I won't wed her."

Celeste blinked, uncertain which report to believe. "God give ye rest this night." She hesitated over his name. Nobility addressed most house servants by their first names, yet Celeste felt shy about treating this man with such informality. "Regretful I am that ye're saddled with this nonsensical post, but. . .but I dinna promise to be an easy charge."

"I ne'er expected ye would be."

Celeste nearly jerked open the door to demand an explanation for that remark but decided to wait until morning. After extinguishing her remaining candles, she climbed into bed. Firelight from the adjoining chamber shone through cracks in the door and beneath it. Celeste laid her eyeglasses on a bedside table, knelt on the counterpane, and tugged at her bed curtains. They refused to move. Rather than relight a candle and discover the reason, she gave up and left the curtains open.

Beryl had forgotten to warm the bed linens. Teeth chattering, Celeste waited for her body to heat them.

Could he hear every little sound from her chamber? How embarrassing!

Sometime during the night, she awakened with a start. Only after a moment of terror did she remember her whereabouts. The castle lay in deadly silence except for a strange noise. Celeste lay rigid beneath her coverlet. Rats? Bats? Ghosts? Fear made her hands clammy and formed a lump in her throat. "Mr. Croft?" she squeaked.

No reply. Had some assassin dispatched her bodyguard? Did a threat to her life lurk in one of the room's dark corners? Or had everyone else vanished in the night, leaving her alone in the ancient fortress? "Allan MacMurray!" She panicked, sitting bolt upright. "Where are ye?"

The sound stopped. Had her cries frightened it away? She heard rapid steps, and the door creaked open. "Did ye call, my lady?"

"I heard a noise. It has stopped now," she admitted, holding her coverlet beneath her chin.

"D'ye wish me to search your chamber?" he asked in a groggy-sounding voice.

"Please." She found her glasses and hooked them over her ears.

Allan knelt at her hearth to light a candle at the banked embers. He cupped one hand around the flame as he rose. His cropped hair, no longer hidden by a wig, appeared dark. Celeste watched him check behind her curtains and screens, then lean out each of the two windows. His bare feet padded silently as he returned to the doorway and faced her. He still wore his knee breeches and a full-sleeved white shirt, partly untucked and unbuttoned.

His white teeth flashed as he spoke. "Naught to fear. Perhaps ye heard the call of a wild creature in the hills." Dared the rogue laugh at her?

Celeste swallowed hard. "I thank ye," she managed to say.

When he was gone, she lay back. How strange to have a man in her bedchamber, and at her father's behest! "He wouldna dare touch me," she whispered to calm her turbulent emotions. "I needna fear him. He is my servant. Mine to order as I will." The idea had its attractions. She imagined him wild with desire for her. How she would laugh and spurn him, her devoted slave! He would learn that woman was not intended solely for man's amusement. He would learn not to speak to her in that contemptuous tone, as if she were a silly child having night terrors.

And again she heard the sound—a rasping, rhythmic purr. She opened her mouth to call, but then a suspicion entered her mind. Slipping into her bed gown, she braved the darkness and crept to the door. Sure enough, the noise came from her drawing room. She pulled open the door.

Allan stretched full length on his back beside a freshly stoked peat fire. One arm pillowed his head. His mouth was ajar, and he snored.

The snoring ceased. Celeste froze.

" 'Tis hazardous to creep up on an armed man, my lady." She saw silvery eyes glitter between his lashes.

"Ye were snoring."

"Ye're mistaken. I wasna asleep. Go back to bed."

Stunned by such arrogance, she returned to her room. While lying in bed, she heard movement in the drawing room. Inconvenient though his presence was, she felt secure. A giggle welled up and spilled over. *Not asleep, he says. Ha!*

Chapter 3

"You have been paid for the job; get on with it." The cultured voice held a dangerous edge.

"I need more. 'Tis a risky piece of work. I willna take the chance of holding the blame." Green-and-gold moonlight shining through stained glass patterned the speaker's cloak. Silver eyes glittered beneath his hood.

"I've pledged you my protection."

"And what value has the pledge of a traitor, I'm asking meself?" Disgust colored the man's thick brogue.

Instead of working her embroidery, Celeste watched Allan prowl the library. His wig was askew. He pulled out a book, thumbed through it, and replaced it. Rubbing a hand over his scalp, he jerked off the maltreated tie wig, dropped it on a chair, and stalked the length of the room once more. Celeste admired the glint of his auburn curls. Never would she have guessed that his hair would be a hue entirely at odds with his thick black brows.

Sunlight barred the carpets, and birdsong wafted through the open windows on a balmy summer breeze. On such days, even Kennerith Castle seemed to echo with songs of joy.

"Will ye read to me while I do my needlework?" Celeste requested, lowering her lorgnette. " 'Twould pass the time and employ your idle hands."

He spoke with a hint of asperity. "My lady could endeavor just once to exercise something other than her tongue and her hands. Ye've been at Kennerith these four weeks, and not once have ye ventured farther afield than the rose garden."

Celeste lifted her lorgnette and attempted to intimidate him with a cold stare. "If my indolence vexes ye, 'twould trouble me not at all if ye were to seek gainful employment elsewhere."

Allan met her gaze. His lips twitched.

"What amuses ye now?" she asked.

"Naught, my lady."

Her irritation increased. "I insist upon knowing the source of your amusement."

He gave a little bow. "If ye insist, your servant must obey. Each time ye gaze at me through those lenses, your eyes startle me—like an owl's they seem, huge and solemn. Why dinna ye wear the wire eyeglasses to do your fancywork? They stay put upon your face so ye needna forever be picking them up and putting them down."

"I see well enough to do needlework without spectacles." Celeste pouted. An owl? "Eyeglasses make me appear scholarly while the lorgnette is stylish."

Allan grunted. "I shall read." He approached the stand holding a large Bible.

Celeste picked up her embroidery and discarded the lorgnette. She heard Allan turn pages, then begin to read: " 'In the beginning was the Word, and the Word was with God, and the Word was God. The same was in the beginning with God. All things were made by him: and without him was not any thing made that was made. In him was life; and the life was the light of men.' "

"What are ye reading?" Celeste interrupted when he paused for breath. "This is from the Holy Bible?"

"The Gospel according to John. Chapter one. Ye've ne'er read it?"

Although his voice held no derision, she felt defensive. "I must've heard it in kirk, but I dinna recall. Is it. . .important?"

His tone softened. "Listen and see."

"This Word it speaks of was a person?" she inquired.

"Aye. So ye did listen. God communicates truth about Himself through the Word—the written word, the spoken word, and the living Word, who is Jesus Christ, God in the flesh. 'So then faith cometh by hearing, and hearing by the word of God'—that is a verse from the book of Romans. Let me begin again and see what ye think."

He read several chapters before his voice began to crack. "My throat is dry."

Celeste laid aside her neglected needlework, rose, and tugged the bell-pull. " 'Twas thoughtless in me, but I became engrossed in the story. . .and ye say this is true? It happened just as ye read?"

A servant appeared in the open doorway.

"Will ye bring us refreshment?" Celeste requested. "Are ye. . .Dougal?" From this distance she could not be certain.

"Aye, m'lady." He bowed and disappeared from view.

Allan answered. "Every word I read is truth. I should be

pleased to read each day with ye, my lady."

Celeste wished she had worn her eyeglasses so she might better assess the facial expression accompanying his tentative offer. "If it pleases ye, I'll not object," she said. "As I expected, your assignment as my bodyguard has proven tedious. I quickly repented of my promise to make your life miserable, yet every day I unwittingly make good the threat. We've few interests in common, I fear." She smiled wistfully. "I could wish ye admired me a wee bit."

"My lady, 'tis my honor to attend ye."

The servant returned with a tray, which he set upon the table.

Celeste's skirts engulfed her tiny chair as she sat down. "Thank you, Dougal." She poured soft cider from a flagon.

Motion caught her eye. Allan appeared to be shaking his head. She thought she saw the footman direct a rude gesture at her bodyguard, then exit in haste. "Is it my imagination, or does that man hold ye in disfavor? Papa recently spoke to Mr. Ballantyne about discharging those of the servants whose manner seems. . .insolent. I believe Dougal was mentioned."

Allan approached to take his mug. "Thank ye, my lady. Dougal and I are presently at odds, but I trust the rift will mend." Sipping the juice, he moved toward one of the rectangles of sunlight upon the faded rug.

The sun's reflection off his brass buttons nearly blinded Celeste. "Dougal. Mason? Is he brother to Beryl?"

"Aye." Allan appeared to be gazing outside.

Nodding as she mentally connected facts, Celeste sipped her drink. Dougal resembled his sister. For that matter, the footman was a rougher, wilder version of Allan. The two shared identical coloring and height, yet there the resemblance ended. Cynical lines bracketed Dougal's craggy features, and bitterness clouded his silver-gray eyes; Allan emanated poise and control.

Tired of viewing only Allan's vague outline, she once again lifted her lorgnette to study his profile. Her gaze shifted to her uncle Robert's portrait hanging over the doorway. Although Allan's ruddy, freckled complexion in no way resembled the swarthy Galbraith men, his classic features and graceful carriage suggested a strong influx of noble blood.

Every servant, every townsman—everyone who sees him must know his origin and pity him. He is Galbraith to the core. And I am not.

Rising, she flounced toward the window and stared out at high green hills beyond the castle walls. The manor grounds extended for miles southward, although only the first half-mile consisted of gardens and lawn. "This land—wild and barren, yet its intensity could break your heart," she mused aloud. "Ne'er before have I seen a sky so blue or grass so green. Though I fear these Highlands, I could learn to love them."

" 'Tis a bonny summer day. Nary a cloud in the sky." She felt him behind her. Not close enough to touch, yet near enough to send tingles down her spine.

"If ye could do aught ye chose this day, what would it be?" she asked in a rush of generosity.

"I would ride among those hills and let the sun beat upon my head, the wind beat upon my face, and my heart beat upon my ribs," he said without hesitation.

Amazed by this poetic outburst, Celeste turned. He still stared out the window. For a moment the longing in his eyes filled her with jealousy, but she shook off the unworthy emotion.

"I shall ask my father to release ye from duty this afternoon," she said. " 'Tis cruel to keep a wild creature penned like an ox."

"I'd prefer to have ye along," he said.

Celeste's heart swelled. She lifted her hand to her throat and turned away.

"My lady? If I spoke out of turn, accept my apology."

She waved a hand. "Nay. 'Tis only. . ." She could not tell him. He would think it ridiculous of her to become choked up because he desired her companionship. "I dinna ride well."

"Then we shall ride slowly." The anticipation in his voice quickened her blood.

Celeste spun around. "Order the horses while I change into riding attire. I'll meet ye at the mounting block." Whatever the cost to her pride and comfort, Celeste determined that Allan MacMurray deserved one afternoon of happiness.

Allan's smile gleamed. "Aye." Halfway to the door, he stopped in his tracks and turned back. "Nay, I'll send word to the stable."

Celeste sighed. He took this bodyguard role far too seriously.

"And, my lady, kindly bring your eyeglasses."

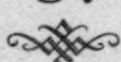

A breeze caught the ends of the wrap holding her bonnet in place and sent them streaming over her staid mount's hindquarters. Celeste dropped her reins to tighten the silken knot under her chin.

With a startled exclamation, Allan leaned over and caught the falling reins. "My lady, no matter how gentle the steed, ye must keep hold."

She retrieved the leather straps and shifted her riding whip to her other hand.

"Ye also must hold the crop in your right hand. 'Twill do ye no good in your left."

Celeste gave a disdainful huff as her dignity ebbed. "I canna see that it matters. My steed follows yours no matter what I tell it. I thought ye wished to enjoy the day." She waved a hand to indicate the surrounding vivid green turf, Scots pines, tufts of broom, and rocky outcroppings topped by blue sky.

"Will ye not heed your horse so I may give notice to the day?"

Celeste's horse dropped its head to graze, jerking the reins from her gloved fingers. "See what the beast has done now!" Surely Allan must recognize the animal's malevolent intent.

He dismounted and hauled her horse's head up. Patting the cob's speckled gray neck, he gave Celeste a rueful look. "We might enjoy ourselves more on foot."

She wilted. "Ye're sorry ye brought me."

"I am not. Come. We shall tie up the horses and continue on foot. Ye've a treat in store."

Celeste placed her hands upon his shoulders and let him lift her down. But when she stood before him, looking up into his face, he immediately turned to the horses. "I'll give them loose rein to allow grazing. That will please your Robin and my D'Arcey."

"Robin certainly seems content to eat," Celeste observed.

"His one joy in life." After attending the horses, Allan dropped his tricornered hat and his wig on a rock.

Celeste looked up at Allan as he approached. Smiling, he met her gaze. Her heart leaped. His smile faltered, and he veered off toward the hill. " 'Tis a stiff hike, but the view is worth seeing."

He strode on, leaving her to follow. Tripping over rocks and ridges, she held up her skirts and silently grumbled. The trees became more numerous, shading the pathway. "I hear running water." Celeste gasped for breath as she emerged from the trees.

Allan stood tall, chin lifted, curly hair blowing in the wind, fists planted on his hips. "That ye do." His smile mocked her gently.

Then she saw it. White water cascaded through a gap in the hills, swirled over rocks, deepened, and flowed past just inches from Allan's boot toes. "Oh!" she gasped, expressing both awe at its beauty and chagrin at her tardy perception. Wildflowers grew in profusion around her feet. Rising mist dampened her face and fogged her eyeglasses.

Allan spoke above the water's roar. " 'The earth is the Lord's, and the fulness thereof; the world, and they that dwell therein. For he hath founded it upon the seas, and established it upon the floods. Who shall ascend into the hill of the Lord? or who shall stand in his holy place? He that hath clean hands, and a pure heart; who hath not lifted up his soul unto vanity, nor sworn deceitfully. He shall receive the blessing from the Lord, and righteousness from the God of his salvation.' "

Celeste listened with a sense of awe. To Allan, God seemed real and present. She looked upon the rushing river and felt God's presence for herself. She closed her eyes, then opened them to marvel anew at the beauty of creation. " 'Who shall stand in his holy place?' " she echoed. Not Lady Celeste Galbraith, if clean hands and a pure heart were requirements.

Bowing her head, she pulled out her pocket and searched it for a handkerchief. "The mist," she muttered, although he probably could not hear. Rubbing her glasses dry gave her a chance to blink back tears.

"My lady, pleased I'd be to instruct ye in the ways of God's salvation, if ye've a mind to learn."

He wore a distant expression and avoided her gaze. Was he truly concerned for her eternal soul? "I am so minded," she confessed.

Allan turned toward her, glanced away, started to speak, and faltered. Finally he nodded. Celeste followed him back to the horses.

Throughout the ride home, she felt the warm imprint of his hands upon her waist. It was worth coming out for a ride if only to have him lift her into the sidesaddle. She determined to make this a daily occurrence.

Chapter 4

"Ye must do this tae defend my honor."

"I'll do naught of the kind, Woman. Do the deed your ainself." He shoveled porridge into his mouth between sentences. "I'll show ye a secret way to the tower, and none will be the wiser. Ye slit her throat in the night, back down the steps ye go, and ye're avenged."

A strong hand gripped his shoulder and gave him a shake. "Nay, 'tis ye must do this thing. If ye'll rally the clan to take the earl's carriage on the road to Aberdeen, ye can slay the twain at once, plus Ballantyne, too."

"*He* will be angry if she dies, but then, die she must since she's a Galbraith." He paused, then crammed in another spoonful of porridge. "A pity."

"Hellooo?" Celeste stepped through the open doorway. Instantly she backed out, waving off flies. Despite the open doors at each end, the atmosphere within the stable was pungent. She straightened her bonnet. "Is anyone about?"

"M'lady, ye dinna belong here alone."

The sound of that reedy voice spun her around. A man with

a face of wrinkled leather sat upon a bench, leaning his back against the stone stable wall. A harness lay across his lap. Squinting in the sunlight, he touched his cap but made no move to rise.

"Quentin." Celeste acknowledged the old servant who frequently assisted her to the mounting block for her rides upon Robin.

"I'm guessing ye've come in search of the lad." Quentin smiled, revealing a few lonely teeth.

"The lad?"

"Your bodyguard."

The shrewd expression in his faded eyes annoyed Celeste. "D'ye ken his whereabouts?"

"That I do. He went for a gallop while ye took luncheon in his lairdship's chambers."

Allan's only private moments occurred while Celeste spent time with her father. She fingered the lapel of her riding habit, feeling guilty. "Mr. Ballantyne complained of the gout. We made a hasty meal of it. Besides, 'tis too bonny a day to remain indoors. I had begun to think we'd ne'er see the sun again."

Quentin let out a cackle. "So ye dinna keer for the fog, m'lady?"

"I thought 'twould never lift." Even the thought of the depressing mist that had shrouded the castle for weeks on end made her shiver and rub her arms.

"Ye'd best enjoy this sunlight while ye may."

Rhythmic hoofbeats caught Celeste's attention. "He returns. Dinna tell him I was here, please?"

Quentin looked quizzical, but he agreed. "If it please m'lady. And I'll give Robin your respects."

Celeste nodded. "Many thanks, Quentin." Picking up her skirts, she slipped into the stable, intending to escape out the far end.

The sound of Allan's voice hailing Quentin stopped her. Poised with one hand against the stone stable wall, she eavesdropped without compunction, hoping her name might enter the conversation.

"How was D'Arcey today?" Quentin asked.

"Prime for jumping. 'Tis a pity the new laird has no taste for the hunt." Celeste heard the slap of leather and clink of metal.

"Seems his lairdship has taste for naught about Kennerith. The crofters ne'er see him, and they with harvest coming soon."

"His lairdship enjoys his studies. The man loves his daughter, and he takes thought for the needs of others," Allan said as if in defense of his master. "At present he watches o'er my lady's safety to give me time to myself."

Celeste cringed. She had left her father and Mr. Ballantyne dozing in their chairs.

"Tell me how ye fare, Lad. I've sensed trouble in your spirit."

A long pause. Celeste leaned forward, straining her ears to hear Allan's answer.

"My life is like unto riding a green-broke horse on the edge of a cliff."

"The lady is difficult tae guard?" Quentin sounded surprised. "I expected the worst of a highborn wench, but her ladyship fooled me. She seems agog to please. Her eyes follow ye, worshipful as a hound pup's, though they be blue as the summer sky."

Celeste smothered a gasp. How dare Quentin say such things!

Clop, clop, clop.

The men must be walking the horse around the stable yard, for their voices receded into the distance. Celeste caught only the end of Allan's reply: ". . .fright the first night, she's given no alarm. Except for our horseback outings, she does little but read, sleep, sew, and stroll about the castle gardens."

"Then why the cliff?"

"Between my lady and Beryl, I'm apt to lose my sanity. Women!"

Never before had Celeste heard so much animation from her stoic bodyguard. His frank opinion stung her pride.

The voices grew loud again. "And how does Beryl torment ye?"

"She spins tales—entirely her own inventions—about me. I hear every word through the chamber walls yet can say naught in my defense. If my lady believes these tales, she must think me the most reprobate of men."

"And ye think she believes them?"

"I fear she is uncertain what to believe," Allan said. "I have spoken to her of my faith in Christ and my desire to live a life pleasing to God."

"And?"

"Each morning while we sit in the library, I read to her from the Holy Scriptures. She has a lively mind and an interest in things of the Spirit. But then Beryl regales her with tales of my supposed exploits, and. . ." The voices faded out of hearing.

A horse in a nearby stall snorted, and Celeste nearly yelped aloud. Her chest heaved in the effort to repress emotion.

" . . . Galbraith?" She heard Allan's voice as the men and horse approached the stable.

"I have," Quentin answered.

"She desires to wed the scoundrel. I canna remain here to see it." Allan's voice cracked. "The earl plans to take her with him to Aberdeen tomorrow for a gathering of his academic friends. I should run while she is away and ne'er look back."

Celeste shook her head. Allan could not leave! Panic filled her at the thought.

"Escape, then, while ye may," Quentin said.

Celeste scampered out the far end of the stable. Pinching her lips together and shaking her head in denial, she sought a path through the outbuildings to the castle gardens. Which way? Brilliant orange roses draping over a stone wall beckoned her onward. After shoving open the garden gate, she rushed between flowerbeds to the castle's kitchen door. Already panting for breath, she ran to the great hall, up the main staircase, along the gallery, up the spiral staircase, and then burst into her sitting room. Darkness and flashes of light alternated within her head as she collapsed into a chair. With a thin wail, she dropped her head back, pulled off her glasses, and began to gasp.

"M'lady?"

In reply to Beryl's startled inquiry, Celeste could only shake her head and whimper. She felt as though her body must either burst the bonds of her corset or expire.

Beryl grabbed her by the arm, hauled her into the bedchamber, and began to strip off her riding habit. Only when the constricting corset had been removed could Celeste weep freely. She flung herself across the bed and let loose her anger and frustration. Articulate speeches took shape in her mind, words she would never dare speak aloud to that exasperatingly reserved man. Above all, she resolved he must not leave. Not ever.

Beryl brought in warm water, a sponge, and soap, leaving

them on the dressing table. She laid out an afternoon dress of fine white lawn sprigged with forget-me-nots. "Ye'll recover your spirits after ye freshen, m'lady." Beryl's tone was gruff, but Celeste appreciated the thought.

"I dinna ken how I would ha' survived these months at Kennerith without ye, Beryl. Ye're more a friend to me than a maid." She caught hold of Beryl's callused hand, squeezed it, and smiled.

To Celeste's surprise, tears sparkled in Beryl's eyes, and her lips quivered. She tugged her hand away and retired, leaving Celeste to bathe alone as she preferred.

While she sponged her body, Celeste pondered. Despite Beryl's tales of his immoral exploits, Celeste knew Allan to be a man of high principles and strong character. The maid's lies sprang from insecurity or misplaced jealousy.

Celeste dried herself and donned a clean chemise, her busy brain planning a rendezvous with Allan. She would summon him to join her in the garden, and there she would assure him of her absolute faith in his integrity and inform him that she would not be traveling to Aberdeen on the morrow.

Celeste positioned herself on the garden bench and arranged her skirts. If Allan entered from the west gate, he would see her framed by sunset-hued roses. But no, the late afternoon sun shone full in her eyes. She hopped up and sought a better venue. A small alcove near the gate held a curved bench. Ivy would make a lovely backdrop for her gown. Smiling, she hurried to position herself upon the bench, leaving room for him at one end.

An angry male voice from beyond the garden wall reached

her ears. Someone approached from the stables.

"My sister is a comely woman, but few wenches could compete with that dainty piece o' yours. I've a mind to tell his lairdship about the way ye've wronged Beryl, just as your worthless father left your mother alone and with child."

"Beryl's wretched tales come out of her blighted imagination." Allan's brogue was more pronounced than Celeste had ever heard it before. "I've heard her tell enough of them tae my lady whilst I was helpless to defend my honor."

"Ye'd accuse your ain kin of lying?"

"Has the whiskey scorched your brain? Beryl delights in mangling the truth. She's done it since we were bairns together. Ye must understand that ne'er will I wed a first cousin—I canna think it right. Beryl is as a sister tae me. Can ye imagine marrying your sister?"

Celeste heard the sound of clashing steel. "Ye're a traitor tae the clan. We all suspected it when ye ignored the call from our bonny Prince Charlie and left my father Angus tae lead the clan tae glory at Culloden. Beryl pled for ye, so we left ye be, thinking ye'd rally to the cause in good time, but now your true colors show through. Ye've turned traitor—a Galbraith lover. First cozening up tae the old laird and now breaking your pledge to marry Beryl."

"Put the knife away. Ye dinna understand, Dougal." Allan's voice sounded sad. "I love my clan. It nigh broke my heart tae refuse Uncle Angus's command and watch ye all ride off tae battle, but I couldna fight against the rightful government of Scotland. The Jacobite cause was doomed tae defeat ere a man set foot upon the battlefield at Culloden."

"Prince Charlie would ha' returned Kennerith Castle tae

the MacMurrays," Dougal said.

"Perhaps, had he the power. But that is neither here nor there. The Stuarts lost the throne during the Glorious Revolution, and our clan lost its castle hundreds of years ago after an inglorious battle. These are the facts, plain and simple. And short of a miracle, thus the case will remain."

"Ye're no Highlander and no MacMurray. Ye're no longer one of us." Dougal spat noisily.

" 'Tis a lie!"

"Then prove your loyalty and join us in taking back our own!" Running footsteps faded into the distance.

Celeste sat with one hand pressed over her mouth, breathing hard, staring at a dandelion in the lawn.

Steps crunched on the garden path. Allan passed her alcove, moving toward the rose bushes at the center of the garden. Celeste hopped up and hurried after him.

He turned at her approach, smiled, and bowed. "My lady. I trust your luncheon was pleasant?"

"It was." Uncertain where to look or what to say, she touched a vivid rose and bent to inhale its fragrance. "Some of the roses had a second bloom this summer. Are they not lovely? Quentin once told me a legend about the lady who planted this garden. Have ye heard it?"

"The tale of the beautiful serf? The laird she married was a MacMurray."

Celeste pushed her glasses higher on her nose. "Your ancestors owned this castle?"

His eyes seemed to search her soul. "Ye o'erheard Dougal at the gate."

"I did." Her fingers tugged at the curl lying upon her

shoulder. "I am truly sorry your family lost the castle. And to think, my father doesna' want it." She studied the effect of afternoon sunlight upon the castle's turrets and experienced her first genuine affection for the place.

"The Lord gives, and the Lord takes away. In His wisdom, He removed the castle from my family and awarded it to yours. I yield to His will. Would that my family might shake off its obsession with the past! Many MacMurrays have emigrated to the colonies or to the continent and started life anew. But others bide their time amid the hills, ever hoping fate will once again award them lands and titles. My uncle, Beryl and Dougal's father, perished at Culloden. Since I had no father, Uncle Angus had helped raise me until my mother's death."

"I am sorry. I wonder why my father allows MacMurrays to work for him. Not you, of course," she amended. "I meant your cousins."

"They use assumed surnames, as do I." Allan paused, frowning. "I wish I hadna recommended them to Crippen."

Celeste seated herself upon the stone bench in the middle of the garden. She reached out to pull an overhanging rose close to her face. "I received a letter today from my cousin Roderick, who is shortly to arrive. He tells me to trust no one, that my life may be in danger."

"He knows of the threats your father received?"

"He tells me to beware the MacMurrays." Still sniffing at the rose, she studied Allan's impassive face.

He opened his mouth as if to speak, then closed it.

"The day I arrived here, Mr. Ballantyne gave ye a letter from your. . .from my uncle. Have ye discerned its meaning?"

"I hope he meant to tell me that he'd made his life right

with God. Ye canna be unaware of the rumors concerning my birth. Despite the evidence, I find it difficult to accept. My mother was a godly woman. She ne'er revealed my father's identity. To anyone."

"Uncle Robert claimed to be a religious man?" Celeste brushed the rose's petals against her cheek.

"Nay. He turned his back on God during his youth. But in later days he seemed ridden by guilt. Whene'er I spoke to him of God's forgiveness, he would shout me from the room. I believe he felt himself beyond redemption. Although he ne'er told me of his conversion, I hope he and God were reconciled."

"I begin to understand your meaning," she said, looking up at him. "The Bible says 'tis sin that separates us from God, and 'tis Jesus' sacrifice upon the cross that reconciles us. Ye read me the passage from Romans, and yesterday I read it again for myself. The Bible is a dusty old book—yet when I read it, my spirit comes alive. Since I arrived here at the castle, I have felt alive in a way I never knew before."

"I, too."

"Ouch!" Celeste released the rose, and it swung back into place. She popped the stinging finger into her mouth and leaped up. Her heart pounded as if to escape her ribs. Bending over a bush of delicate white blooms, she asked, "What d'ye mean, 'I, too'?"

He said nothing.

"Ne'er did I believe the vile tales Beryl told. Your virtue contradicts her lies."

Silence.

Rattled by his lack of response, Celeste allowed her mouth to babble on. "I'll not travel to Aberdeen with my father on the morrow. I shouldna be surprised if Mr. Ballantyne, too, remains at Kennerith. He is unwell." She feared to meet Allan's gaze lest he read her heart. "Thus your trial continues with no end in sight."

"I thought ye desired a respite from my attendance. Why d'ye choose to remain?"

She kept her face averted. "I abhor traveling." The lie stuck in her throat. Her skirts snagged in a bush as she spun to face him. "Truth be told, I feel safest with you, despite Roderick's warning. Though I ken ye dinna watch o'er me of your free will."

Allan released her dress from the rose's thorns. He snapped a sunset-orange bloom from its stem and handed it to her. Celeste accepted the flower, lifting her gaze to meet his. She sucked in a quick breath. Clutching the rose to her breast, she moved closer until her skirt brushed his boots. "Allan." His given name tasted sweet upon her lips.

A muscle jerked in his cheek. He blinked and broke their gaze. Taking a step back, he bent to pull a weed from the black, crumbly soil. "Would ye care to help me tend the roses?"

Celeste felt as if she had run up yet another flight of stairs. She drew a deep breath and smiled. "Like the fair lady of legend? I shall be pleased." She knelt at his side, shoving mounds of fabric out of her way. "Perhaps I should change clothing so I can find the ground."

Chapter 5

My plan has gone awry! She remained here."

He rumbled a humorless laugh that reeked of whiskey fumes and shrugged off her clutching hands. "Then ye must kill her." His horse shifted and sidled as he mounted heavily. "Or leave her for my pleasure. She must die in the end whether ye do the task or nay."

"But *he* wants her left safe!"

"Many things he wants, he may not get." He chuckled again.

"So ye intend to betray him, Dougal?"

"No more than he intends tae betray me."

"Allan would turn back tae me if she were safely wed to another."

"Ye've gone soft on the wench, and Allan is a traitor." He attributed a few filthy epithets to Allan and spat on the ground, narrowly missing his sister's skirts. "Ye concern yourself with a lover, while I've a realm to reclaim. I go now tae rally the clan tae my side! Death tae all Galbraiths!" He reeled in the saddle and grabbed his horse's mane to right himself.

"A realm? Whiskey has addled your mind! Kill the earl, take the money, and let us all flee this cursed place! Allan will join us once she is lost to him."

"Allan must die with the rest of the wretched lot, since all ken he carries Galbraith blood. Why not wed Adam MacKinnoch, who's pined after ye these ten years, and rid your mind of our misbegotten kin?"

At her cry of protest, he kicked his horse into motion and jounced off into early morning darkness.

Celeste drooped while Beryl unbuttoned her gown. "The house seems empty with Papa away."

"Poor man. He'll be missing your care and company." Beryl shook out the gown with a snap and laid it over a chair.

"And I'll be missing his." Concern for her father's safety creased Celeste's brow.

"Why'd ye stay?"

Pulling pins from her hair, Celeste met the maid's gaze in the mirror. "Why does it concern ye, Beryl? I thought ye intended to remain at Kennerith whether or not I left. Perhaps 'twas the prospect of arranging my own hair again that stayed my wanderlust." She let her hair fall over her face in disorder, then pulled it apart to reveal a grimace.

Beryl's lips twitched in response as she reached for the tousled locks. "If ye've a mind tae snare the viscount for your husband, ye'd best leave the task of hairdressing tae me. He's one with an eye for a pretty face, and we'd best see that he pays heed tae yours, my lady."

"Roderick? I hadna realized ye knew him."

A furtive expression crossed Beryl's face, and for the first time Celeste could recall, the Highland woman's cheeks flushed red. "I. . .ye must have spoken of him. . .or Dougal," she sputtered.

"Ye seem to ken more of him than I do. Roderick is a handsome man. He must attract many women." While Beryl prepared her for bed, Celeste tried to recall Roderick's flashing dark eyes and sardonic smile. During his brief but assiduous courtship, not once had she considered the implications of his evident romantic expertise. She had been too flattered and thrilled by his attentions to think clearly.

"Ye should marry him quick and make him take ye tae London or Paris where ye'll be safe."

"Safely away from Allan," Celeste concluded. "Are ye certain ye love your cousin as a woman loves the man she would take as husband, Beryl?"

Beryl's lips tightened into a pink slash across her freckled face. "I'll see him dead ere he weds another. What's mine is mine!" She spun Celeste around and vigorously brushed out her hair.

Celeste considered her maid's proprietary attitude. Despite Beryl's shocking lies and brusque comments, Celeste was fond of her. Yet Beryl, her brother Dougal, and Allan were all MacMurrays, members of the ancient clan that had once owned Kennerith Castle. If even half the accounts of clan battles and feuds held truth, the blood of a Highlander must run hot as molten steel, making a jealous woman such as Beryl a dangerous enemy. Although a clan uprising sounded like the stuff of legends and ballads, the venom Celeste had occasionally seen in Beryl's vivid blue eyes and heard in Dougal's gruff voice warranted caution.

"Will ye be needing aught else this night, my lady?"

Celeste blinked and turned. Beryl waited near the door.

"Ye'd ne'er harm me, would ye, Beryl?"

Beryl's jaw dropped. Her gaze shifted to one side. Her lips trembled, then set into a firm line, and her gaze met Celeste's. "Nay, my lady. I'll ne'er cause ye harm."

Celeste sighed. "I thought not.

The door closed behind Beryl with a hollow boom. Celeste heard her speak to Allan but could not make out their words.

Celeste extinguished her candles and climbed into bed. The castle's dank chill seemed to seep into her bones. She rose to pull the curtains and glimpsed the glow of firelight from her antechamber. Allan gave a little cough. He must have overheard her conversation with Beryl. He must overhear all their discussions, but Celeste hoped perhaps he could not distinguish every word.

Allan. To Celeste, he had become the embodiment of Jesus on earth—kind and selfless and considerate. His polite conduct allowed her to enjoy privacy despite his constant physical presence. Last night in the rose garden, her hopes had flown higher than the clouds, for his eyes had seemed to speak to her of. . .

But his subsequent behavior put the lie to her imaginings. Pleasant, friendly, yet detached—that was Allan.

Roderick's warning about MacMurrays returned to haunt her. Did Allan detach himself out of respect for her, or did he maintain emotional distance because he anticipated her imminent demise? She shook her head in denial even as her hands crept up to grasp her throat. *Can anyone be trusted? Do the MacMurrays all desire my death? Even the earl may plot my death since I am not truly his daughter.*

Her pulse pounded beneath her icy fingers. A sense of her own weakness swept over her. What chance would she have against a woman like Beryl, let alone against Dougal? She rubbed her hands up and down her arms. Skinny arms. No muscle there. No strength anywhere.

Jesus, are You here with me? Please, protect me from mine enemies!

A realization struck her. All the qualities she had seen or imagined in her bodyguard were exemplified in the Jesus of the Bible—kindness, strength under control, and selfless love. Allan might offer her protection, but Jesus had already sacrificed His life for her eternal soul.

A soft snore reached her ears. Allan slept. A little smile curled her lips, and her body slowly relaxed.

God had guided the earl to choose Allan as her protector. Allan, despite his MacMurray blood, was the best human protection Celeste could have. And even if Allan failed her, Jesus held her safe within His mighty hands. Because of Jesus, God would forgive her sinful self and make her His child. At that moment, Celeste put her complete trust in God's salvation.

It seemed mere moments later that Beryl swept back the bed curtains to admit morning light. "Arise, m'lady. A guest has arrived and is eager tae see you."

"A guest?" Celeste mumbled. She rubbed her eyes, stretched, and yawned. "At this hour?"

"Nay. He arrived late last night and slept in the southwest tower chamber. 'Tis the viscount."

Celeste sat up, blinking. "Roderick is here?" Ignoring the bed gown Beryl held ready, she hopped up and ran toward the blurry door. As greater awareness dawned, she turned back. "Last night he arrived? I must dress in haste and greet him. I must be hostess while my father is away."

Beryl handed over her spectacles and assisted her into the

bed gown. Her mind spinning, Celeste buttoned its bodice carelessly while Beryl unraveled her braid. Allan must be told. What would he think of Roderick?

"My lady," Beryl protested as Celeste rushed back to the door. "Your hair. . ."

Celeste flung open the chamber door and nearly collided with her sentinel's back. He turned around. Eyes like polished silver regarded her coolly.

"Oh, I–I. . ." Her startled gaze took in his flawless livery, his brushed wig, and his hand resting upon the sword hilt at his side.

He bowed. "My lady."

Heat rushed to Celeste's cheeks. Allan's magnificence made her own state of dishevelment seem the greater. Hair straggled around her shoulders, and her bare feet cringed upon the threshold. She gripped the door, ready to slam it shut.

"Pardon if I intrude." A voice broke the silence. Roderick Galbraith paused in the drawing-room doorway. "I climb the tower to awaken my lady with a kiss and find another before me, a jester in scarlet raiment. Pray, introduce us, my love."

"Ye must know by the livery that he is my father's servant, my bodyguard," Celeste said. "Allan Croft is his name."

Allan again bowed.

Roderick's full lips curled in scorn, and his voice held mockery. "Aye, that I do know. Such irony! A misbegotten Highland knave in my darling's chambers, beholding her unbound hair? He'll soon rue the day."

"What nonsense!" Celeste's attempt at laughter sounded flat. "Roderick, why ever didna ye tell us the date of your arrival? Now Papa is away a fortnight, and ye've caught me unawares." She ran one hand through her braid-kinked locks. "But welcome, dear cousin." Extending her hands, she tried to smile.

"My love, you look ravishing. How many nights have I lain awake, imagining the glory of your hair? Yet every dream fell short of its resplendent reality." He brushed past Allan and lifted her hands to his lips. "As I explained once before, those eyeglasses mask the glorious hue of your eyes. For my sake, resume the lorgnette."

Celeste stared at the curling black hair on his ungloved fingers. A faintly fetid aroma rose from his bowed head, and she saw grime ingrained around his neckcloth. When had the man last bathed?

Giving Allan a sideward glance, Roderick yanked Celeste into a close embrace and buried his face in her neck. "And where is the kiss I've dreamed of all these lonely weeks?" Strong arms squeezed her body against his, and hot breath moistened her throat.

Burning with indignation and shame, Celeste pushed at Roderick's constricting arms. "What kiss is that, Cousin? Ye've ne'er coaxed one from me! Unhand me ere my bodyguard rends ye limb from limb!" She tried to maintain a teasing tone.

"I'd run him through ere he took two steps in my direction." Although Roderick released her, his grin resembled a sneer. He patted his sword. "I'll soon put an end to this farce."

Celeste trembled in every limb. Sustaining a pleasant expression and tone, she sidled closer to Allan, noting that he gripped his sword hilt. "Enough talk of violence, Roderick. Allow me time to dress and welcome ye properly in the great drawing room."

Roderick moved in. "Why not send this boor away and

welcome me properly right here?" He trailed a finger down her cheek. "Ye've no need of a bodyguard now that your Roderick has come." A hint of brogue crept into his cultured voice.

Sensing Allan's strength at her back, she shook a chiding finger under Roderick's nose. "Such a thing canna be done, even if I wished it. Papa hired Allan to watch o'er me, and only Papa can order him away."

Roderick scanned Allan dismissively. "I could knock him over the head and dump him down the garderobe hole if you but say the word. I'd have done it years ago if that rat Ballantyne hadn't caught wind of the prank and stopped me." He chuckled. "My own, to see your mane flowing free nigh takes my breath away!" He reached out a trembling hand.

Flinging her hair behind her shoulders, Celeste backed up until her heels bumped Allan's boot toes. All pretense left her. "Enough, Roderick. Your intimations insult me! Begone. I shall greet ye downstairs within the hour, and we shall pretend this scene ne'er happened."

Eyes flaming, Roderick appeared to deliberate between challenging Allan upon the spot or biding his time. Caution prevailed. "Within the hour, my own. And leave the churl behind lest I slay it before your tender eyes." He paused to give an ugly laugh. "Keep in mind, Highlander, that those who lift their eyes too high oft fall to ruin."

When she heard Roderick's shoes upon the spiral stairs, Celeste slumped back against Allan. His forearm slid across her back as he released his sword. "What has happened to Roderick? He is a stranger, not the man I thought I–I thought. . ."

How could she ever have imagined herself in love with Roderick? That dirty, lecherous, shifty-eyed beast! No wonder

Papa had objected to the match. She shook her head. Turning, she gave a yelp of pain and nearly fell against Allan. Her hair had tangled on his waistcoat buttons.

"Alas, I appear to be trapped." She attempted a jest despite her heart's pounding, but he did not respond. With quaking hands, Celeste unwound her snarled hair, trying not to touch him any more than necessary. Allan's gloved fists clenched at his sides. His rapid breathing ruffled the curls framing Celeste's forehead.

Allan stood like a statue, enduring the exquisite inferno caused by Celeste's touch. As soon as her hair was free, he stepped back. "I shall call Beryl to help ye dress." He scarcely recognized his own voice.

"No need. I'm here." Beryl waited beside the bedchamber doorway, staring daggers into his heart.

Beryl knew. She had always known.

Celeste turned and dashed into her room. When Beryl would have followed, Allan caught her attention with a wave. She closed the door and approached him, her eyes hooded.

"D'ye wish my lady harm?" he whispered.

Beryl lowered her gaze and shook her head.

"Will ye aid us?"

A slow nod.

His tension lightened, and he whispered directions into her ear. "Can ye do this for me? For her?"

"Beryl?" Celeste opened her door and peeked out.

Allan stepped back, met Beryl's gaze, and received another nod. Beryl entered her mistress's chamber. The door closed, and another chunk of plaster hit the floor.

The next morning, Beryl did not appear in Celeste's chamber. Celeste dressed herself and wound her nighttime braid into a fat bun. Her eyes burned and her stomach ached. Evidence continued to mount that Allan did not return her growing attraction to him. He was impervious to her feminine allure, if she possessed such a thing. Slipping on her spectacles, she studied her reflection in the mirror.

Roderick was right—the glasses did hide her eyes. Not that her eye color could compare with Beryl's anyway. Her simple gown matched her eyes, but its gray-blue shade seemed to lend her cheeks a deathly cast, and her mouth puckered in a distinct pout.

Placing her hands on her hips, she twisted from side to side to examine her figure. Even without a corset, her waist appeared trim. The lace ruffles of her chemise peeped above the morning gown's low neckline and fringed its elbow-length sleeves. A ruffled cap topped her brown hair, its lappets dangling at the back of her neck.

How was a woman to know whether a man preferred willowy grace or plump curves? Celeste was uncertain which description suited her best—probably neither. Did Allan admire a petite woman or a lady of elegant height? Celeste's gloom deepened. Her height was somewhere in between.

She clasped her hands, bowed her head, and squeezed her eyes shut.

Dearest Jesus, my Friend, please help me! Keep Allan here to protect me and teach me about You. Beryl does not love him as a wife should, so please do not let them marry. Keep him safe, and do not allow Roderick to mock him today. And keep Roderick from touching me. I fear Allan will feel obliged to kill Roderick, and that would cause such trouble for him. For Allan, I mean. Amen.

Even while praying, she remembered Allan and Beryl with their heads close together, his gloved hand brushing ruddy curls from Beryl's ear. Had he reconsidered his objection to marrying a cousin? Had Beryl and Allan run off together? Did Allan believe his duty ended now that Roderick had arrived?

Lifting her chin and throwing back her shoulders, Celeste opened her chamber door and stepped into the antechamber.

Allan rose from an armchair and laid aside his book. "My lady." He bowed.

Celeste's face crumpled, and tears began to pour down her cheeks. She covered her face with her hands. Sobs lurched her body.

"My lady." His breath tickled her forehead. "Are ye ill? Have I failed ye in any fashion?" Distress colored his voice. "Come and be seated. Shall I send for wine?"

She shook her head.

He grasped her upper arm. "Please, come and sit. Can ye tell what ails ye?"

She allowed him to seat her in his chair. He pressed a handkerchief into her hands. "Where," she gasped while dabbing at her eyes, "is. . .Beryl?"

He went down on one knee and peered into her face. His thick brows met in the middle of his forehead, and his gray eyes looked dark with concern. "Beryl has gone, but I shall care for ye as best I can. Shall I summon a physic? D'ye hurt anywhere, my lady?"

She nodded and pressed one fist to the center of her chest beneath her bosom. "Here."

He started to reach toward her, clenched his hand, then returned it to his upraised knee. "Is it something ye ate? Is the pain constant, or does it throb?"

"Both." She tried to draw a deep breath, but another sob snatched it away. "I–I was so afraid!"

She saw his eyes flicker back and forth as he studied her face, which must look dreadful after her bout of weeping. "What did ye fear, my lady?"

"I prayed that God would keep ye here. . . ." Her body jerked with leftover sobs. "That ye wouldna leave. . .me, but I feared ye'd gone. . .gone away with Beryl."

"As ye see, I am here. Aught else?"

"Roderick. . .he frightens me. I–I dinna think I can con–control him long, and Papa. . .Papa willna return for many days!"

He switched knees and rested one elbow on the upraised leg. The tip of his sword scabbard rapped the floor. "My lady, in honesty I canna tell ye that your fears are groundless."

"Ye do intend to wed Beryl?"

A smile twitched his lips. "Nay, I willna marry my cousin, and I believe she now accepts it. Her temper is as fiery as her hair, and she indulges in unseemly fantasies, yet her heart is tender toward you, my lady. Against fearful odds, ye've won her loyalty by being a friend to a servant maid. I pray the Lord will reach her heart through your love."

His eyes narrowed. "I believe you intended, at one time, to wed the viscount."

Celeste squirmed. "I believed it myself until I met him again. He had convinced me of his sincerity, and he claimed to love me despite unpleasant family secrets. I now wonder if the tales he related held any truth." Her breathing gradually became more even. "I had even begun to wonder if you, Beryl, and Dougal intended to kill me." She tried to chuckle.

"D'ye trust me now?"

She met his gaze. "Entirely."

He thumped his hand upon his knee and arose. "Pray that good will prevail o'er evil, obey my every command, and dinna allow your cousin to touch ye. Can ye do this?"

"Aye."

"I'll escort ye downstairs when ye're ready, my lady."

Chapter 6

Pacing back and forth across the library, Celeste glanced toward her cousin and wished for the hundredth time that he had never come. The three days since his arrival had seemed endless. Roderick divided much of his time between secretive meetings with the ailing Mr. Ballantyne and intrusive encounters with Celeste. His dark eyes held mysteries that seemed to give him great amusement and satisfaction. Only when he looked at Allan did his face harden and his self-assurance waver.

Roderick's nose was deep in a book, but Celeste suspected him of feigning interest.

"Where did ye go this morn, Roderick?"

"On an errand. Be seated. You make me dizzy."

Celeste sat and picked up her needlework. The first stitch jabbed her finger. "Did ye go to o'ersee the harvest? Is it true that the villagers are unhappy because this recent wet weather spoiled much of the harvest?"

He gave her a disbelieving look and flung one elegant leg over the arm of his chair. "Why would I care? They'll pay rent out of their own lazy hides, if need be. If you must know, I was researching records at a nearby kirk. An ill-favored edifice. I prefer a fine cathedral or even Kennerith's wee chapel."

"People matter more than the building. Vaulted ceilings and intricate woodcarvings canna substitute for fellowship with other believers. I've learned to enjoy the simple services at the village kirk. I understand much more than e'er before, and understanding brings me joy." Celeste glanced toward Allan, who stared through one of the tall windows as rain drizzled down its panes.

"Some people would benefit from greater understanding, but others would only come to realize what they had lost." Roderick aimed the remark at Allan's back.

"There is hope for a man's repentance so long as he draws breath," Celeste said.

"If such belief comforts you, I'm glad of it."

Celeste blinked. "Either a thing is true or it is not."

"Aye, but some will believe it true and others will not."

"I believe Jesus is the Savior of the world, as He claimed."

"How charmingly archaic of you, my love. Religion is good for a woman as long as she doesn't let it harden her." Roderick closed the book over his finger and yawned, patting his lips. "Anything taken too far is a fault, including religion."

"But Jesus is not a religion—He is the Son of God."

Roderick rolled his eyes. "Women are more agreeable when their mouths are closed. Do you not agree, Highland scum? Especially that wench you plan to wed—the one with manly arms and womanly charms. A fitting bride for a weakling knave who would allow his wife to run the house. Do you know his origins, Cousin? It seems our uncle took a passing fancy to—"

"Be still!" Celeste cried, standing up and rounding on her

cousin with a swirl of skirts. "You take every opportunity to mock him. Canna ye see that he turns the cheek as Christ commands? My Allan could slay a feeble gentleman like you in an instant, but he is above senseless killing."

"*Your* Allan? What talk is this? I will not have it!" Roderick leaped from his seat and grasped her arm with iron fingers. "Remove those spectacles and use the lorgnette I bought you." He grabbed for her face, but Celeste twisted away. Spouting imprecations, he spun her back to face him. "You're mine alone, as will be this castle, the title, and all!"

A squawk of pain escaped before she realized what was happening. She heard the ring of steel and felt Roderick's body stiffen. A sword point hovered near the cleft in her cousin's chin. Roderick stared down the shimmering length of the saber. With Celeste pressed against him, his own sword was out of his reach.

"Release the lady."

Roderick swallowed hard. "She is my intended." His voice wavered.

"I am charged with her protection. Unhand the lady. Now."

Roderick let go and backed away. Celeste had thought he might draw his own sword, but he kept his hands lifted. "You'll regret this. I'll neither forget nor forgive." Once out of reach, he regained insolence. "When I am earl, all MacMurrays will die painfully or be deported. I swear it!"

He bumped into the door, turned, and made a hasty retreat. Allan sheathed his sword.

Celeste let her questions spill over. "How does he know you're a MacMurray? What mean these threats he shouts? Has he gone mad?"

Allan frowned. "The viscount spent much of his childhood here. He and I are auld acquaintances. He might ha' learned my true identity almost anywhere. The secret is no real secret."

He turned away and stood with arms folded across his chest, his jacket pulled taut across his shoulders. "As for his threats, I darena' leave your side long enough to discern their significance. The serving staff whispers, yet none will speak openly. Dougal disappeared the morning his lairdship left the castle, and now Beryl is gone."

Celeste shivered despite the fire's warmth. "I wish Papa hadna gone away. E'er since Roderick's arrival, I've had a sense of impending doom. Something dreadful will happen, I ken."

When Allan did not respond, Celeste sank into a chair, remembering conversations she had overheard concerning the indolent tendencies of her uncle Alastair and the disagreeable repute of his son. Alastair had lived off his eldest brother Robert's reluctant largesse most of his ill-spent life, leaving Roderick to run wild.

"Papa has never cared for Roderick," she said. "Until this past spring, I had seen my cousin only twice before, and then I was a small child. When he came to pay me court, he seemed agreeable. I thought Papa was mistaken." The memory that Roderick's attentions originated immediately after Celeste inherited a small fortune obtruded itself once again.

"Allan, did he truly nigh stuff ye down the garderobe? I should think the holes too small." The idea made her shudder. In her mind, the shaft beneath the castle's antiquated latrine terminated somewhere near the center of the earth.

"He might ha' succeeded but for Mr. Ballantyne's intervention. I was a wee lad of ten; the viscount was fifteen." Allan's tone was matter-of-fact.

"How despicable!" Celeste whispered. "This castle would frighten me if you werena here. Almost I expect to become lost someday and happen upon a skeleton in a dungeon. Where is this chapel Roderick spoke of?"

"Ye've not seen the chapel?" Allan turned.

Celeste shook her head. "Will ye take me there?"

"With pleasure." A smile flickered across his lips. "At your leisure, my lady."

She hopped up and followed him from the library and down the main staircase. When he opened the front door, she asked, "Shall I need a bonnet?"

"Nay. 'Tisna far, and the rain has ceased."

He led the way down the castle's front steps and turned left. Then up another set of broad stone steps and along a covered walk beside the partially crumbled curtain wall. "Take my arm, my lady. Many flagstones are broken or missing."

Celeste gladly laid her hand upon his forearm. "It has a musty, moldy smell, this walkway." Large gaps in the sidewall revealed the castle courtyard and outbuildings. A cat stared at them, wide-eyed, then drifted up the wall and out a window like a gray mist.

"I suspect it supports a thriving population of mice, hence the cats." With that comment, he hauled open a wooden door. "The priest's entrance in days of old."

Celeste stepped inside, then waited for Allan to lead the way. A vaulted ceiling with arched enclaves displayed five intricate windows of stained glass. "How beautiful!" Celeste forgot the smell and the cold, gazing upward in rapt appreciation. Her fingers caressed a velvety walnut bench.

Allan strode down the aisle and stepped behind the raised lectern. An enormous Bible lay open before him. "We might have our daily readings here, my lady, if ye can bear the chill." His voice rang hollow in the expanse.

"Is the chapel nevermore used for services?"

"Not to my knowledge. Your ancestors—and no few of mine—lie beneath us in the crypt."

Celeste shook her head. "Not mine." Instantly regretting the slip, she turned to read the inscription on a brass plaque. " 'In memory of Adelaide Ballantyne Galbraith, beloved wife.' I wonder how many generations back are these ancestors."

"Many of the monuments bear dates."

Celeste read the verse inscribed beneath the name. " 'When Christ, who is our life, shall appear, then shall ye also appear with him in glory.' I pray these people were true believers in Jesus. I should be pleased to meet them in heaven someday."

Allan spoke at her elbow, his voice soft. "Did ye mean what ye said to your cousin about Jesus, my lady? Have ye accepted His salvation?"

She rubbed her upper arms against the pervading chill. "Aye. When I hear ye read Scripture aloud, my heart tells me 'tis truth. And your life is proof to me that God exists. I know that Jesus willna fail me, no matter what men may do or say."

He swallowed hard, stared up at a magnificent rose window, fingered his sword hilt, and looked back down at Celeste. "Naught ye could say would please me more. The Lord will keep ye safe, whate'er happens."

"I canna imagine a man hearing the Word and not believing," she said.

She saw his chest expand and deflate in a deep sigh. "I and

my mother before me have oft spoken with family members about the Christ. They listen to the Bible stories, debate theology, decide which kirk the clan will support—and apply none of it personally. Only the Holy Spirit can convict a man of sin and persuade him to accept redemption. This I ken, yet my heart aches at the emptiness and hatred I see consuming my people. 'Twas not always so, and I pray God will once again reach the MacMurrays."

"Ye dinna hate my family, do you?" Celeste touched his arm.

He avoided her gaze. "My lack of hatred alienates my clan. If I am reviled for the sake of Jesus Christ, so be it. I loved your uncle, and I—" He broke off, strode away, and bowed his head, gripping the back of a bench with both hands until it creaked.

"And?"

When he turned his head to answer, she again saw him swallow hard. "I canna betray his trust. My lot is cast with the Galbraiths, though it cost my life."

He bent farther over the bench, eyes narrowing, then reached down and hauled a plaid woolen blanket from beneath it. Mutton bones, fruit pits, and a knife clattered upon the bench and floor. "Someone has been living here."

"Who?"

"I canna tell, unless he died and these be his bones. If so, he was a sheep."

Celeste grimaced then smiled. "Ha ha. How droll. But what shall we do?"

"Depart in haste." He replaced the items and hurried her out the chapel's main door. "Turn back and exclaim o'er the windows again. We may be watched."

She obeyed, shivering. "But the windows appear dull from

the outside. I have lived here for months, yet I know little about Kennerith Castle. What other wonders does its forbidding exterior conceal?"

"Perchance ye'll learn more of its secrets, but not now. It commences to rain again, and, fool that I am, I advised ye tae bring no bonnet. Make haste." He plopped his tricorn hat on her head and rushed her back to the castle as a sharp wind blew the mist into their faces.

That evening, while dining with Roderick and Mr. Ballantyne in the small dining room, Celeste noticed her cousin's boisterous manner. Coming as it did so soon after his humiliation at the point of Allan's sword, this behavior struck Celeste as peculiar.

She felt Allan's presence at her back like a solid wall of reassurance. If she had noticed Roderick's odd behavior, it would not escape Allan's detection.

"A good day's work, eh, Ballantyne?" Roderick said around a mouthful of venison. He sopped oatcakes in the gravy.

Mr. Ballantyne seemed more wizened and miserable than usual. He picked at his food and drank quantities of wine. "The gout," he murmured. "Canna abide this rich fare. I keep telling his lairdship, but he doesna wish to disturb the servants. . . ."

Candlelight flickered in Roderick's eyes. "Uncle Malcolm was never meant to be earl. The value lies not in the castle but in the land! These crofters pay half the rent they should and could if the Highlanders didna steal our rightful earnings."

"My father will be fair and good to his tenants and to the Highlanders," Celeste said. "They owned this land before we Galbraiths did, at any rate."

A cruel smile curled Roderick's lips. "*We* Galbraiths? Have you forgotten your true parentage so soon, my love?"

Giving a start, Mr. Ballantyne spilled wine on his waistcoat. "Sir, ye've ne'er told the lass that tale? 'Twas intended a secret!"

Roderick chuckled. "And you've now confirmed its veracity. Ah, Mr. Ballantyne, what an invaluable source of information you are! Drink up, aged cousin. Enjoy what pleasure is left you."

Celeste clenched her hands together in her lap and felt Allan shift his weight behind her chair. "If ye'll excuse me, I believe I shall retire early this night." Her voice trembled despite every effort to control it. Rising, she curtsied to the gentlemen, who both rose to bow.

"Sweet dreams, my love. Soon you'll be mine in every sense."

Allan closed the door behind her. She rushed into the great room, stopped, and stamped her foot on the flagstones. "I hate him!" Her voice echoed among the beams high overhead. Immediately she repented of the childish display. "But it is wrong to hate."

"My lady, I grapple with the same sin. God is able to deliver us both."

Chapter 7

The new maid assigned to Celeste's service plaited her hair silently, warmed her bed linens, regarded her with proper respect, and curtsied before she left the room. . . yet Celeste missed Beryl. She lay awake with one candle burning long after the maid retired. Light from Allan's fire glowed reassuringly through the cracks in the heavy door.

Lord Jesus, forgive my hateful thoughts. I know I should love Roderick as You do, but I find it difficult. Allan is easy to love because he is like You. I wish to spend every day of my life with Allan.

Her eyes popped open. An idea slipped into her mind. She could bundle up in blankets and join Allan on the floor in the antechamber. They could sit beside the fire and talk. So many things Celeste wished to learn about her bodyguard, her dearest friend. Which foods did he favor? What were his fondest childhood memories? What was he thinking when he gazed at her, as he sometimes did, with his eyes of softest gray like lamb's wool and a hint of a smile about his lips? How would it feel to be held in his arms? Would he wish to kiss her? Roderick's caresses made her flesh creep, but the thought of Allan's hands upon her skin produced entirely different thrills.

Lord, my mind wandered again. Is it evil for me to have such thoughts? Surely I may sit and talk with Allan in the antechamber. . . and yet, somehow I know You and he both would disapprove. Perhaps this is the wisdom You promised to give me if I asked. I know it is impossible that Allan and I could ever marry, but if he could even be with me for the rest of my life, I think I should be content. Or would I? You know my heart better than I do. Please do with me, with us, as You deem best. I beseech You in the blessed name of Jesus.

Oh, and please help me to sleep. I am frightened to the depths of my soul this night! Since I mayn't have Allan's arms about me, I ask You to hold me in Your hands. Amen.

Despite her earnest prayer, Celeste's mind merely wandered in and out of consciousness, and strange dreams wafted through her thoughts. True sleep eluded her.

Sometime during the night, her eyes opened wide. A sound had awakened her. Allan still snored in the antechamber. The banked embers of her fire occasionally popped, but that ordinary sound would not have disturbed her peace. Someone was breathing nearby, breathing heavily but trying to muffle the sound. A footstep scuffed on the rug beside her bed, and the bed curtain rings scraped along the pole.

Summoning all her strength, Celeste rolled over and over to her right. She felt a blow upon the bolster, and a gruff voice cursed. *Thunk.* Cocooned in blankets, she fell off the far side of the bed and tried to roll beneath it. Heavy footsteps rushed around the bed.

Dust filled her eyes and nose, yet she freed her mouth of blankets and rug long enough to scream with all her might. "Allan! Allan! Please God, help me." Her screams turned to weeping, and her imagination felt a knife slide between her shoulder blades.

With her ear against the floor, she heard footsteps like crashing thunder.

Allan rolled from sleep to his feet and drew his sword at the first thump and angry shout. Celeste! The warped door boomed against the wall as he burst into her bedchamber.

Darkness. Silence but for Celeste's muffled sobs. Did the invader have her in his clutches? Allan's bare feet padded on the hardwood and rug. He sidestepped left to avoid being back-lighted by the fire. His sword point drew tiny circles in the dark.

Glass shattered to his right. He turned, recognized the distraction ploy, and feinted left, sword extended. Something struck the wall behind him. His sword point caught on—flesh?—then sprang free. A shadow deeper than its surroundings passed between Allan and the hearth. He lunged low. His saber slashed. A grunt. The assailant landed prostrate on the floor. Allan pressed his sword point against the heaving mass. "As ye value life, be still."

"Allan?" Celeste's voice quivered.

"Aye, Lass. Rise and give us light."

Shuffling sounds from the area of the bed.

"My lady, are ye injured?" Allan inquired, becoming restive.

"Nay, I am tangled in the bed linens until I can scarce move."

"Make haste."

"I'm making all possible haste, if ye please. I must find my eyeglasses!"

Her testy response pleased him.

"I'm coming now. Dinna slay me!" Her footsteps padded

behind his back. She tossed a peat block on the fire and poked the embers into a blaze. Allan focused on the man beneath his sword.

"Allan, look!"

He glanced up. Celeste pointed to his left.

He returned his attention to the would-be murderer. "What is it?"

"A door in the wall."

"Close it, please."

"But should we not first learn how it works?"

"Later, when danger of this rogue attempting escape through it is past."

She obediently closed the door. "I see how it works! A lever hidden beneath the—"

"Clever lass. Now stay back near the bed." He nudged the invader with one foot. "Rise slowly and turn about."

The man clambered to his feet, lifted his gloved hands, and faced Allan. "I'd ha' killed ye both had I been whole, Cousin." A sneer disfigured Dougal's countenance. Dark stains upon his breeches, hose, and coat glistened in the firelight and dripped to the floor. "Two days past, the earl's outrider caught me with a ball in the side, but not ere I'd shot his lairdship!"

"Ye're insane!" Celeste said. "Why would ye want to kill my father? Why would anyone kill Papa?" She began to weep again, and Dougal laughed.

"This castle belongs to MacMurrays by right of inheritance! The young master schemed to inherit, but I had my ain plans. Death to all Galbraiths! Death!"

Knocking Allan's sword aside, Dougal stumbled toward the chamber door. Only then did Allan see his objective—the point of a dagger was embedded in the wall. In one motion, Dougal gripped the dagger, spun, and flung it at Celeste.

Allan's sword knocked the knife aside. But in that moment, Dougal had staggered to the window, pushed open the casement, and climbed upon the sill. Allan dropped his sword and dove after him, catching his cousin by the coattail. "Dougal, ye're mad! 'Tis a rainy night—the roof will be slick. Come and let us tend your wounds."

"Ye'd heal me to hang me, traitor that ye air!" Dougal punched Allan in the head, then beat at his grasping hands. "I'll run to the hills or die a free Highlander!"

A kick caught Allan in the inner thigh, and pain made him see stars. Dougal left his coat in Allan's grasp and slid through the window. *Thud!* He hit the roof ten feet below. His scrabbling attempts to catch hold ended in a despairing scream that faded into the distance.

Celeste wailed.

Allan gripped the stone sill and pushed himself to his feet. Grief for his cousin and for the earl weighted his heart, but first he must see to comforting Celeste.

She was a wraith in white beside the bed, her eyeglasses reflecting the firelight, her hands clasped beneath her chin. She took one step toward him, then another.

The antechamber's outer door slammed open, and a stream of servants poured into the tower. Roderick entered last, dazzling in a violet-striped banyan robe. "What has happened here? We heard shouts and screams. . . ." His gaze fell upon Celeste, and his eyes widened. He then studied Allan, the open window, and the disheveled state of Celeste's bed.

He pointed at Allan. "Arrest that man for the attempted

murder of Lady Celeste Galbraith!"

"Nay!" Celeste ran toward Allan. He caught her in one arm and grabbed her bed gown from its hook on the wall. Keeping his gaze averted, he wrapped her in its concealing folds.

"Roderick, ye dinna understand!" Celeste slipped her arms into the bed gown's sleeves. " 'Twas another man tried to murder me. Allan saved my life!"

"Murder? Where is the body?" A strange voice asked.

Celeste buttoned her bodice, staring up at Allan's face. Why did he not refute the charge? She whirled about. The village sheriff stood at Roderick's side, looking almost as confused as Celeste felt.

"The body of the murderer lies in the courtyard," she said. "He fell off the roof while attempting—"

"The darkness and the late hour have bewildered your thoughts, my lady," Roderick said. "I sent for the sheriff when word of a heinous scheme reached my ears." He stepped forward, keeping a wary eye on Allan. "Sheriff, this man is part of the MacMurray plot to steal Galbraith lands and title. Are you a man of the law or not?"

The law officer wavered. "I am, but I see no evidence of murder, and the lady says—"

"If you neglect your duty, I'll have the wretch thrown in the castle dungeon until a scaffold can be built. The laird of the castle's word is law, and I am he. Charlie? Ian?" Roderick beckoned forward two young men, strangers to Celeste, who grasped Allan by the arms.

"Nay, ye canna take him!" she cried, but a large hand shoved her aside, and they dragged Allan toward the door.

"My lady!"

She met Allan's gaze. He glanced at the dagger on the floor. Celeste quickly seized it. When she looked up, he was gone. Heavy footsteps sounded on the stairs.

"Clear the chamber, the lot of you!" Roderick shouted. "Dumb sheep." Several servants glanced in evident bewilderment from Celeste to Roderick, but obeyed without protest.

Roderick fixed Celeste with a glittering stare. His silken turban and robe gave him the aspect of an Oriental potentate. He extended a hand. "The dagger, my love."

She clutched it, turning away, but he caught her and wrested the knife from her grasp. "I canna allow you to despoil either your breast or mine." She struggled to free her arm. His smile twisted into a sneer. The point of the dagger snagged in her lace chemise as he traced it along her neckline. Celeste stilled but could not restrain a shudder.

"Perhaps I'll keep you alive after all, safe in this tower until I tire of your charms. Come what may, I shall inherit your fortune, for you have no other living relatives."

"The Lord knows your black heart, Roderick," she said.

"More religion. I have used God's house as mine these past months, and it served me well. Either He doesna care, or He canna intervene, or He doesna exist."

"Ye've been living in the chapel?"

"Aye. Accomplices inside the castle saw to my care and feeding. The MacMurrays played easily into my hands; I fed upon their resentment and superstition. Dougal killed your father, but it should be easy enough to switch the blame to your bodyguard, since Ballantyne will back my word that Allan Croft went missing these past three days. A prompt hanging, a few legal ends to secure, and all will be mine. Including you. If you'll join me, I shall marry you. If not, I fear you'll pine away for loss of your father and die here in the tower."

Celeste studied his features and wondered how such a heartless soul could exist. "My heart pities the void it senses in yours, Roderick, and I pray the good Lord will touch ye ere 'tis too late."

He swore and flung her away. "I'll give you until the morrow to ponder your fate. A laird of the castle has many tasks to occupy his time, but I might think to visit you. Be grateful for small mercies—I might have chained you in the dungeon with your lover. Dinna attempt to leave the tower; I've set my loyal guard upon the tower stair."

Celeste stared at the closed door and listened to his footsteps on the spiral staircase. As soon as silence met her ears, she sprang into action. First, a warm woolen gown and cloak. Sturdy shoes. A simple candle would not do; she lighted two lamps.

Then, standing at the closed portal, she pressed the lever inside a recessed candle sconce.

Chapter 8

With the grinding of stone, a black crack opened in the wall. Narrow steps led down a stairway barely wide enough for Celeste. Blinking and taking deep breaths, she lowered her chin. Dougal had traversed it; so could she.

The air tasted dead. She bent to keep from bashing her head on jutting rocks. With a lamp in each hand, she could not balance herself against the walls. The staircase must wind around the thick outer wall of the tower, leading down—she would find out where. Her legs shook from fatigue by the time she reached the bottom step. A stone-lined passage lay before her. Something ran ahead, squeaking; its feet pattered on the uneven floor. Her own shadow loomed double on the walls, moving as she moved.

What lay at the end of this eternal tunnel? Dougal had entered it; she could exit it. The temptation to run back up the stairs to her familiar bedchamber passed through her mind, but she dismissed it. Allan was imprisoned in a chamber possibly less cheery than this. She must find a way to rescue him.

The tunnel ended. Celeste glanced around. Had she missed

a door? The walls seemed solid. Perhaps another hidden door? She set her lamps down and searched for a lever.

Nothing.

Lord Jesus, please give me aid! She backed up and bumped her head. When she reached up to rub the spot, her hand connected with a hanging metal ring. A wooden door lay above her. She remembered to say a quick word of thanks for God's guidance before she pushed upward. The door gave, but its weight frightened her. Although the tunnel's ceiling was low, she might lack strength enough to push the trapdoor all the way open.

Allan. She could do it for Allan. Groaning with the effort, she gave a mighty shove. The door popped open but slammed back down. "No!" she shouted and pushed again. This time, to her surprise, the door lifted easily and swung back to hit the floor above.

A white face gazed down at her. She shrieked.

"Lady Celeste! Thank the guid Lord above, ye're alive!"

"Mr. Ballantyne? I thought ye were a specter!"

The little man reached a shaking hand to take the lamps from her. Celeste feared she might pull him into the tunnel if she accepted his aid, but for his pride's sake, she allowed him to assist her. Once seated on a stone floor with her legs still dangling into the tunnel, she glanced around. "Where are we?"

"In the crypt beneath the chapel."

Celeste froze. The stone blocks had a different aspect once she knew their contents.

"Why are ye here?" she asked.

"Where is Dougal Mason?" he asked at the same time.

Celeste looked at Mr. Ballantyne with sudden suspicion.

"Ye waited here for him?"

"Aye. I told him of the secret passage, to my regret. I didna tell Roderick." His shoulders bowed. "Come into the chapel, and I shall reveal all. I must atone. You carry one lamp."

Celeste gripped his elbow and let him lead the way among granite monuments and marble effigies. He seemed barely able to climb the steps into the chapel. Once in the sanctuary, he dropped upon a bench and covered his face with his hands.

"I carena if they kill me; I must confess all. God has granted me no peace since the business began, and I canna spend eternity in such torment of soul!" he moaned.

"Mr. Ballantyne, what have ye done?" Celeste laid a comforting hand upon his shoulder.

" 'Twas Robert's doing. Had he not looked upon a MacMurray wench, none of this would have come about." Mr. Ballantyne sounded angry.

"Uncle Robert?"

"Aye, Lass." Mr. Ballantyne lowered his hands. "He loved Laura MacMurray and married her in the village kirk, with me as witness. Fearing the wrath of his father, the third earl, he kept the marriage secret, promising Laura to own her as his wife once he became earl. But the hatred against Highlanders in these parts kept him silent even after his succession to the title, and ere he made up his mind to claim his bride and wee son, Laura died. She sent her innocent lad, him not knowing his ain father, to Robert's care."

Celeste felt a strange heaviness in her breast. "He never acknowledged his rightful heir!"

"Cowardice destroyed him from within. He nigh burst with pride and love for the lad, yet he couldna look Allan in the eyes and tell what he'd done to the lad's mother. Robert laid the charge upon me to set up Allan as heir upon his passing."

Celeste shook her head. "Why did ye not? My father doesna care to be earl."

"Ah, Lassie, the shame of it! I couldna bear the thought of a MacMurray taking back Kennerith! A Highlander." He nearly spat the word. "I told Roderick where to find the kirk marriage record so he might expunge it."

"Roderick knows! No wonder he hates Allan. He is—Allan is our cousin."

"Not yours by blood, my lady. Yet I'll not have ye thinking shame on your mother. She was married and widowed ere she wed Malcolm. Your father was a French army officer."

Celeste grabbed Mr. Ballantyne in a quick hug. "My mother and Allan's were both good women. I knew it! Truly, I did."

" 'Tis all accounted in the family Bible there upon the stand. I didna yet reveal that record's existence to Roderick."

Celeste stared at the huge book, visible now in the morning light streaming through stained-glass windows. "Uncle Robert told Allan in his note: 'All ye need know is contained in the Holy Scriptures.' " She ran up the steps to the lectern and turned to the family record in the front pages of the huge Bible. A sealed paper lay inside the book's leather cover. It bore a spidery inscription. Celeste read aloud, " 'Allan MacMurray Galbraith.' " With a thrill of satisfaction, she slipped the letter into the front of her gown.

The ground seemed to rumble. "Horses arriving. A carriage." Mr. Ballantyne tottered to open the chapel door.

In the courtyard, a sea of mounted horses surged around

the earl's carriage as it slowed to a stop. "Papa!" Forsaking caution, Celeste ran down the stairs, across the cobblestone drive, between startled horses, and flung herself into her father's arms as he stepped down. "Ye're alive! They told me ye were dead."

"I might ha' been, but for Dougal's ineptitude with a firearm." Malcolm's voice held the ring of steel. "Thank the guid Lord, ye're safe! That maid Beryl warned me of a plot against your life. Where is Roderick?"

Celeste glanced around, noting uniforms, guns, and swords. The earl had returned to Kennerith in the company of a military unit. Her heart sang. "Papa, ye must hear Mr. Ballantyne's tale. Ye'll be thankful."

Cold from the stone wall seeped through Allan's torn shirt and drove deep into his bones. No matter how he strained his eyes, no glimmer of light relieved the dungeon's darkness. He wondered if he would live long enough to lose his power of sight.

Heaving a sigh, he tipped his head back. *Protect Celeste from that monster, Lord. I cannot see Your plan in this adversity, but I must trust that You remember Your children.*

He heard a clank overhead and running footsteps echoed. "Allan?"

"Celeste!" Was he dreaming?

Light appeared as a tiny square in the door to his cell. "Where are you?"

"Here." He rattled his chains and a moment later heard a key turn in the rusty lock.

The door creaked open, and Celeste stopped to stare. "Oh, Allan!" An iron key ring hung from her hand.

He blinked in the brilliant lantern light. "Ye're safe?"

She set the lantern on the floor and began to try keys in his wrist shackles. "I am well. My father returned safely, and I used the secret door in the tower to escape and—oh, Allan, how could he abuse ye so?"

Losing patience with the keys, she knelt upon Allan's bench and wrapped her arms around his neck. Smooth, lavender-fragranced skin filled his senses. He tugged at his fetters. "My lady—" She cut him off with a kiss that eradicated the dungeon's chill.

Her hands caressed his hair and rasped over his stubbled chin and throat. "Allan, I love you."

Helpless, he simply savored her kisses. As soon as he was free, he must run to the hills and never again lay eyes upon his beloved lady—but at the moment, this dungeon cell was paradise.

"Allan, I have a letter for you from your father." She slipped a note from her bodice and held it before him. "He married your mother! Ye're his true heir, not Papa. We're to hurry upstairs and hear Papa's announcement."

Allan wiggled his hands. " 'Twould help if ye'd release me, my lady."

In Kennerith Castle's great hall, Malcolm Galbraith confronted his two nephews. Soldiers gripped the arms of Roderick, whose twisted features expressed rage and defeat.

Allan stood alone. Despite his bare head and filthy, tattered clothing, the assembled company regarded him with evident awe.

Anxiety pinched Celeste's pounding heart. Since he had read his father's letter, Allan had spoken not one word. Heat seared her cheeks, and she avoided his gaze. What had compelled her to declare her love while he was unable to escape her advances? Nevertheless, come what may, she had memories to treasure of Allan eagerly returning her kisses.

Malcolm spoke. "After hearing Mr. Ballantyne's testimony and reading the surviving record of my brother Robert's legal marriage to Laura MacMurray, I declare Allan MacMurray Galbraith the true fifth earl of Carnassis. Let each man present stand as witness."

A murmur rose among the assembled servants and soldiers, quickly breaking into a roar of approval.

Epilogue

A carriage stopped before a modest row house on a street near the university. The coachman placed the step and held the door. "Shall I wait, your lairdship?"

The earl of Carnassis stepped down. "Ye needna stand about in the cold. Return for me in three hours, John."

In the entryway, a maid took his cloak. "Step into the study, your lairdship. I'll tell the professor and miss that ye've arrived."

"Thank you, Beryl. A certain crofter of mine asks about ye regularly—Adam MacKinnoch. Fine fellow."

She returned his smile and blushed. "I'm thinking I'll soon be following my lady back to Kennerith."

He grinned and chucked his cousin under her chin.

Beryl left him in a book-lined study. An embroidery, partially completed, lay on the arm of a chair.

"Welcome, your lairdship!" Malcolm Galbraith stepped into the room. He clasped the earl's hand and shook it.

"Ye look well, Uncle," Allan observed.

"Pleased to be where I belong." Malcolm drew his daughter forward. "I know ye've come to see my lass, but first I'd hear the news. What has come of Roderick?"

Allan bowed over Celeste's hand and lifted it to his lips. "My lady."

The lacy fichu crossed upon her chest seemed to flutter, and her face turned pink. "I am no longer to be addressed so, your lairdship," she said. "Kennerith Castle has a fresh heir. I am simply Miss Galbraith."

She sat down and picked up her needlework, but her gaze remained on Allan. He relaxed upon a horsehair sofa and attempted to direct his attention to her father. "Roderick has run to the Continent. I thought it best to show mercy."

"Did the minister at Dalway testify that Roderick rifled the kirk's marriage records?"

" 'Tis true enough."

Allan could scarcely keep his eyes off Celeste after three months' deprivation. She appeared rosy and healthy. Her blue eyes glowed behind their thick lenses.

"What happened to your MacMurray kinfolk?" she asked.

"Dougal, of course, perished that night. Many of my kin decided to emigrate to the colonies; others I have granted crofts on the manor. I pray God will reclaim the MacMurray clan, starting with Beryl."

"She is an amazing woman," Celeste said. "We are fast friends now. She favors a young man from Dalway, however, so I may soon lose her."

"Perhaps." Allan restrained a smile.

"And Mr. Ballantyne?" Malcolm asked.

"He remains at Kennerith. His health deteriorates; he seldom leaves his rooms. Although I have forgiven him, he seems consumed by remorse. Only the Lord in heaven can remove such a weight of guilt. 'Tis joy to know that my father did accept God's forgiveness before his life ended, according to his letter. I regret he didna find courage to confess to me; nevertheless, all is forgiven."

"Your poor mother," Celeste sighed.

"Aye, yet now she lives in paradise and suffers no more earthly pain. I moved her body to lie beside her husband's beneath the chapel."

"Although their story is sad, I trust their son will have great joy in this life as well as in the life to come." Malcolm laid his pipe upon the mantelpiece. "If ye wish to address me, Lad, I'll be in my drawing room. God bless ye both."

As soon as the door closed, Allan knelt at Celeste's feet, enveloped in her voluminous skirts. "My lady, how I have missed ye!"

"And why should the earl of Carnassis miss the likes of me?"

"Because he loves ye more than life itself."

"Och, I dinna believe it. All those months guarding me, and nary a word ye said." One dainty finger touched his waistcoat.

He caught her hand and clasped it to his heart. "Nary a word, but ye must have read all in my eyes."

"I'm short-sighted. I must hear these things to know them."

"Every time I said 'my lady,' I claimed ye as mine."

She leaned forward to touch her lips to his forehead. "Ye seemed cold at times. I thought ye loathed me."

" 'Tis a fearful thing for a servant to love his mistress. How I prayed for immunity to your beauty and charm!" His arms slid around her waist.

"Ye speak as if I were a disease." She framed his face with her hands. "And now ye're a great laird. What would ye need with a clumsy, sharp-tongued, bespectacled lass like me?"

He ignored her question. "The castle is cold and dank and falling to pieces about my ears. Without ye, I'd soon take ill and die of loneliness. I need ye to help turn a fortress into a home. I need ye with me to ride in the hills and to work in the Lady Fayre's rose garden. I need ye to read Scripture and to pray with me and to raise our children to love and serve the Lord Christ. I need ye with me to shine the light of God's love upon this dark world."

"I prayed. . .that ye'd want me," she confessed. Her lips met his, warm and soft.

Allan nearly lost his balance in the effort to bring her closer. Admitting defeat, he rose, gripped her hands, and pulled her up with him. Now he could hold her close without hoops digging into his thighs. She twined her arms about his neck and melted against him.

"We'd best ask your father's permission to marry," he murmured between kisses. "He's expecting us."

"Be warned that should ye choose to be my husband, I shall try to make your life wonderful," Celeste said.

JILL STENGL

After fifteen years of military life, Jill and her husband, Dean, built a log house beside Lake Kawaguesaga in northern Wisconsin and are happily putting down roots. Their oldest son, Tom, is at the Air Force Academy, hoping to become a pilot like his dad. Three other children, Anne, Jim, and Peter, are still at home. Jill's two shadows, Fritz, a miniature schnauzer, and Myles, a Siamese lap warmer, keep her company at the computer while she writes. Although she was born and raised in southern California, the Midwest is now her home. Home schooling, scrapbooking, sewing, visiting with friends, and housekeeping keep Jill occupied, but she always finds time in her schedule to write.

Jill's e-mail address: jpopcorn@newnorth.net

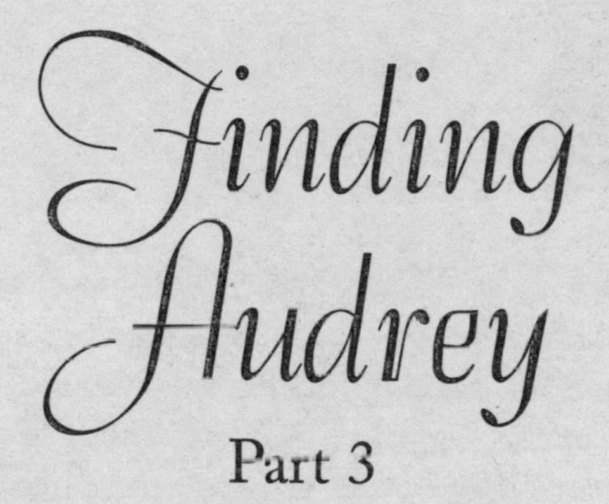

Part 3

by Tracey V. Bateman

Chapter 7

The second Audrey entered the church, her palms began to sweat, which was doubly distressing because everyone wanted to shake her hand. But the sight of Cassie, pink-cheeked and smiling again, was worth any price, even if it meant attending church service—once.

"Audrey! I can't believe you really came!"

Audrey gave the girl a weak smile. "A promise is a promise."

Cassie gave her a teasing grin. "It was shameful of me to force this on you. But whatever it takes to get you in church."

Audrey looked at her with mock scandal. "Cassie! Did you go and get appendicitis just to get me here?"

They laughed together, and Cassie looped her arm through Audrey's. "Come into the sanctuary and we can find a seat. Church will be starting in just a few minutes. Oh, and thanks for the box of stuff from the shop. We made enough yesterday for two of us to go on next year's mission trip to Mexico. Just thirty-four more kids to sponsor, and we're good to go."

Audrey shook her head at the girl's enthusiasm. She wasn't crazy about helping to fund a missions trip but hadn't been able to refuse Cassie's request for donations. "Glad I could help," she lied, then swallowed hard as they entered the sanctuary. She shared halfhearted smiles with passersby as she made her way down the aisle to a pew about halfway to the front. Sitting next to Cassie, she allowed her gaze to scan the nicely decorated but far from ornate room. Soft greens and mauves gently accented each other. Seasonal flowers and sturdy plants, strategically placed in corners and in front of the podium, lent a natural, comfortable feel, leaving no room for anyone to think they were sitting in a cold, heartless place.

Warmth. The decor exuded warmth.

Or was it the people? She could barely speak two consecutive words to Cassie as what seemed like a swarm of people stopped at her pew to introduce themselves and shake her clammy hand.

From the platform, the soft strains of "Amazing Grace" filtered through the sanctuary. Subconsciously, Audrey sang the familiar song in her mind, and to her horror, hot tears sprang to her eyes. She blinked them away, but the moisture clung to her eyelashes.

Cassie squeezed her hand, and Audrey wanted to cry more. Somehow the thought of being part of this. . .family appealed to Audrey in an odd way. She knew these sensations were most likely caused by all the emotional stress she'd been under. First making a fool of herself with a man clearly wrong for her, then finding out so much about her family so quickly. Not to mention Cassie's little adventure. No wonder Audrey was such a wreck—clinging to anything that might calm her down.

Get ahold of yourself, Audrey MacMurray. This isn't real.

Squaring her shoulders, she patted Cassie's hand to let her know she was fine. The girl took the hint and turned her loose.

Audrey's breath caught as Brett walked to the podium. He scanned the crowd. When his gaze lit on her, his brow rose, and his jaw dropped. Next to her, Cassie giggled.

"You didn't tell him I was coming?" Audrey whispered.

"No. I thought it would be more fun to watch his face."

In spite of herself, Audrey grinned.

Thankfully, Brett recovered and went on with opening the service.

The service was painfully long. It seemed as though every song sung and word spoken were directed toward her. It was as though Brett whispered into the song leader's ear and they changed the lineup at the last minute. And the sermon. "The Family of God." How could that have happened without prior knowledge?

As she stood for the closing prayer, a smile twitched the corners of her lips.

God had pulled a fast one on her.

Brett practically tripped over a baby stroller in the aisle in his haste to reach Audrey and Cassie before they left the church. He composed himself just as Audrey was saying good-bye to the Perrymans, Cassie's new foster parents, and spied him.

She smiled.

"Hi." And then his mind blanked out. *Hi* was the only word in the English vocabulary he remembered, so he repeated it. "Hi."

"You said that."

Heat crept up the back of his neck, and he gave her a sheepish grin. "Yeah. So, I'm surprised to see you."

A wry grin tipped the corner of her lips. "Don't get used to it, Rev. I was just keeping a promise to the kid." She moved her head sideways toward Cassie.

Cassie gave her a quick hug. "Yes, but she loved the service; I could tell. You'll be back." Without waiting for an answer, she dashed off to catch up with her foster parents.

Audrey watched her go. "She looks so healthy and happy."

Brett took hold of her elbow and steered her toward the doors. "The Perrymans are talking about adopting her."

"Really? It's unusual for kids her age to be adopted. That's great."

Sensing rather than hearing her hesitance, Brett frowned. "Except for?"

"Except for what?"

"That's what I'm asking you." He opened the door and hung back as Audrey walked through. He followed her into the brilliant sunlight.

"Well, if you *have* to know, I was considering looking into adopting her myself."

"I see."

She shot him a glance, the sun shining off her eyes nearly taking his breath away. But her tone brought him back to earth. "You see what?" she demanded. "Don't you think I could raise her?"

Wishing he'd just minded his own business, Brett nevertheless recognized a challenge when he heard one. And since he wasn't the type of guy to back down, he shrugged. "I think she's better off with a two-parent family. And there's the issue of God."

"God? What's He got to do with whether I should adopt Cassie or not? I wouldn't stop her from going to church."

"Maybe not. But she'd be unhappy in a home where she was the only one serving God."

Audrey hesitated a moment, as though pondering his words. She leveled her gaze at him and shrugged. "Well, I don't suppose it matters anyway if those people plan to adopt her."

"Right." Brett reached out and opened her car door. An invitation to lunch was on the tip of his tongue, but he thought better of it. Nothing had changed really. And it wouldn't be right to start down the same path they'd just vacated. One that had already caused them both pain. They'd end up in the same place, only this time, the damage might be irreversible.

As though reading his mind, she smiled. "Good-bye, Brett." She slid behind the wheel. Brett shut her door. An ache settled over his heart as he watched her drive away. Her good-bye had been final. And as difficult as it was, Brett knew he had to let her go. "Please, dear Lord. I surrender her to You, but please keep her in Your hand and continue to woo her to You."

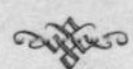

Audrey stepped into the dark flower shop and headed directly to her office. She switched on the light and walked to her desk. Coming down to the shop at two-thirty in the morning probably hadn't been the smartest idea in the world, but she'd lain sleeplessly in bed, staring at the ceiling, her thoughts running back to the service that morning. The joy on the faces of the congregation. The apparent sincerity in every single face that had smiled and welcomed her. Finally, in an effort to squelch her longing to return and become part of that group, she pushed aside the covers and headed to her desk at home. She decided to move on in her research, past Allan Galbraith and his beloved Celeste. But she needed her book about Kennerith

Castle to look for a starting place to resume. Only, she'd looked up and down and the book was nowhere at home. Then she remembered she'd had it at the office.

Drawing in her lower lip, she glanced around, her heart beginning to race. The book was right here yesterday morning when she'd gathered up things for the youth group rummage sale.

A gasp began deep inside her. "Oh, no!" She flew to the desk. The book had been under a stack of magazines. Then it all came back to her. She'd been busy with a customer when Cassie came through the door to pick up the box. Audrey had offhandedly mentioned the stack of old magazines might bring a dime each. Cassie thanked her. She must have grabbed the book along with the magazines. Cassie had told her just about everything sold, and the things that hadn't were already hauled away.

Tears sprang to her eyes, and she sank helplessly into her leather desk chair. The book was out of print. She knew because she'd looked it up online to see if there were any follow-ups to the 1939 edition.

With her elbows resting on her desktop, she covered her face with her hands and allowed the tears to flow. Despair washed over her. She had been at a standstill for so long until Brett had given her this book. Now she felt as though she'd never finish her research. Instinctively, she knew that the rich heritage she'd already uncovered was more than most amateur genealogists ever uncover, but the drive to delve deeper hadn't abated. Feeling more alone than ever before, Audrey looked up toward the ceiling. Staring into the artificial light, she took a quick breath. . .and prayed. "God, I don't want to stop now. This is part of who I am. If You are truly able to do anything and if You really love me like Brett says You do, then help me to take the research further back."

Silence permeated the room. Feeling guilty, as though she'd been caught stealing, Audrey sat back in her chair and waited. For what, she wasn't sure, but the monumental event that had just taken place struck her mute. She had actually said a prayer. Not an accusation or a bitter prayer, but a real one. She knew she had no right to ask anything of God. Her heart hammered against her chest and inside her ears. Verses from the Bible, seared into her memory by her minister foster parents, came flooding back like a rushing tide.

"Be still and know that I am God."

"The Lord is my shepherd, I shall not want."

"I have come that you might have life, and have it more abundantly."

Her breath caught.

"For God so loved the world that he gave his only begotten son, that whosoever believeth in Him should not perish but have everlasting life."

Her life played before her eyes, years in home after home, working hard in college, meeting Aunt Tavia. Suddenly the pain was more than she was willing to bear.

She shot to her feet. "Enough!"

Chapter 8

"Oh, Audrey, we're so glad you made it! Come in."

Mrs. Perryman stepped aside to allow Audrey entrance into the split-level yuppie home. She wore a bazillion-dollar smile—that of a new mother.

Audrey had been prepared to dislike the woman, but she couldn't help but respond to the warm welcome. "Congratulations on Cassie's adoption. You're a lucky mom, Mrs. Perryman."

"Please, call me Nan. You're part of the family."

"I am?" Audrey's cheeks warmed. Cassie must not have told them she wasn't a Christian and therefore wasn't part of the little "family of God."

The woman snatched her up into a quick hug. When she pulled away, tears sparkled in her eyes. "I am so grateful that God sent you to save Cassie's life. If you hadn't gone to that house that day. . ."

Feeling like a major fraud, Audrey cleared her throat and decided to keep it honest. "I just. . .I don't believe in God," she blurted, then felt foolish.

Nan smiled. "And He still used you to save my daughter's

life. What an amazing God He is. Well, come on. Cassie's been prowling the house like a crazy woman, waiting for you to get here."

"Am I late?"

Her pleasant laugh lingered in the air. "Not one bit. She's just a typical teenager. Impatient."

Audrey followed her down the hall and through an open doorway. She scanned the room, looking for Brett. Her heart leapt to her throat as she spotted him in the center of a group of teenage boys. He didn't notice her. So much for being able to feel when someone you love is in the room.

She forced her attention back to her hostess. "You have a lovely home," she murmured. The spacious living room, decorated in tans and forest green, buzzed with the sounds of at least two dozen guests talking and laughing. Nan led her around, introducing Audrey to Cassie's large, extended family. Two sets of grandparents beamed in the excitement and took turns kissing Audrey's cheek and thanking her for saving Cassie's life.

Despite the embarrassment, Audrey couldn't help relishing the approval.

"Audrey, you're here!" Cassie's cheery voice greeted her a second before Audrey saw her.

She embraced the girl. "Congratulations on officially becoming a Perryman, Sweetie."

"Thanks." Cassie eyed the gift in Audrey's hand. "That for me?"

"Of course."

"Can I open it now?"

"I don't see why not. Unless. . ." She glanced at Nan. "Did you want her to wait?"

"Not at all. I'm dying to see it."

Audrey held her breath while Cassie unwrapped her present.

"Oh, Audrey." Cassie stared in wonder at the gift. "I can't believe you did this. H–how did you know the names?"

Audrey glanced at Nan. "Your mother gave me all the names and dates of your family tree all the way back to the Revolution." Together they studied the painting Audrey had ordered for Cassie. The professional family tree document had been painted onto an eleven-by-fourteen canvas and framed in oak.

Cassie smiled, first at Nan and then Audrey. "It's perfect. Thank you." She turned. "Hey, Pastor Brett, come check out my present from Audrey."

Seconds later, while Audrey was trying to slow her racing heart, Brett stood only a couple of feet away, admiring the painting. "It's beautiful." His tender gaze swept her face. "Perfect."

Unable to look away, Audrey gave herself to the depth of the love shining from his eyes.

"That's exactly what I said," Cassie gushed. "Perfect."

Nan glanced from Brett to Audrey and cleared her throat. "Let's get the cake, Cass."

Audrey barely noticed them walk away.

"So how have you been?" Brett asked, his voice laced with emotion. "I've missed you. Four months is a long time."

"Yes." Too long. *Oh, Brett. I miss you so much it hurts.*

"Did Cassie give you the news?"

"You mean about the adoption?"

"No." His face reddened. "I meant about me."

Please don't tell me you found someone and are getting married.

Bracing herself, Audrey shook her head. "No. She hasn't

told me anything." She refrained from mentioning that she'd banned any mention of Brett at the flower shop.

"Well, my pastor has resigned from the church. I was voted in."

Audrey felt the blood drain from her face. "Y–you're the pastor now?"

"Not officially. But I will be after tomorrow. Pastor is sort of passing the baton after he preaches his last sermon there. And we'll have a farewell dinner afterwards. I would have called you to do the flowers, but I didn't think you'd want to have anything to do with me."

"I never turn down business."

"I'll remember that for future events." His familiar chuckle sent a wave of pleasure down Audrey's spine.

"So. . ."

Whatever he was going to say was cut off as Nan and Cassie returned to the family room carrying a huge cake. Audrey's heart sang at the look of rapture on Cassie's face and the matching smiles on the faces of her new parents.

If this was Your handiwork, God, then I guess thanks are in order.

Audrey jerked away at the sound of her ringing phone. Four in the morning? What sort of creep called at four in the morning? She grabbed her whistle to be ready in case it was a pervert calling. Then she snatched the receiver. "Hello?"

"Audrey! Did I wake you?" Brett groaned. "That was a dumb question. Of course I did."

"Slow down. What's wrong?" Audrey gasped. "Is Cassie okay?"

"Huh? Oh, yeah. Cassie's fine. I'm not though."

Audrey swung her legs over the side of the bed. "What happened?"

"My florist's shop burned to the ground with all my flowers in it!"

"What? Brett, I'm trying to follow you, but you're not making any sense. Calm down and start over."

Over the line, she heard him take a couple of steadying breaths. "Okay. Remember I told you the banquet is today after services? A farewell dinner really."

"Yes."

"The lady who was hired to do the centerpieces for the tables and the corsages for the pastor's wife and the women staff members had a fire in her shop. All of our flowers are gone."

"That's awful. That poor lady. I hope she had good insurance."

"She did, but that's not the point. Audrey. Think about why I'm calling you at this ridiculous hour. Can you help me out?"

"You mean you want me to come up with centerpieces and corsages by noon?"

"They have to be on the tables and looking presentable by eleven-thirty, when services are over. People will begin trickling into the fellowship hall directly after that. I know it means you'd have to start right now, but we'd pay you above the going rate for the rush."

"Oh, for crying out loud. How many do you need and what color scheme? Fresh or silk? What about the corsages?"

She heard the relief in his voice as he launched into the fall flower arrangements. The rose-carnation corsages wouldn't be a problem.

She hung up the phone ten minutes later with a page of notes to work from. With a sigh, she dressed, pulled her hair back into a ponytail, slipped on her gym shoes, and headed to the shop.

Help me do this, God. Audrey had settled into a sort of give-and-take relationship with God over the past weeks. She found herself calling on Him for help on occasion. And she took the help if He gave it. She always felt a bit guilty asking for anything, but in this case, she felt the situation warranted. After all, it *was* for church.

For the next four hours, she worked frantically and created four centerpieces—thankfully Brett had settled for centerpieces on only the main tables—and six corsages, one that stood out with a combination of white and red rosebuds. She surveyed her handiwork critically. It had been a rush job, and it showed, but she doubted anyone else would notice.

Wearily, she headed to her office for a cup of coffee. She'd brewed the pot before she'd started working and hadn't stopped long enough to pour herself a cup. The four A.M. wake-up call was definitely catching up with her. She figured she had time to sit and have some coffee before stopping home to clean up and get over to the fellowship hall to deliver the centerpieces and set them up for Brett. After pouring her favorite almond-flavored coffee into her "Flowers make me smile" mug, she sat and began thumbing through her latest issue of *Gardens of the World.* She'd received it only yesterday just before closing and tossed it along with the other mail onto the desk in her haste to get ready for Cassie's party.

As she perused the pages, she suddenly caught her breath at the familiar sight of her beloved ancestral home, Kennerith Castle. Her heart raced like a runaway train. "Oh. Oh."

"One of the loveliest rose gardens in Scotland is found in the Highlands at the legendary Kennerith Castle," she read. "The rose festival wouldn't be complete without a tour of Fayre's Garden and the famous MacMurray roses. These roses are said to have survived over seven hundred years of wars and natural disasters. Legend has it that each time a new owner has restored the castle, they have found one rose bush living."

Tears sprang to Audrey's eyes. And this time, she thanked God honestly, knowing this was too much to be coincidence. Forgetting all about the arrangements in the next room, she became engrossed in the legend of her ancestor for whom the garden was named. . . .

by Tamela Hancock Murray

Dedication

To my husband, John
My knight in shining armor for twenty years.

Chapter 1

Scotland, 1348

"Please, Laird Kenneth. Have mercy!" Witta Shepherd touched one knee to the ground and bowed his head. "If I had the few farthings ye request, I would hand them over without question." He trembled despite the summer heat.

Why do they ask for more than we can give? Fayre felt her own body tense and then shake as she witnessed the scene between her father, Laird Kenneth, and two of his knights. The longer she watched her aged father's humiliation, the hotter her emotions became. Rage and fright threatened to display themselves, but as a mere serf, she couldn't afford such luxury. Only a fine lady of the king's court could dare express displeasure to an exalted laird and his vassals.

Mounted upon fine stallions, the knights were an intimidating lot. The animals looked grand, dressed as they were in horses' cloaks depicting the familiar plaid cover the laird wore, a yellow background nearly covered with horizontal and vertical stripes of varying widths in red, black, blue, and green. Whenever Fayre saw the cloth, she couldn't help but feel prideful that her father's land was part of such a powerful and prestigious kingdom. Yet she chafed under the complete obedience the laird demanded.

She didn't mind so much for herself. A woman's lot in life was to be considered nothing more than chattel. Didn't the priest say that the heavenly Father commanded men not to covet their neighbors' wives? If she doubted a wife's status as property, the Lord God's words left no uncertainty.

She knew that several of the men in the village had an eye for her, but Fayre returned none of their interest. Her friends thought her silly and vain. They tried to convince her that marriage wasn't about affection. The arrangement was a contract made between two families for the betterment of both parties. She knew her friends were right, but even watching them take their vows—the first one when she was twelve—left her with not enough envy of their status to convince her to follow. Why would she want to leave her father, who in his kind ways would never lay a hand on her, for a rough man who would think nothing of beating her should she oppose his will? Fayre shuddered and said yet another silent prayer of thanks to God that even though she was nearing the age of twenty, her father hadn't demanded that she wed.

Witta Shepherd didn't deserve to be embarrassed, to be treated by the laird as nothing more than a stubborn beast. Fayre had never hated the tartan as much as she did at that moment. Her eyelids narrowed so much that they hurt. She could just see out of the slits they had formed. She widened them before the laird could see her sign of ire and command his men to kill her, too.

Laird Kenneth, wearing a suit of light armor minus the headpiece, sat bolt upright, surveying the flocks and fields that

Fayre's father had tended all these many years. He placed a flat palm and extended fingers above his eyes and studied the rolling hills, covered with fine grass for the sheep to feast upon. His gaze stopped and rested upon the two-room cottage in the distance where Fayre and her father had lived as long as she could remember. She thought back to the days when her mother sang songs—happy tunes she remembered from the traveling minstrels playing in the village—as she spun wool at the wheel. Those days, the ones before Fayre's mother went to live with the Father in heaven, were the happiest she had ever known.

Ever since Fayre's mother had died, sadness had followed Witta. His hair turned from gray to white almost overnight. The skip left his step. Her death extinguished the fire in his eyes. He was left with a gentleness of spirit, but one that was more resigned than joyful.

Fayre forced herself to stop daydreaming, to bring her attention back to the present moment. The knights wore contempt on their faces, regarding Witta like a faded flower whose time to be discarded had arrived. If only he would say something, anything, to defend himself and her. But Fayre knew he didn't dare. A serf, even an elderly male serf who enjoyed respect among the local villagers, dared not speak against the laird.

Fayre watched Laird Kenneth's appraisal travel from the hut to the vegetable and herb garden Fayre maintained for their subsistence. She could just make out their rooster strutting near the garden and hut. Hens clucked and scratched at the ground, unaware that one of them would be snatched for the evening's dinner come sundown. The two goats they depended upon for milk and cheese bleated in between chomping on clumps of thistles and grass.

Such a humble existence could hardly be the envy of a prominent laird, yet the greedy look in his eyes was unmistakable. He would gladly seize everything the poor shepherd owned so he could grant the land to one of his arrogant vassals, no doubt. The thought caused flaming ire to rise in the pit of her stomach, leaving her feeling volatile. She forced herself to put aside her feelings long enough to send up a silent prayer.

Heavenly Father, dinna let the laird take away what little my father has left.

At that moment, Fear tapped its icy finger on her shoulder, reminding Fayre that humble possessions were the least of her worries. The laird and his knights could easily slaughter the two of them on the spot, leaving their lifeless bodies to wilt in the sun-drenched field, undiscovered for days. Even then, Laird Kenneth and his vassals would go unpunished. Who would dare approach such an important man, a member of the landed gentry, a member of the king's court, with accusations concerning an insignificant shepherd and his virgin daughter?

With a renewed attitude of humility, Fayre murmured, "Blessed Savior, my divine God from whom all courage and strength is gathered, protect us."

"How dare you challenge me!" Rich with authority, Laird Kenneth's voice cut through the air.

Fayre startled. Was the laird forbidding her to utter a small prayer? She wondered how to respond until she realized the great man was looking directly upon her father. Her plea had gone unnoticed, at least by Laird Kenneth.

"King David has a war to fight," the laird said. "Victory will ensure he is granted his rightful position as king of France. Do you not see that by neglecting to pay your taxes, you are denying

His Majesty's army the means to fight for the independence of our fair Scotland?"

Fayre could see the distress on her father's face. "My laird, I would happily give every coin in my possession to the king if I were in possession of any." He sent the laird a begging look. "Wouldst ye accept as payment my best ewe?"

The laird straightened himself in his saddle, his body stiffening into a rigid line. "I know we settled on a ewe as payment last time, but I cannot accept an animal in exchange for your rent on every occasion. In any event, you cannot afford to give away so much livestock, and the king needs gold to exchange for supplies and men."

A frantic light pierced Witta's dim eyes. "My laird, the season hasna been good. The Black Death has taken so many people that the need for wool and mutton is less. The marketplace stays empty." He looked at the goats. "Nanny will be giving birth soon. Her new baby will take her milk, leaving even less food for us." He bowed his head. "I beg yer forgiveness."

After making his plea, Witta allowed his other knee to fall to the ground. With agility uncommon for one so elderly, he leaned his head, sparsely decorated with white strands of hair, over his bent knees until his nose met the ground. Outstretched palms, touching the soil, trembled. The sight caused Fayre's heart to feel as though it were tumbling into the abyss of her abdomen.

"Silence!" Laird Kenneth raised his hand. "Perhaps a few weeks in the dungeon will teach you a lesson." He nodded once to his knights.

In haste, they drew their lances from their leather sheaths. The long poles were now trained forward in the direction of her father. The knights readying themselves to commit murder, their eyes took on a cast as cold as Fayre imagined their hearts must have been. She gasped and looked in the direction of her father. He prostrated himself on the earth.

"Nae!" Shouting, Fayre hastened toward the men with such fury, she felt her long braids slap on her back with each step.

The unexpected motion scared Laird Kenneth's horse into rearing. The others startled and snorted in response. As the riders soothed the animals with comforting clucks of their tongues, Fayre was thankful she had stopped the vassals from taking her father into custody—at least for the moment.

After his white stallion's front hooves returned to the ground, Laird Kenneth snapped his head in her direction. His gaze caught Fayre's, the metallic silver hue of his eyes matching the point of his javelin. His unremitting gaze left her feeling no less wounded than if she had been stricken by the forked lightning of God's wrath. He addressed Witta. "Who is this maiden?"

Fayre curtsied so low she thought she might topple.

"My laird." Though he remained in his obsequious position, her father's voice was strong as his eyes met Laird Kenneth's. "She is my daughter, Fayre."

Rising, Fayre looked into Laird Kenneth's face. Golden eyebrows arched, indicating his interest. A straight nose gave way to full lips that were parted to reveal a nobleman's even, white teeth. Fayre averted her eyes to the reed basket in the crook of her arm. It contained a lunch of milk and a sliver of cheese, plus bread and mutton baked in ovens provided by Laird Kenneth.

"Fayre," she heard Laird Kenneth say. "Fair indeed."

Fair? Her rage and fear liquefied into curiosity and unfamiliar stirrings. *How can he think me fair? I am but his serf, and my plain brown garment tells him so.*

Her doubts seemed to be confirmed by the knights' boisterous laughter. "Aye, my laird," one of the vassals agreed. His voice was hearty in a way that made her wish to throw her arms over her body in a vain attempt to shield herself from his lusty stare.

Feeling her cheeks flush, Fayre nevertheless summoned the courage to hold up her head. She deliberately ignored the plain-spoken knight and set her gaze upon Laird Kenneth's face. Where she expected to see a vision of greed and desire, she saw instead the soft look of compassion and kind interest. His benevolent expression gave her the courage to speak.

"I most humbly beg yer pardon, my laird." Fayre wondered if her voice, soft with fright, was loud enough to conceal the sound of her racing heart. "I bring my father his food each day when the sun is high in the sky."

"And the flower you hold?" Like his countenance, Laird Kenneth's voice was soft. Was that a flicker of tenderness she spotted in those steely eyes?

She had forgotten the rose from her garden, even though she brought one to her father each day. "Fayre Rose," Father always said. "Ye bring beauty tae the world around ye."

"My laird," she answered, "the rose is from my garden."

"Never have I seen a rose with such brilliance, the color of the setting sun," the knight with reddish hair observed.

"Nor have I," agreed the other knight.

Laird Kenneth extended his hand to take the bloom, which Fayre willingly sacrificed. He studied its petals, touching each one with the gentleness a besotted bridegroom would reserve for his beloved damsel according to songs she had once heard traveling minstrels sing in the village. An approving smile touched his lips. "Lovely."

He tossed the flower back to Fayre. Too frightened to move, she allowed it to land at her feet. Filled with compassion upon seeing the bruised bloom, she bent and retrieved it. She felt the eyes of the men upon her but ignored them.

"Do you have a brother who can tend these sheep?" the laird wanted to know.

"Nay, my laird, she doesna," Witta answered on her behalf.

Laird Kenneth nodded for him to rise to his feet. "And why not?"

"The plague," he whispered and bowed his head toward the ground in a manner of defeat.

"Aye." Laird Kenneth nodded to show he understood. He redirected his attention to Fayre. "Then I fear you shall be spending less time among the blooms in your garden. You shall need to take your father's place here in the fields. Perchance you can produce profit enough to render his debt. Only then will he be released from prison."

"Then he shall never be released!" Her voice rising in pitch, Fayre motioned toward Witta. "Can ye nae see my father is old? Ye, my valiant laird, are a man whose honor lies in following the teachings of our Lord and Savior, Jesus Christ. How can ye consider taking a man so well along in years tae a filthy prison? Surely the Lord would not wish my father tae die in the dungeon! And die he will, if he maun spend even a moment among the dirt and rats!" Passion intense, Fayre stamped her foot. At that moment, she realized her hands had fisted so tightly that her fingernails dug into her palms. She knew she looked like a tempestuous child, but her anger was too great for her to exercise more self-control.

"Then perhaps the bonny lass has favors she would care to exchange for her father's freedom," the redheaded knight offered.

Fayre shivered despite the heat. She glanced sideways at Witta. Her father was too feeble to defend her. She would be forced to submit to whatever they desired. And with Witta so near, yet so helpless.

Father in Heaven, please—

"Please!" Witta's voice, stronger now, echoed aloud her silent prayer.

"Enough!" Laird Kenneth's voice slashed through the innuendo. "Have you forgotten the knight's code of honor?"

"Nay," the redhead admitted. He nodded toward Fayre. "But this one is a mere serf."

"Do you not remember Saint Paul's epistle to the Galatians?" Laird Kenneth reminded him. " 'There is neither Jew nor Greek, there is neither bond nor free, there is neither male nor female: for ye are all one in Christ Jesus.' "

Fayre was just as quick to recall a pertinent verse: *"Hypocrite, cast first the beam out of thy own eye; and then shalt thou see clearly to take out the most from thy brother's eye."* She wished she could tell Laird Kenneth then and there about the large beam in his eyes, but her life depended upon her silence. She swallowed.

To her relief, the laird's words brought a shamed look to his knight's face. "I beg pardon," he muttered.

Fayre breathed an inward sigh of relief. Perhaps he was a hypocrite, but the laird's words had saved her from an unspeakable fate.

Despite Fayre's previous display of temper, a soft light flickered in Laird Kenneth's eyes as he returned his attention to her. "And my apologies, Fayre. My vassals can be obtuse at times." He paused.

"I beg pardon, Woman," the knight said.

"Very well." The laird nodded to his knight. "As for the matter at hand, I do not wish the death of your father. But since he cannot pay his taxes, I fear he leaves me no other choice but to confine him to the dungeon until the debt is paid."

"But of course ye have a choice!" When she heard the shrewish tone of her own voice, Fayre knew she risked her life with such words. Nevertheless, she held herself upright, to her full height.

"Nay, I do not. If I were to favor your father, every serf in the kingdom would expect leniency."

"Then I shall go," Witta said.

Fayre shook her head at her father, despite the disobedience the gesture represented. "Nay," she whispered.

"But the rose, my laird," the second knight interrupted.

Laird Kenneth turned his attention to the knight. "The rose? What of it?"

"If I may be so bold, I am of the opinion that the royal court would be pleased by such lovely blossoms."

Laird Kenneth returned his gaze to the rose that Fayre held. He nodded. "Indeed."

"I propose we take the maiden to your estate," his vassal said. "Let her cultivate the roses in your garden. When you present them to the ladies of King David's court, the whole of them shall be delighted and look upon my laird with even greater favor."

Laird Kenneth's expression became thoughtful. He turned back to Fayre. His eyes searched her face. "Could you do that?"

"Aye, my laird. But. . ." She hesitated to raise an objection, but the thought of leaving her father alone so she could go live in a castle was not agreeable.

"But?"

"Ye need not cultivate the roses at yer estate," Fayre offered. "Ye may take as many as ye desire from my garden, any time they should offer ye and the ladies pleasure."

"Of course. But your cottage is far away from my castle. And having such roses in my personal garden would please me more. Can you grow them for me?" His voice held more humility than she had ever imagined was capable of a laird. His question seemed more of a request, a plea, than the demands and edicts so commonly dispensed from rulers.

Even though a feeling of disappointment engulfed her being, Fayre nodded. "I am certain of it."

"But my laird," Witta objected. "The lassie did nae harm. I am the one who has wronged the king. Take me and spare my child."

"Nay." Laird Kenneth stiffened. "The decision has been made. Your daughter will go with me in your place." He gave a nod to his knights, but before they could seize her, Fayre rushed to Witta and embraced him.

"God preserve ye," he said.

"And ye, my father." Breaking away, she looked into Witta's aged eyes. "Dinna despair. I shall be back as soon as the first roses bloom in the garden of Kennerith Castle."

Before he could answer, Fayre felt the grip of a knight squeezing her forearm. Witta tightened his hand around her fingers. His eyes misted as the knight drew her closer to his white steed, forcing her to break the hold. With a nod, he instructed her to mount the horse.

Before her bare foot reached the stirrup, Laird Kenneth intervened. "The lass shall ride with me."

To Fayre's surprise, Laird Kenneth mounted his steed and then gestured for her to come near. After she obeyed, he placed his hands on each side of her waist and lifted her with an easy motion until she sat in front of him on the horse.

Though his victories in battle were fabled, Fayre hadn't expected him to be so strong yet still handle her with a tender touch. His gentleness was small consolation when Laird Kenneth clicked his tongue, commanding the horse to trot away from the shepherd's field, away from the only home she had ever known. Terror knotted inside the pit of her abdomen and sent an ugly wisp to the base of her throat. Fayre turned and glimpsed her father one last time. As he waved farewell, she prayed she could keep her promises.

Chapter 2

Not far into the journey, Kenneth discovered that he enjoyed the sensation of his arms loosely enveloping the serf maiden. Her body was rigid, as though she was afraid if she moved, Dazzle would throw them both. As a serf, she would naturally be unaccustomed to riding upon any steed, let alone a beast of such quality and experience as Dazzle.

Though as a serf, she was far below him in station, Kenneth sought not to take advantage of her. He wouldn't be so bold as to hold her more closely than necessary for her safety. Since he could only see the back of her head, he had to content himself by forming a portrait of Fayre in his mind. Long, reddish blond hair, unencumbered by hats and jewels, was appealing in its free style. No woman he knew, whether maid or titled, would think of letting her hair catch a breeze. Perhaps that is why when wisps flew away from Fayre's face, they framed it in such a way as to make her seem fresh. And fresh she was. He could tell by her countenance, her innocent and questioning looks, that she was not yet cynical, not yet acquainted with the ways of the world. Perhaps such a young spirit wasn't meant to become as hard as some of the women of his acquaintance. He let out a breath. Was he wrong to expose the virgin to the wiles of the king's courtiers?

Yes. Yes he was.

But what of the roses? Without Fayre, there was no hope that he could ever impress the king or his courtiers with such brilliant orange blooms.

I shall just keep her away from King David's castle, that is all. I will keep her confined to Kennerith. That will be easy enough to do.

He nodded once. Even as he made his resolution, he drew a second internal portrait of Fayre. This time she was dressed in the ornate clothing of a member of the court. He pictured her in blue. No, not blue. Gold. Yes, cloth the color of gold would suit her and would reflect the light brown of her eyes. Her hair had disappeared under a conical shaped hat decorated with a crimson cloth that hung from its tip and was caught up again on the back side of the corded brim, then allowed to flow partially down her back so that it blended with the red girdle she wore in his imagination. And shoes. Fayre couldn't be permitted to run barefoot in the castle, as he had found her in the fields. She would wear wooden clogs or shoes tailored of kid leather. One pair of each would be in order.

A pang of guilt lurched through his belly. When he first glimpsed her that morning, Fayre had seemed happy enough amid the squalor that she called a life. Not that her surroundings were worse than any other serf's. If Kenneth could have provided grand houses for all of his people, he would have done so gladly. If only he weren't obligated to extract what little money the serfs had to finance this war.

"My laird." The knight with hair the color of ebony pulled up alongside them.

"Yes, Ulf," Kenneth answered and drew Dazzle to a halt. He heard Walter, the other knight, stop his horse not far behind them.

Ulf followed suit. "We are just upon another house that is delinquent in tax payment."

Kenneth knew the house of which Ulf spoke without even looking. Like Witta Shepherd, these serfs were poor, too poor to pay what the king wanted. No surprise that Ulf pointed out the hut. He always viewed the prospect of a conflict, even a joust with an unarmed serf, with more vigor than Kenneth liked.

"We might stop there upon our next journey, perhaps," Kenneth answered.

"But my laird, we didn't spare Witta Shepherd. Or his daughter." Ulf peered at Fayre in a bold manner. Kenneth controlled the urge to give him a lashing with his tongue. Most men of Kenneth's rank wouldn't care in the least how his vassal looked upon a serf maiden.

But he did.

"Ulf is right," Walter, his second knight, agreed.

"Right," Kenneth blurted. Walter's observation brought him back into the present, a present that was none too savory.

Kenneth let out a sigh that he knew all around him could hear. Of the two knights, Walter was the one who didn't let emotion rule the day. If passing the next house offended Walter's sense of fair play, then Kenneth had no choice but to stop. Especially since Fayre was privy to his actions and decisions.

"All right, then." Tiredness colored his voice. Not only was Kenneth in no mood to undertake a disagreeable task, but also he was eager to return home. The longer they journeyed, the more he noticed that Fayre leaned more heavily upon him.

Obviously, the long ride was taking its toll upon her body and spirit. But he couldn't ask her if she wanted to stop. If he did, his knights would never let him forget that he let a woman make his decisions for him. No, they would have to visit the cottage.

He pulled on the bridle. Obeying, Dazzle veered to the right. As they neared the house, a young woman exited the hut. Kenneth imagined she wasn't much older than Fayre, but her sunburned countenance and rough hands suggested her physical appearance had been hardened by work. She held an infant, and four children followed behind her. The smallest clutched at her drab wool clothing. Judging from the heights of the children, the woman had given birth annually over the past five years. A protruding belly suggested another new arrival was imminent. Despite her girth, she managed to drop a curtsy.

"Good day, Lass. And where is your husband?" Kenneth asked.

Her face clouded and she tilted her head toward the ground. "He is ill in bed, my laird."

"I am sorry. May he soon gain robust health. Shall we pray for him?"

Her eyes lit as she looked up at him. In her obvious gratitude, years seemed to melt from her face. "Would ye?"

Kenneth nodded. He bowed his head, along with the others, and made a brief petition to God.

"Thank ye, my laird," the woman said after the prayer's conclusion. She paused. "But ye dinna come here tae pray. You are here tae collect the taxes we owe."

"Aye. But I can return when your husband is better."

She shook her head. "But I ha'e the money. We sold a sheep

at market just this past week tae pay ye."

Her words caused him to feel a pain no less sharp than that of a piercing lance. Yet he had to do his duty to his king.

"May I approach?" she asked.

Kenneth nodded. Still holding the child, the expectant woman took a few steps toward the horse. The effort left her winded, her breathing audible. She extended her hand. When she opened her palm, he counted the coins owed by the master of the house. He extracted them from her sweaty palm and then secured them in his pocket. "Very good. Tell your husband he owes no more for now."

She nodded and curtsied. The woman's glance darted to Fayre. The light in her eyes bespoke curiosity, but she didn't ask questions.

Guilt caused a lump to form in Kenneth's throat. Would the whole kingdom believe he was apt to steal women away from those who didn't pay? Yet every time he felt regret about his decision, a feeling of gladness that she was with him soon washed it away. Kenneth had a nagging feeling that God planned for Fayre to come to the castle. Divine intervention or wishful thinking?

"Twenty farthings and a pretty lassie," Ulf declared two hours later into their journey, as twilight fell. "Not much to show for a day's ride."

Fayre shuddered as she felt Ulf's stare bore into her. Yet his boldness seemed the least of her problems. Her precious rose bushes, gathered earlier when they stopped by the garden next to her father's cottage, had made an arduous trip. How could they survive?

Against her will, her thoughts returned to the prospect of her own survival. How could she elude Ulf while she lived at the castle? And were the other men even worse? What about the laird? Was he hiding his true reasons for wanting her to come and live in his castle?

No. He was not that type of man.

Fayre had been touched by the laird's gesture to the woman whose husband lay ill in bed. The idea that such a great man would bother to pray for one so far below him in station was sobering to her. Perhaps the laird really was sincere in his love of God.

She wondered about the spiritual state of his vassals. They seemed so different from one another. One was eager to collect all he could from each house, while the other expressed no feeling one way or the other. Fayre resolved to pray for them both.

If stopping at the first cottage wasn't enough, Ulf had convinced the laird to make yet another stop. The last cottage they visited had been in even worse condition than the one she and her father shared. She couldn't imagine the laird and his knights could collect any coins from its inhabitants. When they could find no one at home or in the nearby fields, she had breathed an inward sigh of relief. The knight called Walter seemed reasonable enough, but Ulf was too quick to draw his lance. Fayre could only pray that she and her party would arrive safely at the castle, despite her fear and dread.

She had selected four of her best bushes in hopes of transplanting them in the laird's garden. Fayre had no idea that the journey to the castle would take so long. The break for a meal had taken up a good part of the day. Not that she minded; her stomach had been begging for food for a full hour before they finally stopped. Her belly was rewarded for its wait. Rather than a humble meal, the men had in their satchels delicacies she had never seen, let alone eaten. Breads and meats flavored with exotic spices and herbs she could never afford to buy. They tasted odd to her palate at first, but she quickly realized she enjoyed the pungent flavors. She hadn't expected Laird Kenneth to share his fruit tart, but when he offered her half, she didn't hesitate. Such sweetness! The expression on her face must have shown her delight, for as she let the pastry melt in her mouth, the knights let out bawdy laughs. She didn't mind that she appeared unwise to the world. Let them laugh. Truly, the lairds and ladies feasted upon delicacies fit for the Lord above.

Perhaps the scrumptious food was but little reward for their travels. After bouncing for hours on a rugged pathway that could hardly be called a road, Fayre's backside reminded her with an unrelenting ache that it would not soon forgive such abuse. Fayre had clung to Laird Kenneth as though her life depended upon it during most of the journey. When the horse's hooves hit ruts and stumbled over rocks, she thought she might be tossed to the ground. She had no intention of falling so the knights could laugh and make sport of her, even though that meant holding the laird more closely than she wanted. At least he didn't flinch at the touch of a mere serf.

A waterfall flowing out of the gray rocks caught her ears with its sound. Since her eyes had adjusted to the dark, she could still discern its beauty. She pointed. "Might we stop for a bit?" she asked the laird. "I would welcome a drink of water, and I would like tae water my rose bushes, if I might beg your indulgence."

"Nay. We all must wait for refreshment. Darkness is upon us, and we are close to the castle now," Laird Kenneth answered. "To stop now would merely be an unnecessary delay. I promise you may drink of all the water you like once we arrive at the castle in but a wee bit of time."

Fayre didn't argue. The thought of reaching the place she would be calling home, at least until she could coax new blooms from the bushes, was welcome. Her tired and sore body needed a bed no matter how uncomfortable or modest. Aye, she could sleep on a bare floor this night.

As the laird promised, she didn't have to wait long. With a grateful eye, Fayre caught sight of the castle she would be calling home until the roses blossomed. Modest though it was, her own little cottage, the one she had shared with Father since Mother's death only a few months past, seemed like a piece of paradise in comparison.

Kennerith Castle loomed immense. Stones the color of tan comprised the building. Fayre counted four towers, one on each corner. She imagined herself in one of the overlooks, her gaze drinking in the land that was her beloved Scotland. If Laird Kenneth would let her roam. She cast a brief gaze at his shoulders, obviously broad even though they were protected by armor. Someone as powerful as he could squelch her as easily as a horse tramples a cricket. She quivered, almost wishing she were anywhere else.

What was my poor mind thinking, tae promise the laird perfect roses? What if there is a drought or too much rain, or what if the bushes simply fail tae bloom? What fate will befall me then?

She stroked a wilted petal of the vivid orange flower she held, the one originally meant for her father to enjoy over a simple meal of bread and cheese. She remembered stopping by the garden long enough for the two knights to wrench her beautiful bushes from their place in the soil. Hard and rugged warriors, the men seemed not to notice how lovingly the soil had been plowed or how each plant had been pruned so the blossoms bloomed on them just so. If they had been more observant, they would have never tossed the tender plants carelessly into leather satchels meant for the provisions of war.

Now her roses would delight the ladies of the court. Titled ladies who would otherwise have no use for a mere shepherd's daughter. The beauty of the flowers she devotedly tended so that none could compare would be wasted on them. How she wished the flowers would still offer joy to her aged parent. But instead, they had become a mere tool to gain the laird newfound respect. She almost wished she could destroy each blossom, just to prevent Laird Kenneth's mercenary wishes from coming to fruition. But for the sake of her father, she kept her feelings in check.

After the brutal assault upon her roses, none of the men had spoken to Fayre. Even Laird Kenneth had remained silent as she rode with him on his horse, whose name, she had since learned, was Dazzle. She had observed the way Laird Kenneth said the name, his intonation lying lazily on the *z*s, but curtly enunciating the rest of the letters so his voice sounded like a whip slashing through the dusk.

The tired horses seemed to gain momentum as they drew closer to the castle. Perhaps they anticipated a warm bed of straw and plenty of oats to eat. The watchmen were obviously adept at their job. A massive wooden drawbridge descended so the travelers could cross safely over the murky moat. Fayre surmised the water was deep and wide enough to house the fabled

Loch Ness monster, reputed to live in the loch beyond the Grampian Mountains that rose up behind the castle. She had often fantasized about Nessie, first seen centuries ago. To have Nessie herself protecting the castle! Ah, but no doubt Laird Kenneth had plenty of vicious sea creatures lying in wait should an enemy fall into the water.

They crossed over the bridge and into a large courtyard, where three stable boys awaited to tend to the horses.

"Welcome to Kennerith Castle," Laird Kenneth said as he dismounted. He extended his arms to help her dismount as well. "I promised you water to drink. Are you hungry as well?"

Too apprehensive until that moment to think about her growling stomach, Fayre suddenly realized she could use a bite to eat even though the delicacies she had enjoyed at dinner had tamed her appetite throughout most of the journey. So as not to seem eager, she merely nodded.

"Come, then." Though he stood beside her, Laird Kenneth loomed over her, reminding her once again of his might. She wondered if this were an intentional ploy until he smiled. Under other circumstances, she might have thought him handsome. But not now.

"Might I first see how my roses fared? The journey was no doubt as difficult for them as for us."

The smile didn't leave his face. "Indeed." With a silent nod, Laird Kenneth commanded his vassals to retrieve the four plants from their satchels. The first had shed the petals from each blossom, with the exception of one or two on the stray bloom. Fayre felt her body tense as the remaining plants were taken from the bags. Each had suffered the same fate. Anxiously she touched their roots. They had become parched over the course of the day. She was unable to conceal her distress.

"Ah, my lass. Do not despair," she heard Laird Kenneth console her. "Surely someone with your skill can revive the plants, aye?"

Fayre didn't answer. She had made too many promises already.

Thankfully, the squire chose that moment to distract his master. "Laird Kenneth," he said as he bowed. "I pray your journey was a success." Lifting his head, the squire sent an admiring glance in Fayre's direction. "I can see my prayers were answered."

Kenneth cut his glance her way and then answered, "Would you have Fayre shown to the most agreeable guest bedchamber in the castle? She will remain with us for some time." Laird Kenneth looked at Fayre. "At least until the roses bloom."

"Aye, me laird." He handed Laird Kenneth a letter. Burned into the sealing wax was the outline of a coat of arms. Was it the herald of the MacMurray clan?

"From Lady Letha, no doubt," Ulf taunted Laird Kenneth.

The look that crossed Laird Kenneth's golden face was one of satisfaction. Could Lady Letha be the one whose favor Laird Kenneth sought?

Chapter 3

If Lady Letha was the one he wished to impress, Laird Kenneth showed no indication of his intent on his face. Not a muscle moved.

At the mention of Lady Letha, a strange feeling hit the pit of Fayre's belly. She didn't remember feeling that way before. She wasn't sure she liked whatever it was.

For an instant, Fayre wondered what Lady Letha looked like. Surely if she had attracted Laird Kenneth's attention, she was fine and lovely indeed. Would her roses please Lady Letha? And if they did not? She didn't want to think about that possibility.

At that moment, Fayre realized the urgency of her situation. Under normal circumstances, she would never have uprooted her flowers, but the laird had no patience to wait for new bushes to grow from slips. If she were to be honest with herself, Fayre would have to admit that she had no patience for such a wait, either. Fayre wanted nothing more than to return home. The more quickly she could grow beautiful roses for the laird, the more hastily she could return to the life she knew. In the meantime, her father would have to make himself content remembering her by the two bushes, planted beside the small window of the cottage, that she had left to bloom in her absence.

"What is the matter, Fayre?" Laird Kenneth asked.

She swallowed. He must have seen the distressed look upon her face. "The roots. They are a wee bit dry." She wasn't given to understatement, so her conscience pricked her. Fayre sent up a silent prayer for forgiveness.

The laird stepped beside her and investigated the plants for himself. "Are all of them this dry?" He touched the roots with his fingertips.

"Aye." She tried to keep her countenance from revealing the depth of her distress. She looked into his silver eyes. "I maun plant them right away. Please, show me the spot in the garden where they might grow."

Laird Kenneth peered west, in the direction where she supposed the flower garden was planted. He shrugged. "That is for the gardener to decide." He returned his attention to her face. "You and Norman can meet tomorrow morning and make your plans then."

"Nay, my laird." Then, realizing she was out of order, Fayre gave a curtsy so low that she feared she might tumble. "I beg yer greatest indulgence, my laird, but my task canna wait. I maun plant the roses tonight, even in the dark."

Otherwise, they will surely die. Then Father will be thrown in the dungeon, where he will surely die. What will I do then?

She looked up in time to see Laird Kenneth's eyebrows shoot up. "Indeed," he said, "I promised that you would have water for the roses as soon as we arrived here. I shall keep my word." He nodded toward the squire.

"Yes, my laird," he responded. "I shall summon Norman right away."

Relieved, Fayre stood upright.

"Perhaps you shall have some fortification as you wait," the laird suggested.

"I offer tae ye my greatest gratitude, my laird." Fayre forced her sense to overrule the rumblings of her belly. "But I canna. I maun plant these bushes as soon as I can."

"Then at least allow me to accompany you to the garden."

The laird's generosity surprised her, but she accepted his offer willingly. Fayre had never ventured more than three miles from her own little cottage. She couldn't remember a night she didn't sleep in her own bed. Humble though it was, her home offered comfort in its familiarity and warmth in its love. Fayre did not yet know whom, if anyone, she could trust in her new surroundings. Of those she had met, Laird Kenneth had shown himself the most compassionate thus far. She was willing to stay near to him as long as he was amenable.

Laird Kenneth took a lantern from one of the servants and led Fayre to the garden. As she expected, it was located in the courtyard behind the kitchen. Yet she didn't expect the garden to be so grand.

He chuckled.

"What do ye find so amusing?" she asked.

"Your eyes," he answered. "They are so wide they nearly constitute your entire countenance."

She bowed her head in shyness. "I–I just have never seen such, such. . .glory."

"Indeed?" He chuckled, then his face turned thoughtful as he surveyed his surroundings. His eyes took on a light that suggested he was seeing his garden for the first time, although Fayre knew full well that couldn't be. "I suppose you have not." He turned a kind gaze toward her. "This bailey garden is rather modest, in actuality. This is nothing in comparison to the king's."

Fayre gasped in wonder. "Then he maun have many gardeners."

"Aye. Many more than I."

"Will I be expected tae help tend the rest of the garden?"

"Nay. Norman is quite proud of his work. Do not be surprised if he resists your encroachment. I must caution you. He has worked here, alone, for many years. Those who help him are all men, so he is unaccustomed to working alongside women. Do not expect to be welcomed." He sent her a smile of assurance. "Do not fear. He is harmless enough."

Fayre nodded. She was all too aware that her position as a serf woman caused many men to look upon her as little more than a beast. If a man was rough and uncouth, he might not think twice about taking advantage of her tenuous standing. Her spirit calmed as she determined not to call attention to herself. "I shall try not tae be the source of any trouble."

To her amazement, Laird Kenneth took her chin in his thumb and forefinger and lifted her face so that her gaze met his. The gentleness in his touch astounded and delighted her. "How can one such as yourself instigate any trouble? Nay, such a prospect would be impossible."

She let out a little gasp, then an uncertain laugh escaped her lips. For the first time, she gained a glimmer of understanding as to what her friends meant when they tried to tell her about marriage.

Marriage? What am I thinking? Never.

No laird would marry her. No, she was here to coax life into the rose bushes so that the laird could find favor with the king.

Or with a lady. Or perhaps both. The thought left her unhappy.

"Ah, here comes Norman now." The laird took his fingers away from her chin, leaving Fayre feeling even more unhappiness than before. With the other hand, he lifted his lantern to greet a wizened old man whom Fayre surmised was the gardener.

If the man noticed the laird's quick motion, he made no indication. He bowed.

"My laird. Why summon me tae the garden after fall of night?"

"I know this is an unusual request, but the matter is of the utmost urgency." The laird held the rose bushes up for the gardener to inspect. "You see, these must be planted with the greatest of haste."

Norman rubbed his chin, which was decorated with dark but scraggly hairs. "Fine roses, they are. Such color!" He leaned closer to study the plants. After a moment, he shook his head. "They're dry, they are. Even though I'll be fetchin' water right away, they will never survive."

Fayre's intake of breath was louder this time. She clamped her hand over her mouth. "Please. Do not say that."

Norman took in her plain brown frock and decided he could address her without fear of reprimand. "And who might ye be?"

"She is Fayre. She is here to grow these roses upon my orders. You are to treat her with the utmost respect and see to it that the rest of the servants do the same."

"Aye, my laird." Norman touched one of the fading blooms. "I can see why you desire such a flower. I have never seen such a color."

"Nor have I until today," Laird Kenneth agreed. "You must

give Fayre the best spot in the garden to assure that at least one of these bushes survives."

"But—"

"I care not how long the planting takes or even if you must uproot other bushes to make room for these. You are to assist Fayre in any way possible."

"Aye, my laird." His obedient words denied his sour expression. Fayre almost felt sorry for him.

"Likewise, I will assist ye in any way I can," Fayre told him.

"Humph." He twisted his mouth into a doubting line. "Come on with you. I think I know a good spot ye can have. I had planned the row for some of my best roses, but I can see that is not to be."

"Thank ye."

"Don't bother to thank me. Any favor ye get from me, ye owe tae my master."

As she helped Norman dig, Fayre wished he could find a way to be congenial. Laird Kenneth was right; the gardener was a wee bit grumpy. She decided that her best course of action was to ignore him. For that matter, perhaps her best course of action would be to make herself as invisible as possible. The less trouble she caused, the more likely she would survive her stay at the castle.

Heavenly Father, please grant my roses life so that my father and I might also live.

An image of the expectant woman whose husband lay sick in bed came to mind. She realized how self-centered her prayers had become ever since she had been taken upon Laird Kenneth's horse that day.

Lord, heal the ones who are sick. Protect those in this house, so that they might be spared from any sickness. Especially the plague.

She shuddered at the thought of anyone close to her being stricken with such a deadly disease that had already taken so many lives.

"Cold?" Norman asked.

"Cold?" She snapped back into the present. "Nay. I am nae cold."

"Then why do ye shiver?"

"Just praying."

"I never shiver when I pray." Norman shook his head as he tamped dirt around the roots of one of the bushes. "Who can understand a woman?"

Fayre thought better than to challenge Norman. As long as she was expected to work with him, she saw no need in angering him. He was already grumpy enough. Yet underneath his gruff exterior, she could see his love for the garden. Perhaps he was a gentle soul in his way.

As soon as the roses were planted and Norman had bid her an unenthusiastic good night, Fayre exhaled, letting out pent-up emotions of uncertainty, fear, and exhaustion. She didn't care whether her quarters were as magnificent as the laird's or a stall shared with Dazzle. All she wanted was to lay her weary body in a horizontal position and fall into a deep slumber.

Eager to reach this goal, she ambled to the back door and entered the palace through the kitchen. Not even the smell of the night's dinner, long since served but its delicious aromas still filling the air, enticed her to ask for sustenance. She hadn't been at the castle long enough to know the cook from the chamber maid, so she addressed the first person she eyed, a portly woman who looked as tired as Fayre felt.

"May I be shown tae my quarters?"

The woman folded her arms, cocked her head, and inspected Fayre. "So, would ye be the lassie that my laird brought home with him?"

"Aye."

Her gray eyebrows rose so high that new wrinkles were temporarily added to her forehead. "I can see why."

Fayre felt color rise to her cheeks as she squirmed.

"He'll be seein' ye now."

"Seein' me?"

The woman nodded toward a younger version of herself who was entering the kitchen, apparently having finished some task unknown to Fayre. "She's here."

"Good." The servant motioned for Fayre to follow her.

Fayre didn't bother to look at her clothing. She knew the dust needed to be shaken from it and that her face was surely smudged with dirt. She rubbed her fingers together in a vain attempt to whisk away a few particles of soil. "But I am in no condition tae enter a fine room, much less tae see the laird. Might I take a moment tae refresh myself? Can you nae show me tae my quarters first?"

The maid shook her head. "He wants tae see ye right away. Follow me."

The kitchen door led to a narrow and dark passage. After they passed through, the servant opened a door that led into a large hallway. Fayre stared upward at the arched ceiling that loomed high above her. The passageway was so wide that she and four other women could have stretched out their arms and touched fingertips and still not made contact with the opposite walls.

"I have ne'er seen such," Fayre noted.

"It don't seem so wonderful when ye're the one that's got tae scrub the floors and do the dustin'," the maid observed.

Fayre peered at the walls. "No, I suppose it wouldn't."

The maid paused in front of a massive wooden door. "Here we are. The laird awaits."

Fayre swallowed. Even though she had been with him all day, the prospect of seeing him again left her anxious. The maid's expression offered neither sympathy nor compassion as she announced Fayre to the laird.

Fayre could see she had no choice. She had to face him.

What did he want?

The laird was standing when she entered, a gesture she didn't expect from one of such elevated rank. She marveled at how she had seen him treat others with kindness, even serfs. But then, Laird Kenneth was well regarded in the land. She had heard talk of his fine countenance and fine form. Light hair was exposed, forming longish waves that made him appear young and carefree. Aye, and his silver eyes! She watched them reflect the nearby flames. The flickering light made his eyes glisten even more than they had in the sunshine earlier that day. Softened features suggested his mood was relaxed. Perhaps he was as tired as she. What would it be like to be a lady, to sit by the fire with Laird Kenneth after a long day and to touch his cheek, comforting him?

Is my mind unsound tae think such a thing?

She shook the thought from her head and curtsied.

The wooden chairs in front of the fire looked appealing, but he didn't offer her a seat. Fayre hoped that meant the visit would be brief. A wooden table by one of the chairs held a mug along with a plate that was empty save a chicken bone.

"I trust all is well and that Norman showed you a good and proper place for your roses?"

"Aye, my laird."

"And you have had your sustenance?"

"Nay, my laird."

"What? No sustenance?" The edge of anger that entered his voice unawares left her taken aback. This was a man who could be brought to ire in an instant. Fayre realized that if the laird were to do battle, he was sure to emerge victorious.

"Food was offered, my laird. I declined."

"Do you mean to say that nothing in the kitchen tempted you to eat? Surely my cooks could prepare something to your liking."

"I am quite certain any food in yer home is much finer than anything tae which I am accustomed. The midday meal was evidence of that. I am too tired tae eat at present, if I may be permitted tae say so. I am sure I shall regain my appetite tomorrow."

"I know you must be exhausted from such a day. I would not have summoned you here if it were not important. I surmise your expectations are to be treated as a servant while you are here."

"I–I dinna ken what my expectations are, Sir."

He chuckled. "I suppose not. So much has happened today. I want you to know that as long as you remain here, you will be treated as a special guest."

Fayre felt her mouth drop open. A guest!

"Tomorrow morning the seamstress shall set upon sewing you a decent frock."

Fayre looked down upon her garment. The brown wool was

plain, but no plainer than any other serf's. And it was clean. Well, as clean as it could be considering she had been on a horse all day. She swiped at the loose soil that had penetrated the cloth on the two spots where she had knelt in the garden to plant her roses.

"There is no need for that," Laird Kenneth interrupted.

She stopped. Perhaps he didn't want her to dirty the floor. For the first time, she noticed the stones were covered by a runner woven in a fine botanical pattern of threads in hues of red, purple, and gold, colors that could only be afforded by the rich. She looked up long enough to apologize. "Forgive me, my laird." She returned her stare to the floor and added, "But I am nae deserving of such honor."

"That is for me to decide." His voice conveyed a request rather than a command. "Brona—that is the seamstress—shall meet you in your chamber tomorrow morning."

When Fayre awoke the next day in a strange bed, her stomach felt as though it were leaping into her throat. Where was she?

Just as quickly, she exhaled and placed her right hand at the base of her throat. "Kennerith Castle."

She studied the room. In the light of day it proved larger than the entire hut she shared with her father. Tapestries depicting festivals and celebrations of lairds and ladies adorned the walls. And the fine fabric under which she lay! She had never dared try to barter with merchants to purchase soft material dyed in rich hues. Fayre imagined them throwing their heads back and laughing with unbridled mirth at the thought that someone as inconsequential as she would dare think she could own such luxury. The fine things in life were reserved for royalty and gentry. Still, she wished she were back in her humble dwelling all the same.

She heard a knock on the door. Before she could answer, a servant she had never seen entered. Somehow the servant managed to balance a tray loaded with food while opening the door at once. Fayre leapt out of bed and rushed to assist her.

"There's no need tae help me. I'm here to serve ye. At least, that's what I ha'e been told." She surveyed Fayre with beady eyes and sniffed through her hooked nose as though she smelled an odor. She set the tray on the small, oval-shaped table beside the bed. "I'm Murdag, your ladies' maid."

A ladies' maid! Fayre had never fantasized that she should enjoy the services of a ladies' maid—ever. Judging from the way Murdag frowned as she scrutinized her, the servant was none too happy with her new mistress.

Not knowing what else to do, Fayre resolved to be friendly. She caressed the sleeve of her lightweight night shift. "So ye are the one who left this for me?"

She nodded.

"Thank ye." Fayre smiled.

Murdag turned away and regarded Fayre's brown clothing. The garment was neatly folded and left on the bed. "Ye won't be putting that thing back on, are ye?"

"I most certainly am." Fayre's voice reflected her indignation. "My duty here is tae work in the garden. I am aware that Laird Kenneth will be sending the seamstress this morning, but I canna imagine that I would tend tae my roses wearing a fine frock." When Murdag didn't answer Fayre's logic, she continued. "And I know Brona will nae possibly sew a garment in a matter of minutes. I maun wear something while she works on my new clothing."

"As ye wish. Is there anything else, or may I leave you tae your breakfast?"

"Ye may go. Thank you." The words felt and sounded strange falling from her own lips, unaccustomed as she was to giving anyone permission to do anything.

Fayre shivered as she watched Murdag exit. She wasn't sure which of them was the more unfortunate: Murdag, for being forced to serve a woman below her own station, or herself, for being looked down upon by her maid.

Despite her hunger, Fayre didn't want to greet Brona in her nightclothes. She donned the simple frock that shouted her lack of position. As she slipped the rough woolen garment over her shoulders, she felt defiant. Why should she be ashamed of who she was? God had known her since she was formed in her mother's womb. He had put her exactly where He wanted her to be, for His own purpose.

The door creaked.

Fayre controlled the urge to display her ill mood.

Why didn't the seamstress knock?

She looked in the direction of her visitor and gasped.

"Sir Ulf? What are you doing here?"

Chapter 4

Ulf ran his tongue over his lips and leered. Even though he wasn't close enough to touch her, Fayre stepped away from his outstretched arms.

"What is the matter, my pretty lassie? You should be grateful that a vassal, especially one as close to the laird as I, would even look at you twice."

"If ye are of such importance, would you nae be able tae find many willing ladies tae do yer bidding?"

"Aye, I can have my way with any lady in the king's court." Ulf ran his fingers through a few strands of his curly hair. "But you! You are exceptionally fine, exceptionally fair. Fair like the roses you grow." He took in an exaggerated whiff with such force that his nostrils folded almost shut. "You are honest, of the earth. The smell of God's soil clings to you, to your hair, tae your frock."

He regarded her brown clothing, and then let his gaze travel to her bare feet. "Aye, you are different from the fine ladies I am accustomed to. I am expected to woo them with poetry and words o' love." He opened his mouth and patted it three times, feigning a yawn. "But with you, I need not display pretense."

The expression on his face as he watched Fayre reminded her of how a lion must look when surveying his dinner.

Fayre shook her head and stepped back. Her bare heel made contact with the foot of the bed. Her heart made her aware of its presence by its rapid beating. Since she had nowhere to go, she stood in place, trembling.

Father in heaven, protect me!

Ulf swiped his arm toward her waist. She stepped aside, evading him.

Please, Father, hear my prayer!

"So you want to put up a fight, eh?" The glint in his eyes grew more evident. "I like a lass with spirit!" His chortle made her squirm.

Her answer was to make a run for the door. To Fayre's dismay, her foot caught on the end of the bed covering. She tripped. Although she managed to keep upright, she stumbled long enough for Ulf to catch her in his arms. Red lips puckered and made their way toward hers.

Nay! My first kiss canna be like this!

She screamed, her voice high-pitched with urgency.

Obviously surprised by her resistance, Ulf jerked his head back. "What are you making such a fuss for, Lass? 'Tis only a kiss." An evil smile covered his face as Ulf brought his lips closer to hers.

Fayre moved her head away from his, but caught up in his grasp as she was, she knew resistance was in vain.

A welcome sound of footsteps was followed by the door creaking open.

Ulf stopped in midmotion, cursing under his breath.

"What is the meaning of this?" Murdag's face held an

expression of curiosity and disbelief.

" 'Tis none of your affair," Ulf answered. Still, he let Fayre go and stepped back.

Murdag's beady eyes shifted so that her gaze bored into Fayre. "Is he here by your leave?"

"Nay," she whimpered.

"She lies!" Ulf protested.

Murdag's eyelids sharpened into narrow slits. She said nothing for a moment, then nodded. "Nay, I believe she speaks the truth, Sir."

"How dare you accept the word of a mere serf over the declaration of a knight! If I werena a gentleman and you were a man rather than a maid, Murdag, I would be forced to draw my sword in my defense."

"I beg pardon, Sir Ulf." She curtsied and withdrew.

Nay! Now I ha'e no chance at all. Fayre's uncontrolled trembling resumed.

"Where were we?" Lust returned to Ulf's eyes.

Fayre watched the open door, hoping against hope that Murdag would return.

Ulf's gaze followed hers. "Aye. 'Twould be a good idea to shut the door, would it not? We cannot have everyone in the castle knowing our secret."

Fayre glanced around the room. Where could she run? Although the room was large, it had no hiding places. The only door was the one Ulf was shutting at this moment. Could she jump out of the nearest window? No. Shaped like keyholes, they were too narrow. And even if she could squeeze through one, surely the jump to the ground would kill her. Perhaps she could pick up an object and throw it upon his head? Nay. That would be too rash. Besides, Murdag had already seen her with Ulf. Her quick exit indicated she accepted Ulf's story that Fayre had invited him to be in her bedchamber. If she injured Ulf, he would have her thrown out of the castle, and her father was sure to go to prison.

"Nay!" she shrieked, more at the thought than at her captor.

"Silence!" Ulf cautioned.

At that moment, she heard the door fly open with such force that it hit the opposing wall. Fayre gasped when she realized that Laird Kenneth stood in the entryway.

"Ulf?" Laird Kenneth planted his feet on the floor and stood erect.

Ulf blanched, then bowed. "Aye, my laird?"

"So it is as Murdag said." Laird Kenneth lifted his chin and surveyed his vassal. Tightened lips suggested disapproval. "What do you have to say for yourself?"

"She wanted me to be here."

Wanted him to be there? How could Sir Ulf, a knight who was sworn to valor, bear false witness in such a blatant manner? The words flew off his lips as though he lied every day. She wouldn't have believed it possible had she not heard with her own ears.

"Nay!" Fayre objected. "He entered my bedchamber without my permission or my desire."

"The wench lies," Ulf said.

"Does she?" Laird Kenneth asked. "Then why is her body shaking?"

"In fear of your ire, no doubt," Ulf retorted. "She knows you can never believe the word of a serf over your own devoted vassal."

"It is my hope that you would not lie, but I fear you disappoint me."

"Why would I lie about a mere serf?" Ulf looked at Fayre as though she were a dead rat, before returning his attention to the laird. "And even if I did, what does it matter? She is but property."

Fear gripped Fayre's torso. Ulf was right. According to the law, she was nothing more than the laird's possession, to do with as he pleased. In spite of the fact that the laird had ordered the seamstress to sew her a new frock, in spite of the fact that she was ensconced in a guest chamber, she was his servant. The word of a chattel would never override the declaration of a knight.

Fayre braced herself to be punished. What would the laird decree? Fifty lashes? Banishment to the servants' quarters, where she was already resented? Or would she be spending her stay in the dungeon, no doubt among rats that would fight her for a piece of molded bread and unclean water—the fate she had tried to spare her father? She struggled not to shake.

"I shall not have any untoward behavior toward a woman who is in my care, regardless of her station." Laird Kenneth paused, studying them both. Finally, the laird looked his vassal in the eye and proclaimed, "Ulf, you may return to your home to await my summons."

Fayre's heart beat faster, but this time with victory rather than anguish. The laird believed her over his own knight!

Ulf's mouth dropped open in obvious shock and upset. "But my laird—"

"You heard what I said." The laird's tone showed that he would brook no argument. "I am the laird of this manor. You shall obey me."

"Very well." Ulf threw a hate-filled look her way, then bowed to Laird Kenneth and exited.

Ulf was gone! Fayre clutched her hands to her chest in relief. As soon as she realized she was safe once again, curiosity overcame her. "What will happen tae him now?"

The laird's eyebrows shot up and he folded his arms. "Do you really care?"

She wasn't sure how to answer. "I–I don't wish tae be the cause of hardship for anyone."

Laird Kenneth's eyes widened and he shook his head slowly. "How can you be so forgiving?" He paused. "Unless you really did wish his presence—"

"Nay, my laird. Ne'er." Fayre felt her face flush at the thought that she would ask a knight into her bedchamber. At the thought of what might have happened, unwelcome tears streamed down her cheeks.

"How scared you must have been." The laird's eyes were alight with compassion. He closed the gap between them and took her in his arms.

Nay! Not him, too!

She looked into his silver eyes, thinking she might protest. Anything she could say would be feeble since she was in his complete control. But when she studied his face, she saw no leer, no untoward lust, no puckering of the lips—just kindness. Truly he sought to comfort her, not to take advantage. At that moment, she realized she liked the feeling of his arms around her. Never had she felt more protected, more safe.

How can that be? I was once afraid of Laird Kenneth. Now he is my redeemer?

Gently she broke the embrace. "I praise my heavenly Father

that ye entered when ye did."

"Only because Murdag told me."

"I praise God that she believed me."

"How could she not? Honesty exudes from you."

The compliment would have pleased Fayre any other time, but Laird Kenneth's words were too close to Ulf's earlier observation to give her solace.

"I only regret," he said, "that my vassal is not as chaste as you are. And he is not likely to be as forgiving either."

Fayre shivered.

"I assure you, he will not be permitted near you again as long as you remain here." A light of kindness entered his eyes. "You are righteous to forgive him."

"The Lord said for us tae forgive offenses, no matter how often they occur."

"You know much," the laird said. "You must listen to the priest rather than daydreaming during worship as many young girls do."

"My favorite uncle was a cleric. He taught me at his knee." Fayre felt her eyes mist. "He is gone now. Gone tae a better place, where the Lord has built many mansions." She bowed her head. "Perhaps even one for Sir Ulf."

The laird thought for a moment. "He seems to repent not. Remember, we are not required to forgive unless we are asked." The laird's voice was soft.

"Nay, but I choose tae forgive him nonetheless."

Laird Kenneth shook his head. "You are a stronger person than many who reside in the king's court."

A knock on the door interrupted them. A young woman stood in the entryway and curtsied.

"Brona," Laird Kenneth said. "Good. I want you to begin on Fayre's frock immediately. Her garment should be fine but sturdy enough for every day."

"Aye, my laird. In what fabric?" Brona inquired. "Is the gold cloth we already have suitable for your pleasure, my laird?"

"More than suitable. Perfect." With his broad smile, Fayre had never seen him look so happy. She realized how handsome he appeared when his expression was touched by glee. "But we have no fabric for the second garment, I am sure."

"Second garment?" Brona gasped.

"Of course. What colors do you prefer, Fayre?"

Fayre didn't know how to answer. In the past, her only decision regarding the color of the wool she spun herself had been whether to dye it with vegetable juices or to leave it in its natural state. "I–I canna imagine, my laird."

His mouth twisted into a sympathetic line. "Nay. Nay, I suppose not. Very well, then. You and I shall travel to the marketplace on the morrow."

Fayre was struck speechless. Travel to the marketplace with the laird? She couldn't imagine such a privilege!

"Brona," he was saying, "discuss with Fayre what type of frocks she would prefer and determine how much fabric I should purchase." The laird turned his attention back to Fayre. "Once you begin to dress in a more suitable manner, you shall be treated in a more suitable way. With respect. The type of respect a godly woman merits."

Respect? Could he think of her as more than mere property? His words seemed to indicate that he did.

"Brona," he said, "consider what you will need for three sets of clothing."

"Three!" The women exclaimed in unison.

For an instant, Fayre thought she might faint with joy. Never in her wildest fantasy did she think she would ever own one fine garment. But three? Had she heard the laird correctly?

"Aye," said Laird Kenneth. "Two shall be for everyday and one for the king's ball."

Fayre gasped. "The king's ball?"

He nodded. "The event will be held two weeks from today. You, Fayre Rose—and your wonderful blooms—shall be present."

Later that day, Kenneth felt a pang of guilt as he left the castle with his falcon to meet his hunting party. Because of his actions, a serf maiden had been whisked away from the only home she had ever known and taken to an imposing castle that must have seemed strange and forbidding. His decision, made in a fit of tough compassion, had placed her in jeopardy from one of his vassals.

Father, forgive me!

Fayre was the only woman ever to inspire him to experience such an extraordinary number of emotions in such a short time. Certainly, her outward beauty showed through her mean garment. Yet he didn't fully see her inner spirit until she forgave Ulf so quickly after he displayed himself to be a beast. Had his vassal, a man he had trusted for years, always treated women as such? Or was Fayre subjected to his disdain just because of her low status?

Kenneth knew that his own father would chastise him if he had been present. A man given more to the material world than the spiritual one, his father would have found Ulf's pursuit of

Fayre a source of amusement. What was a pretty serf if not a diversion?

The idea of following in his deceased father's footsteps repulsed Kenneth. He could not look at any woman and think she was something to be trifled with. The Lord Jesus Christ had made plain in His teachings that women were valuable in His Father's sight. Kenneth couldn't bring himself to treat any woman as chattel, no matter what the laws of the land said he could do.

Especially not Fayre. Fair as the roses she grew, she had caught more than his fancy. In the briefest of times, she had captured his heart.

The following day, Fayre ventured out into the garden to check on her roses. Yesterday she wished they would live to assure her father's survival. Today she wanted them to bloom into mature beauty to please her laird.

Her laird. He had rescued her, had believed her word over a trusted vassal. Her word! She never thought she would be of any value to a laird, but Laird Kenneth treated her as a prize. And to think, he wanted her to enjoy respect, so much that he was willing to buy her pieces of fabric at the marketplace. The thought was so lovely that it pained her to imagine it, to dream of such privilege.

She touched a green leaf of a surviving rose bush with a gentleness she reserved for her flowers. Of the four that had made the arduous journey, only one looked as though it had any hope of survival. Yet that one remaining plant looked hardy. Hard green balls on the tips of several branches promised flowers for the future.

Father in heaven, please allow my flowers tae bloom and for Laird Kenneth tae be pleased.

"Prayin' won't get ye anywheres with the flowers," Norman's sharp voice interrupted. "Only good soil and fair weather will get you good blooms."

She opened her eyes. "Prayer always helps, even if the Lord dinna see fit tae answer as we might wish."

"If He dinna answer as we like, then I dinna see how it helps much. That's how I see it."

"I am certain that God will change your mind one day. At least, I hope He will."

Norman shrugged. "I doubt that. Nae with this awful plague. It has struck the castle now. All of us are doomed."

"The plague? Nay, please say ye speak in jest." Fayre clutched her throat in shock and despair.

"I would never speak in jest aboot such a thing."

Fayre could tell from his monotone that he spoke the truth. She ran down a mental list of those she knew in the castle. The list was short. Since the laird had decided for reasons unknown to her to treat her as a guest, Fayre wasn't permitted to socialize with the servants. Yet Ulf and Walter, the vassals who had been with the laird the day he brought her here, told all they knew of her lowly status. As a result, the laird's friends treated her with civility, but no warmth. Her only real companion was her maid, Murdag. Even she had been unsympathetic to Fayre until the incident with Ulf. Contemplating what could have occurred was still enough to make her shudder. "Then who among us is sick? The dairy maid? Or one of the squires?"

"Nay. Much worse." He leaned toward her and whispered. " 'Tis the laird himself."

Her stomach lurched in distress. She took in an audible breath. "The laird himself?"

"Aye. He was feeling ill last night. This morning, he dinna rise from his bed." Norman shook his head. " 'Tis a shame. No one will go near him. Nae e'en his most devoted servants."

"They mustn't be devoted enough if they refuse tae help him in his time of need." Fayre remembered a time, not so long ago, when the laird had come to her rescue.

"The servants love him very much," Norman argued. "But tae go near him the noo is t' write one's ain death sentence."

Fayre imagined the laird, so strong, so bold, now lying helpless against a dreaded disease. "I maun see him!"

"See him?" Norman laid his hand on her shoulder. "Dinna be more foolish than the court jester, Lass. If ye go near tae him, ye are sure to die."

"Perhaps I shan't die."

"Men of God have died while nursing plague victims. What makes ye believe ye are stronger than they?"

"I make no such claim. But if I die, so be it. I will go and see tae him now."

Chapter 5

"Ye canna go in the laird's bedchamber," Murdag cautioned Fayre. "Not e'en his most loyal servants dare enter except tae get food tae him with the greatest of haste."

"They hurry in and out without a word? Does he nae deserve better?"

"He has been the image o' kindness tae me," Murdag admitted. "No finer example save the Lord Jesus Himself, I expect."

"Aye. Ye have witnessed his compassion toward me as well," Fayre said.

"I know. And I ken ye want tae repay him," Murdag said. "But the laird is already sick, and ye arenna. Maun ye make a deliberate effort t' place yourself in danger, thereby further endangering everyone else in the castle? Did I save ye from Sir Ulf only tae have ye die of the plague?"

Fayre looked down at the hem of the fabric that concealed her legs. She had already expressed her gratitude to Murdag, and she could understand the maid's distress. Yet she had to listen to her own heart. "Ha'e ye so little faith?" Fayre asked.

"Faith I ha'e, but certainly no more than men of God. Even some of them ha'e died while ministering tae victims in their flocks."

Fayre swallowed when she remembered how one of the priests in her parish had contracted the disease after praying over dying plague victims. "So no one is ministering tae the laird?"

"Our priest prayed o'er him this morning," Murdag said, "I imagine for the last time."

Fayre wondered whether Murdag meant that the laird had so little time left or if the priest feared returning to the bed-chamber, or both. She decided that either thought was too dreadful for words and held back her urge to inquire.

She herself had been in prayer since Norman first told her about the laird's illness. Fayre was well acquainted with the power of prayer. God had chosen thus far to answer her puny petitions with mercy. Her father remained in their hut rather than being thrown into prison. Her best rose bush had survived uprooting, a long journey, and transplanting. Those who lived in Kennerith Castle had been kind. Even the one person who meant her harm had been thwarted. How could Fayre not follow Scripture's admonition to pray without ceasing?

She had no intention of giving up now. But if a priest was not immune to death from this gruesome sickness, why should she be? The heavenly Father did not promise anyone tomorrow. How long would His mercy endure?

Questions, questions. Her priest said that the faithful should not ask questions but should trust in the Almighty. Obediently, she shook the questions out of her mind long enough to answer Murdag. "The laird, for reasons unknown, has treated me far better than I could have expected for someone in my lowly station."

"He is kind tae everyone, but I think he has taken a special liking tae ye," Murdag said.

Unaccustomed to flattery from anyone except perhaps her own father, Fayre looked at her lap to keep from answering.

"Word is all over the castle aboot how the laird defended ye," Murdag informed her. "If Laird Kenneth finds ye worthy, then so do I."

Fayre looked into Murdag's eyes. "Then ye understand why I maun return the favor."

"But tae sacrifice yer life—"

" 'Tis no sacrifice, when I feel such a strong leading tae be with him."

Murdag raised her hands in surrender. "I can see there's no talking tae ye." She motioned to the low-backed wooden chair in a nearby corner. "Come now. Let me fashion yer hair. Brona may not have finished your garment yet, but ye can at least have a few pearls woven through yer pretty locks."

"Pearls?" Fayre inhaled so strongly in delight that her breath whistled between her lips.

"Only a few. Nothing too fancy with that awful brown garment." She wrinkled her nose. "Even one of mine would look better than—" Murdag stopped herself for a moment. "Would ye like tae wear one of my frocks?"

Although Fayre knew that under normal circumstances a ladies' maid would never dare make such a suggestion to her mistress, Fayre was grateful for the gesture. "Do ye think. . ."

Murdag inspected her. "Aye, I believe one of my garments might do. 'Tis only for awhile. As soon as Brona sews yer own frock, ye'll be wearin' that one. Let us hope ye can wear the one she sews at least once before you are laid t' rest in yer grave."

"Ye cheer me so."

"I beg pardon. 'Tis my fervent prayer that ye will wear yer new frocks for many years. And that most especially, ye'll be able tae dance in the gown at the king's castle someday." Murdag sighed.

"Someday. I am only glad that the laird discovered his illness before we went tae the royal palace."

"Aye." Murdag sent her several quick nods. "I shall retrieve the pearls the noo. And my best garment." The maid smiled with more warmth than Fayre had seen from her. "Surely the laird will believe he has seen an angel before he makes his final journey intae heaven."

Despite her faith, Fayre couldn't help but feel a twinge of fear as she approached the imposing door that led to Laird Kenneth's bedchamber. She set down the tray, burdened with a light meal, on the table beside the door.

Since she had never adorned her hair with anything other than the occasional wildflower, the elaborate braids with pearls woven in her locks felt strange and new. She touched the side of her hair now and again, fearful that one of the pearls might fall out. But Murdag's expert skill assured that they remained anchored in their splendor.

Murdag's clothing was heavier than she expected and fit tightly around her midsection. The garment had uncomplicated lace on the collar, ornamentation that made her feel as though she were wearing clothing far above her station. Two layers of white undergarments, wool stockings, and simple leather shoes with a button cover flap finished the outfit. The fabric of the outer garment was far less scratchy than the brown wool she had been wearing. The color reminded Fayre of the color of the Highlands on an early summer morning—a deep but muted green.

The kitchen maid instructed her not to knock; the laird was too feeble to answer. Fayre peered into the room. Her gaze traveled to a large canopied bed situated on the other side of the unlit fireplace.

God in heaven, I pray that I shall find favor with Thee. I ken I am selfish tae ask, but I ask Thee tae heal Laird Kenneth and t' protect me as well.

A lump underneath a pile of covers moaned. "Luke?"

The weakness of his voice made her feel as though she had been pierced through the heart with a lance. The magnitude of Laird Kenneth's illness struck her at that moment.

Lord, grant me courage.

"Nay, 'tis I," she answered aloud. "I ha'e come tae bring ye dinner." Fayre leaned partway out of the entrance and retrieved the tray.

"Fayre?" His voice sounded stronger. "It is you?"

Even in his puny state, the sound of his voice lifted Fayre's spirits. "Aye."

The covers moved and Laird Kenneth emerged from underneath them. He tried to sit upright, but only managed to prop himself upon his elbows. His hair was tangled and damp from fever. Fayre worried about his ashen skin and how he shivered, though she tried not to show it.

"I am glad tae see ye are feeling well enough to sit," Fayre noted as she set the tray on the table beside his bed. "I was expecting tae feed ye lying doon."

"Lying down, sitting up. In either position, I want no food." As if to demonstrate that he spoke the truth, he let his body fall back onto the pillows. "You should not be here."

"Aye, I should. I am determined tae nurse you back tae health. Whether you feel like it or not, ye maun eat." She lifted the cover from the largest dish. "Pheasant and turnips." She inspected the second dish. "And bread. Surely that will tempt ye."

"Nay."

She eyed a dessert. "Here is a fruit tart. If you dinna eat it, I surely shall."

"Go on with it. Why should I bother to eat? All is lost. I am doomed to die and take my entire castle with me."

"Do not speak like that!" The strength of her voice, daring to issue a command to her superior, surprised even herself.

"But it is true, is it not? I am doomed to death?"

"Nay. Ye arenna. By God's great mercy, I shall help make ye well." She pulled a chair up to the side of his bed. After she sat, Fayre tore a piece of bread from the small loaf and brought it close to his lips. "Here."

He shook his head. "Drink. May I have a drink?"

Saturated strands of hair hung above his eyes. He looked like a little boy who had just gone for a swim rather than a powerful man stricken with a dreaded disease. If only. . .

"I shall give ye drink," she said, "and then bathe your face with cool water."

Through half-closed eyes, Laird Kenneth looked upon her. "You are an angel."

She smiled. If only Murdag's image of her were true. If she

were an angel, she would look upon the face of God each day. She could not.

Or could she?

"Thank you." Laird Kenneth's faint smile was her reward for cooling his face. She hadn't noticed until that moment, but his features were fine, as fine as any of the sculptured statues in the laird's gardens. Yet even in sickness, his eyes sparkled with the promise of fun.

He coughed.

Fayre could hear wheezing in his chest. The sounds frightened her. "Ye maun sit up. Ye maun clear yer lungs."

"Nay, it is too hard to sit," he said in between coughs. "I want to lay back down. Please." He let his head flop back onto the pillow.

"Nay. Ye maun let me prop you up."

"Nay." He pouted.

Fayre chuckled in spite of her frustration with him. "Did ye use that pout tae charm yer dear mother?"

"Aye, and she always let me have my way."

"Surely yer jesting is a sign that ye're feeling better already. So you should nae mind if I do this." She yanked the pillow from under his head.

"Say, what do you mean by that?"

"I mean tae rearrange the pillows so ye can breathe better. When I am through, ye'll feel so comfortable you will nae realize you are no longer lying doon."

"Since the plague has not killed me yet, you plan to finish the task?" He coughed as though for emphasis.

"Ye arenna a very good patient. 'Tis a sign ye're getting well." Fayre looked toward one of the small windows. Judging from the rays shining through, the sunlight was at its strongest. "Every minute ye live is a good sign. Many people are dead within hours of falling ill, ye know."

"I think of that every waking moment," he assured her. "God would not grant me a quick death. He decided I should suffer."

You should remember that the next time you collect the rents.

Fayre didn't dare speak aloud her private thoughts. Did the laird really deserve to suffer? Probably not. She had heard nothing but good about him since she arrived at the castle. Why else would she subject herself to the chance of becoming as ill as he?

"I'll have ye t' know, I've been praying for the whole castle," Fayre told him. "I dinna ken everyone's name, but the Savior does, and He answers prayer."

"You are praying for the whole castle?" he muttered.

"Aye."

"Then let us hope that the Father in heaven will indeed answer your prayers. Not a finer woman than you would be found among the ladies at the king's ball." His voice was soft. He gasped. "The king's ball. You should be there, dancing the night away, instead of here with me."

"Nay, I wouldna think of such a thing. What festivity would a ball be without ye?" Immediately she regretted her outburst. What was she thinking?

She was just about to apologize when his smile stopped her. "Next time, then," he murmured.

Perhaps her true feelings were what he needed to hear after all. She smiled in return. "Next time."

The next day, Kenneth opened his eyes. He could tell by his

increased strength and improved humor that the plague had left his body.

Fayre's petitions to God had worked!

Imagine, the pleas of a mere serf. Then Kenneth remembered how Jesus healed the multitudes. Certainly everyone He touched wasn't a leader. And He listened to the pleas of women, even prostitutes.

Of course He heard Fayre!

Despite Kenneth's improvement, he felt weak and feverish and thought it best to remain in bed. As he recovered, shadowy nightmares haunted him before he awakened to the sound of singing and then fell asleep to the sound of sweet melodies. Fayre's voice was much prettier than any bird's song. She chose to sing psalms. The words comforted him, reminding him that the Lord was near. Her hands tended the withered laird much like they must have cared for her roses.

Too near, perhaps. Some nights, he thought for certain that he would be touched by death's icy hand. But that hand was stayed. Surely the heavenly Father heard his cries in the night. Cries in petition to preserve his own life—and Fayre's.

Kenneth barely remembered the first day he fell ill or when Fayre first arrived. All he knew was that she provided a constant presence for him, a presence of love and caring that confounded his reason for her sacrifice and courage in facing the unknown course of the plague.

"Fayre?" he called softly.

"Aye?" She left the window from which she had been peering and traveled swiftly to his bedside.

As she walked toward him, he noticed she wasn't wearing the brown garment. The new one wasn't as fashionable as the ones he'd seen in the king's court. Fabric dyed an indifferent shade of green hung on her small frame yet seemed tight around her waist. Even in such condition, the clothing was an improvement over the mean frock she once owned. "Is that the frock that Brona made for you?"

She looked downward. "Nay. It is Murdag's."

"Murdag's?" He laughed, filling the room with the sound of his mirth. "I never would have thought she would do you any favors."

"Neither did I, at first. She was a wee bit chilly toward me. I think she was insulted tae be assigned to one as lowly as I. Yoer high opinion of me encouraged her tae do me a good turn." She averted her eyes to the floor. "I ne'er did thank ye for taking my word over Sir Ulf's. If ye hadn't entered just at that moment. . ."

The thought of his boisterous knight clutching at Fayre as though she were a pawn in a game rather than a woman to be cherished enhanced his fever. "Let us not mention it again." His voice grew strong with resolve.

She sent him a smile that displayed the comely shape of her mouth. "What do ye need? A bite tae eat? Or drink tae quench your thirst?"

"Neither. I should like for you to summon my knight Walter."

She paused. "Why do ye need him? If there is something I can do for ye—"

"I doubt it. Unless perchance you can read." He made the suggestion knowing the prospect was unlikely at best. "I might try, only I still feel a bit weak."

"I wouldna ha'e ye try. Ye are still too ill."

"Walter, then. . ."

She answered with several rapid shakes of her head.

Why was she so reluctant to summon his knight? He had to admit, he hadn't missed his servants and squires much since he took ill. The past few days were nothing more than a fitful memory. Then a frightening thought occurred to him.

"Walter is not. . ." He didn't want to give voice to his fears. "He is not. . ."

"Nay," Fayre answered, obviously reading his thoughts. "He is well, as far as I ha'e been told."

"Thank our Father in heaven for such a blessing." He exhaled with relief.

"Aye, I prayed for him by name."

Kenneth felt his eyes mist with gratitude. He turned away so Fayre wouldn't see him in a moment of weakness. "So you will summon him?" he managed.

"There is no need. I can read to you," she answered.

Shocked, he turned his face back toward her. "What? But you—pardon me—are but a serf maiden." As soon as the words left his lips, he regretted them.

She lifted her chin in pride. "I am quite aware of that fact."

"Surely you cannot read Latin."

"Aye. Latin is the only language I can read. I told you aboot my uncle, the cleric. He taught me tae read."

So that is why her speech was closer to that of a lady than a serf! Certainly, her voice lilted with the Highland dialect, but it was nothing like the rest of the servants. Fayre's speech showed she was educated.

"Well, then," he said aloud, "would you be so kind as to read a bit of Scripture to me?"

"I wish I could. I ha'e not a copy. We were too poor tae have one of oor ain."

Of course they were. No serf was wealthy enough to own a copy of Scripture. Fayre was a prime example of what a person of low birth could achieve with the guidance of someone who cared and with the desire to learn and to remember.

Kenneth pointed to a wooden coffer in the corner of the room. "You will find one in there."

He watched as Fayre followed his instructions. When she opened the heavy chest and looked inside, she stopped for a moment. She reached for the book, but her motions were hesitant, as though the Words of God might impart judgment upon her in just the touching. She stroked the leather cover and took the tome in her arms, then held it to her chest as though it were a small child. Her excitement over touching a copy of sacred Scripture ignited his own.

"Open the book before me." Kenneth could hear the pitch of his own voice grow higher.

She complied, sitting in the chair beside him and examining several pages. Each one brought a gasp of delight. "I–I dinna feel worthy."

He understood. He knew from his own reading that the illuminations were startling in their detail. The monks at the monastery at Dryburgh had labored over the artwork for years. Kenneth extended his hand and touched hers. "You have come to nurse me at great risk to yourself. Surely you know I never would have asked that of you."

She nodded.

"Yet where are the others? I have many in my employ. Do you see them?" He paused. "That is the real reason why you were reluctant to summon Walter, is it not? You knew he did not want to take the risk of being too near me."

Fayre looked at the Bible in her lap. Her reticence only confirmed his suspicions.

"I would have expected as much from Ulf but not Walter." He pushed unwelcome thoughts from his mind and grasped Fayre's hand. Her fingers seemed so tiny in comparison to his own. When he gave them a gentle squeeze, she did not resist. "You nursed me all this time when no one else would. In my eyes, you are indeed worthy."

"Let us not be too quick tae judge the others," she answered. "Fear is a powerful emotion, and perhaps they dinna rely as fully upon God as I do. Nevertheless, I ha'e kept everyone in the castle in prayer. As of yet, I ha'e heard of no one's death."

"That is a blessing indeed. Thank you, Fayre," he said. "You are wiser than most learned men. I would be honored if you would read to me."

As Fayre's gentle lilt passed over the familiar words, Kenneth prayed for himself but said an especially fervent prayer for her.

Chapter 6

The rose bush has many blooms," Kenneth said weeks later as they inspected the flowers in the garden.

"Aye. Norman took good care of them while I tended tae ye," Fayre agreed. "And they have flourished under my continued care, if ye dinna think me too vain tae admit."

"You are never vain." He observed the bright orange blooms and then looked into her eyes. "They are beautiful, but not nearly as beautiful as you."

Fayre felt herself blush. "Are ye delirious once again? Shall I return ye tae yer sick bed?"

"Never." He shuddered. "I have better plans for my future. Now that I have a future, thanks to you."

"Dinna give me such honor. 'Tis the heavenly Father who saw fit tae save ye."

"Your humility is charming in its sincerity." Kenneth took her hands in his. She liked the feel of his fingers wrapping themselves around hers in such a protective manner. "Fayre." His voice was almost a whisper. "I have a question to ask."

The way his voice dropped in pitch on the last word indicated he had turned serious. Her heart began thumping. "Aye?"

"Though I have never given voice to my feelings, surely you know by now how much I love you."

"Dinna say such a thing. I ken ye believe what ye say, but we have just seen the miracle of healing together. Ye were close to death, and our Creator breathed fresh life into ye with His ain breath. I believe that with all my heart."

"But you prayed for me."

"Aye." She averted her gaze to the roses, although the blooms no longer held any interest for her. "I ken yer love is felt only out of gratitude."

"Nay, 'tis not." With a gentle touch, he took her chin in his strong hand and tilted her face toward his. "My love for you is strong, Fayre. Stronger than any I have ever felt."

His cloaked reference to another stirred an unwelcome memory in Fayre's mind. "Even for Lady Letha?"

He jerked his head slightly, as if she had slapped him across the face. "Lady Letha?"

"Aye." She looked down at her feet, now shod in kid leather. "Dinna ye want me to grow the roses for her?"

His mouth dropped open. "For that foolish and idle woman?" Kenneth threw back his head and laughed. "Is that what you thought?"

Surprised by his reaction, she looked back up at him. "Aye. Yer knights said so on that first day ye brought me here."

"Did they now?" He chuckled. "Why did you let a little bit of jesting toward me throw you into such speculation? Nay, a match between the lady and I is but wishful thinking by my vassals, who value outward beauty far more than a lovely spirit. A marriage to her would add to my earthly riches but leave me hungry for spiritual food. Nay, such a woman will not suit. I am a free man, unwilling to tether myself to any but the finest woman." He looked her squarely in the eye. "No matter if she must barter a rose bush for her father's freedom."

The gravity of what he proposed struck her. "And if we were tae wed, I would be free."

"Aye."

"I could be marrying ye just tae gain my freedom," she challenged, although she knew her tone and expression indicated the opposite was true.

"I shall know you are not because your freedom does not depend on our marriage," he said. "Fayre, I grant you freedom now, whether or not we marry."

She gasped. "Truly?"

"Aye."

"Then I shall return the favor by releasing ye from any sense of gratitude. Ye need not marry me. By yer leave I shall take my freedom and depart." She curtsied.

Kenneth did not answer right away. He knew he had not asked her hand only out of gratitude for her devotion to him during his illness. Yet if she believed as much, he could only set her free. "Why, aye, you may depart," he managed. "I shall instruct Walter to escort you home."

"Thank ye, Kenneth," she said as she curtsied again. "I shall always be grateful tae ye."

Before he could answer, she ran back to the castle. She was free! She was going home!

Kenneth's countenance fell and his feet felt heavy in his boots. Fayre had run away from him. Was his company so horrible that she could no longer endure him? Had she been patient with him as a nursemaid during his sickness, praying for him to recover only so she could leave his presence?

Father in heaven, did I misread her? Was our time together of no more significance than that of a laird and a faithful servant?

Kenneth felt no sense of peace after his prayer. But he knew there would be even less serenity in his heart if he insisted on a wedding to a woman who ran from him.

He looked at the rose bush once more. Seeing the flowers brought rage to his being. Kenneth couldn't remember a time he wished he could tear an innocent plant from the ground by its roots and destroy it with his bare hands.

Resisting the urge, he turned away and headed toward his bedchamber intent on retiring early. To keep his promise, he was obligated to instruct Walter to escort Fayre home. Walter was the only knight that Kenneth wished to see. He was too proud to face anyone else in the moment of his darkest defeat.

Several hours later, Fayre and Walter approached the mean hut. Her heart pounded with joy. To see her father again! How many times had she thought about him and petitioned God for his continued health and well-being? Finally, she would look upon his face and hear his voice again.

Walter had barely stopped his horse when she jumped off, thanked the knight, and ran into the cottage. "Father! Father!"

"Fayre!" Witta rose from the small table where he was eating bread and vegetable soup and hurried to greet her. "My lassie! I ne'er thought I'd lay eyes on ye again." He wrapped his arms around her and squeezed her in a loving embrace. "This can only mean the roses bloomed, eh?"

"Aye, and Kenneth granted me freedom! I am free! Our

debt has been paid." She stretched out her arms as though she could fly.

"Free! It canna be!"

"But 'tis!"

"Then we dinna pay rent t' the laird any longer." Witta's smile faded, and he furrowed his brows. "Free or not, ye maun call the laird by his title."

Fayre glanced at her feet in embarrassment, which only caused her father to look at them as well.

"Shoes!"

"Aye. A gift from the laird." She returned her gaze to his face. "I tended tae the laird when no one else would. He told me tae call him by his Christian name. I ken 'tis a privilege."

"A privilege!" Fear and suspicion entered his eyes. "What other liberties did he try to take?"

"None. I promise."

"Are ye sure, my lassie?"

She decided to omit the incident with Ulf. Why anger Father with a story about how she hadn't been entirely safe during her stay?

"Aye, Father," she responded. "Kenneth never touched me except to take my hands in his upon occasion." The memory of his strong hands holding her smaller ones sent a feeling of warmth through her body. She would miss such gestures, their conversations, and the life they shared however briefly. She couldn't think of that now. She was home.

"What, then?" he prodded. "Every gift from a man bears a price."

"A price! Many women would be happy tae pay such a price as he asked." She paused. "He asked me tae marry him."

"Marry him!" Witta chortled and slapped his knee with an energy she had no idea he could summon. " 'Tis no need tae jest with me, though the laugh has done me good, it has."

" 'Tis nae jest. He asked me tae marry him."

" 'Tis no jest?" He scratched his balding head, then smiled. " 'Tis no jest! My bonny lassie, 'tis a dream come true! And ye have come here tae take me to Kennerith Castle."

Fayre shook her head.

The happiness drained from Witta's face. "I see. 'Tisn't fitting for a lowly man like me tae be present at such a time."

She put her hands on his shoulders. "Nay! I told Kenneth I wouldna marry him."

"What? You denied him?" Witta's eyes widened. "And ye live tae tell the tale?"

"I dinna wish for a marriage based on gratitude alone. His gratitude, Father. I ken I do love him."

In Kenneth's eyes, the castle seemed desolate since Fayre's departure. Its dreary stone ramparts seemed even darker on this day. Walter had returned without Fayre, unable to convince her to change her mind. How could she think that Kenneth had wanted her only out of appreciation for what she had done, however brave and good? Naturally, he felt grateful. But never would he propose marriage to any woman on such a weak foundation.

He loved her well beyond gratitude. How could he make her see? Desperately he wanted to chase after her, to make Dazzle gallop to the little hut she and her father shared. But when he asked the Lord for permission, he did not receive the Savior's leave. He would have to wait.

Father in heaven, what is Thy will for me? Surely the feelings I have must be love. But I wish not to marry her without Thy leading. I pray it is Thy will to send her back.

A month later, Fayre was silent as she brought the day's milk into the hut. She set the worn wooden bucket on the table. "Care for a bit of warm milk, Father?"

"Nay, 'tis better tae save all we can for the cheese."

"The cheese." Fayre sighed.

"What's the matter? Ye ne'er minded making cheese before. Why do ye mope aboot, Lassie?" her father asked. "Ye seem more enslaved than e'er, instead of the free lass ye are."

"Aye, but I dinna feel free."

"I ken. 'Tis love that enslaves ye, 'tis. Love that ye canna live the way God intended, as a man and wife should. Yer sitting here, all silent and miserable. That's nae way to be." He finished stoking the fire and came closer, then took her hands in his. "I remember how much I loved yer dear mother. I'm sure your laird is just as unhappy as ye, all alone as he is in that big castle."

His words brought a smile to her lips. "You dinna believe he proposed only oot of gratitude?"

"No man in his position would ask ye tae marry him out of thankfulness alone. Yer freedom would have been enough if that's all he felt. Nay, my lassie, he loves ye. And ye love him. Why dinna ye accept his proposal, Fayre?"

She looked around the hut. "But ye would be alone."

"I've been alone before, and I can be alone once more. 'Tis better for an old man set in his ways, anyhoo." He surveyed the tiny cottage. "This little cottage is all I've e'er kent, and I'm right fond of it. It's always been my life, and 'tis my life the noo. I know it was once all ye kent, but noo, there's nothing here for ye."

Fayre swallowed. If only he didn't speak the truth!

"Go," Father prodded. "I beg ye."

"Oh, Father." She hugged him around the neck. "Yer guidance is what I've been praying for all these weeks. Now I know I ha'e release t' return tae Kennerith Castle."

When she broke the embrace, she saw tears in her father's eyes.

"There we go, Dazzle. Good boy." Kenneth stroked the horse's neck. "Time to survey my properties toward Loch Tay." Despite his cheerful demeanor, he'd been dreading this day for weeks. He desperately wanted to visit Witta's hut, but should he? Could he?

No. Fayre had fled at the prospect of wedding him. All was lost.

Kenneth and two vassals exited the courtyard, crossing the drawbridge that kept them safely out of the moat. The day promised to be long and hard.

They had only traveled a mile or so when in the distance, he heard horses' hooves clomping on the crude path ahead. "Halt," Kenneth instructed his vassals. "Let us wait and see who approaches." He stiffened, ready to draw his lance for battle.

When he recognized the coal black steed favored by Sir Rolfe, tensions eased. His knight and the two others who were with him, approached.

"A profitable day at the marketplace, I presume?" Kenneth asked.

"Aye." Rolfe's smile told him that he had a surprise that would please Kenneth.

"Good bargains, eh?" he guessed. "You always were good at bartering."

"Better than that. I found quite a prize." Rolfe tilted his head toward the last knight. At that moment, Kenneth realized that a woman rode with him. The last knight disembarked and assisted her.

Fayre!

He drew a sharp breath and leapt off Dazzle. "Fayre?"

The maiden he had come to love ran toward him. " 'Tis I!"

"You have returned!" He wanted to take her in his arms with more passion than he had ever displayed, but he hesitated. If he was mistaken, if she hadn't returned to accept his proposal but for some other reason, to greet her as a lover would make him appear foolish.

"Have I waited too long?" she asked.

He noticed that she trembled slightly. "Too long?"

She opened her lips to speak, but then seemed to remember that their actions were being witnessed by five knights.

" 'Never' would be too long." Kenneth extended his hand. "Lead on, my faithful men. Your lady has my favor. To Kennerith in haste that this joy may be welcomed to all within and beyond."

Despite the rapture she felt at riding upon Dazzle with Kenneth once again, Fayre quivered in anticipation and dread as they approached Kennerith Castle. What would he do once they were inside the castle?

The courtyard they entered was now familiar. Memories of

her first encounter with the castle flashed through her mind. The circumstances were so different, yet the stakes were equally high. Perhaps even higher.

Kenneth helped her from the horse. "Are you in need of sustenance?" he asked as her feet touched the ground.

Fayre couldn't have eaten had her life depended upon it. "Nay."

"I wonder why you do not waste away to nothing," Kenneth teased. He snapped his fingers at a nearby squire. "Tell Cook I want the midday meal served to Fayre and myself in my private quarters."

"Aye."

"And have her send plenty of fruit tarts." Kenneth smiled at Fayre. "Before we retire to dinner, I want to show you something."

He walked in the direction of the garden.

My roses!

The brilliant blooms shone from the entryway. Sunlight filtered through the clouds above. Fayre quickened her pace so she could examine them more closely. As soon as she neared the bush, she touched one of the rose petals. "These blooms are beautiful! Even more beautiful than before." She turned to Kenneth and saw that he wore a pleased expression. "The king will love them."

"Aye. But I care less about what the king thinks of them than what you think. I am glad to see you are delighted with the care they have received in your absence." He motioned his hand toward the bush. "Go ahead. Pick one for yourself. Such a bloom would look pretty in your hair."

Fayre hesitated.

Not one to wait, Kenneth plucked the largest bloom and placed it over her ear.

Just the simple movement bringing him in such close proximity to her filled her with anticipation about the future.

Kenneth escorted Fayre to a small sitting room within his residence. When they entered, she knew she was home.

The fire was lit, and this time Kenneth suggested with a wave of his hand that she take the seat opposite his. She obeyed, though she was unaccustomed to the pillowed bench. She noticed that Kenneth shifted forward in his seat.

"So," he said, his voice a wee bit too cheerful, "Rolfe found you in the marketplace?"

"Aye. Father and I searched until we found one of yer knights." She hesitated.

"You did?" He leaned toward her, his eyes bright.

"Aye. I–I wanted to return." She peered at the stone floor and studied it to avoid his inquisitive gaze. Fayre couldn't bring herself to look him squarely in the eye. Not yet. "I hope my return doesna distress ye."

"Nay," he whispered.

The one word gave her courage to look at him. "I am here for a reason." Not knowing what else to do, Fayre stood and then curtsied so low that her nose nearly touched the floor. "If I am not too late. . ." She lifted her eyes toward his face. "I would be honored to accept yer proposal of marriage."

Her legs quivered and her heart beat wildly. What if she was too late? What if he had already found a lady? Or worse, become betrothed in her absence?

No, she would have heard.

"Fayre?" he said. "Why do you not answer? Can you not

understand what I say?"

She had been so busy thinking terrible thoughts that he might not want her anymore, she must not have heard him nor noticed that he was standing before her. Suddenly unable to utter another word, Fayre managed to shake her head.

He took her hand and guided her to her feet. "Aye, I still want to marry you. This castle is nothing but a shell without your shining presence. I am the one who would be honored for you to be my wife."

As Kenneth entwined her in his strong arms, Fayre looked into his handsome face and saw that his lips were nearing her own. Again she quivered, but not with dread. Rather than the fright she had felt with Ulf, she welcomed her first kiss—a kiss from the man she had grown to love.

As his warm mouth touched hers, the heat of love filled her. At that moment, she realized that her sacrifice, which now seemed so small, had given her rewards beyond her most treasured hopes and dreams.

TAMELA HANCOCK MURRAY

Tamela Hancock Murray lives in Northern Virginia with a godly husband and two wonderful daughters, and is privileged to write for the only true kingdom—that of the Lord Jesus Christ. She finds Scotland fascinating, particularly since her husband's family tree includes Duncans, Barclays, and Murrays.

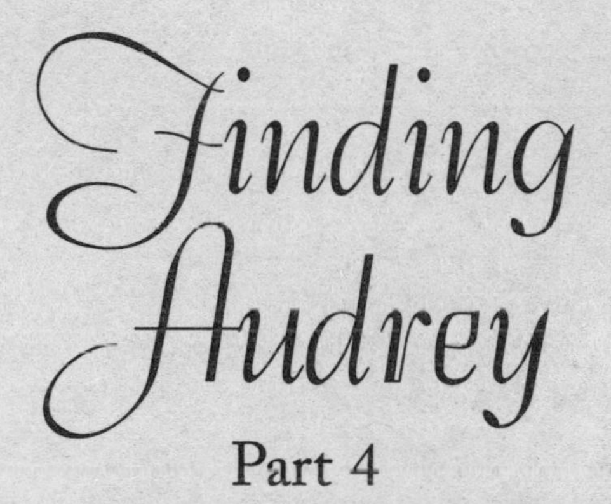

Part 4

by Tracey V. Bateman

Chapter 9

Audrey sat back with a sigh and smiled. After discovering the information about Fayre's rose garden, she now knew where she'd gotten her love of flowers and of roses in particular. She'd have to remember to tell Brett. After all, without his help, she never would have made it farther back than the nineteenth century in her research.

Brett!

She catapulted to her feet and ran into the front room where the only clock in the place hung on the wall.

Ten o'clock.

Why had she ever booted up that computer? After reading the two-page story of Fayre's rose garden, Audrey had grown even hungrier to know more, so she'd logged onto the Internet and started searching for rose gardens.

The legend of at least one of Fayre's rose bushes surviving for each new owner had filled the pages, and she'd been able to read more about Fayre. She'd become so engrossed in the history surrounding the time period of Fayre's life, that she'd completely lost track of time. She'd printed documents and saved sites to her favorites file to look over later, but the treasure chest of information she'd discovered about her ancestry filled her with joy and a sense of peace that had eluded her for her entire life.

But at the thought of Brett, that peace had been replaced with panic. She lamented her appearance. No makeup. Faded jeans and a sweatshirt. Hardly the kind of thing a professional would wear to deliver flowers. Even worse than appearing unprofessional was the thought of Brett seeing her like this. But it was that or let him down and not have the fellowship hall decorated when the service concluded.

Loading up her midsized car, she made the only decision she could. Get in, get out, don't let Brett see her—under any circumstances.

The twenty-minute drive across town seemed to take hours. To her dismay, she hit every red light between the flower shop and the church. Finally she arrived in the parking lot, unloaded the car, and went to work—determined to give the fellowship hall just the right touch for Brett's big day.

The speakers were on, and she could hear the service. It never occurred to her to be annoyed that she had to listen to a sermon. Rather, she was grateful for the heads-up. At least this way, she'd know when the service concluded.

Someone had already spread linen cloths on the tables, so Audrey only had to arrange the sprays, flowers, and plants in a manner that looked completely natural and unhurried.

And she had to do it in—oh, brother—less than an hour.

The preacher's voice came loud and clear through the speakers. "God leads us even when we don't understand or acknowledge that He's leading."

"Yeah, yeah," she muttered. "God's in charge of my life. Yada yada."

Audrey felt uneasy in the pit of her stomach, and she felt ashamed. Looking back over the past year, she had to admit that some mighty strange coincidences had occurred in her life, starting with meeting Brett at the library and becoming his friend. All the pieces of her history had begun to slowly fall into place, even as she'd lost her heart to the only man she would ever love.

And then there was Cassie. She smiled, thinking of the girl. God had certainly placed her in the right home. Mrs. Perryman even shared Cassie's love of painting and the gorgeous blond curls. Mr. Perryman shared her love of corny jokes, science fiction, and Raisinettes. She couldn't have fit better in that home if she'd been their child from birth.

I have a place for you, too.

"It's a little late for me. I'm all grown up. Too old to be adopted."

Not into My family.

She pushed aside the nudges she knew were from God as the preacher began wrapping up his sermon. Audrey kicked her tasks into high gear.

His words crackled over the speaker. "It's difficult for me to say good-bye." His voice broke, and his breathing increased as he fought for control. "I've known many of you since you were babies. Some are new friends. We are part of a precious family, bound together by the blood of Jesus Christ. There's never a need for a Christian to feel as though he or she has no one as long as we are part of God's family. We have brothers and sisters all around us."

Audrey placed the last arrangement on the table and stopped. Part of her wanted to bolt from the fellowship hall, but her soul yearned to hear what the preacher was saying. Her soul won. She stared at the speakers.

"Before I close the service and officially turn the church over to Pastor Canfield, God's new man to shepherd this flock, I would like to give one last opportunity for anyone who doesn't know Christ to receive Him now. To become part of this precious family to which we've been called."

Audrey's heart charged. Her palms dampened. More than anything, she wanted to answer that call. To be adopted into the family of God. To become part of this incredible, warm church family.

As the last few months flashed through her mind, she realized that God had become a part of her life, and slowly her anger against Him had begun to melt. Still, surrender was hard. The fear that she might have to go to the mission field or give up her flower shop or something like that made her hesitate. Was she really ready to give it all?

As though God was soothing her heart's fears, the preacher spoke again, "I'm about to give anyone an opportunity to receive Jesus Christ, but first I'd like to read a verse. Romans 8:15 says: 'For ye have not received the spirit of bondage again to fear; but ye have received the Spirit of adoption, whereby we cry, Abba, Father.' The joys of being adopted into the family of God far outweigh the hardships that come with sharing in Christ's suffering."

He paused. For what seemed like an eternity, nothing came through the speakers. Panic welled up inside of Audrey. Had someone turned off the speakers?

No! Not now!

She nearly cried out in relief when his voice resumed. "Will you set aside your fear and allow God to adopt you into His family?"

Without another second of resistance, Audrey knelt on the gray carpet and surrendered.

Wired from too little sleep and too much coffee, Brett could barely keep from tapping his foot until the service was over and he could make a beeline into the fellowship hall to see if Audrey had delivered the flowers. As soon as the final prayer was said, he slipped out the side door while the praise and worship leader led the congregation in the old favorite: *"I'm so glad I'm a part of the family of God."*

He reached the fellowship hall, and his heart lurched. Audrey was just leaving through the outside door, arms laden with boxes. "Audrey, wait!"

She turned.

"What's wrong?" he asked. Her eyes and nose were red. Obviously, she'd been crying her eyes out. "Did something happen to the flowers?"

Her laughter surprised him. No—stunned him.

"The flower arrangements are fine. I'm fine. Better than fine actually."

Joy shone from her beautiful silver eyes. A sudden urge to wrap her in his arms nearly overcame him, and had she not been carrying empty boxes, he'd have probably done just that.

The sound of voices filtering into the fellowship hall as service was dismissed sufficiently squelched any chance he had to discover what was happening with her, so he quickly changed tactics. "The hall looks great. Thank you for doing it on such short notice."

"You're welcome."

"Do you want to stay for the dinner? There's going to be plenty of food."

She shook her head but not in the defensive, don't-ask-me-to-church way she normally refused his invitations. This was a gentle refusal. "I need to be alone," she said. "To sort through a few things. But call me later, please."

"You want me to call you?" Brett hesitated. Should he respond to the obvious love exuding from her? His own feelings hadn't slackened in the slightest, and seeing her now, he realized they were only getting stronger.

"Please. I have some news, but you need to go and be with your congregation, and I have some things to sort through."

"All right. I'll call you this afternoon."

She nodded. "Congratulations on becoming the new pastor. You're going to do a dynamite job."

Perplexed, he watched her go, feeling like the last one privy to a secret.

Audrey read and read and read some more, devouring the Gospels. Thrilling to every red-lettered word spoken by her newly found Savior. She'd memorized many, many Scriptures during her teen years, but they'd been nothing more than ink on a page to her back then. Now as she read the familiar verses, they took on meaning she'd never expected. She thrilled to the life-giving, life-changing words.

A knock on the door startled her, and she stood, glancing at the clock as she did so. She'd been reading for five hours.

"Who is it?"

"Brett. I couldn't get through on the phone."

She unlocked the door. "Sorry. I unplugged it. But I meant to plug it back in after a couple of hours."

He hung back when she opened the door wider. She didn't blame him. Last time he'd been inside her house, she hadn't behaved very well. "Let's go for a walk," she suggested.

His brow lifted in surprise. "Sure. Sounds great."

Grabbing her keys, she followed Brett through the door and locked it behind her.

They walked in silence for two blocks, until a deep breath from Brett signaled he'd really like to have his curiosity satisfied.

Audrey had been trying to formulate the words. But suddenly her trademark eloquence evaded her, and she heard herself blurt out, "So, I became a Christian today."

Brett stopped dead in his tracks. "Huh?"

Turning to face him, Audrey suddenly felt shy. She stuffed her hands into her back pockets. "Yeah. It was while I worked on the tables."

"You got saved arranging flowers on the tables?"

She nodded. "I listened to the service over the speakers."

"Wow."

Joy bubbled up inside of her. "Oh, Brett. I can't believe how different I feel! It's like that hole inside me is all filled up for the first time in my life. I thought finding out my family roots would make things change, and I admit I've felt more of a sense of purpose since discovering what a neat heritage I have, but that feeling is nothing like what I've experienced since this morning at your church."

Brett recovered enough to step forward. With a whoop of joy, he snatched her up into an embrace, lifting her off her feet in the process. "Audrey. This is wonderful news."

He held her firmly until Audrey pulled gently away from his arms. "I–I just want you to know that I'm going to be attending your church. But I don't expect you to. . .I mean, except for Cassie's party, it's been months since we've spoken, and I realize things have probably changed for you. And I'm perfectly fine with that. I–I just thought you should know. I'm not chasing you."

Audrey clamped her mouth shut. So becoming a Christian hadn't made her any less a rambling idiot when she was with the man she loved.

Reaching forward, Brett trailed his finger down her cheek. "You don't have to chase me. You caught me a long time ago. And if you still feel the same way about me, I'd like for us to start over. Let's do things the right way this time."

"Oh, Brett. I would love that."

"How about going for coffee?"

"Like a date?" She grinned.

"A lot like one."

"Mocha latte?"

"With white chocolate added."

"White chocolate. You remember the way to a girl's heart, don't you?"

"I know the way to yours."

She grinned. "I think this is the beginning of a beautiful friendship."

Taking her hand, he laced his fingers with hers. "I think it's more than that. I think it's the beginning of a very meaningful and lifelong relationship."

"We'll need to take things slowly. I have a long way to go. A lot to learn before I could possibly be the kind of wife you'll need and that your congregation will need."

"We'll take it as slow as necessary. But I want you to know I plan to marry you someday."

Audrey's heart lifted. "In God's time."

Brett's eyes misted, and he drew her close. "I love you."

Without awaiting her response, he brought his lips down to meet hers. Audrey settled into the security of his embrace, knowing she was right where she belonged.

Epilogue

Audrey pushed back a lock of hair as she stood inside Fayre's Garden with the other tourists. She wanted to shout, "This is my heritage! My family legacy! You're all looking at my castle!"

But she kept quiet and closed her eyes instead, trying to imagine Alex and Fiona exchanging their vows, Allan and Celeste working the soil. Fayre's beautiful roses that had captured the attention of Laird Kenneth in the first place.

The familiar comfort of Brett's arm enveloped her. Turning, she opened her eyes and smiled at her husband of less than two years.

"Is it everything you've dreamed of?" he asked.

Audrey observed the beauty of the garden. She drank in the sweet fragrance of the roses as the gentle breeze blew through. Her mind went to the secret she'd protected until this moment. Taking her husband's hand, she whispered, "Everything I've dreamed of is right here."

"It is beautiful." The tenderness shining from his eyes filled Audrey with a comforting warmth.

"Yes, but I'm not talking about the garden."

"You're not?"

She shook her head. "How would you feel about being a daddy?"

His eyes widened and his gaze dropped to her flat stomach. "Are we?"

Laughing, she nodded. "In about seven months."

Cupping her face, he bent and kissed her tenderly. Audrey had never felt such peace. She looked forward to the years to come. Years of family, friends, and church family. She saw the rich natural heritage from whence she'd come, but more importantly, she saw the future she and Brett were going to build.

A rich legacy of faith and love for the generations ahead.

TRACEY V. BATEMAN

Tracey lives in Missouri with her husband and their four children. She counts on her relationship with God to bring balance to her busy life. Grateful for God's many blessings, Tracey believes she is living proof that "all things are possible to them that believe," and she happily encourages anyone who will listen to dream big and see where God will take them.

E-mail address: tvbateman@aol.com
Web site: www.traceyvictoriabateman.homestead.com/index.html

A Letter from the Authors

Dear Reader:

It has been our joy to bring this anthology to life. Thank you for traveling to Gretna Green with Alex and Fiona and watching their journey toward love. For sharing Allan Galbraith's happiness as he took his rightful place as the earl of Carnassis and married his beloved Celeste. And for kneeling in Fayre's garden as she cultivated her beautiful roses and the love between serf and laird grew.

We chose to connect these stories through one woman's quest for her legacy. The spiritual emptiness inside Audrey manifested itself in a loneliness that spurred her to search for her roots. But no matter how far back she went in her family tree, she wasn't satisfied. The reason? Life without Jesus is empty. And as important as earthly family is, our ultimate heritage is found only in one common bond: the blood of Jesus, poured out on a cross.

If you don't know Him, it is our hope that you, too, may come to experience the strong faith that we share in belonging to the family of God. Because the most important message we can ever deliver to you, dear reader, is the one about Jesus loving you so much that He chose to die—so that you could live. He asks only that you receive His gift and accept Him into your heart and life. Before you close this book, we leave you with one last thought:

Audrey wanted a family. . .Fiona wanted acceptance. . . Celeste wanted respect. . .Fayre wanted mercy. . .And all four girls wanted to be loved. All these things can be found through Jesus Christ, our Lord.

If you would like to contact us with any questions about this, we will be happy to answer them. God bless and keep you.

Tracey V. Bateman: tvbateman@aol.com
Pamela Griffin: words_of_honey@juno.com
Tamela Hancock Murray: TamelaHancockMurray@juno.com
Jill Stengl: jpopcorn@newnorth.net

A Letter to Our Readers

Dear Readers:

In order that we might better contribute to your reading enjoyment, we would appreciate your taking a few minutes to respond to the following questions. When completed, please return to the following: Fiction Editor, Barbour Publishing, Inc., P.O. Box 719, Uhrichsville, OH 44683.

1. Did you enjoy reading *Highland Legacy?*
   - ❑ Very much—I would like to see more books like this.
   - ❑ Moderately—I would have enjoyed it more if ______________

____

____

2. What influenced your decision to purchase this book? (Check those that apply.)
   - ❑ Cover ❑ Back cover copy ❑ Title ❑ Price
   - ❑ Friends ❑ Publicity ❑ Other

3. Which story was your favorite?
   - ❑ *Finding Audrey* ❑ *Fresh Highland Heir*
   - ❑ *English Tea and Bagpipes* ❑ *Fayre Rose*

4. Please check your age range:
   - ❑ Under 18 ❑ 18–24 ❑ 25–34
   - ❑ 35–45 ❑ 46–55 ❑ Over 55

5. How many hours per week do you read? ______________

Name ____

Occupation ____

Address ____

City ____________________ State ___________ Zip ___________

E-mail ____